Please return/renew this item by the last date shown

**Herefordshire
Libraries**

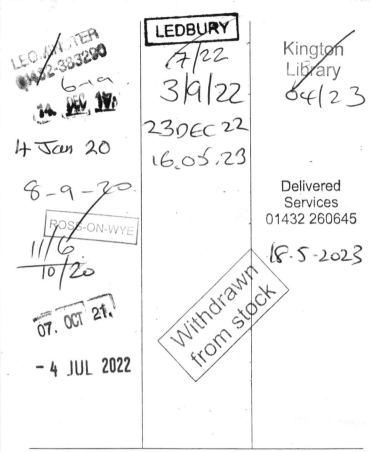

*Herefordshire
Council*

SPECIAL MESSAGE TO READERS

THE ULVERSCROFT FOUNDATION
(registered UK charity number 264873)
was established in 1972 to provide funds for research, diagnosis and treatment of eye diseases. Examples of major projects funded by the Ulverscroft Foundation are:-

- The Children's Eye Unit at Moorfields Eye Hospital, London
- The Ulverscroft Children's Eye Unit at Great Ormond Street Hospital for Sick Children
- Funding research into eye diseases and treatment at the Department of Ophthalmology, University of Leicester
- The Ulverscroft Vision Research Group, Institute of Child Health
- Twin operating theatres at the Western Ophthalmic Hospital, London
- The Chair of Ophthalmology at the Royal Australian College of Ophthalmologists

You can help further the work of the Foundation by making a donation or leaving a legacy. Every contribution is gratefully received. If you would like to help support the Foundation or require further information, please contact:

THE ULVERSCROFT FOUNDATION
The Green, Bradgate Road, Anstey
Leicester LE7 7FU, England
Tel: (0116) 236 4325

website: www.foundation.ulverscroft.com

Lucy Clarke has a first-class degree in English Literature, and is a passionate diarist. She has worked as a presenter of social enterprise events and a creative writing workshop leader, and is now a full-time novelist. Her debut novel, *The Sea Sisters*, has been published internationally, and was selected as a Richard & Judy 2013 Summer Book Club read. Together with her husband, a professional windsurfer, and their two young children, she spends her winters travelling and her summers at home on the south coast of England. Lucy writes from a beach hut.

You can discover more about the author at www.lucy-clarke.com

YOU LET ME IN

Elle Fielding has taken the literary world by storm, with her first book hitting the bestsellers lists and making big money. But now she's under pressure from her publisher to produce a follow-up that's just as compelling. Having spent a chunk of her earnings remodelling her dream house on the cliffs, she decides to take a break to try to cure her writer's block, renting the property out on Airbnb while she's away. Upon her return, however, she realises something has changed. Despite her friends' reassurances that everything is fine, and her vivid imagination must be running away with her, Elle is increasingly convinced something is seriously wrong. As fear and paranoia close in, her own home becomes a prison. Someone is unlocking her past — and she's given them the key . . .

Books by Lucy Clarke
Published by Ulverscroft:

THE SEA SISTERS
A SINGLE BREATH
LAST SEEN

LUCY CLARKE

YOU LET ME IN

Complete and Unabridged

CHARNWOOD
Leicester

First published in Great Britain in 2018 by
HarperCollins*Publishers*
London

First Charnwood Edition
published 2019
by arrangement with
HarperCollins*Publishers*
London

The moral right of the author has been asserted

This novel is entirely a work of fiction. The names, characters and incidents portrayed in it are the work of the author's imagination. Any resemblance to actual persons, living or dead, events or localities is entirely coincidental.

A catalogue record for this book is available from the British Library.

ISBN 978–1–4448–4117–6

Published by
F. A. Thorpe (Publishing)
Anstey, Leicestershire

Set by Words & Graphics Ltd.
Anstey, Leicestershire
Printed and bound in Great Britain by
T. J. International Ltd., Padstow, Cornwall

This book is printed on acid-free paper

For my parents, Jane and Tony.

Prologue

I'd like to offer you one piece of advice. It's just a small thing. It won't apply to many of you — but it is important.

It changed everything for me.

It's this: if you're considering letting someone into your house, pause first. Think.

Think about what it means to give a stranger — or strangers — the keys to your home.

Think about that stranger drifting through your house; a hand slipped into a drawer; fingers trailing through the clothes hanging in your wardrobe; the bathroom cabinet opened, examined.

Think about where their gaze may linger; the photos of you and your family hanging on the walls; the calendar in the kitchen outlining your plans; the file you keep at the bottom of a trunk.

Think about that person lying in your bed; the mattress moulding to their warm body; tiny cells of their skin shedding on your sheets; their breath moist against your pillow.

What other parts of themselves will they leave behind?

What parts of you will they discover?

1

Elle

'What happens in the first chapter of your novel should be like an arrow pointing to the last.'

Author Elle Fielding

I slow the car into the curve of the lane, feeling it bounce over ruts and channels, loose gravel spraying from beneath the tyres.

As the track climbs, I straighten, peering beyond the hedgerows to catch a glimpse of the sea. In the muted light of dusk, I spot whitecaps breaking across the water, the sea ruffled by wind. Already, my breathing softens.

I flick off the radio, not wanting the presenter's voice to dilute the next moment. I've been looking forward to it during the long drive from London to Cornwall.

As I turn the corner, I see it: the house on the cliff top, standing like a promise at the track's end.

★   ★   ★

Pulling into the driveway, I cut the ignition, and sit for a moment, engine ticking.

It still feels entirely incredible that this is where I live.

3

In the first meeting with the architect, I'd no idea what I'd wanted beyond the number of rooms and a space to write. Over the months that followed, those untethered ideas began to weave together into a vision, which now stands three storeys tall, overlooking the wave-pounded bay.

The house is painted dove-grey, with large windows framed in natural wood. 'Contemporary coastal heritage', the architect said. I'm glad the weatherboarding is starting to lose some of its stark newness, and the windows look pleasingly salt-licked. I still need to soften the exterior, perhaps train some wisteria to climb around the entrance — if it can survive the bracing sea winds.

I've never owned a house before. Or a flat. Growing up, my sister, mother and I always lived in rented accommodation. Words like *house* and *mortgage* were for other people, not us.

The car door swings wide as I step out, the sea breeze causing my dress to billow and flatten around my thighs.

Gravel crunches underfoot as I cross the drive, hauling the case onto the flagstone doorstep, then searching the depths of my handbag for my house keys. I'm one of those people who carries too much — purse, phone, pens, a novel, my notebook.

Always a notebook.

Slotting the front door key into the lock, I hesitate.

There is something unsettling about returning home knowing strangers have been staying here.

4

My fortnight in France was laced with worry over the decision to Airbnb the house, so much so that twice I'd clambered onto the roof terrace of the farmhouse in search of mobile reception. Thankfully there were no cries for help from them, or my sister.

Standing on the doorstep, I have the unnerving sensation that when I open my front door, I will find the family who rented it still inside. The mother — an attractive woman with an expensive-looking hairstyle, I recall from her Airbnb profile — will be at my butler sink, water sluicing over pale hands that hold a plastic beaker. Behind her, I imagine a child in a high chair, pudgy fingers pushing a strawberry into its mouth. At the breakfast bar, a father will be cutting slices of toast into soldiers, lining them onto one of my stoneware side plates, before carrying it to a girl of three or four, who will count the pieces carefully with a fingertip.

There will be music playing. Talking and laughter. The side-step of parents' feet as they avoid a toy car on the floor. All that noise and energy and movement that a family generates pulsing inside my house.

My heart contracts: it should be my family.

★ ★ ★

Pushing open the front door, I'm immediately aware that the air smells different. Something earthy and damp, mixed with the residue of someone else's cooking.

The wind sucks the door shut, slamming it

5

behind me with a startling clang.

Then silence.

No one to call out to. No one to greet me.

I drop my handbag onto the oak settle beside a pile of neatly stacked post. I glance at the bill resting on top, then look away. I slip off my shoes and walk barefoot into the kitchen.

Sea and sky fill the windows. Even at dusk the light is incredible. Two gulls wheel carelessly on the breeze, and beneath them the sea churns. This is why I fell in love with the house, which was originally a rundown fisherman's cottage that hadn't been modernised since the sixties.

I read somewhere that the beauty of a sea view is that it's always changing, no two days are the same. I remember thinking the statement was pretentious — but actually, it's true.

Pulling my gaze from the water, I scan the kitchen. The long stretch of granite surface is clean and empty. A note is tucked beneath the corner of a terracotta basil pot. In my sister's handwriting, I read:

Welcome home! All went well with the Airbnb. Pop over for a glass of wine when you're settled. Fiona x

I missed her. And Drake. I'll go over tomorrow, suggest a beach walk, or a pub lunch somewhere with a play area so Drake can roam.

Right now, all I have the energy for is taking a long bath with my book.

I reach into the cupboard for a glass, and as I draw it towards the tap, a movement by my fingertips causes me to drop it, the tumbler smashing into the sink. A thick-legged house spider scurries from the broken pieces to take up a crouching position in the plug hole.

I shiver. There's just something about the way spiders move — the jerkiness of all those articulated legs. With a sigh, I resign myself to the new task of removing the spider from the house. Catching it in a spare glass, I head for the front door.

The flagstones are freezing as I climb down the steps barefoot, then wince as I pick my way across the gravel to the far end of the driveway. This bugger isn't getting back in. I set down the glass, then nudge it over with my toe, before hopping back. The spider remains motionless for a few moments. Then, with a flurry of black legs, it scuttles away.

I turn back towards the house just in time to see my front door catching in a gust of wind, slamming shut.

'No!' I hurry across the driveway and grab the handle, yanking at it fruitlessly. My palms slam against the door; I'm furious with myself.

My handbag is on the settle, my keys and mobile zipped within it, my jacket hanging from its hook. *Idiot!*

Fiona is my spare key holder, but her house is a good half-hour walk away. I can't do it barefoot and coatless in November — I'll probably freeze to death before I get there.

I look over my shoulder towards the bungalow that crouches beyond my house. It is the only other property on the cliff top and belongs to Frank and Enid, a retired couple who've lived there for thirty years.

I remember walking to their door that first

time, my hand pressed in Flynn's, filled with an excited anticipation that we were homeowners, that we were meeting *neighbours*. It all felt so impossibly grown up, as if we were play-acting. Frank had a brusque manner and looked at us through the corners of his eyes, as if trying to get the full measure of us. Enid fretted over the strength of the tea and that there were dishes in the sink from breakfast. But Flynn always had an easy, relaxed way with people and by the end of the visit a friendship had been made.

Now those visits are over. I haven't been inside their home in months. If we pass on the single-lane road, Frank ensures it is me who reverses to a pull-in, or if he catches sight of me while putting the bins out, he looks determinedly away.

With a sinking feeling, I cross the driveway, framing my request for help.

★   ★   ★

My hair whips around my face, and I gather the long twist of it in one hand. I'm about to press the bell when the door swings open and a man steps out, shrugging on a black leather jacket.

He stops abruptly, hooded eyes fixed on mine.

'Oh. Hi,' I say, taken aback. 'I'm Elle. I live next door.'

Through a curtain of thick, dark hair, his gaze flicks towards my house. The set of his features shifts, tightens. He looks to be a few years younger than me — in his late twenties, perhaps — the first scribblings of lines settling around his eyes, his jaw grazed with stubble.

'The author.' There's something about his intonation that makes it sound like an insult.

'That's right. You must be Enid and Frank's son?'

'Mark.'

That is it. They'd mentioned a son some time ago — when we were all still on good terms. I think Enid had said he'd left Cornwall for work, but I can't recall the rest of the details.

'Here's the thing, Mark. There was an incident with a spider ... I was evicting it from the premises, when the wind caught me unawares and the door slammed shut. Stupidly, my keys and phone are inside.'

His gaze travels down my body, over the pale blue summer dress, down my tanned legs, settling on my bare feet, which are set together, my toenails painted a shimmering pearl. I want to explain, *I don't usually dress like this in November. I've come from the airport. I —*

'Shoes.'

I blink.

'Your shoes are locked inside, too.'

'Oh. Yes. They are.' I hug my arms to my chest. 'Would you mind if I used your phone to call my sister? She has the spare key.'

He waits a beat, then steps aside, holding the front door open. I move past him into the narrow hallway.

The smell of fried onions hangs thickly in the air, alongside something pungent. *Weed,* I realise, a warm burst of memory swimming back to me.

'Are Enid or Frank home?'

'No.' There is a heavy clunk as Mark shuts the door. He stands with his back to it.

I shift. I always need to know where an exit is, to plan how I could get out of a room, a building — a habit ignited at university, which now seems impossible to shake. My gaze travels to the lock. Yale. No key on the internal side of the door.

'So, are you visiting for a few days? You live in the city, don't you?' I ask, my friendly tone overlaying the first prickle of fear. 'What is it you do? I think your mum mentioned something about computers, or I may have made that up.'

'Why would you make that up?'

I can feel myself shifting uncomfortably beneath his gaze. I am a thirty-three-year-old woman. I don't need him to like me. I just need to use his phone.

The landline sits on an old-fashioned telephone table, set below a brass-framed mirror. 'May I?'

'Not working.'

'Do you have a mobile?'

There is a pause before he reaches into his pocket and pulls out a mobile. He taps in a passcode, then holds it out to me. There is an odd moment of resistance — no more than half a second — where he holds onto the phone as I go to take it.

Flustered, I try to recall Fiona's number. I don't want to look up, yet I'm certain Mark's gaze is on me. Heat is building in my cheeks.

'I can't remember her number. I used to know everyone's numbers, but now they're all pro-grammed in our mobiles, aren't they?'

He says nothing.

I clear my throat. I begin entering the dialling code and, as I do so, the rhythm of the rest of the number comes to me. Relieved, I hold the mobile to my ear, listening to it ring. I make a silent prayer that Fiona will be there.

The leather of Mark's jacket squeaks as he leans against the door, checking his watch.

'Yes?' Fiona whispers, Drake most likely asleep nearby.

'Oh, thank God! You're there! I'm calling from someone else's phone. Listen, I'm locked out. Tell me you have my spare key? That you're home?'

'I'm home. I have the spare.'

'Can you come over? Or I could get a taxi to you if Drake's in bed?'

'Bill's here. I can come. Gets me out of bath-time.'

'Perfect, thank you.'

'Whose phone is this?'

'I'll explain later.'

I can imagine Fiona's expression as she tells Bill that she has to go and rescue her sister. Again. Getting locked out of the house is not the sort of thing that happens to Fiona. There will be some sort of system in place, a back-up key meticulously hidden, or a syndicate of neighbours with spares.

I return Mark's phone. 'My sister is on her way. She'll only be ten minutes.'

There are several beats of silence. Then Mark says, 'I'm going to be late.'

'You . . . you want me to wait outside?'

He doesn't answer, instead he opens an

11

under-stairs cupboard and spends a moment rummaging within it. He turns back to me holding out a woman's purple fleece.

Then he opens the front door. There is no mention of whether I'd like to borrow shoes. I step out onto the freezing concrete step noticing that dusk has slipped into night.

I push my arms into the sleeves, a musty, lavender scent filling my nostrils. 'I'll drop this back later.'

He shrugs as he moves past me, pulling the door closed behind him.

A black motorbike is parked at the edge of the property. I almost laugh. Of course he'd ride a motorbike! I watch as he pulls on his helmet, straddles the bike, then guns the engine.

★ ★ ★

Crossing the driveway, I'm grateful when the security light flicks on. I perch on my doorstep, the cold of the flagstone seeping through my seat bones.

'Hurry up,' I mutter to myself, imagining my sister sitting stiffly behind the steering wheel, sticking religiously to the speed limits.

I pull the fleece tighter, my shoulders hunched towards my ears.

I can feel the house behind me, looming, empty. I half wonder if it's punishing me for abandoning it — like a dog put into kennels who ignores its owners when they return.

The security light switches off and I'm left shivering in the darkness.

Previously

A single-lane track carves through tall hedgerows, climbing towards the cliff top.

'It's at the very end,' I tell the taxi driver.

The driveway is gravelled with grey and white stone, no doubt selected to complement the exterior paintwork and natural wood weatherboarding.

The house sits imposingly on the cliff top, steel struts bored into the rock so that the sea-facing side of the house seems to hang suspended above the cliff. There is something in the contrast of the fresh warmth of the house, versus the jagged dark hues of the rocks below. It is an incredible feat of architecture.

'Lovely place you've got here,' the driver says as the taxi crunches to a halt.

'Yes, indeed,' I say with a private smile.

I pay the fare, tipping him more than is necessary.

I carry my holdall to the front door, setting it down on the flagstone steps. I wait until the taxi has circled from the driveway and disappeared within the tunnel of hedgerows. Then I cross to the edge of the property where, as described in the email, the wheelie bins are stored within a discreet fenced area.

I drag the green recycling bin aside, which clinks with bottles. Beneath it lies a large pebble. I lift it carefully, feeling like a child turning over

13

rocks in search of a treasured glimpse of woodlice or bugs.

There it is: the key to the house.

I return the wheelie bin into position, then cross the drive to the doorstep. My fingertips meet the solid wood door, painted in a grey-green shade that recalls the sea. I pause for a moment, aware of the magnitude of this moment stretching around me, raising the beat of my heart.

I glance once over my shoulder, just to be sure that there's no one watching. I take a breath, then slot the key into the lock.

2

Elle

'Thank God you were in,' I say, refilling Fiona's wine glass, then sinking back onto the sofa.

'And if I hadn't been?'

'Flynn's the only other person with a key.'

'He still has a key?'

I shrug. 'It'd feel churlish to ask for it back.'

Fiona doesn't say anything. She never needs to. Her eyebrows — dark and angular — speak for her.

'How did Drake get on at Bill's parents?' I ask. 'I missed him. Maybe he could come over this weekend? I got him a little treat while I was away.'

'He needs a treat reprieve. Bill's parents let him watch cartoons for two hours a day — and took him for ice cream every afternoon. I'm surprised he hasn't asked to be formally adopted.'

'You must have missed him.'

'You're kidding? I had lie-ins. I didn't cook. I got more work done than I've managed in months. I've asked if they'll make it an annual thing.'

'Is that right?' I say, my turn to arch an eyebrow. Drake has just turned two and it's the first time he's stayed a night away from home. Bill spent months carefully negotiating the week-long visit to his parents in Norfolk.

'What about you? How was France?'

15

'Oh, fine.' I'd been invited as a guest-speaker on a writing retreat. I'd deliberated over going, anxious about my approaching book deadline, but equally the retreat was so well paid that it would have been a mistake to turn it down. 'They put us up in this stunning old farmhouse in the middle of the countryside. There was a beautiful pool. I swam every morning.'

'If you've come back skinnier than you went, then you didn't eat enough cheese.'

'I ate cheese for breakfast.'

'Good girl,' she says, taking a drink of wine. 'What were the guests like?'

'Interesting, intelligent, passionate about books. One or two were a little intense. Deadly serious about word counts. In bed by ten o'clock.' I pause. 'You'd have liked them.'

Fiona laughs — a laugh I've always loved, loud and unapologetic.

'Yes, but did any of them take revision notes into the shower?'

During her A Levels, she used to tuck her revision notes into a plastic sleeve, so that she could continue to study while showering. She's always been the one with the focus, the drive.

'Can't say I witnessed it.'

'And what about . . . ' Fiona pauses dramatically, ' . . . your work in progress?'

I glance towards the window, lamplight reflected in the dark pane. Just the thought of my second novel makes my stomach tighten.

'Still floundering in the wilderness.'

'Will you make the deadline?'

I lift my shoulders. 'It's in six weeks' time.'

Fiona assesses me closely. 'What if you don't?'
'I lose the book deal.'

And then I lose this house, I think, panic beating its wings within my ribcage. I can't let that happen.

Fiona knows the energy I've committed to this house, the long process of architectural drawings and planning applications, the months and months of builders clambering over scaffolding, craning in huge glass panels, drilling into rock to fit unyielding iron struts, the hours I spent studying bathroom fittings and flooring and paint charts.

It was all so unlike me — the me who drifted through my twenties owning little more than I could squeeze into a backpack. But I wanted it more than anything. Cornwall was where Fiona was. *A house overlooking the sea* was our mother's dream. It was putting down roots, it was stability.

One evening, mid-build, when I'd returned to our rented flat in Bristol, Flynn kept his back to me, watching the flames dance in the fireplace, as he'd said, 'I wonder if you're putting too much energy into that house.'

That house. Never *our* house.

I wish I'd noticed the distinction back then.

I replied, 'I want to make it perfect, so we never have to leave.'

★　★　★

'Thank you for looking after things while I was away,' I say to Fiona. 'The house looks immaculate.'

'Surprised?'

'Very.'

'It's because I hardly had to do a thing. It was spotless.'

'Was it? I was worrying about it while I was away. It just felt so strange knowing there was someone in my home that wasn't *me*.'

'I knew you'd be like that.'

Bill was actually the one who'd suggested I rent the house.

'You know, if money is tight,' he'd begun while we were barbecuing on the bay one evening, 'you should think about putting the house on Airbnb over the summer.'

'Remember my friend Kirsty from university?' Fiona had asked.

I must have looked blank.

'The English teacher. Had sex with the headmaster in his office — and a parent walked in.'

'*That* Kirsty!'

'She has a three-bed house in Twickenham and goes away over the school holidays and rents her place. She gets two grand a week for it.'

'Two grand?' I crouched down to examine a shell that Drake had brought to me. 'It's beautiful, baby,' I said, planting a kiss on the smooth curve of his forehead, then folding my fingers around the shell. He trundled off in search of more.

'Everyone's doing it,' Bill said. 'Easy little earner.'

'Yes, but this is Elle.' Fiona threw me a look. 'She took three days to choose the right handles for her doors.'

'I can handle it,' I said, grinning.

'Anyway, don't encourage her, Bill. You know who'll have to look after it when she jets off on another book tour and some porn company decides to use it as the location for their next shoot — '

'God, don't!' I laughed.

'Contract cleaners in that case,' Bill said.

'Kirsty puts all their valuables in their study and locks off the room. Easy.' Fiona plucked a piece of mint from her glass of Pimm's and tore it between her teeth. 'You know that place Bill and I stayed at when we went to Pembrokeshire? That was an Airbnb. They left everything. The wardrobes were full of this woman's clothes. I think she was a ballroom dancer.'

'Tell me you tried on something sequinned.'

'She was more Bill's size.'

'I do love a leotard,' he said, patting his stomach fondly. 'Seriously though, you could charge a fortune for your place. You should think about it.'

And I had. I thought about it as I stared at the final invoice from the builders, my fingers trembling as I tapped numbers into my calculator. Fiona and Bill didn't know — they still don't — that I had to remortgage to pay the builders.

So this first Airbnb rental is a trial, a test run. The idea is that I rent out the house again in the summer and bugger off somewhere. My two best friends both live on the other side of the world; Nadia has moved to Dubai to teach English, and Sadie lives on a farm in Tasmania with her husband's family.

19

I turn to Fiona, asking, 'What were the family like who rented it?'

'Yes, fine,' she says, setting her wine glass on the lounge table.

'Did they seem nice?'

'I only met them briefly.'

I detect a tightness in her tone, which makes me ask, 'Everything did go okay?'

'Yes, absolutely. No breakages. I've released the deposit. They left a couple of bits and pieces behind.' As Fiona unfolds herself from the sofa, I notice she's lost weight. We've both always been slim, but there's something angular about the breadth of her shoulders, her sternum pronounced at the open neckline of her shirt.

Fiona moves to the sideboard, picking up a pot of nappy rash cream, and a well-chewed plastic giraffe.

'These were the only things I came across,' she says, squeezing the giraffe until it squeaks.

Unexpectedly, sadness swells in my chest.

'I've washed all the bedding — hot wash,' she adds with a wink, 'and taken Drake's high chair home.'

'Oh yes, thanks for the loan.'

'I dropped it in the evening before they arrived and almost had a heart-attack as the alarm was on. I'd forgotten you'd told me you'd set it.'

'You turned it off okay?'

'On the sixth attempt. My eardrums bled. Right,' Fiona says, sweeping across the lounge towards the doorway. 'I'm going. Told Bill I'd only be half an hour.'

'Sorry for stealing you.'

'It's fine, he has the television. Three's a crowd.'

I stand and kiss my sister, our cheekbones clashing.

★   ★   ★

Locking the door behind Fiona, I move into the kitchen, flicking on all the lights and the radio.

I take my notebook from my handbag and position a pencil beside it. I take a step back, looking through the screen of my phone at the configuration. I snap the picture, then upload it to Facebook, adding the caption:

After a lovely fortnight tutoring on a writing retreat, I'm back home and SO excited to be diving into my novel — on the home straight now! #amwriting #authorlife

Then I put the props away.

Opening the fridge, I inspect its contents, hoping Fiona might have left a pint of milk or a loaf of bread — but it's bare.

Too tired to contemplate getting back in the car, I root around in the pantry and pull out a bag of pre-cooked quinoa and toss it through with tahini and lemon juice. I eat standing up, flicking through the post.

I glance at the bills, trying to ignore the words FINAL REMINDER blazoned across my electricity statement. Next there are a couple of packages from my agent containing proof copies of other authors' books requesting advance praise. The remainder of the mail includes requests for charity donations, two fan letters forwarded on from my publishers, and an invite to a friend's birthday. Nearing the bottom of the pile my hands reach for a thick cream envelope embossed with a gold logo. It's from Flynn's solicitor.

In France I'd been reminded of our first trip together in our mid-twenties, when we'd taken the ferry to Bilbao and then driven north to Hossegor in Flynn's battered Seat Ibiza with a surfboard strapped to the roof and a tent in the boot. We'd camped in the shade of thick pine trees and lived on noodles and warm batons of French bread. We drank cheap stubby beers and wine from cardboard containers, and spent the evenings playing cards by headtorch, or lying in the tent, the door unzipped, salt and sun-cream glossing our entwined limbs.

On that trip Flynn had talked about all the places he wanted to travel — and I had said yes to it all, knowing that I wanted to be anywhere but home. When I was with him, the rest of my life seemed like something that had happened to a different person, someone I was happy to leave behind in the campus of a university town I'd never return to.

I scrape the rest of the quinoa into the bin, then collect my suitcase and go upstairs. Flicking on my bedroom light, I pause in the doorway, my gaze on my bed.

Fiona has done a half job of making it, of course. The cushions aren't plumped, the soft olive throw is stretched across the entire bed, not just the foot of it. These tiny details remind me that I wasn't the last person to sleep in this bed — rather another woman and her husband.

I set down my case, then wander round my room, eyes scanning the clean surfaces. I slide open my wardrobe door; my clothes are still hanging in one portion of the wardrobe just as I'd left them, the rest of the rail clear for the other couple's clothes. I move to my bedside drawer and pull it open. Empty, as I'd left it — oh, except for a small pot of men's hair wax pushed right to the back. I twist off the lid and, seeing it is almost empty, drop it into the bin.

Taking out my washbag, I move to the large free-standing mirror at the foot of my bed, where I dab cleanser onto a cotton pad and sweep it gently around my face. I've picked up a little colour in France, and my hair has been lightened by the sun to a warm caramel shade.

As I lean in, that's when I notice them: fingerprints. Larger than mine. I look closer: a hand has been pressed flat to the mirror, the smear of a stranger's skin marking the glass.

Standing here with the empty room reflected behind me, an unsettling feeling creeps over my skin. Someone else has been in this room. Been in my house. The woman who'd rented it — Joanna — must have stood where I am, her image caught in the mirror. It feels as if this stranger's gaze is still here, watching.

As I step back, a hot pain bursts into my heel.

I snatch up my foot, reaching out for the wall for balance. There is a deep puncture in the very centre of my heel, a bead of blood springing to

23

the surface. What the hell have I stood on? I crouch down, searching the carpet, running my palms across it until they meet the waspish scratch of something.

A shard of glass, knife-sharp, is lodged deep in the plush carpet. I grip it between my fingers and carefully pull it out. The downlights illuminate a beautiful blue icicle, something vaguely familiar in the glitter of the glass.

Has something of mine been broken? I can't think of anything in my bedroom that this piece could've come from. I keep the surfaces of my bedside table clear, except for a tripod lamp and a jug for flowers. My bottles of perfume have been packed away with the other breakables and valuables, which I'd locked in my writing room. It's unsettling to not be able to place this lethal dagger of glass.

I wrap it in a tissue and, as I drop it into the bin, I glance down at the cream carpet and see it is marked with the crimson blush of my blood.

Previously

Oak, jasmine and something citrus — those are the smells that greet me as I step inside. There is a clean, fresh quality to the air that is different to my house: it is dry, free of cooking smells, or that earthy dampness that comes from washing dried on radiators.

I can't help myself. 'Hello?'

There is, of course, no reply. I smile. The quiet is beautiful, softened by the distant sound of the sea.

My black holdall looks incongruous on the solid oak floor. I kick off my shoes and leave them discarded. Yours, I see, are placed neatly beneath the oak settle.

I walk through the entrance hall, which leads straight into the spacious kitchen. The walls are a warm shade of white; I think the paint has been chosen with light-diffusing particles so that it feels as if the walls are breathing air into the room. The splashes of colour — chalky pastel shades — come from the painted wooden cabinets, the well-chosen artwork, the pottery carefully displayed.

The style is graceful, calming. It's as if a handful of sea-bleached pebbles have been gathered and used as the basis for the palette. The modern, sleek lines of handle-less cabinets and a granite work surface have been married with a beautiful old farmhouse table, the wood

25

ring-marked and age-worn. A long bench seat is set against the wall, strewn with hessian cushions. It's a table for a family, or for dinner parties. Not a table for one.

I smile to see that the high chair, as requested, is placed at the end of this table, although it won't be used, of course. On the kitchen counter there is a small bunch of wildflowers in an old honey pot, tied with brown string. Leaning against it is a handwritten card addressed to Joanna and family.

A thoughtful touch.

I pick up the card, tracing a finger across the elegant handwriting, but I don't open it.

Setting it back down, I move past an aged dresser painted duck-egg blue, where earthenware mugs hang from neat iron hooks. Seagrass-speckled pots are stacked artfully between mason jars containing nuts, pulses and attractive spirals and ribbons of pasta. I slide open the dresser drawer and, as I reach into it, I experience the sharp sensation that someone is going to snap the drawer shut on my fingers, a child caught snooping.

I feel like a trespasser. Yet, in my pocket, I'm aware of the small but solid presence of the front door key resting against the top of my thigh.

I am no trespasser, I remind myself. You let me in.

3
Elle

'If you're going to throw a ticking bomb into the story, light the fuse at the beginning, and let us hear it tick.'
                    Author Elle Fielding

In the charcoal-coated dark of three a.m., I am awake. The cut to my heel throbs; my pulse seems to tick there.

Over the years I've tried a wealth of tips and tricks to soften insomnia's grip: a soak in a lavender-scented bath; listening to an audio book; blackout blinds; a warm, milky drink before bed; that sodding meditation app that I'd thought was the key but eventually stopped working, too; no screen time; no sugar after dinner; sleeping pills; homeopathic remedies; acupuncture. Everything. I've tried everything.

People don't understand that it's not *falling* asleep that's the problem. It's *staying* asleep.

If only there was just a switch for my mind, some way of turning it off, or at least turning down the volume; instead, as the night draws deeper, worries begin to stir, stretch, wake. Harmless, innocuous happenings take on a different shape — the shadows they cast, stretching.

The chef I used to work with when I was

27

waitressing in a pub called them the heebie-jeebies.

'Don't trust any thoughts you have between two a.m. and five a.m. It's like listening to your drunk self.'

Reminding myself of this advice doesn't settle me tonight. I inhale and exhale slowly, following the path of my breath.

But I can still feel it: the ice-sharp point of that shard of glass as it pierced my skin.

★ ★ ★

I lean against the kitchen counter, listening to the low gurgle of the coffee machine as the water begins to heat. What would I do without coffee? I finally stumbled into a deep, dreamless sleep at around five a.m., but now I feel thick-headed, disjointed.

Beyond the window, mellow white clouds blanket the sky, thin swatches of blue glimpsed beyond. A kayaker is powering across the bay, the paddle lifting and dipping with pleasing fluidity.

On the shoreline there's a lone birdwatcher, collar pulled to their chin. They are standing with their head tilted back, binoculars raised towards the cliff. There's a stillness about them that I admire — lovely to be so enraptured by bird life that you'd want to dedicate hours of your day to simply observing it.

I follow the direction of the birdwatcher's gaze to see if I can locate what they've spotted.

As I follow the angle of their binoculars,

unease trickles down my spine. Their gaze isn't focused on the cliff. It is set higher.

They are watching my house.

A memory, match-bright, flashes through my thoughts: his slow smile; the dark, knowing eyes that followed me, hawk-like with exacting focus; the pleasure in his voice as he said my name.

I extinguish the memory with a blink, yet feel the shiver it leaves behind.

Course they're not watching the house, I tell myself. The binoculars must be trained on a bird; sand martins nest nearby, and there are rare but occasional sightings of a pair of peregrine falcons.

The stranger's hair is covered by a hat pulled low to their ears, but something about the way they stand, the straightness of their posture, a narrowness of shoulders, makes me wonder if it's a woman.

The stranger seems to become aware of me at the window, as they lower their binoculars and, just for a moment, our eyes meet. There is a beat of time — no more than a matter of seconds — when we are looking at one another. Then the stranger turns, moves on.

★　★　★

Sliding my mobile towards me, I see my editor's name flashing.

I adjust my face into a smile. 'Jane. Hi.'

We exchange niceties about my writing retreat and Jane's visit to the Frankfurt Book Fair, and then Jane takes a breath, signalling the inevitable slide from small talk to business.

'So, I just wanted to touch base and check we're on track for next month's deadline.'

My shoulders stiffen. The book is already months overdue. I've cited house renovations and marriage difficulties — and in fairness to Jane, she has been understanding, extending the deadline twice. Her patience, however, is starting to thin — and I can't blame her. A final deadline has been set for the tenth of December and, if the new novel isn't handed in, I'll be in breach of contract.

During the writing retreat, I'd made time to think about the novel I am writing — or more accurately, am not writing. I've been switching between ideas for months, with so many false starts that I've lost my confidence, my instincts. The ideas aren't big enough, aren't exciting enough to carry a reader through. If I'm not inspired or excited by a story — why should readers be?

Second novel syndrome, David, one of the other tutors on the creative writing retreat, had called it.

'If you have a big success on your hands,' he'd said, while spreading sun-warmed brie onto a cracker, 'then it's like all those generous words of praise from reviewers and readers are stacked up in front of you. Your debut was an international bestseller — it scooped every bloody award going. Readers are desperate for whatever's coming next. It's hardly surprising that every time you attempt to write, the expectation towers over the page. You're writing in a book shadow.'

Book shadow, I'd thought afterwards as I'd lain in the cool of my room, red wine making my head swirl, the shutters thrown open so I could catch the sound of birdsong beyond the window.

'It's coming on well,' I say to Jane now, the tightness between my shoulder blades spreading down my spine.

'We're all so excited to read it,' Jane says brightly. 'Would you be happy to send across what you've written so I can start to get the flavour of it? I'm eager to brief the designers for our cover development.'

I picture the plain black notebook, a tangle of words jostled into paragraphs, sentences scribbled out, entire pages slashed with a single pencil line.

'Actually, I'm in the middle of revising a plot thread. If you don't mind, let's stick to the tenth of December.'

Jane accepts — what else can she say? We talk a little about an upcoming interview my publicist is in the process of securing with *Red* magazine, the date yet to be confirmed. Before Jane signs off, she says, 'I'm looking forward to your Facebook Live debut shortly.'

I glance at my watch. Just under an hour to go.

Before I left for France, Jane talked me into doing a series of live videos, telling me it would be a good way to connect with readers and build up pre-publication buzz.

When I said I had no idea what I'd talk about, she sounded genuinely surprised.

'Elle, you're a confident, eloquent young woman. You'll be fine. Readers just want to know more about you — where your ideas come from, how you write. That sort of thing. Keep it informal — maybe start each week with a writing tip, you know, like 'Things I've learned as an author'. Then answer any questions.'

I couldn't think of a good enough reason to say no.

Now she says to me, 'We've been pushing it across our social media channels, so we're hoping you'll have several thousand people tuning in live. We'll all be cheering you on at the office.'

All those people watching me. Asking me questions. Live. No room for mistakes. No possibility to edit. Nowhere to hide. Just me — Elle Fielding, author — in my writing room.

I put down the phone, aware that I'm sweating.

* * *

The air cools as I climb the stairs to the top of the house.

I kept my writing room locked during the rental; I needed somewhere to store my valuables — but also, I didn't like the idea of a stranger sitting at my desk. Odd of me, I know.

I slip the key from my pocket and spend a moment fighting the lock, turning it back and forth until I hear the bolt release. I push the door wide open.

Light fills the space, the shimmering scales of the sea pouring through the glass wall, streaming over the stripped wooden floorboards and across white walls. When I'd designed this room, I'd wanted to create a space where my imagination could travel beyond a desk, beyond a computer screen, beyond the walls of the house — for it to sail off towards the endless promise of the horizon.

I've kept everything purposefully pared back and unadorned. The only pieces of furniture are an aged oak desk, a simple bookshelf constructed from reclaimed scaffold planks, which display a collection of my favourite novels, and a ceramic oil burner. In the far corner of the room, there's a wingback chair turned to the view, and beside it an oak trunk that houses notebooks, photographs and diaries.

I cross the room, surprised to notice the fresh scent of salt in the air. I thought it would be stuffy up here after keeping the room locked for a fortnight.

Then I see it: the small window at the edge of the glass wall is open. I'm surprised — I always double-check the doors and windows. I must have somehow overlooked it. I know no one could have accessed the room during the Airbnb as I left it locked and took the only key with me.

I let the thought go as I settle myself at my desk. I love this desk. I came across it at Kempton Market four years ago. At the time, Flynn and I were living in a rented flat in Bristol, and I'd just begun working on my first novel — carving out slices of time to write in lunch breaks, or after I returned from a shift. I kept my ambition secret — except from Flynn — as somehow the dream felt too new, too fragile to be spoken about, as if a misplaced remark could have the power to damage it. As we'd left Kempton Market, I'd told Flynn, 'If I ever get a book deal, the first thing I'm going to do is buy a writing desk.'

Unbeknown to me, Flynn called the seller and arranged for the old desk to be delivered to his mother's garage. On the weekends when he visited his mother, he spent hours restoring the desk, treating it for woodworm, sanding it right back, working into the grooves of the ornate legs, removing the layers of varnish that had been reapplied over the years. He'd changed the handles, waxed the runners, and sealed the cracks.

A year later, when my novel was finally finished, I printed out six copies ready to send to prospective literary agents. That's when Flynn took me to see the desk.

'I was going to wait till you got your first publishing contract,' he said, as we'd stood in his mother's garage, the smell of turpentine spiking the air, 'but I think this day is more important. You finished your book, Elle. Whether this one's published, or whether it's the next one, or the one after that — you're a writer now.'

★ ★ ★

The timer on my phone beeps.

One minute to go.

My stomach turns over with nerves. *Several thousand people tuning in live.*

I sit up straighter, pull my shoulders back. I know what I need to do. What everyone is

34

expecting from me.

I reset my focus, drawing my gaze to my laptop. My own face glares back at me on screen using the laptop's camera. Perhaps it's just the tilt of the screen, or the way the light pours into the room, but for a moment, I don't recognise myself.

I reach for the mouse, hovering it over the GO LIVE button.

I click.

My smile stretches across my face. I can hear it in my voice as I say, 'Hello, everyone. I'm Elle Fielding, and I'm live today from my writing room here in Cornwall. Thanks so much for joining me. For those of you who don't know me, I'm the author of Wild Fear, a psychological thriller that was published last year.

'Over the coming weeks I'm planning on chatting about my writing journey, sharing tips of what I've learned so far, and answering any of your questions.

'Right, I suppose a good place to start would be with today's writing tip. It's something simple that we can all do: get a notebook. Keep it with you at all times. Our short-term memory retains information for three minutes, so unless it's written down, ideas can be lost. This is my current one,' I say, holding up a plain black notebook. 'I keep it in my handbag, or by my bed at night, or anywhere I go. It reminds me that I'm always a writer, wherever I am, whatever I'm doing.'

I'm careful not to open it.

Not to show what is inside.

I take a breath. 'Okay, so now it's over to you and your questions.' I peer at the left-hand side of the screen, where viewers are typing them in real-time. 'I'll do my best to answer as many as I can. The first one is from Cheryl Down. She asks, *Your debut novel was an international bestseller. Does that put pressure on you for your second novel?*'

I'm aware that Jane and her team will be watching. 'Yes, there is some pressure — but, the good thing is that I began my second novel before *Wild Fear* was released, so I didn't have any expectation at that point. I must admit, I'm a little behind in delivering — there was a house move and a big book tour — but things are finally settling, so I'm planning on getting my head down now.'

Tick.

'Next up, Adam Grant asks, *What did you do before you became an author?*' I smile. 'What didn't I do? I waited tables, served coffees, worked on a reception desk, manned a night-club cloakroom, cleaned offices. I travelled as much as I could afford. I lived in New Zealand for a while, and later, Canada. I pretty much spent my twenties bouncing from one thing to the next trying to work out what I wanted to do.'

Who I wanted to be.

'And then I found it: writing. It just clicked. I felt stupid for not recognising it earlier. The moment I started to write, I fell in love with it. I didn't know if I was any good at it, or whether I could ever make my living from it. All I knew was that I loved it.'

That is the truth.

I answer half a dozen more questions, then take a sip of water and glance at the clock.

'Time for just two more questions today. Amy Werden asks, *Do you have any writing rituals? PS You have the perfect life!*'

'Perfect life? I'm obviously using too many filters! With regards to writing rituals, something that is important to me is writing down my early ideas by hand. There is something about the germ of an idea, when it feels too precious, too delicate to be tapped into a computer screen and locked there. I like the curve of words on the page, a lack of uniformity, the scratch of a pencil on cream paper. The ideas can flow and find their rhythm.'

If Fiona is watching this, she'll be rolling her eyes.

'The final question is from Booklover101.' I immediately recognise the username. The accompanying profile picture is of a bike, its wicker basket filled with books. Booklover101 has followed me from the very beginning, commenting on almost every post I write. She tweets me, sends me direct messages, has sent me handwritten cards via my publishers.

'*As your no. 1 fan,*' I read now, '*I'm interested to know, does an author need to have a dark mind to write dark books?*'

I should have skipped it — chosen a different question.

I keep my face set in a smile.

'What you need,' I say slowly, giving myself a moment to think, to get it right, 'is an enquiring mind. To be able to look at any situation and see the possibility for shadows. To always ask, *What if?*

I leave it there. I thank everyone again for tuning in and remind them that I'll be live again next week.

My face disappears from the screen.

★　★　★

I sit for a moment, taking several deep, slow breaths. Almost pitch-perfect, I think. Jane will be pleased.

Then I push to my feet, moving away from the desk, and I open the window wider. Hooking a finger under the neckline of my top, I shake it to let air circulate to my flushed skin.

I stand there, gaze mapping the waves, waiting for my heartbeat to settle.

2003

Sitting in the passenger seat of her mother's old Renault, Elle turned the silver star stud through the cartilage at the top of her ear. Around and around she twisted it, like a rosary, as she ran through each of her worries. *Would her new housemates like her? Would she be homesick? Had she chosen the right course? Was her outfit okay?*

She didn't know then, as she wound down the window, pushing her face into the salty, marshy breeze as they crossed the Severn Bridge, that none of those questions were the ones she needed to ask.

The event that would change everything was marked out for later. For a time when she was settled and happy, her life ready to bloom.

That's when it would blindside her.

★   ★   ★

Elle arrived first. They pulled up on the pavement, leaving the hazard lights blinking as they trooped back and forth with Elle's belongings: a duvet spilling from a torn bin liner, a cardboard box heavy with food raided from the cupboards at home, a lava lamp wrapped in a towel, a duffle bag bulging with clothes, two posters rolled into tubes that had bent in the car.

She didn't mind the dreary pebbledash

student house that backed onto a trainline, or the stretch of damp on the wall behind her bed. She looked at her student house and saw freedom.

Her mother helped her tack up posters of Bob Marley and Lenny Kravitz, and postcards from Fiona who was interning at a news desk in Santiago.

'You're going to be so happy here,' her mother said, holding Elle's face in her hands. 'I'm so proud of you. I hope I tell you that often enough.'

Elle could sense the emotion brooked in her mother. It was the first time in two decades that her mother would be returning to an empty flat.

'You know, Mum, you could do this, too. Study. Make more time to write. You could get a student loan . . . '

Her mother had waved a hand through the air. 'This is your time. You enjoy every moment of it.'

And Elle would do.

Until she met *him*.

4

Elle

In the moon-streaked dark of one a.m., I twist onto my side, pulling the covers under my chin.

When I was a girl, if I couldn't sleep, I'd slip into my mother's bed and ask her to tell me a story. She'd pluck ripe characters from the branches of her imagination and I'd lie on my back, eyes open, a forest of snow leopards or daisy fairies dancing across our ceiling.

It's been four years since she died, yet some nights, it's still hard to believe that she's gone.

In those awful first weeks after her death, when Fiona and I were both reeling, I'd read everything I could about sepsis. I'd pick up the phone, outraged to tell Fiona: *Did you know, eight million people worldwide die every year from sepsis? How, how have we not heard of it? How can our mother no longer be alive because of something that began with a urinary tract infection?*

I flick on the light, too agitated to sleep. From my bedside drawer, I pull out my copy of *Wild Fear*, and turn to the front.

I read the dedication.

For my mother.

I run a fingertip beneath those words.

Your mum would've been so proud, a reader

41

once said at a book signing.

They were wrong.

★ ★ ★

Wind funnels along the side of the house as I step from the back door into the morning's cold bite. Beneath bare soles, the paving stones are ice. Tightening the cord of my dressing gown, I feel the glossy kiss of my swimsuit beneath.

At the end of the pathway, private steps carve into the rock face, which I share with Frank and Enid's property. I concentrate on each footstep, avoiding the puddles of seawater pooling in grooves, the rock edges furred with seaweed.

Last night I only managed to snatch an hour or two's sleep. It felt like there was an axle out of alignment in my mind, causing my thoughts to over-steer, almost imperceptibly, in one direction so that, no matter how far I travelled, eventually they'd turn a circle and I'd arrive exactly where I started.

Out here though, buffeted by the blast and sting of salt air, my head begins to clear. Reaching the beach, the sand is compact, cold against my feet. Whitecaps rise and crumble beneath blustering clouds.

'You're mad,' Fiona always tells me whenever she hears I've been in for a winter swim. 'No one knows you're out there. You don't even wear a wetsuit. What if something happened?'

'It won't,' I reply, confident in my ability to judge conditions, to know my own limits. I've always loved to swim, but there is something intoxicating about swimming in the depths of winter. When I moved here, I made a bargain with myself that I'd get in the water once a week — all year round.

As children, we used to holiday in Cornwall, renting a caravan set back from the beach. I remember a particularly cold April, books and blankets scattered across the caravan, and a sense of restlessness at having spent too long indoors. I'd looked up from my page to watch a group of elderly people in swimsuits gathered at the water's edge. There was no squealing, no tiptoeing, no fuss. They simply walked into the sea and swam.

'That's what dementia does to you,' Fiona had declared, clambering onto the sofa beside me to watch.

'They're brave,' I countered, chin resting on forearms.

'They're like, a hundred. They'll get pneumonia.'

Our mother, who'd been writing in the gold-edged notebook we'd bought her for Christmas, glanced up.

'Cold water boosts our white blood cells because our bodies are forced to react to the changing conditions. It's good for you.' She'd always had a knack for casting a relevant, articulate fact into almost any stream of conversation.

Fiona turned to me, eyes glinting. 'I dare you to join them.'

Four years older than me, her approval was hard to gain. I thought about the sharpness of

43

the cold, the feel of the icy waves lifting and dropping me, the way my skin would pucker with goose bumps. I placed a bookmark into the spine of my novel.

'Sure.'

I lasted a minute and a half, the cold squeezing the air from my lungs, but Fiona had clapped and cheered from the shoreline and I felt like a hero. Afterwards our mother warmed a pan of hot chocolate and I sat cross-legged in front of the electric fire watching the wiggling red lines of heat, the mug cupped in my hands, a surge of endorphins pumping in my body.

Now at the shoreline, I step from my dressing gown, the cold nicking my skin. I set the gown on the damp sand, then snap a picture of it, typing a quick post:

My drug of choice for getting the brain cells firing. #wildswim

Then the phone is away, and it is just me and the sea.

The trick, I've learned, is not to rush. To set a pace that doesn't falter. I walk purposefully to the shore and straight into the sea. I don't focus on the cold gripping my ankles: I concentrate on my breathing, keeping it level as the water climbs to my waist.

I push off, kicking away from shore. The bitter sea wraps around me, stealing every thought in my head. It is all I can do to remember to breathe.

I'm careful to remain near shore, not wanting to chance my luck against the stronger currents that pull and suck towards the horizon. I can taste the salt on my lips, feel the pleasing sting of it against my skin.

I look back towards my house. I realise that I've left the light on in the writing room and I can see straight inside, the empty desk eyeing me.

It looks, just for a moment, as if someone passes behind it.

I tread water, blinking saltwater from my eyes, looking again. It is a trick of the light, of course. A strange reflection, because now the shadow has gone.

★   ★   ★

The first time I saw the cliff-top house was with Flynn. We had come to Cornwall to be introduced to a ten-day-old Drake. Fiona seemed shell-shocked that this tiny pink creature with tightly curled fists and a fierce cry was hers. She moved around the house in a daze, a muslin flung over her shoulder, patches of her shirt stiff with leaked milk.

'Take him,' Fiona had begged, when I passed the nursery one evening and found her jigging him wearily.

Pressing him to my chest, I slowly circled my palm over the curve of his tiny back. I began to sing in a low, half-whispered voice, words that unravelled from some distant song that our mother had taught us. The rhythm seemed to soothe

45

him, and I placed my lips against the soft down of his head and breathed in. Longing bloomed like blood rising to the surface of my skin.

When I turned, I saw Fiona still standing in the doorway of the nursery, watching. Her eyes shone with tears that didn't fall.

'I can't even stop him crying.'

'You're doing brilliantly — but you're exhausted. Get some sleep. I'll wake you when he's hungry.'

Fiona didn't seem to hear. Her gaze was on the empty cot.

'There are so many things I want to ask Mum. She did it on her own. The two of us.' She shook her head. 'Dad left when you were six weeks old. How the hell did she manage with two kids and no family nearby to help? I can't even imagine. She was a hero, but I didn't . . . I didn't tell her how incredible she was . . . it's only now . . . ' She pulled back her lips, as if baring her teeth. 'I just, I miss her so much.'

'I know you do,' I whispered.

It was no surprise that the cruelness of our mother's absence revisited us again with the birth of Drake, in the way that life and death circle each other. She would have loved rocking Drake to sleep in her arms, examining those tiny pink toes, carefully dressing and undressing him, bathing him, washing the blankets he used, the Babygros he soiled, the muslins he posseted on. She would have made meals, stocked freezers, emptied bins, folded washing. She would have praised Bill's easy competency at changing nappies, or with manning the sterilizing station.

46

She would have looked at Fiona and known that sleep deprivation was sinking her, that the baby blues were in danger of growing into something more serious.

She would have done all those things because she was a mother herself, and she knew.

I tried to fill that role as best I could, but each time I held Drake, my own longing sharpened. Flynn, sensing I needed a break, removed the pile of clean vests and white hats and delicate cardigans I'd been folding, took my fingers in his and told me, 'Let's walk.'

We weaved down a footpath in the direction of the coast, eventually coming to a steep path of switchbacks leading to a small bay hugged by cliffs.

I had a vague memory of visiting this beach years before. I could recall the red tassels of a picnic blanket, my mother sitting with a hand shading the sun from her eyes, marvelling at something. I could picture the black rocks that lay exposed and dripping at low tide.

As we walked, Flynn said, 'It will happen for us.'

I'd slipped my hand into the back pocket of his jeans, leaning into him. 'It's been over a year.'

'Maybe it's time to see a doctor.'

I felt myself stiffen, retract. But I needed answers, too.

When we reached the far end of the bay, we looked up, noticing the squat fisherman's cottage set on the cliff top. 'What a view.'

'It has a For Sale sign,' he said, pointing to the red board at its shoulder.

The owner was home — a retired nurse who didn't mind this young couple knocking on her door — and she invited us to look around. The cottage was hopelessly run-down, the roof sagging, the wallpaper curling at the edges, yet there was magic there.

'Imagine living here,' Flynn had said when we were alone, turning me to face the view, wrapping his arms around my waist, chin resting on my shoulder. 'We could do it, couldn't we?'

The money from my advance had just landed in our account, and Flynn had some savings from a family inheritance.

'Yes, I think we could. But Cornwall? What about your job?'

'I can be a tree surgeon anywhere,' he'd said. 'I think this is where you want to be, isn't it? Near your sister, near Drake.'

I thought of Fiona cradling her new son; I thought of our mother's dream to own a house overlooking the sea; I thought of the chances of stumbling across this cottage, finding the owner home. It seemed serendipitous.

'Yes,' I'd said to Flynn. 'It is.'

Twelve weeks later, we had the keys. We moved in, sleeping on a mattress on the floor while we made plans. A lick of paint. A wood burning stove. New curtains. Fresh carpet. It was everything we'd need.

Now, as I swim looking up at the towering house on the cliff top, I wonder if we'd stuck to the plan — if the idea of the house hadn't overtaken me — whether our marriage would have had a better chance of surviving.

48

Here I am alone, with a house I can no longer afford, and a career that feels like it, too, is teetering on a cliff edge.

★   ★   ★

My feet look bloodless and pale against the dark rock as I climb the cliff steps, shivering beneath my dressing gown. My hair hangs wetly at my neck and I am already anticipating the warmth of the shower.

As I follow the narrow path alongside the house, a plastic bag wheels past on the breeze, brushing my bare ankle. I grab for it, but a gust lifts it out of reach, parachuting the bag beyond me. Hurrying after it, I come to the end of the path and halt.

The driveway is scattered with litter. Used kitchen roll, empty tins, plastic containers, and cereal boxes are strewn across the gravel. Sheets of newspaper dance in the gusts, several more pinned against the fence line. A crumpled page from a notebook rolls past me. At the edge of the driveway, the recycling bin lies on its side, lid open. Although the wind is blowing, I know it isn't nearly strong enough to upturn a bin.

I hurry across the drive, gravel cutting into my feet, and with some effort, I manage to right the bin. I re-knot the belt of my dressing gown, then begin gathering the litter. My wet hair whips around my face, leaving trails of fresh salt.

As I push my hair back from my face, I have the growing sensation that I'm not alone.

Across the lane, I spot Mark standing in the

doorway of his parents' house, a cigarette held between his fingers.

'Foxes,' he calls.

He stubs the cigarette against the wall, then turns and disappears inside the house.

I stand there, open-mouthed. Did that just happen? Had he — a grown man — upturned my bins?

I half-laugh, staggered. Is this a reaction to the house build — a retaliation for compromising the view from their family home? I think of the awful visit six months after we'd bought the house, as I unrolled the architect's drawings across Frank and Enid's kitchen table.

'You said renovate, not rebuild!' Frank exploded, colour bursting into his cheeks.

When I'd worried about the neighbours' reaction, friends reassured me that *No one owns a view! Any other buyer would do the same!* Although they were right, it didn't lessen the guilty heat that crept up my neck.

Enid had moved towards the kitchen window, heavy-knuckled hands worrying the edge of her cardigan. She looked out towards the sea as if her time with the view was waning. If there'd been a moment when I was close to reconsidering, that had been it.

I finish collecting the litter, then drag the bin back into position at the end of the driveway. If I were Fiona, I'd go over and demand an apology from Mark, but I don't have the energy for a confrontation.

My novel, I think. That's what I need to focus on.

Setting myself at my desk with a steaming coffee and salt-damp hair, I am ready. I open the drawer to grab a pencil — but can't find one. I pull the drawer right out, trailing my hand through the mess of pens, Sharpie markers, Post-it notes, and glue sticks. There is a hole puncher, a calculator, a pot of drawing pins, a lighter for my oil burner — but no bloody pencils.

It's a stupid detail, but it bothers me: I always have spares.

I tramp downstairs and locate a pencil from the depths of my handbag. I'm tetchy by the time I return to my writing room. I open the window, settle myself for a second time. I keep a well-thumbed dictionary on my desk and I watch as its cover lifts in the breeze, pages fanning.

Something doesn't feel quite right. I try not to indulge the feeling — I don't want to become one of those writers who demand a certain ambience to create — but I can't shake the thought that something is off-balance.

Then I realise what it is. The dictionary. It is usually secured by a paperweight — a beautiful glass globe that my mother bought on a hiking holiday in Malta three years before her death.

'It looks like it's caught the sea inside,' she'd told me, a wistful look in her eyes. I always keep the paperweight on top of the dictionary — but oddly, it is now positioned beside it.

I pick up the paperweight, turning it through my fingers, feeling its solidity and coolness against my palms. Daylight catches in the silver flecks, making it shimmer like the surface of the sea. As I rotate it, my skin catches on something jagged.

Lifting the globe towards my face, I see the crack — a chip no greater than the length of a fingernail.

I can't remember damaging it.

There is something unsettling at the back of my mind, a sense of discord. I pace for a moment, trying to work it loose.

Then I seize on it: the jagged shard of glass that punctured my foot. It'd looked like a tiny, lethal icicle. The same colour as this.

I hurry from the writing room, descending the stairs, fingers gripping the paperweight. Pushing open my bedroom door, I go straight to the wastepaper basket at the foot of my mirror. Digging through it, I pull out a parcel of tissue.

Opening it carefully, I remove the dagger of glass I'd found embedded in the carpet.

I press the missing fragment against the paperweight.

Like a key slipped into a lock, it is the exact fit.

Previously

When staying in someone else's house, one would have to be incurious not to wonder about the owner. There are clues everywhere — the photos carefully selected for display on the walls, the clothes hanging in the floor-to-ceiling wardrobes, the stock of medicines in the bathroom cabinet, the box file filled with documents in the bureau, the post that arrives with the handwritten address.

I can take my time, enjoy these small discoveries because, for now, your house is mine.

I drift from the kitchen to the lounge, admiring the sense of continuity and flow between rooms. Everything is marvellously tasteful: the low-backed cream sofa, framed by two upholstered tub armchairs, each carefully angled to face the water. The neutral tones and uncluttered lines naturally focus the gaze towards the sea. Even on a dull day, such as this, there is a mesmerising quality to the water. In warmer weather, I imagine sliding back the bifold doors, removing a wall of the room so that it feels as if the house and water are just a breath apart.

It's a truly beautiful home. I'm sure some people would be quick to add, 'Well, yes, easy if you've got the money.'

I disagree. This takes vision.

I could never have created this.

My gaze is drawn to a slight groove in the seat of your sofa, the lightest depression in the fabric. This is where you sit. My eye travels to the adjacent coffee table, where there is a scuff mark close to the edge where you must put your feet up.

I lower myself into the spot that is familiar to you. I find my hand sliding down the side of the sofa. It's the forgotten corners in a home that are often the most revealing. I feel the rough grate of sand or crumbs beneath my nails. My fingers meet something firm and narrow, and I withdraw a pencil. The end of it is splintered, the lead protruding further than the wooden housing. It appears as if the pencil has been snapped in two.

An accident?

Pushing myself to my feet, I turn. Behind the sofa is a library wall. Carefully selected pieces of pottery punctuate the rows of books with the grace of well-placed commas. I stand for a moment admiring your literary choices, many of them classics: Hemingway, Shakespeare, Brontë and Austen. A little predictable, but nice all the same.

I step closer, running my finger along the worn spines of the fiction shelf, passing psychological thrillers, romance novels, literary novels — but no, I still do not see it. I keep looking until I'm sure.

There is only one notable absence on these shelves: your book.

5

Elle

I drop the final piece of naan into my mouth, then gather the takeaway dishes, following Fiona through to her kitchen.

'Avert your eyes,' Fiona instructs, glancing at the sink, which is piled with washing up. 'One of those weeks.'

'I'll do them. It'll take me a minute.'

'You will not.' She blocks the sink. 'You can pour us more wine.'

My sister's relentless bossiness has a nostalgic flavour. I'm used to my actions being channelled, as if I'm something fluid, destined to flow around Fiona.

'I've been meaning to ask,' I say, watching her rinse the plastic takeaway dishes, then jam them into the recycling bin, punching down a cereal box to make room. 'You know when you cleaned after the Airbnb, did you happen to go into my writing room?'

'Oh God, don't tell me I was meant to clean in there, too?' She forces the bin door shut with a shove. 'I had such a busy week that I only got over for an hour. I'm not doing it again, by the way. Next time you can find a cleaner.'

'No, it's not that — it's just, when I went in there, the window was left open and it felt like things were different.'

'Different?'

'Like things had been moved.'

Fiona turns. 'What do you mean?'

'I have this blue glass paperweight on my desk. Do you remember? Mum brought us them back from Malta.'

'Yes, with the swirls of ink.'

'It's been chipped. I found the missing part lodged in my bedroom carpet.'

'And?'

'I think it happened while I was away.'

'Thought you'd locked your writing room?'

'I did.'

'So, you think,' Fiona says, an eyebrow cocked, 'that the Airbnb renters broke into your writing room, chipped your paperweight, then tossed the broken piece into your bedroom?'

I'd anticipated this reaction: dismissive, unperturbed. That is precisely why I decided to tell my sister.

Fiona continues. 'The glass probably got stuck to the sole of your shoe, and then you walked it around the house, and it finally came loose in one of the rooms.' She slots a tablet into the dishwasher and clanks it shut with more force than is necessary. 'I knew you'd get like this after renting your house. You need a dog.'

'I do not need a dog.'

I fetch a bottle of white from the fridge and refill our glasses. The fridge door is covered with photos, notes, and the first of Drake's crayon scribblings. My gaze lands on the picture of me and Flynn standing in front of our campervan, alongside Bill and a heavily pregnant Fiona.

I miss that camper. An old Mercedes Sprinter, which Flynn had spent months converting. We'd pull up at quiet beaches and cook dinner with the slide door pulled wide.

I pluck the photo from the fridge, looking more closely. I remember the first time I'd seen Flynn — the long sandy hair, the sun-tanned face, the skateboard slung under his arm, the carefree curve of his smile. My stomach flipped with desire as I'd served his coffee, slipping an extra biscuit on the saucer. He'd come back to the café every day for a week before he worked up the nerve to ask, 'Fancy hanging out after you finish?'

I was twenty-four years old at the time and felt impossibly lost. I was working shifts in cafés and bars, sleeping at strange hours, barely leaving my rented flat except to go to work. I felt as if I were submerged . . . that life was happening to other people and I was watching it at a distance. I'd lost contact with my school friends and had distanced myself from Fiona and our mother. I didn't know who I was or what I wanted until, on a Tuesday morning in spring, Flynn Fielding walked into the café with his skateboard. I could see the surface again; I could breathe.

Fiona moves to my shoulder. 'Remind me why you're divorcing again?'

I shoot her a look that says, *Don't.*

'You know what I've been thinking?' Fiona says as I pin the photo back in place.

'Here we go.'

'You need to start dating.'

'I thought I needed a dog.'

'Date a man with a dog.'

'Leave it with me.'

We take our wine through to the lounge and settle onto the sofas. In the warmth of the room, I find myself yawning, my eyelids heavy. It's not even ten o'clock.

'So tell me about the tenants. What were they like?'

'Sorry?'

'Joanna and her family. The renters. When you did the handover, did they seem okay? You know, not paper-weight-chipping maniacs?'

Something passes over Fiona's face. She inspects the stem of her wine glass. 'Yes, they seemed fine.'

I know my sister. 'What aren't you telling me?'

'Nothing at all.'

'Fiona . . . '

There is a good three- or four-second pause before Fiona looks up, right at me.

'Listen, I'm sorry, but I didn't meet them.'

'What?'

'I went over the morning they arrived like we agreed, but they were out — so I just left a note with my phone number. I planned to check in with them later in the week, but then things got a bit chaotic and — '

'You said you had! You told me you'd met them.' My palm slams the sofa arm, surprising us both.

★ ★ ★

58

It is just like my sister to not follow through with something that doesn't directly benefit her.

In the bright overhead light of Fiona's bathroom, I'm confronted by how tired I look — the bags beneath my eyes settling into dark bruises. I've learned that you do not say you're exhausted to a mother of a toddler who has been parenting on her own all week.

I wash my hands, forgetting that the cold tap sprays water, which shoots over my top. I snap off the tap. Not finding any towels, I dry my hands on the dressing gown hanging from the back of the door.

I remember offering to pay for a bathroom refurbishment — back when my book advance felt like it might never run out — but Fiona had given me one of her lethal, haughty stares, and I knew not to offer again. In a way, I'm pleased. There's a sense of comfort in the bath edge lined with shampoos and conditioners, the plastic ducks and toy boats spooling from a net suckered to the tiles; there are toothbrushes jammed into a chipped mug, a bowl of tiny bottles of shower gels pilfered from hotels. There are no hidden cupboards for toiletries, or woven baskets to house neatly folded towels. It feels lived in and there is something appealing in that.

I've often thought that people who know Fiona in a professional capacity — who are used to her straight-talking, razor efficiency — would be surprised if they stepped into her home. It is a valve, a little pocket of chaos to relieve the pressure of her exacting approach to her work.

In that sense, I suppose we're opposites. My

house is my sanctuary: uncluttered, ordered. Everything has its place — and that gives me a sense of security, of calm.

It's the rest of my life that's in chaos.

★ ★ ★

Moving onto the landing, I pause outside Drake's room. His door is ajar and my heart lifts at the thought of his little pyjama-clad body, the biscuit smell of his neck, the light raspy sound of his snores. It is so tempting to slip into the room, check his blanket, make sure he has his comforter by his hand — but I daren't risk waking him. It took Fiona an hour to get him down and I don't want to experience her wrath at being dragged to her feet again.

The room opposite is Fiona's study, which is lit by a desk lamp. It is the boxroom in the house — the would-be-nursery, if Fiona would entertain the idea of another child (she won't). Her desk is swamped beneath a sea of papers, notebooks and articles, a computer screen floating above the flotsam.

For years, Fiona worked as a journalist in London, writing ground-breaking exposé pieces about industry professionals. She went after those men and women like a hound following a scent, uncovering illegal fund transfers, tax evasion or any whiff of inequality towards staff. The work appealed to her exacting sense of fairness and she thrived in an industry with punishing hours and high pressure.

Moving to Cornwall and having a baby was

not so much a change of direction, but the squealing of brakes, the burn of tyres on tarmac, a vehicle sliding out into a U-turn. It was impossible to do both; her job was driven by contacts, interviews, sources — all of which needed to happen in London.

Fiona's work has always been central to her identity, so Bill and I were pleased when, on the evening of Drake's first birthday, as party plates were being stacked, Fiona announced that she was going to set up as a freelance copywriter.

Now her working hours are defined by seeking out the perfect word, a crisp turn of phrase to appeal to customers, to draw them to a brand. A pin board is tacked to the wall above her desk, filled with briefs, images, and guidelines about a client's specific language choices. In the middle of it all, there is a postcard. I recognise my own handwriting. *You are so fearless, so talented, that I know you'll succeed. May cutting edge copy fly!*

I smile, touched that my sister keeps this note pinned above her work station.

Behind me, there is the creak of floorboards. 'Not quite a sea view, is it?' Fiona is standing in the doorway.

'I love it in here.'

'What are you looking at?'

'You kept this postcard I sent you.'

'Did I? I'd forgotten it was there.'

Then, from behind Fiona, there comes a wail. 'Mummy!'

★ ★ ★

61

The front door opens, and Bill loafs into the house, a rush of cold air chasing after him.

He throws down a holdall, slinging his suit jacket over the top. His shirt is undone at the collar, tie removed.

'Hey, aren't you that famous author?' He beams at his old joke, then opens his arms, shirt straining across his barrel chest. 'Thought I spotted your car.'

As we hug, I catch the scent of car air-freshener and mints — and the subtle hint of cigarette smoke, too. Fiona banned him from smoking when she gave up six years ago, but we all know Bill likes the occasional secret cigarette. As does Fiona.

'They taste better smoked in secret,' Fiona had once explained. 'Makes us feel as if we're living dangerously.'

'So where's that gorgeous sister of yours?'

'Upstairs. Drake woke.'

'Ah.' He glances at the takeaway menu on the side. 'Fiona's been cooking you lavish meals again?'

'Makes a wonderful korma. Sorry, we didn't know you'd be back early. We'd have saved you some.'

'All I need,' Bill says, moving into the kitchen, me following, 'is one of these.' He pulls a bottle of beer from the fridge, twists the cap free, and clinks the neck of it against my wine glass. 'Cheers. To the end of the week.'

'The end of the week,' I agree, although I don't share his buzz. Tomorrow I'm delivering an author talk at the local library and know I won't relax fully until it is over.

Bill grabs a packet of pistachios and shakes them into a dish. He offers them first to me, then begins snapping the shells, dropping the nuts into his mouth, washing them down with beer.

'How was France?'

'Good. I enjoyed it — although I was ready to come home.'

'House still standing?'

'Thankfully, yes.'

'Fiona said the Airbnb all went well.'

'Think so.'

'Next time you rent it, give me the nod. Wouldn't mind escaping the chaos of this place for a few days.' He laughs, eyes sparkling.

I remember meeting Bill for the first time when Fiona was living in London. He was standing at her sink, thick arms plunged into a bowl of soapy water, the kitchen light reflecting off the curve of his bald head. My first thought was that he was one of her housemates' fathers.

Bill was so unlike the sallow-skinned academics who Fiona tended to date that I'd worried it wouldn't last — that Fiona, with her tendency to bore quickly, would become distracted.

'You know he has a proper job,' Fiona told me later, when we were alone. 'Something to do with sales. They give him a car to drive. This ugly great silver thing with awful tinted windows.' She spoke about their relationship with a tone of quiet amusement, as if she couldn't quite believe she'd fallen for him. 'Bill hasn't read a novel in two years. He watches snooker. He classes a good night out as having 'a few jars' at a comedy club. He's twelve years older than me. He wears jewellery — and I don't mean body piercings. I mean actual jewellery. A gold neck chain. And a signet ring.'

I'd looked at her closely. 'You really like him, don't you?'

She'd smiled, glanced away — a girlish expression I rarely saw in my sister. 'Yes, I think I do.'

Now Bill is asking, 'Everything okay? You're looking a bit tired, m'dear.'

I love Bill's knack for sensing when I'm off-kilter.

'I'm not sleeping brilliantly at the moment, that's all.'

'Ah, the insomnia snake. You've got a lot going on, eh? Flynn. Your book deadline. Maybe you're still adjusting to being in the new house, too.'

I nod, reminded of how intuitive Bill can be.

'You know that we're here if you need us, don't you?' he says, placing a large hand on my shoulder. He squeezes — his grip just a fraction too firm.

★ ★ ★

'Thought I heard the door,' Fiona says, crossing the kitchen and kissing Bill on the mouth. 'No traffic?'

'I had a meeting in Bristol. Finished on time. Came straight here. Drake all right?'

'Fine — but he's yours for the weekend.'

'As long as you're all mine for the weekend, too,' he says, pulling Fiona into his arms and

64

burying his face in her neck.

I move towards the chair where I've left my coat and handbag. 'I'm going to disappear.'

'Don't be silly! Stay!' Bill says, releasing Fiona.

'I'm giving a library talk in the morning.'

'I saw the posters,' Fiona says. 'We're going to try and pop in.'

'Are we?' Bill asks.

'Don't you dare!' I say.

Fiona bats away my resistance. 'It's at eleven, isn't it?'

'Please, you've got better things to do with your weekend.'

'We are immensely boring people, Elle.'

'And anyway,' Bill adds, 'we want to sit in the audience and show off that we're related to you.'

'Just don't ask any embarrassing questions, okay?'

Bill links his arm through Fiona's, wiggling his brows as he says, 'Us?'

★ ★ ★

I step from the warmth of their house and cross the street towards my car. Fiona and Bill watch from the doorway, checking I make it safely to the vehicle.

I start the engine, flick on the heater, turn up the radio. As I move off, I lift my hand to wave — but they are already turning away.

Bill pulls the door firmly behind them, locking his family inside.

65

2003

Elle's skin held the deep tan of a summer holiday spent largely unoccupied. She was running late, still learning to navigate the sprawling campus, and she slipped into the back of the lecture theatre, breathless.

She scanned the sea of heads looking for an unoccupied seat, dismayed to spot only one at the front. As she tiptoed down the central stairway, trying to make herself invisible, the lecturer paused mid-sentence.

He was sitting on the edge of a desk, the screen behind him illuminated with the words *Shakespeare's Tragedies*. He had foppish brown hair and wore a well-cut cord jacket, over a pair of dark jeans.

'I should mention,' the young lecturer said, 'that if anyone is late, they have the regrettable task of being my assistant at the end of the lecture and handing out the day's notes. So,' he said, his gaze finding hers, 'that role is awarded to you, today.' He smiled. A boyish smile that lit up his face and created sunbursts of lines around his eyes.

The attention in the auditorium swung to her, as a hundred pairs of eyes followed his. Perhaps because she was nineteen, perhaps because she was still buzzing from the shots she'd only stopped drinking at four a.m., she had — right there in front of a packed auditorium of English

Literature students — grinned as she curtsied to him.

'At your service.'

★ ★ ★

Luke Linden, he was called, 'but just call me Luke'. He was one of those lecturers, she would learn, who abandoned the lectern and preferred to roam, striding expansively from one end of the hall to the other. He had a flair for using a pause to great effect, causing even those students with a tendency to drift, to suddenly look up as if silence had summoned them. Luke Linden was a man who could talk passionately about semantics and notions of romantic love in Jacobean England — yet still looked like one of them.

Except he wasn't one of them.

And that's where Elle had made her first mistake.

6

Elle

'The best story to tell — the only story to tell — is the one living within you, inhabiting you, insisting that it be heard.'
                              Author Elle Fielding

I push open the car door into darkness, feel the hurried beat of my footsteps across my frost-hardened driveway.

On the doorstep, I fumble in my handbag looking for my key.

Maybe I should have had an extra glass of wine, crashed on Fiona and Bill's sofa, not come back to an empty house.

I slot the key into the lock and slip inside, bolting the door behind me.

There it is, the silence. It pins me, fills my ears with its voiceless boom.

I hate coming home to an empty house — particularly after dark. Jesus, maybe Fiona is right: I do need a dog.

I keep finding myself missing the congestion of my old life in Bristol; the steady thrum of traffic, the stores open all hours of the night, the sounds from other people's lives that filtered through the walls of our flat — voices, televisions, cisterns refilling, plates being stacked, laughter.

I force myself to move briskly through the house, flicking on lights, the radio and television.

It will be my first winter here and I wonder how warm it will be. Underfloor heating doesn't give the same heat as a fire. I must start using the log burner — but each time I think about laying it, I'm overwhelmed by Flynn's absence. It has always been his thing.

In the last place we rented, there was an open fire, and I remember the way he'd carefully select the wood each evening, telling me whether it was apple or silver birch, or a piece of plum chopped down from a job he'd done the previous year. He'd describe how long each piece would burn for, what the notes of the smell might be, how long it had been seasoned.

Before I can talk myself out of it, I slip my mobile from my pocket and dial his number. I want to hear his voice. I want to say, *I'm thinking of lighting the log burner you chose.* I want to tell him, *I miss you.* To hear him say, *I forgive you.*

When he picks up, I catch the low riff of music. Muddy Waters. One of Flynn's favourite blues artists. He plays his music on a record player that used to belong to his father. He loves the ceremony of setting the needle, hearing the fuzzed scratch as the record begins to spin.

'Elle?'

'I just . . . I thought I'd . . . say hello.' I glance at my watch. It is midnight on a Friday. Shit.

'Right. Hello,' Flynn says, lightly amused.

Tucking the phone under my ear, I move into the kitchen to make certain the back door is locked. I press on the handle, check the bolt. Then I follow the perimeter of the kitchen ensuring each of the windows is secure, and the wine cellar is locked.

I tell Flynn about my evening at Fiona and Bill's as I move into the lounge, looking behind the sofa, running my hand along the curtains until I can feel the wall. Every room needs to be checked. Every window. It gives me peace of mind.

When I'm satisfied that the house is secure, I move into my bedroom, sinking down onto the bed, letting myself fall backwards, my head hitting the pillow with a soft *thump*.

Pressing the phone close to my ear, I can hear the slow draw of Flynn's breath, can picture him sitting on the sofa, fire lit, an empty bottle of ale on the side table, the lights low.

The Muddy Waters record comes to its end and our conversation ticks comfortably into silence. I let my eyes close. In our previous life — the version of *us* that runs parallel to this one — I would be stretched out on the sofa, my feet on his lap, the warmth of the fire playing over my shins. We would be making plans for the weekend ahead: a walk in the forest with a pub lunch perhaps, or a drive to the coast to visit friends.

Across the phone waves I hear a door opening, then foot-steps. Quick and light. There is the murmur of a female voice, low, keening.

'Oh,' I say, sitting up, a hand moving to my chest. 'You've got company.'

His mouth sounds closer to the phone, as he

says, 'Listen, Elle, I didn't know you were — '

I try to form words that will make this okay, but I can't think what to say, what to do with this sudden, crushing realisation.

So I do the only thing that comes to me: I hang up.

★ ★ ★

I pace my bedroom, replaying the phone call, over and over.

Flynn.

Flynn and another woman.

It's a fist in my stomach.

I launch my mobile at the bed. It bounces off, hits my cream bedside table and lands on the carpet.

I run a bath, add some essential oils, let the water slip over my body until it is cupping the disc of my face. I concentrate on my breathing, on trying to relax.

But I can't. I climb out, water sloshing over the bathroom floor.

I wrap myself in a dressing gown, then eye my bed. There's no point trying to sleep when I'm agitated, wired.

I'll write, I decide.

★ ★ ★

The lamp casts a white spotlight across my desk. Behind me, the rest of the writing room is in darkness.

I take a breath. Hover the mouse over the

Word document labelled *BOOK 2*.

It's coming along well, I'd told Jane.

Five and a half weeks until my deadline.

Downstairs, I picture the unopened bills piled on the bureau, the mortgage repayment not met this month. Everything is riding on this book, waiting on me. I think of Booklover101's latest post on my Facebook page. A gif of a woman sat at a typewriter, face possessed, keys bashing up and down. *Hope you're working hard. Remember, your no. 1 fan is waiting* ☺

I click.

The document opens onto the title page:

BOOK 2
By Elle Fielding

And below it, nothing.

Whiteness.

All that blank space eyeballing me, waiting to be filled. It's like staring into a black hole — only white — as if I could be sucked into it, lose myself in all that emptiness.

Beneath the desk, my foot jigs up and down.

I remember how excited, how inspired, I felt before I was published. Back then I was writing without expectation or deadlines — writing just for myself. There was such freedom in it. I didn't realise it at the time when I was yearning to get published, but it was a beautiful way to write — out in the wilderness, without a contract.

Now thousands of readers are eagerly awaiting my next novel, a publishing house is primed and ready, the security of my home teeters on it. I rub the skin below my collarbone, pressure tightening in my chest.

This isn't how I imagined it to be.

None of this is how it was meant to be.

'It's going to be fine,' I say aloud to the empty room, my voice unnaturally bright. 'You can do this. You just need to focus, stop doubting yourself. Don't overthink this, Elle. Just write.'

Team talk to self.

Jesus Christ, all this silence. No wonder I'm talking to myself. I play some music, turning it up loud. Then I flick on the large overhead light, too. There, that's better, I think, pacing.

If someone is in the bay tonight, they could look straight into this room, see me up here, alone.

I pick up the paperweight from my desk, pressing my thumb into the jagged crack. I can almost feel the sharp point of the missing shard as if it's still embedded in my heel.

That feeling, the hot breath of fear.

I lower myself into my chair, placing the paperweight beside me. The lamplight bounces off it, throwing my image back at me, distorted by the curvature of the glass.

I know the story I need to write. I think I've known it all along.

I've got it all here, in me. I see that now. My characters are already alive, living under my skin. I just need to get them on the page, pin them there.

So I picture them, I tune into their voices, I invite them in.

And then I start to type.

2003

Elle's second mistake came later.

Glancing up, she checked the librarian was still focused on unstacking her book trolley, then continued deconstructing a Crunchie, biting off the top layer of chocolate before sucking the honeycomb until it turned sticky in her mouth.

Her housemate, Louise, who was sitting opposite, was whispering her plan to spray-paint a roll of bubble wrap and fashion it into a dress for that evening's space-age party.

Louise halted mid-sentence, her eyes fixing on something beyond Elle's shoulder.

'There he goes.'

Elle removed the Crunchie from her mouth, twisting in her seat.

Luke Linden was crossing the library with long, easy strides, a newspaper tucked under-arm. A ripple of attention followed him. At a table to the left of theirs, a group of students waved him over. He paused mid-step to listen to a question, nodding lightly. He delivered his answer into the hushed silence and then, a moment later, continued.

As he passed the table where Elle sat, his gaze lifted, met hers. He smiled, his mouth curling to one side. Then he moved on, disappeared.

Placing her elbows on the table, Louise whispered, 'I'm going to have to do an MA, just so I can look at him for one more year.'

'Take a photo. Less debt.'

'You can't tell me you're not in love with him.'

'I'm not in love with him.'

'But you'd sleep with him in a heartbeat, yes?'

She shrugged.

'You would, of course you would!'

Later, Elle would wonder about what she'd said next. Whether she'd meant it, how it changed things. She would want to go back, edit the memory. Rewrite that tiny detail in her story, because — although it was only a sentence — it would become pivotal.

It would become the hook from which she would hang.

But in that moment, Elle was just a teenage girl, hair to her waist, skin unlined, still bright with the promise of how her life was about to flower.

Elle held Louise's gaze as she finally answered, 'Yes, I absolutely would. In fact,' she added, her mouth spreading into a grin, 'maybe I *will*.'

7

Elle

In the black-velvet darkness of four a.m., I twist onto my side. The sheets are a hot tangle around my waist. The snake in my brain is alive, wide awake.

I listen to the house. I want there to be noises of other people — the purring snore of a child asleep in the nursery, the cast-iron creak of the log burner opening, a hunk of wood fed to the flames.

But it is just me. My breathing. My heartbeat, rapid.

And then my thoughts. They are not silent, but loud and rowdy, like a bad drunk. They seem to echo in my mind, filling my head with their noise and spite.

You invite your story, your characters, into your thoughts — but what then if they won't leave?

I sit up. Eyes open in the darkness.

★   ★   ★

I feel raw this morning, empty. It's that strange depleted feeling you get after you've cried. I wrote five thousand words last night. I couldn't switch off. I still can't. The last thing I feel like doing is giving a library talk. I want to stay here, get this story down.

Pulling on my winter coat, I pause in the hallway, examining myself in the mirror. God, I look terrible. My skin tone is uneven and there are purplish blooms beneath my eyes.

I glance at my watch. One hour until I'll be standing at the front of the library talking about my great life as an author.

Why did I agree to this?

But of course, I know why. I need to start getting more involved locally, putting down roots. Demolishing the original fisherman's cottage hasn't been a popular decision, and I'm sure people think I'm just another city blow-in. I want to make friends here, make Cornwall home.

I need this.

Opening the clasp of my handbag, I check for the second or third time that my notes are tucked inside my novel.

Anticipating the cold beyond the front door, I draw my coat snug to my throat. Something's wrong. My fingers meet the empty space at my collar where a brooch is always pinned. It belonged to my mother — a silver swift in flight — and I never remove it. It was here the last time I wore this coat. That was the day I left for France. Since then the coat's been hanging right here in the hallway. I crouch, searching the line of shoes beneath the row of hooks, shaking each one — but they are all empty.

There isn't time to search thoroughly now, but I don't like leaving the house without it. It's unsettling, a bad omen.

As I get to my feet, an image of Joanna slinks into my thoughts: a pale hand travelling over the collar of my coat, long fingers meeting the silver wing of the bird, then the lightest of movements as the brooch is unpinned, cool metal hidden within a palm.

★ ★ ★

Collecting the box of books from the back seat, I close the car door with a swing of my hip, then fumble with the key fob.

Set back on an expansive lawn, the pebbledash library looks tired in the morning sunlight as I follow the stone pathway towards the entrance. A trail of wisteria, the blooms long dead, snake across the wall, bird droppings staining the concrete beneath.

I shoulder open the door and breathe in the warm pulp smell of books.

A young librarian, wearing a checked shirt that strains at her bust and stomach, abandons her book trolley and races over.

'Welcome! Here, let me take that box!' she says, removing it from my grip. 'I'm Laura. By the way, I loved *Wild Fear*. Literally loved it! I recommend it to, like, everyone!'

'That's so lovely of you, Laura. Thank you.' I smile.

She guides me towards an area where chairs have been set out in a semi-circle facing a small table.

'Does this look okay?' Laura asks, with a faint

Cornish accent. Her cheeks are flushed, wispy strands of hair escaping from her ponytail. 'I've popped a jug of water on your table. There's a microphone on standby if you need it — but I know some people prefer not to use one. Maeve did say there's a lectern in the store room if that'd be better?'

'Everything looks great just as it is. Thank you.' My attention drifts towards the window, the sea glimmering in the distance. I have a burst of longing to be out there, in the water, salt on my skin.

'Oh, I'm sorry. The windows don't open, but if you think it'll get a bit stuffy, I can prop open the fire exit. What do you think? Should I do that now?'

'I think the temperature is just right. I love the event poster,' I say, indicating the noticeboard.

'I just whizzed a few out on our printer,' Laura says, pressing her hands to her chest, pleased.

I remove my coat and drape it over the back of a chair, then set my copy of the novel on the table, opening the cover and checking my notes.

'Oh, look! Here's our library manager, Maeve. I don't think you've met.'

A petite, middle-aged woman in a vintage pinafore dress approaches, a bluebird-print headscarf knotted over deep red hair. Her pale green eyes fix on me.

'Hello.' She smiles.

'Nice to meet you,' I say, offering a hand.

Maeve's is cool and soft in my grasp. There is something vaguely familiar about her.

'Likewise.'

'Thank you for hosting today's event.'

'Laura has done all the work, haven't you?'

Laura beams. 'It's been my pleasure. Not often that a bestselling author moves to town. Everyone is so excited about the talk. It's a sell-out,' she says, turning to look at the seats, which are steadily filling.

The library doors open and Fiona strides in, unbuttoning a high-necked coat, her gaze scanning the crowd. She is dressed in black, a pop of red lipstick adding colour to her otherwise make-up-free face, a large handbag swinging from a shoulder strap. Her utilitarian style looks abrupt in the fusty library setting. Seeing me, she lifts her fingers in the air, then crosses the room towards me. We kiss, and I breathe in the smell of croissants and coffee.

'This is my sister, Fiona,' I say, introducing her to Laura and Maeve.

'We all know each other,' Maeve explains, smiling. 'Book club.'

'It's at your house this month, isn't it?' Laura asks Fiona.

'Oh Christ, you're right! I should warn you that salted caramel brownies will not be on the menu. I can, however, guarantee that there'll be a sea of alcohol.'

'Then the masses will descend,' Maeve says.

Laura turns to me. 'Are you in a book club, Elle?'

'No.' Fiona has mentioned the book club before, but I wasn't offended that she hadn't invited me — we've always kept our social lives separate.

'Then you should join ours!' Laura says, bouncing lightly on her heels. 'It'd be so lovely to have an actual author there. We're doing *The Secret History* this month. Think I'm the only one who's not read it before. You should come. I'd love it. Everyone would love it!'

'Yes, come,' Fiona says, and I find it difficult to tell whether she genuinely wants me there.

'Okay, then.' Glancing over my shoulder, I see that the room has filled, people jostling to find seats, draping winter coats over the backs of chairs, setting handbags on laps. Two young women sit together near the front, notebooks on knees, their heads inclined as they talk. I think, *It was only a breath ago that I was you. That I watched other authors speak, praying, 'Please let that be me, one day.'*

Maeve and Laura disappear to hand out membership forms, and Fiona says, 'Bill sends his apologies. Drake was desperate to go to the beach.'

'That's fine.' Fiona could have been spending the morning with them — but instead she has come here to support me. I reach out and squeeze her fingers. 'Thank you for coming.'

Fiona glances down. 'Clammy hands?'

'Nerves.'

She considers me. She has a penetrating gaze that makes me feel as if she is unpeeling layers of me, seeing deeper than other people are able.

'Juliet. Sandy. The Virgin Mary. You were the lead in just about every school production there was. You owned the stage.'

'That was years ago. And anyway, I was in

82

character. I learned a script.'

'So get in character now. You're an internationally best-selling author. You have one of the most coveted houses in Cornwall. You're young, beautiful and successful. And — on top of all that — you've got one pretty fucking incredible sister.'

★ ★ ★

Standing in front of the mirror in the library toilets, I take a moment to compose myself. My neck is flushed and I fasten an extra button of my shirt, aware that my hands are trembling.

I can do this. I've played this part dozens of times before, on book tours, at literary festivals, in interviews.

In my head, I run through the first section of my talk. I plan to briefly touch on my childhood holidays here in Cornwall, and then I will skirt that strange dark cloud that hovered around my early twenties, and I'll begin the story when I'm in my late twenties. I'll explain about the vague dissatisfaction I'd felt simmering, how I'd tried various jobs but none of them were a valve for the bubbling restlessness. I'll then talk about travelling with Flynn (to mention him by name, or not? *Not*, I decide, unwilling to risk the possible waver in my voice) — and how it was when I returned home, renting a flat in the heart of Bristol, that the idea of writing was seeded.

'There is this night course,' Flynn began one evening as we were eating takeaway pizza straight from the box. 'It's in creative writing. It started last week — but you've only missed one session. I saw a flyer about it. Here,' he said, pressing it into my hand.

It was an abstract image of a wing cutting across a blue sky. *Let your imagination soar,* was the heading in a stylish grey font.

'I thought,' Flynn said tentatively, 'that I could treat you to it. For your birthday. If you were interested.' Flynn had just taken his first salaried position as a tree surgeon, returning home each evening with wood chip clinging to the weave of his jumper, bark staining his jeans.

'It's taught by a woman,' Flynn said. 'She's written a couple of books. You should look her up.'

I'd lain in the bath that evening, candles lit, essential oils making a film on the surface. When we'd been travelling, I kept a journal, filling page after page with descriptions of new experiences and interesting places. Those moments I found myself sitting cross-legged on a beach, or in the back of our van, a pencil scratching across the smooth page of my journal, had filled me with a deep sense of calm. Yet I'd never considered nurturing that passion into something more.

Fiction was my mother's world. She'd always worked as a teaching assistant because the hours suited our schooling, but she'd often set her alarm early 'to get the best of this old brain' before her day began. Over the years she'd had several short stories printed in magazines, but when Fiona had asked if she dreamt of becoming an author, she replied, 'I don't write to get published. I write because I can't not.'

'Yes,' I told Flynn, as I stood in a towel, my feet wet on the lino flooring. 'I'd like to do the course.'

Wednesday evenings became the highlight of the week. I loved my tutor, a woman in her fifties with short red hair and a limitless collection of animal-print neck scarves. She had a wickedly sardonic sense of humour, and she filled the room with her passion for words. Her students were a mix of ages: two men, recently divorced, who wrote wild adventure stories in the realm of Wilbur Smith; an English graduate who'd lost a twin sister; three retired friends who met for dinner before each class, the smell of Thai spices or wine clinging to them. Wednesdays were a beacon for us all.

During the course I had the idea for my first novel. It wasn't a lightning-bolt moment of inspiration; it was simply an image. I could picture two women standing together on a shoreline, their hands gripped, squinting into the distance. I wondered what or who they were looking at. As I encouraged my mind's eye to zoom in more closely, other details emerged: two boys in the water; the flash of an orange life boat; one boy brought back to shore alive — not two.

Once the idea took hold, I worked on it feverishly. I was a receptionist at the time and the jotter by the office phone filled with plot ideas and character notes. I spent my lunch breaks writing in the back seat of my car, not willing to use the staff room for fear of someone disturbing me. Following my mother's example, I set my alarm an hour early each morning to write, and in that quiet dawn hour, I left behind the walls of the studio flat and I soared.

Gradually, gradually, the shape of a novel began to form. It was loose and unpinned, but there was something in it, I'd felt sure.

Authors often talk about that magical moment of securing their first book deal — and I remember every detail of it. Invited to meet an interested publisher, I sat with my agent in the spacious atrium of the publishing house reception, staring up at a metallic sculpture of a globe suspended from the ceiling, a disco ball without the party. My outfit, which I'd spent an entire afternoon deciding upon — corduroy yellow skirt with embroidered detail, and a green silk top — now seemed oddly provincial.

I watched other visitors streaming into the atrium, being ushered through security: handbags and briefcases conveyored through an X-ray machine, lanyards swinging from visitors' necks. Everything was so removed from the process of writing the book that I suddenly felt like I was in the wrong place. I reached into my pocket and pulled out my mother's fountain pen. I turned it through my fingers, exploring the faded patch near the nib, where the gloss had worn away with use. I remembered the way my mother wrote with it, the slant of her hand, her elbow sliding along the table edge. As a girl, I used to be fascinated by the empty black ink cartridges, containing a tiny glass bead, like the eye of a vole.

Holding it between my fingertips, I knew my mother would have been proud that I had got this far, that I, Elle Fielding, former barista, waitress and travel bum, had written something good enough to draw the attention of a publisher.

My literary agent and I were collected by an assistant and taken by lift, up twelve storeys, and deposited in a glass-doored meeting room that overlooked a sprawling open-plan office. I had never seen so many people working in one place.

A few minutes later, a woman in a simple blue dress and ankle boots walked in, clutching papers.

'Elle, I'm Jane — one of the publishing directors here. It's so lovely to meet you.' She kissed me warmly. I liked Jane immediately. She was sincere, intelligent, and passionate about books.

'Let me just tell you, I *loved* your story. I got lost in the characters. Those women — I felt like I wanted to pick up the phone, call them. You have a wonderful eye for observation.'

A surge of delight rushed through me and I began to relax, talking with ease about how the idea came to me, why I ended the book as I did. My agent smiled at me enthusiastically. *Yes, it was going well.*

Jane briefed me on the next steps: she'd be pitching the book at their acquisitions meeting that week.

'One of the questions that will be asked,' Jane said, 'will be what other ideas you have.'

I'd poured every ounce of energy into that story, those characters. I hadn't dared step outside of them, in case they shut the door behind me while my back was turned.

'If you've got anything you could share with me ahead of the meeting,' Jane said, 'even if it's just a very loose idea or two — that would really help my pitch. We like to be able to look ahead to see how we can establish your brand in the marketplace.'

Marketplace. Acquisition. Brand. My stomach fluttered with excitement. I allowed myself the smallest butterfly of hope: this could be the start.

★ ★ ★

Now, standing in the library toilets, I wipe my damp palms against my jeans. I take a deep breath, feel my shoulders pulling back.

'Hello, I'm Elle Fielding,' I say to the mirror, fixing on a smile.

Looking at myself, I think about the author the audience are expecting to see. A thirty-something woman with a successful, glittering career. A woman who is confident, composed, happy.

Who do I see? I wonder, leaning closer to the mirror, looking right into the dark centre of my irises, seeing the skein of red lines mapping the edges of them.

I blink. Push her away.

'Hello, I'm Elle Fielding,' I say again, brighter this time, with more volume. 'It's lovely to be invited here to — '

I stop short at the sound of a toilet flushing. A bolt is unlatched, and Maeve appears from one of the cubicles.

Her gaze meets mine in the mirror.
I have the feeling of being caught out.
'Pre-talk warm up,' I say.
Maeve moves to the sink, letting cold water stream across the backs of her pale hands. She flicks off the tap with her wrist, then pats her hands carefully with paper towels.
'Practice makes perfect.'

Previously

Even though you're not in the house, I feel close to you.

There are traces of you everywhere. Earlier, I found one of your hairs clinging to the sleeve of my shirt. I held it up to the light, examining the caramel shade, surprised to see the root bearing a hint of grey.

In the recycling bin, I found a screwed-up Post-it note, reading, Focus! No internet! I smiled at that because I can imagine how much self-discipline must be required as an author. What pressure you must be under to deliver an exceptional second novel.

We are all waiting for it.

I remember reading your debut for the first time. It blew me away. I read it in one sitting, pinned to the chair. The beauty and skill of the story, the racing pace. It left me breathless.

You've signed my copy at the front, a looping signature with a kiss.

I went to one of your book signings, I watched you from the back of a snaking line.

I studied the dip of your head as you bent to sign each copy, hair falling forward over your shoulder. You were smiling, chatting to readers as you asked their names, asked who you should dedicate each book to.

It was only when I looked closer that I noticed it — the way your legs were shaking beneath the table.

8

Elle

'A novel is about truth: both seeing the truth and writing the truth.'
Author *Elle Fielding*

'It's my pleasure,' Laura says, addressing the room, 'to introduce local author, Elle Fielding. Her debut novel has sold over half a million copies and has been translated into a dozen languages.'

My gaze flits across the room, taking in the audience. Every single seat is occupied — and a cluster of latecomers are standing at the back, obstructing the exit.

Breathe, I remind myself. *Smile.*

As I scan the crowd, a face on the front row causes me to freeze. Mark is sitting with an arm slung over the seat back, one ankle balanced casually across his knee. He smiles lazily.

What the hell is he doing here?

I snap my gaze away. Laura is now saying, 'Not only is Elle a bestselling author, but if you happen to follow her on Facebook, you'll also know she's a passionate sea swimmer and has a killer eye for interiors. Be warned: house envy may ensue.'

There is a ripple of laughter from the audience. I don't need to look at Mark to know he is smirking.

93

'Also, if there are any budding writers in the room tonight — like me,' Laura adds with a giggle, 'Elle shares brilliant writing advice in her weekly Facebook Live videos — so tune in.' She snatches a breath. 'Before I sound any more fan-girl, please put your hands together for the very lovely and incredibly talented Elle Fielding!'

I propel myself forward, nodding my thanks at Laura, then anchor myself beside the small table where my novel and jug of water are positioned. As the applause settles, I reach for my notes.

They're not there.

A swell of panic rises, hot and rapid.

I fan through the pages of my book, trying to maintain my smile. The notes were inside the cover when I arrived — I checked.

I can feel my heart pounding against my ribcage. *I cannot do this without them.*

'Just a moment . . . ' I say, crouching down and casting around beneath the table, in case the notes have slipped from the leaves of the book. Then I check my handbag, but they are not there either. All the while I can feel the collective stare of the audience pinned to my back.

My notes had been in the book when I'd placed it on this table — I know it. Someone must have moved them.

I get to my feet. Face the audience.

Has someone here taken them?

'I seem to have misplaced my notes.'

Mark catches my eye, smiles.

'Did you move them?' The words have escaped before I can stop them.

The attention in the room shifts to him.

94

He opens his palms. 'Course not.'

Someone clears their throat loudly. I turn and see Laura twisting the pendant of her necklace, nodding at me lightly as if to say, *Go on*.

'Who needs notes anyway?' I say, attempting to sound light-hearted, but I can tell from the expressions in the audience that it comes out wrong.

Breathe. Smile. Speak slowly.

I need to get my nerves under control, buy myself a minute to think. 'Where do ideas come from?' I ask, tossing the question to the room.

A hundred pairs of eyes look at me blankly. Maybe the question needed context. Sweat is building under my arms.

'I . . . I'd like to talk about where ideas originate — and how we turn those into a story. So, where do you think authors — or indeed artists or musicians or . . . or other people — get their ideas from?'

There is a murmur among the audience as they seem to consider answering. Eventually an arm is raised at the front. From the periphery of my vision I know it is Mark. I wait a few moments, but when no other hands are lifted, I have to say, 'Yes?'

'From a sea view.'

A ripple of anticipation travels through the crowd.

In a slow, cool voice, Mark continues, 'I've read that the sea helps people think creatively. It's healing, apparently, to have a view.'

I murmur something in response. I don't even know what. There's a pressure building in my chest. I look towards the exit — but it's blocked by a small crowd who are standing at the back of the room. The pressure tightens, reaches into my throat, squeezes. I cannot get enough air.

Everyone is watching. Waiting for me to say something. To be Elle Fielding, bestselling author. But I'm frozen. That person has left me.

'Perhaps,' someone in the audience says, 'ideas come from the people around us.'

It is Fiona.

'It could be a snippet from an overheard conversation,' she suggests, coming to my rescue, 'or a story someone tells.'

'Yes.' I seize on this, pulling myself back from the edge. 'You're right. Anything like that could be the spark. I'll be talking today about the idea that inspired my debut novel, so perhaps I should start by reading you the opening page.'

The familiar rhythm of the words begins to lend my voice confidence, soften my nerves. I concentrate on speaking slowly, getting my breathing under control. I can do this. I have done this dozens of times, to bigger audiences.

I manage it, planting my feet firm, speaking in a clear voice, pulling my shoulders back. But just as I think that I am going to be okay, my eye catches on a mark on the page. A word has been circled in red pen.

I have absolutely no recollection of when I'd have done this, or why. I never write on my books — there is something sacrosanct about the printed page.

I hurry through reading aloud the final few lines, yet all the while my thoughts are pinned to that one strangely circled word.

You.

★   ★   ★

The talk careers on, with me skidding and sliding from one topic to the next, only pausing to snatch breath. I'm running on adrenalin and can feel the tension in my shoulders, in the small bones at the back of my neck.

There is a brief round of Q&A, but the audience — perhaps sensing my desperation to be freed — keep the questions to a minimum. After that there is a small queue of readers wanting signed copies, then the thank yous and goodbyes with the library staff, and then, finally — finally, I am released from the building.

Fresh air spikes my skin, the damp shirt cooling on my back. My car is parked on the roadside under a treeline of poplars and, as I pull my keys from my handbag, Fiona appears, a cigarette between her fingers.

'Need a drag?'

I nod, then lean against my car taking a long draw of smoke into my lungs. It's been years since we've shared a cigarette, and the rush of nicotine fills my head.

'Who did you bum this from?'

She taps the side of her nose.

I take another drag, then hand it back. 'Aren't you going to say something polite about my talk, like, *There were some good moments once you found your stride?*'

'Do you need me to?'

I exhale hard. 'I think what I need is alcohol.'

'It wasn't as bad as you think.'

'Thank you for coming to my rescue.'

'What happened to your notes?'

'They were inside the cover of my book, which I left on the library table. Someone must have moved them.'

Fiona arches an eyebrow. 'What, like that man on the front row who you accused?'

'I didn't accuse him. I *asked* him. That's Mark — Frank and Enid's son.'

'Oh. The bin tipper.'

I can hear the light tease in her voice and can't quite tell whether it is helping, or whether I'm annoyed by it.

'I can't believe he had the gall to sit on the front row. He must've loved seeing me die on stage.'

'Maybe he was genuinely interested in what you had to say.'

'There's nothing genuine about him.'

'Speak of the devil,' Fiona says, nodding her head.

Mark approaches us, his gaze on me.

Fiona's hands move to her hairline, pinning her hair from being whipped by the wind.

'Interesting library talk,' he says without a smile.

'I'd no idea you were so interested in my writing career,' I respond with icy politeness.

'It's important to support the local community, don't you think?'

'I thought you lived in London.'

'This is home.'

There is a pause and his gaze flicks to Fiona. He extends his hand. 'I'm Mark, Elle's neighbour.'

Fiona places the cigarette between her lips, then shakes his hand. 'Fiona.'

A private smile flickers at the edges of his mouth.

'Ever find your notes?' he says, turning to me. 'You took them, didn't you?'

He laughs then, rolling back slightly on his heels. 'If only I'd thought of it. Struggled a bit, didn't you?'

Then he lifts a hand in goodbye, and saunters past us.

'Arsehole,' I mutter beneath my breath.

'Albeit a vaguely attractive one,' Fiona says, dropping the cigarette on the pavement and twisting the heel of her boot over it. 'Right, I best get back to my boys.'

I try not to feel it, but it is there, the low pulse of envy that my sister is returning to her family life.

'Have a lovely weekend,' I say, kissing Fiona goodbye with extra warmth to make up for it.

As I climb into the driver's seat, that's when I feel it: the crease of paper in the back pocket of my jeans.

My notes.

I tug them out and hold the warm, crumpled card on my knee. Blood rushes to my face: I must have taken the notes into the toilets to glance at before the talk.

I lower my head until my forehead is resting against the cold steering wheel. The horn blares, a long note of exclamation.

★　★　★

I open my front door, then hesitate. Something is different. I can sense it immediately. The air is sharper. A draught weaves past me from within the house.

Leaving on my coat, I move along the hallway, a hollow feeling spreading across my abdomen. It can be no later than two o'clock, but the dull sky has leached the light from the day.

I pause outside the lounge, listening. A low ruffling sound is coming from within. A breeze snakes beneath the door, reaching my ankles.

I want to turn, leave. But I force myself to swing the door wide. My movements are jerky rather than bold, as if I'm expecting someone to come running at me.

The lounge is icy cold. The curtains are lifting in a breeze, catching against the windowsill. I can see from the doorway that the top window is gaping open, the wind rushing through the room. The cards that were on my mantelpiece have been blown to the floor.

I'm usually fastidious about checking everything is locked before I go out, but this morning I'd felt dazed, the lag of another bad night's sleep. Perhaps the catch hadn't been fully depressed, and the sea breeze sucked it open.

I force myself to cross the lounge and shut it firmly. I pause for a moment, listening intently. But all I can hear is the thrum of my heartbeat, and beyond it, silence.

Then I propel myself into action, making a thorough sweep of the rest of the downstairs. It's

100

only when I'm satisfied that all doors and windows have been double-checked that I finally take off my coat.

In the kitchen I slide a bottle of wine from the fridge and pour myself a large glass. Standing by the fridge, I drain half of it, the tension between my shoulder blades beginning to ease.

Fiona is right: I do need a dog. The house would feel so much warmer if I were returning to a dog, seeing it turning circles of excitement, letting it curl on the sofa with me, or lie at my feet as I write. Flynn had suggested getting a dog a couple of years earlier, but I'd been resistant to the idea then — as if owning one were an admission of something: a dog instead of a baby.

I finish my glass of wine and pour a second. I need it to settle my nerves. God, the library talk had been humiliating — to flail around so publicly. I could feel the heat of a panic attack closing in on me. It wasn't just the lost notes that tangled me, but also the strangeness of seeing the word *You* circled in my novel.

Opening my handbag, I pull out my copy of *Wild Fear* and turn to the first page of the story. There it is, clear as anything, that innocuous three-lettered word ringed in red pen.

You.

Why? Why would I have done that? It's such a small thing — yet its oddness marks it out.

I turn through the next few pages, scanning them carefully, looking for another hint of red pen, anything else that has been circled or underlined, but there are no more annotations. Perhaps I circled it when I was prepping for the talk — marking the place I'd read to. God, maybe this is another of the damaging effects of insomnia — losing my notes, leaving windows open, drifting through my waking hours.

I continue to flick all the way through the book, but just as I reach the end, another flash of red catches my eye. On the last page of the final chapter, a second word has been circled in red.

I am rigid.

I squeeze my eyes tight, then open them to be sure.

Lied.

I turn from the first page to the last, the blood draining from my face as the two circled words eye me.

You Lied.

★ ★ ★

In the winter-deep dark of four a.m., I sit up, pushing my hair from my face. Sweat beads between my breasts. I drag the duvet free. My breathing is shallow, like I have just finished a race.

You Lied.

Those circled words won't leave my head. They're following me, tracking me through my dreams, getting closer and closer, until they are upon me.

I can see a pale hand — the same hand that unpinned the brooch — but this time it holds a red pen The hand hovers for a moment, before dipping low to the page, ringing those words in red.

Leaving me a message.

I launch myself from the bed, cross the room, throw open the balcony doors. I step out, the deck damp with dew. The sudden cold is a shock against my skin. I grip the railing hard. Breathe.

The sea coils in the darkness, restless. I sense the tide is high, swallowing the bay, encroaching on the rocks.

I push onto tiptoes, lean forward, looking down at the black rock and beyond it the surge of the sea.

I experience a strange echo of someone else standing here before me. Joanna? Her husband? That pale hand again, gripping the railing, considering the distance between where my feet are placed, and the hardness of the rocks below.

Previously

Your bedroom mirror is larger than my front door. It leans casually against the wall, the ornate silver frame worn at the edges.

It is an overcast day, yet the mirror gathers up that particular quality of light that is unique to the coast, and playfully casts it around the room. It glitters across your king-sized bed with its rich cream sheets and the plump scatter cushions.

I take a step forward so that I am standing directly in front of your mirror. My feet are planted squarely in front of it, the thick pile of your carpet soft between my toes. I am standing exactly where you do as you apply your make up — I can tell this from the fleck of mascara on the glass where you've leaned too close.

Do you like what you see, I wonder?

The rest of the world does. I scrolled through your Facebook feed yesterday, looking at the comments from readers.

You're amazing, Elle. Keep doing what you're doing!

I've read your book THREE TIMES. You're my new favourite author.

You have a beautiful smile ☺

I slide open the wardrobe door and find an empty space on the rail for my things. I can't quite picture them hanging here. I'm more of a drawer person.

I glance at a mid-calf-length dress in a soft blush hue. Silk, I think, my fingers touching the neckline, caressing the material. I can't claim to know much about fashion, but I know the dress will complement your willowy figure, will pick out the caramel tones in your hair. I know how heads will turn when you cross a room.

These aren't guesses: I know, because I've seen you wearing it.

9

Elle

The tide is out and the packed sand glimmers in the thin morning light. Drake runs ahead, chasing sea foam buffeted by the breeze. Fiona and I watch as he spots a clump quivering on the shoreline, and jumps on it, red wellingtons sending bursts of foam skyward.

Two surfers cross the beach ahead of us, jogging with their boards underarm, gazes mapping the waves, studying the pattern of the sets, picking their course for the paddle out.

Pushing my hands deep into my coat pockets, I draw back my shoulders and take a deep breath. My lungs fill with fresh, salted air. Out here, my head feels clearer than it has in days. After hours of lying awake last night I finally gave up on my bed and sat in front of the television, trying to drown out the noise in my head. I woke there this morning, neck cricked, hands bloodless and cold.

After two coffees, I forced myself to my writing desk, but nothing felt right. I'd lost my nerve, found a hesitancy in my writing, as if I wasn't ready to go back to the story. In the end I'd called Fiona, suggested a walk.

'Elle?'

When I turn, Fiona is looking at me.

'Sorry, miles away.'

'I asked if you'd heard from Flynn.'

'I called him on Friday night — after dinner at yours. There was a woman in the background.'

'Oh.'

'Has Flynn mentioned anyone to Bill?'

Fiona glances away.

'So he has.'

'If you want to know, I can tell you. But, Elle,' she says, opening her hands, 'do you really want to know?'

'I do.'

Fiona sighs. 'All Bill's told me is that the last time they spoke, Flynn said he was trying to get out and about. Meet people.'

Meet women, I think, my stomach folding in on itself.

'Flynn's been low. I think it was good advice.'

'Advice? You mean Bill told Flynn to get out there? Sleep around?'

'They're friends. Bill's just trying to look out for him.'

'What about looking out for me?'

Her attention is diverted by Drake, who is scooping a handful of sea foam to his face, fashioning a quivering beard of bubbles.

'Not in your mouth!'

He shakes his head, foam flying loose in white droplets. Watching him backlit by the sun, I smile, thinking how beautiful, how vital he looks. Whenever I doubt the wisdom of my decision to move to Cornwall, Drake is the one thing that makes absolute sense. I want to be part of his life, see the small shifts of development, be

108

someone he can come to as he grows older.

I slide my phone from my pocket and centre him in the frame, snapping his picture.

'Don't you dare put that on Facebook.'

'I wouldn't,' I say, stung.

'Good, because you never know who ends up with all those pictures you post. Anyway,' Fiona says, 'what were you doing ringing Flynn at midnight?'

So we are back to Flynn. 'I just wanted to hear his voice.'

'If you're lonely — '

'I didn't say I was lonely.'

An eyebrow arches. 'Then let me rephrase that. If you feel like company, the sofa bed is yours. Stay over whenever. Just know that Drake will be using your head as a cushion by about six a.m., cartoons howling.'

'Sounds tempting.'

'My life is. It really is.'

There is something about my sister this morning — a tautness, as if she's been stretched too far.

'Is Bill away for the week?'

She nods. 'Single mum again.'

'If you want a night off, you know I'd love to have Drake.'

'By the time Drake is in bed, I just want to crash — but then there's also that pull of thinking, *This is the only time I have to myself*, and I feel like I should be doing something, even if it's just having a glass of wine in the bath, you know?'

I nod — although, of course I don't know. I

have all the time I want to myself. Too much time. I think how different our lives are right now. I ask, 'How's the copywriting?'

'Thought-provoking. Engaging. Stimulating.'

'Really?'

'I'm writing brochure copy for a cruise-liner. I use words like *aspirational* and *well-appointed*. How do you think it's going?'

'I thought you were pleased you won the pitch.'

'Only because we need the money. It's hardly intellectually challenging. Anyway, I'll have finished it in a couple of days.'

'Could you pick up any freelance journalism, more like your old stuff?'

'Cornwall may as well be a different continent. And motherhood hasn't exactly enhanced my CV. You don't always get the life you'd imagined.'

The way Fiona says that last remark, her gaze distant, her tone subdued, serious, makes me pause. Consider what that comment means to her.

'Fiona,' I begin.

But she is striding towards Drake, who is dancing on the spot saying, 'Need wee-wee!'

I watch my sister as she begins dismantling layers of Drake's clothes. It still catches me off-guard that Fiona is a mother. She'd always maintained that she didn't want children, didn't hanker after marriage — and yet here she is, a wife, a mother.

I turn slowly on the spot, taking in the vista. As children, when we holidayed in Cornwall, we loved it when a low pressure blew in, sending huge rollers pounding onto the beach, the boom sounding thunderous from our caravan. When the waves mellowed, leaving the shore strewn with driftwood and treasures churned from the seabed, Fiona and I would go beach-combing. One autumn, Fiona found an unopened can with a Japanese label still intact. She'd carried it reverently back to the caravan and set it on the table like a centrepiece, and we spent hours speculating about its possible contents. It was enticing for its exoticness — yet also for demonstrating that somehow, through the ocean, the world was connected.

With no small degree of ceremony, Fiona opened the mystery can, then peered in, brows knitted. She reared back, clamping a hand over her mouth.

'That's disgusting!' she cried beneath the clasp of her fingers.

I peered at the opened contents and found something jellied and mollusc-like, slippery and saltine. I poured them into a bowl to inspect more closely, using a toothpick to stab one and hold it up to the daylight. Fiona had insisted that they be gotten rid of immediately. I remember carrying these strange dead creatures towards the door, Fiona shuddering theatrically at my side. At the exit there was a misstep. The wind snatched the door, or perhaps I misjudged the distance, but I remember wobbling, the bowl teetering in my hand, the fishy liquid sloshing over the rim and splashing onto Fiona's lower legs and sliding down the tongue of her new purple Dr. Martens.

There had been a howl, a huge great drama of pulled-off boots, of claims it had been done on purpose. There were numerous apologies and attempts to wash out the boots, but Fiona's mood remained black — that was, until I later put on my wellingtons and found the nose of them stuffed with an entire can of tuna. Even as Fiona was being reprimanded by our mother, she'd tossed me a self-satisfied smile, as if to say, *There you go.*

The memory is dislodged by my ringing mobile. It's my editor. I'm tempted to let it go to voicemail, but at the last minute, I pick up.

Jane's voice is abrupt. 'Elle, is everything okay? *Red* magazine's features editor has just called. You haven't turned up for the interview.'

Interview? My skin flames. I knew it was coming up, but I don't remember it being set for today.

'I thought you were going to send through the details?'

'I did, last week.'

I have no recollection of receiving them.

'I'm sorry, but I didn't get them, Jane.'

There's a pause. 'You replied, Elle. Said you could make it.'

Did I? I think of a stream of emails that have rolled in over the preceding days and weeks, a dam of them that needed responding to. Now I remember tackling a clutch of them in the middle of the night when I couldn't sleep. I must have responded on autopilot, not put it in my diary.

'I'm so sorry, Jane. I've completely messed up. I've been so absorbed by my manuscript. I'll get in touch with *Red*, apologise.'

'Yes, do that.'

The call ends. I curse under my breath, furious with myself.

Fiona has returned to my side, Drake still playing near the shoreline. 'What was that about?'

'I'm meant to be in London right now. I missed an interview with *Red* magazine,' I say, eyes on my phone's screen, scrolling through my emails, looking for the proof of my reply.

And there it is. Sent several days ago.

To: Jane Riley
Date: Friday 5 November
Subject: Re: Red magazine interview
  Thanks for this, Jane. All sounds great.
  Looking forward to it.
  Elle x

I tip back my head, groaning. I know how hard my publicist works setting these things up. The chances of rescheduling are slim.

'You okay?'

I run a hand over my face. 'I can't believe I forgot. Jane sounded pissed off.'

'We all forget things.'

'You've never missed an appointment in your life,' I say, but it comes out sharply. 'Sorry. I'm just so exhausted. I hate not thinking clearly, making mistakes. Bloody insomnia.'

'This patch will pass,' she says reassuringly.

'It's just the pressure of your deadline.'

'Yes,' I say, my gaze sliding away.

★ ★ ★

We climb the dune path, back towards Fiona's car. I try and shake off the bad feeling about the interview, concentrate on Drake's pudgy hand in mine as I help him up the steeper parts.

Fiona keeps up a steady stream of conversation, trying to cheer me. 'Are you planning on joining our book club on Thursday?'

It's the first time she's mentioned it since Laura and Maeve's invitation at the library talk.

'I'd like to. As long as you don't mind?'

'Why would I?'

'You've got your own life down here. I don't want you to feel like I'm piggy-backing it.'

'Don't be ridiculous. I hadn't mentioned it sooner as I thought you'd find it all a bit provincial now that you're an international literary talent.'

'You will be serving canapés?'

'We'll need something to go with the Bollinger.'

Drake frees his hand from mine and races ahead up the dune, the bobble of his hat bouncing.

Where the path widens, Fiona catches me up and we walk side by side. In a few minutes we'll be back at our cars. Fiona and Drake will return to their house — and I'll go back to mine.

I think of the silence waiting for me beyond my front door. The white-washed walls echoing

114

with it. I don't want to be there, I realise. I'm looking for reasons to stay away.

I don't know why I'm feeling like this. The cliff-top house has always been my sanctuary. Yet . . . ever since I returned from France, something feels different. As if it's no longer *mine*.

I turn to Fiona. 'I haven't told you, but Mum's brooch has gone missing.'

'The silver swift?'

I nod. 'I think it's been taken by the Airbnb tenants.'

'What?' she says, shocked. 'Where was it? In your jewellery box?'

'No, pinned to this coat. I left it hanging in the hallway while I was in France.'

Her concern is replaced by amusement. 'Isn't it more likely that it's just fallen off?'

'It's possible, but I just have this feeling — '

'A feeling?'

Fiona doesn't work on sensations. She works with facts. She would never use the words, *I just have this feeling . . .*

'I can't explain it. I just feel like it's been taken. Anyway, it's not only the brooch — there was the cracked paperweight, and — ' I'm about to tell her about the two words circled in my novel, *You Lied*, but I stop myself.

It raises too many questions.

Instead I say, 'I'm thinking about contacting Joanna.'

'To say what?'

'I don't know. I just . . . I want to get the sense of her. Make sure she checks out.'

'Checks out? Elle, you do realise how that

sounds? Joanna and her family stayed in your house, paid their bill, left it beautifully. And now you're wanting to investigate her?'

'Not investigate. Make contact. Just for peace of mind.'

'I know it's hard being in the house on your own. It's natural to be jumpy. Just don't live too much in your head, okay?'

'What does that mean?'

'Look, I'm not going to patronise you by saying you're reading too deeply into these things, but equally I don't want to fan your fears because — that's what they are. You're a writer, Elle. Imagination is your tool.'

★ ★ ★

I need to get it out of my thoughts, I tell myself, as I return home and open my laptop. Logging into my Airbnb account, I find the most recent correspondence with Joanna, where I finalised the details of the rental and passed on Fiona's number in case of problems while I was abroad. Joanna had responded with thanks, saying that their family were excited about their visit.

Continuing the message thread, I begin to type.

Hi Joanna,
Thought I'd drop you a line to see how you enjoyed your stay. I hope the weather was good for you and the family. Do feel free to leave a review, if you have a chance.
I just wanted to let you know that you left

behind some nappy rash cream and a toy giraffe. I'm sorry not to have been in touch sooner. Do let me know your address and I'll pop them in the post.

    All best wishes,

    Elle x

I just want to make contact, that is all.

I'm about to put away my laptop when an auto-generated reply pings straight into my inbox. It says only: *This user is no longer a member of Airbnb.*

Joanna's account is no longer active. Her details have gone.

My fingers drum against the desk. I don't like this.

Is there another way to get in touch with her? All our communication has happened via the website. We've never spoken on the phone, and I'd had no need for Joanna's address.

I type *Joanna Elmer, Winchester*, into Google. The search pulls up several Joanna Elmers: a mental health nurse, a seventeen-year-old Joanna pouting in purple lip-gloss on Facebook, a pug breeder in her late sixties. But no images that match Joanna's Airbnb profile picture.

Next, I open my online banking to see whether there is any information on my payments. I find the dates: two payments, as per the terms and conditions, on the correct dates. The only discrepancy is that they weren't made by a Mrs Joanna Elmer, but by C. Elmer. Of course, the payment could have come out of her husband's account, so it isn't particularly unusual.

I've learned nothing illuminating. I run a knuckle back and forth along my lip. What else can I do? If Joanna has closed her account, I can hardly beg Airbnb to track her down. I have no complaint to make.

I close the lid of my laptop. It is ridiculous to be speculating about this when I should be writing. I need to put it out of my head, focus.

Yet somehow, a steady beat of unease continues to build in my chest: Joanna has deactivated her account. There is no trace of her online. It's as if she no longer exists.

2003

It was three in the morning when Elle finished her shift, stepping out of the nightclub onto a rain-slicked pavement, ears ringing. She pulled up the hood of her jacket to keep out the mizzling rain and stuffed her hands deep into her pockets.

She'd spent six hours sitting on a plastic stool in what was effectively an oversized closet, handing out coat tickets to clubbers who, hours later, searched for those pink rectangles of paper in purses, in the zipped nooks of handbags, in cotton pockets that jangled with loose change, before pleading with her, to just *Give me my coat. It's that one. There. The red one. The fur-lined one. It's got a badge on the collar. I'm sure I checked it in. No? Maybe I wore the parka, actually. Shall I just come around, have a look myself?*

A taxi drove past, an arc of water lifted by its wheels. Its 'Vacant' sign glowed temptingly. The fare home would be half her wage. It wasn't even a consideration.

As she walked, she wondered how her mother was, whether she was lonely in the rented flat with its empty rooms. Elle would ring her tomorrow, see if she wanted to come and visit for a weekend. They could have a picnic in Bute Park. Or maybe if her mother came by car, they could drive out to the Gower for the day, walk the beaches together.

A vehicle slowed alongside her, windscreen wipers swishing. She imagined another taxi, but when she glanced across she saw a dark car, its headlights beaming across the black surface of a puddle.

There was a whir as an electric window slid down.

She felt herself stiffen. The street was empty. She didn't know anyone in Cardiff who drove.

'Elle?'

She recognised the timbre of the voice — had heard it in the dry air of a lecture hall.

She adjusted her hood so she could see better. Luke Linden was leaning towards the open window.

'It is you.' He smiled. 'Do you need a ride?'

Glancing up towards the night, she felt the rain splatter across her forehead and cheeks. Then she looked towards the dry warmth of the car, at Luke Linden smiling.

It seemed like nothing at the time. Just a yes or a no. Months later, when she'd returned to Bristol, trying to forget Luke Linden, she would think back to that moment and wonder how things would have been if she'd walked on, rather than smiled, said, 'Yes, that'd be great.'

She ducked around the back of his car and climbed in.

The car smelled of cigarette smoke, a menthol brand that made her eyes burn. Pearl Jam was playing on the radio. He leant forward and turned down the volume. The heater was blasting air from the vents and as she clicked the seat belt in, she sighed.

'Busy shift?'

She looked at him.

'You work in the club,' he said, pointing to the lanyard around her neck.

'Eight hours,' she told him. 'I do the cloakroom. And then a walk home in the rain.'

'Lucky I spotted you.'

She didn't ask him what he was doing outside the club at three in the morning, or why he'd slowed when he'd seen her.

As he pulled away, she watched his hand on the gear stick, a gold wedding band catching in the passing beam of a street light.

She had only ever seen Luke Linden in a lecture hall, a library, a university corridor — places imbued with a professionalism that reminded her of their roles: he lecturer, she student.

But in his car, in the blue-black hours of the night, her skin damp with rain — everything felt different.

He glanced at her sideways, just once. He didn't ask her how she was enjoying her second semester, what she thought of the course. He said nothing — and neither did she. They travelled in silence and there was a thrill in it, the possibility in the unsaid.

'So,' he said, pulling up outside her student house. 'This is where you live.'

10

Elle

*'When you are considering your villain, re-
member the old adage holds truth: 'It's usually
someone you know.' The job of the author
is to explore how well your protagonist ever
really knew them.'*

Author Elle Fielding

I move through my lounge offering wine and
glossy chilli-flecked olives from a wooden bowl.
Two women are sitting on my sofa, knees angled
towards each other, laughing. A woman in an
elegant waist-cinching skirt rests her wine glass
on the bookcase, as she talks enthusiastically to
an artist from St Ives. Music plays throughout
the downstairs and chatter rises above it,
washing through with laughter.

I feel as if I'm watching the scene from under-
water, everything holding a slightly refracted quality.
I hadn't anticipated hosting book club. Hadn't
imagined my home suddenly being filled with
strangers.

'Listen,' Fiona had said when she'd called
earlier, 'our central heating has crashed. It's like
the bloody Arctic here. Not only that, but there's
a sickness bug doing the rounds at Drake's
nursery, and I'm terrified he's brought it into the

house. I can't fell the entire book club in one swoop. Even if they survive the sickness, they'll probably be hypothermic after an evening in this frigid house. We need to come to you.'

I'd started to protest, but Fiona cut me off, saying, 'You don't need to do a thing. Not a thing. I've got everything ready: wine, cheese, those chocolate nibbly sticks women go misty-eyed about. All you need to do is open your front door and usher people to seats that aren't booby-trapped with Duplo. Say yes?'

My sister has never liked having people to her house. When Bill's parents visited in the summer, she booked them into a B&B up the road.

'Is it wrong to like a little privacy?' she'd snapped when Bill had challenged her.

I wouldn't be at all surprised if the central heating was fine.

'Can I top anyone up?' I ask, approaching Maeve and Laura who are talking together by the hearth.

'Driving,' Maeve says.

'Don't try and lead astray a bobby's wife,' Laura says, holding out her glass instead.

Laura can only be in her early twenties and I can't help wondering if she doesn't have something she'd prefer to do with her evenings. I refill her glass, then open the window, letting a refreshing blast of sea air blow through the room.

'You're lucky to live right on the cliff,' Maeve says. 'The views must be incredible in the daylight.'

'It's the first time I've ever lived by the sea — and I've completely fallen in love with it.'

'The house is *amazing*,' Laura says. 'I mean, I knew it would be from Facebook — but it looks even more beautiful in the flesh.'

We are joined by a third woman, Ana, who runs a coffee house in town. She has luminescent skin and a striking crop of blonde hair. Her wrists are ringed in silver bangles, which jingle as she raises her wine glass and clinks it against mine.

'Here's to our newest book club member. Good recruitment skills,' she adds to Maeve and Laura.

'It's so nice to finally have people over,' I say, with meaning. I'm enjoying my home being filled with people and noise and laughter. I've found it hard to meet friends since moving here. I don't have work colleagues. I don't have a partner to draw me into their group of friends. I don't have a child to make those easy connections that seem to flower between mothers. Maybe I should borrow Drake, take him to one of those soft-play places that Fiona refuses to step inside on the grounds of her sanity.

I laugh, a light snort. God, am I a little drunk? Quite possibly. I had a couple of glasses of wine before the book club arrived, just to help myself ease into the evening.

Ana tucks a hand into the pocket of her wide harem pants, the indigo fabric ballooning from her petite frame.

'Now you've let us in, you'll be struggling to get rid of us.' She smiles, then turns to Maeve, saying, 'I don't think we've caught up since your

125

retreat. How was it?'

'Wonderful. An entire week without cooking or cleaning or ferrying around a teenager.'

'What kind of retreat was it?' I ask.

'A friend of Ana's runs a wilderness centre in Devon. She holds an annual retreat in the last week of October, so it's my chance to escape into the woods and pretend to do yoga and meditate. Really it's just a holiday from real life.'

'We could all do with one of those,' Laura says.

I agree, although there's something about the way Laura says it — sad, wistful — that makes me wonder what she means by it.

The rest of the conversation flows around me. I observe the curve of Ana's mouth as she smiles, the way Maeve looks through the sides of her eyes as she listens. The details pixelate in my mind's eye and I catch myself thinking, *I'll write about this later.*

When the doorbell rings, I slip out into the hallway.

'You're late.'

Fiona moves through the door, shouldering off her coat.

'Sorry, sorry. I'm here now,' she says, through red-painted lips. She thrusts out a carrier bag filled with warm white wine and several bags of crisps and dip. 'All okay?'

'Absolutely fine. Go through. I'll get you a drink.'

In the kitchen, I take a long-stemmed glass and pour Fiona a glass of the wine she's brought. Then I empty a bag of cracked-black-pepper crisps into a bowl, placing a couple into my

126

mouth. I'm swaying lightly on my feet and the sensation isn't entirely unpleasant.

I take out my phone and snap a picture of the wine and crisp bowl, putting out a quick post about book club.

Haven't started discussing the book yet, but the wine is going down nicely. #bookclub #wineclub

I slip my phone away, then wander back to the lounge. Moving through my house, I look around, as if seeing it for the first time. Sometimes it catches me by surprise, the sheer scale of it. The size, the beauty feels overpowering, almost vertiginous. It is too much.

I don't deserve it.

Reaching the hallway, I pause mid-step aware of someone watching me. Maeve is descending my stairway, a hand sliding down the bannister. Her hair is pinned up and fastened with a headscarf, drawing the gaze to her small features.

'The downstairs bathroom was occupied.'

I smile. 'Of course.'

'Thanks for having us over last minute. You know we're all going to want to do book club here every month?'

I laugh, following Maeve back into the lounge — just as Laura is exiting. 'Nipping for a wee! Don't start the book chat without me!'

Fiona has anchored herself to the hearth. Her shoulders look stiff, her chin lifted.

'Thanks,' she says taking the wine. She leans in close and whispers, 'I hope you've served me the crap stuff I bought.'

127

'I have.' I grin.

'The neighbours called the police,' Ana is saying to the room. 'My hairdresser had to fly back early from her holiday. When she opened her front door, she *cried*. They hadn't even attempted to clear up. There were smashed glasses in her sink, cigarette butts stamped into the carpet, the dining table was scratched to pieces from girls dancing in stilettos. I won't even repeat what she said about the state of their bedroom.'

'Not like you to skimp on the details,' Fiona says with a wry smile.

Ana grins.

'You hear such terrible things about those Airbnb stays,' the woman in the waist-cinching skirt says. Katherine, that's her name. She's an Assistant Head at the local comprehensive, and I can imagine her radiating a quiet sort of discipline as she patrols the playground with her stiff-backed posture. 'I read an article about a woman returning home to find her living room had been turned into a setting for a pornographic photoshoot.'

'Sounds like that would make arriving home a lot more fun,' Ana says.

'Let's not scare Elle,' Fiona says. 'She's only just recovering from Airbnb-ing this place.'

'Here?' Ana asks, surprised. 'I can't believe you'd rent out this house. How did it go?'

'It was left immaculately,' I answer.

'I'm not sure I'd like the idea of strangers in my house,' Katherine says. 'It's very brave of you.'

'It was just a test run. I only did a fortnight.'

'Tell them about the paperweight,' Fiona says.

128

I shoot her a look — I don't want my anxieties repackaged as anecdotes — but it is too late; the attention of the room has turned to me.

'Oh, it's nothing really. It's just I have this lovely paperweight that I keep on my writing desk. When I got back home, it was chipped. That's all. I suppose with any rental there'll always be little things like that.'

'It wasn't the chip that was the problem though, was it?' Fiona says. 'It was that Elle kept the paperweight in her writing room — which she'd *locked*.'

'What, you think the renters broke in?' Ana asks.

'Not really, no. It must have happened before I went away. When I mentioned it to Fiona, I was just speculating, letting my imagination run away with itself. Which, as you pointed out,' I say, inclining my head in Fiona's direction, 'is my trade.'

Everyone laughs.

'What I can't believe,' Ana says, her gaze turning to Fiona, 'is that we've been doing book club all this time and you never mentioned your sister was an author!'

Had she not?

'Didn't know myself,' Fiona says. 'Elle kept her book-writing activities top secret, didn't you?'

'When you first start writing you don't actually believe you'll get published. The last thing I wanted to do was start saying, *Hey everyone, I'm working on a book!*'

'Except I'm not everyone.'

My sister is in one of her provocative moods. I can guess there's been an argument with Bill before coming out and she hasn't quite shaken off her viper reflex.

'Is it true,' Maeve asks, 'that it's best to write about what you know?'

The question causes me to pause and I take a moment to frame my response.

'I suppose it lends a credibility, a sense of vividness and emotion if it's something you've experienced. But I don't think authors should be limited by it.'

Katherine says, 'I read a fascinating article about method actors and the lengths they go to to get into role. Have you watched *The Fall*?'

I shake my head.

'Oh, you must. It's a chilling series about a serial killer. The actor — Jamie Dornan, I think his name is — wanted to experience the thrill of the chase. So one evening on the tube, he followed a woman as she got off. Apparently, he kept his distance, so she had no idea she was being followed, but he stayed on her tail for a few streets, experiencing what it felt like to pursue someone.'

'That's just creepy,' Laura says, shivering.

I don't disagree, although I can see why he did it — the benefit of being able to live that emotional experience, to then channel that feeling into playing the part.

'So, have you always wanted to be a writer?' Ana asks.

'I don't think I knew what I wanted until fairly recently.'

'Oh, come on,' Fiona says. 'You've always had a head for fiction. Even your diaries.'

'My diaries?'

'Remember that phase you went through of making up diary entries?'

I explain to the room, 'I thought our mum was reading them, so I started peppering them with fictional entries to try and catch her out.'

Fiona says to the other women, 'Elle made up these wonderful tales about a boy at school who was supposedly infatuated with her. I seem to remember you referred to him by a code name — presumably to cause maximum speculation about his identity.'

I can feel heat building in my cheeks as I recall certain extracts. They began as girlish weaves of fiction, focused on the sweet things he whispered to me, or the way he'd brush his hand against mine if we happened to pass in the corridor. Gradually, the fiction grew into a story of stolen kisses and a declaration of love.

The trap worked. I remember the afternoon that my mother called me into the kitchen. There were two cups of tea on the table and a slice of lemon drizzle cake, which always made my mouth fizz. My mother opened the conversation with the phrase, 'A little birdy has told me . . . ' It seemed a ludicrous thing to say, but I let my mother talk, explaining her worries about the seriousness of an older boy showing such interest in me.

I was waiting for the moment to jump in and say, *Busted! You've been reading my diary.* Yet somehow, I sensed that explaining I'd made the whole thing up — that it was all just a story — would get me in trouble. Anyway, the story

131

was pleasant. I liked living it. So instead I said, 'Yes, I understand.' My mother had looked surprised, then eventually relieved. We hugged, shared a second slice of lemon drizzle cake.

Over the next few days, I began to create new entries about cooling it off with 'R'. I wrote in detail about our tearful parting hug and the long letter he'd slipped into my locker. I could tell from the less watchful way my mother looked at me that she'd been following each instalment closely.

Now I say to Fiona, 'You never told me you'd read them.'

'Older sister privileges,' she says with a wink. 'Anyway, I enjoyed your little tales. Who knew that one day you'd do it for a living?'

I smile, but something about this conversation leaves me humiliated. It's not just that Fiona used to read my diaries. It's that I've been exposed for lying.

★ ★ ★

'All those Plato and Homer references became a bit tedious, I thought,' Laura says, when we finally get around to talking about the book.

We are discussing Donna Tartt's classic, *The Secret History*.

'They were my favourite thing about the book,' Ana counters.

'You would say that,' Maeve says. 'Didn't you do some sort of MA in Ancient Greek or Theology?'

'Philosophy,' Ana corrects. 'Serving coffee is

132

just the cover job; I've got a philosopher's soul.' She grins.

I decide I like Ana, and hope that the two of us will become friends.

'Did you study English?' Laura asks, turning to face me.

I hesitate, wanting to get my wording right. 'I started an English Literature degree at Cardiff University, but I didn't fall in love with the course, so I left at the end of the first year.' I make sure the words come out lightly, a smile in my voice, because in my experience once people detect a hesitation, they poke at it, want to inspect it.

I move to the window, opening it a little wider. I must unsettle the edge of the curtain because from within the fabric there is a flutter of movement that rises to my eyeline. I feel it — the brushing of wings against my cheek.

My reaction is immediate, instinctive. I scream, rearing back, hands raking at the air.

I am not thinking about the silence that descends upon the room, or the way everyone has turned to stare, startled by my violent burst of movement. I think of nothing except white-hot, blinding fear.

I've pinned myself to the wall.

From somewhere across the room, I hear Fiona's voice soothing, calming, as she says, 'It's okay, Elle. You're okay. I'll get it out.' She is on her feet, moving towards the window. 'Got ourselves a moth phobic,' she says to the others, the lightness in her voice attempting to downplay my behaviour.

Above the pounding rush of blood in my ears,

I tell myself that I am safe, there is nothing to fear. My breathing is agitated, eyes blinking rapidly, but the rest of my body feels frozen.

I watch Fiona capture the moth in cupped hands. My eyes track the cage of her fingers, watching as she frees the moth through the open window, then pulls it shut, snapping the handle down.

The moth beats its wings against the glass for a matter of seconds, then disappears into the night.

I keep watching for several more seconds, then slowly I let out the breath I've been holding.

When I turn, everyone is staring at me.

Humiliation burns in my cheeks as I mumble an apology, my voice shaking.

'A moth phobia,' Laura says. 'Didn't even know that existed.'

'Mottephobia,' Ana says, naming it. 'Have you always had it?' she asks gently.

I don't look Ana in the eye as I answer, 'Yes.'

'No, not as a child,' Fiona corrects, she's a stickler for accuracy. 'You were the queen of bug hunts. You'd capture anything that would fit in your little magnifying box — ants, spiders, moths, ladybirds.'

'Was I?' I say vaguely. 'A rogue trait I developed later, then.'

Fiona refills my wine glass and hands it to me. 'Get that down you.'

'I can't believe you're afraid of moths,' Laura says, not unkindly, but as if she is completely bewildered by the idea of it. 'They can't hurt you.'

I remind myself to smile. 'I know.'

134

There is the dance of departure — drinks being finished, bags gathered, coats shouldered on, thank yous being made. I see everyone to the door, standing with a hand anchored to the frame, still on edge after the shock of the moth.

Watching as my house empties of guests, I'm aware of my desire to call them back, ask them to stay a while longer, to not leave me here.

Laura is the last to go and she pauses on the doorstep, turning back to face me.

'I almost forgot. I got you something. Call it a house-warming gift, or a welcome to Cornwall gift, or whatever.'

She rummages in her bag and pulls out a beautifully wrapped parcel.

'Laura — ' I begin, but she waves a hand through the air.

'I saw it and knew you'd love it.'

I unwrap it carefully, feeling uncomfortable that Laura — who is probably earning little more than minimum wage at the library — has chosen to spend her money on me.

'See,' she says, as I pull out a cream mug. 'I had to get it for you.'

Printed in a black typewriter font, it reads, *Careful, or I'll put you in my next novel.*

'Thank you.'

Her expression turns serious. 'I've got to ask: what is your secret?'

I blink, my attention narrowing to the question.

Laura's eyes glitter from the wine. 'There's

something you're keeping from us. I'm just wondering what it is.'

I shake my head. 'I . . . '

'I mean, you can't be much more than thirty, you own *this* house, and you're a bestselling author. Who did you have to kill to get this life?'

I hear the slow roll of waves beyond us, the sound of a car door closing at the end of the driveway — and then Laura's mouth breaks into a smile.

She is joking, of course she is joking.

I match her smile. 'All my killing happens strictly on paper.'

'Well, as your number one fan, I thought it my duty to check!' Laura waves cheerily, then turns and crosses the driveway, climbing into Maeve's car.

Engines start, headlights beam, everyone returning home to their husbands or families. I wait in the doorway, the cold air frigid against my cheeks.

I remain there until the last car has disappeared down the pocked lane. As I make to pull the door behind me, a prickling sensation stretches across my neck.

I turn back, certain I am being watched.

The security lights have flicked off, cloaking the lane in darkness. Wind funnels over the cliff face, creeping through my open doorway as I stand illuminated on the front step.

There is no one there. It's just my nerves jangling.

But then I notice it — a faint orange glow in the periphery of my vision, no more than a prick of light. My gaze narrows, focusing on it.

Suddenly the neighbours' security light flicks on, illuminating the front of their house — and there stands Mark. He is leaning against his door, a cigarette between his lips, gaze locked on me.

There is no smile. No call of a greeting. Just that dark gaze reaching across the night, fixing on me.

Several beats pass as we stare at one another.

Slowly, he raises his right hand. For a moment it looks as if his first two fingers are pointing at me, like the slow draw of a gun, aimed at my head.

My breath tightens.

I blink. But when I look again, it is his open palm facing me, held up in a wave.

11

Elle

In the ocean-deep dark of four a.m., silence is swallowing me.

Only hours ago, the house was filled with the noise and thrum of book club. Now that everyone's left, the stillness has deepened, solidified.

Alone in this island bed, I keep thinking of Flynn.

Keep wishing he was here with me.

When we first met, Flynn was living in a rented house with three friends, and he had the boxroom — just a single bed and a hanging rail for the two pairs of jeans and handful of jumpers he owned. For four months we'd slept in that narrow bed, limbs entwined. I'd press myself against his back, my knees in the warm crook of his, feeling the rhythm of his breathing slowing mine.

I always slept well.

But this bed, this bed is too large. One side of the mattress too cold.

'Fuck you,' I say to nothing, to nobody, shirking off the duvet.

I swing my legs out and sit on the edge of the mattress, the heels of my hands pressing into my eye sockets. One bad night's sleep is standing on the shoulders of the next, compressing me beneath the weight of exhaustion. It will mean another day propped up by caffeine, another day sleepwalking.

I run through my immediate choices: I could watch a film or listen to a radio play. Then I remember the proof of Clare Mackintosh's latest novel that's in my writing room. I'll dive into that, lose myself in someone else's words.

Wrapping myself in a fleecy dressing gown, I drift upstairs, the air cooling noticeably as I rise through the house.

In my writing room, I flick on my desk lamp and see my own image thrown back in the glass wall. By day, the flowing space of this room feels tranquil, a sanctuary, but at night the darkness transforms it into something looming and exposed. There are no curtains to pull, no nooks to cosy within. Up here, the roaring groan of the sea sounds so close, it's as if the waves are beating against the glass.

My hand strays to the paperweight on my desk, tracing a fingertip over the deep crack at its centre. I pick it up, feeling its cold weight against my palm. So strange to find the missing fragment embedded in my bedroom carpet — right in front of my mirror.

It's as if someone knew where I would stand. It's as if someone positioned it there.

I shiver, setting down the paperweight.

I turn, taking in my writing room. If someone had been up here, what would they see, I wonder? Where would they look?

Somewhere below there is a low sound of

140

knocking. I freeze, head angled towards the noise.

Downstairs?

It's not the front door knocker. Too faint. I wait, listening, heartbeat raised.

It comes again, two or three light knocks, like the quick tap of knuckles on a window.

Unease creaks along my spine.

My thoughts trip to Mark standing outside his house, his stare pinning me. Then that strange lift of his hand.

Had he still been watching as I'd turned away, stepped back inside my house, alone?

Another knock — but this time I catch the sound more clearly: a tapping, then a scratch. My gaze lowers to the balcony that rings my bedroom below. In the darkness I can just make out the branches of a potted bay tree bending in the wind, scratching against the. glass doors.

I laugh to ease the tension, but it sounds brittle alone in the room.

★   ★   ★

I cross my writing room, moving towards the oak trunk. Kneeling beside it, I open the heavy lid.

The trunk is filled with old photo albums, a stack of diaries, a clutch of notebooks with faded covers and doodling in the margins. My fingers meet a bundle of cards fastened together with a rubber band and I find myself pulling them onto my lap.

I've kept every card Flynn has written to me. Rolling the elastic band free, I think, maybe this

141

is the real reason I've come up to my writing room — to look at these.

The first card is illustrated with roses, *Happy birthday* written in swirling silver writing. Flynn's card-buying skills have never been notable.

Dear Elle, Happy birthday. Remember, I do have receipts. The benefits of not charity shopping (this year). Flynn x

I smile, the easiness of his words softening something within me. The next card has been homemade on flimsy green paper. On the front there is a photo of me sitting on Flynn's lap on a picnic bench, our gazes on the ground, my long hair falling like a curtain over one side of my face, Flynn's tanned arms loosely slung around me. In the background are the thick trunks of redwood trees, the green dome of a tent. The caption reads: *3 years today!*

1 continent, 2 countries, 4 provinces, 8 states, 8,500 miles, 10,000 mosquito bites and 1 badly made card later, and we are still madly in love. Happy anniversary honey.

Even as my face splits into a smile, my eyes film with tears.

This, this is what's real, I think.

In amongst the cards, I come across another photo of the two of us. I look at the wide stretch of his smile, the way the light catches at the edges of his eyes as he looks towards me, grinning. The photo had been taken on the night I signed the contracts with my publisher. Flynn had met me after work and we'd gone to a bar in the centre of Bristol with some friends. I

142

remember Flynn kept kissing me, telling me how proud he was, that I was amazing. *You've done it!*

I recall another fragment of the evening — it could only have been a few minutes at most — where I'd stepped out of the night, just disappeared like a scene in a story that would never be read. It had been late, after midnight, and the burn of smiling so hard had left an ache in my jaw. I'd left the bar, raising the inside of my wrist towards the bouncer, who'd nodded once as he glanced at the ink stamp. My heels clicked against the road as I'd crossed, my dress dancing against my thighs. The mizzling rain caught in my hair, a crown of liquid beads.

I walked towards the cash machine — but, at the last minute, ducked past it, slipping down the side of the building into a narrow, unlit alleyway. I stood with my shoulder blades pressed to the damp brick, chest heaving, my breath coming too rapidly. I made a cup of my hands, breathing into them, collecting the expelled air and drawing it back into my lungs.

Eventually, eventually, the race of my heartbeat began to settle. I tipped my head back, looked up at the flecks of rain caught in the streetlamps, falling motes that covered my skin with dew. I had known that I would go back inside to Flynn and our friends. That I would carry on like nothing was different.

That was my decision — and I must live with it.

★　★　★

143

As I put Flynn's cards and photos away, my fingers meet a leather-bound file. My heartbeat trips, stumbles. I know exactly what is inside. I know that I won't open it, won't look.

It's dangerous to even keep it — and yet, I must. I push it deeper into the trunk and close the lid.

No, it wasn't a book, or even Flynn's cards that brought me up here. It was that file. I needed to see it. To check it was still there.

⋆ ⋆ ⋆

Ready to return to bed now, I grab the proof copy, then reach across my desk to switch off the lamp. I must misjudge the space as my elbow catches it, toppling it to the floor.

Thankfully the bulb doesn't smash. Bending to retrieve the lamp, my eyes follow the beam of light, which is shining against the leg of my desk. There is a mark in the wood that I haven't noticed before. It takes a moment for my eyes to adjust to the light and, when they do, I see there are letters carved into the pale oak. I think of school desks tattooed with names of students, or declarations of love made with a compass point.

I move closer, angling my head to read the letters.

The hairs on the back of my neck stand on end. I blink rapidly, but the word remains in front of me, etched there in capitals.

Although the desk is second-hand, Flynn had spent hours and hours refurbishing it. He'd sanded the legs — he'd told me about how hard it was to work the old varnish out of the ornate twists. These carved letters look fresh, the gouged wood paler than its surrounds.

I run my fingertips along the other desk legs, feeling for grooves and nicks. I angle the lamp towards the underside of the desk, scanning it closely. But there is nothing else, no carvings, or marks. Just one word singeing my thoughts.

LIAR.

2004

In the spring semester, daylight hours slid by in a blur of lectures and lie-ins, of afternoons spent slinging a frisbee in the park. It was only at night, when there was no shift to work, or party to be at, that Elle would finally open her course books and think, *Right then. Essays.*

Her thumb and forefinger pinched her brow as she struggled to focus. She was trying to write something discursive about post-modernism, but was restless, her attention waning. Maybe she would go out after all, just one quick drink with her housemates at the students' union.

Rummaging through her wardrobe, she picked out a new T-dress in dusky blue that she could wear with Converse.

It was as she was wriggling into the dress that she became aware of it — the feeling of being watched. The hairs on the back of her neck rose and her gaze travelled to the window. Their student house backed onto a valley railway line, where litter gathered at the base of the bushes.

It took her eyes a moment to adjust to the darkness, and then she saw it — the shape of someone walking along the edge of the track, then cutting between the shrubs and disappearing through the shadows.

A drunken student wandering to a party? Someone taking a short cut home? If they'd caught a glimpse of her changing, so what? Let them look. She was nineteen and newly beautiful. She'd been a late bloomer — braces, a short but intense affair with acne, and a fringe that never suited her had kept her off boys' radars — but over the past eighteen months there'd been a metamorphosis. Straight white teeth emerged from beneath metal tracks, hormonal skin was replaced by a clear youthful glow, the fringe had grown out into long waves of caramel-blonde hair.

Dressed now, she returned to her desk to check the deadline for her essay, the figure by the track sliding from her thoughts. The essay didn't need to be handed in for another couple of days. She'd party tonight. Work tomorrow. She'd pull an all-nighter if necessary — the pressure of a deadline always made her focus. It was a good plan.

As it turned out, her essay score wouldn't matter. In fact, none of her essay scores or exam results would.

But she didn't know that yet.

Just like she didn't know, as she admired herself in the mirror, a hand balanced on her hip, that she would wear the new dress only once more. Or that, afterwards, she would shed it like a skin, knotting it within the depths of a bin liner. Because all Elle would want, would be to forget the girl in the dusky blue dress.

12

Elle

*'With every reveal, raise a further question.
Intrigue is what keeps the pages turning.'*
Author Elle Fielding

In the cloaked darkness of one a.m., I lie awake,
picturing her. The girl I was in my twenties. The
one who left Cardiff and moved into a rambling
house-share in Bristol. The girl who cut her hair
to her chin, and ringed her eyes with kohl. The
girl who stayed in a room with no curtains
— because it didn't matter if there was light or
not, she so rarely slept.

I think of that girl, who would've been awake
in the middle of the night, just like I am now.
Unravel ten, twelve years and here she would be,
lying on a single bed, mattress springs digging
into her back, eyes open to the darkness. Her
insomnia is just starting, just worming its way
under her eyelids, making a home in her mind.

What would I tell that girl if I could reach her?
I could show her the beautiful house where she'd
one day live, with its king-sized bed and
duck-feather pillows. I could tell her about the
career she'd have, show her the awards engraved
with her name. I could point to the sea beyond
the window and say, 'Look. Look where I am.

Everything will be okay.'

But she would see through me. She would ask, *Then, why are you still lying awake?*

★　★　★

Morning eventually arrives. I drag myself from bed, my senses feeling like they've been shaken, disordered. Some too acute, others muffled. The daylight feels too sharp, the shower streams needles over my skin.

Then I am downstairs and there is a coffee in front of me that I don't even remember making. I scald my lips not waiting for it to cool.

An hour later, I am sitting in a windowless office talking to my bank manager. Sweat gathers in the small of my back as I watch his pale eyes dart over the sheaf of papers on his desk.

He shakes his head and my stomach twists. 'It clearly shows that we already adjusted your mortgage payments last October to an interest-only rate for a fixed period of twelve months. Since then you've missed the last two payments — '

'The final bill for the builders came out,' I interrupt, not quite succeeding in keeping my tone neutral. I've never been good at this sort of thing — banks, offices, spreadsheets. 'I hadn't realised they'd need it all in one go. I'll be back on track for next month's payment.' I force myself to smile.

'I must make you aware, Mrs Fielding, that if you don't meet your mortgage repayments, the bank is legally within its rights to repossess your house.'

I absorb the enormity of this statement. I've known this. I've read these words on the letters I've been pushing to the back of the kitchen drawer. But now here I am, face to face with the manager of the bank from which I've borrowed an eye-watering sum of money.

Throughout my twenties, Flynn and I rarely earned much more than minimum wage — we were used to living within our means; there was a sense of pride in it. Yet, somehow, when it came to the cliff-top house, reason was swallowed by the desire to create the perfect writer's home. Why, I wonder? To prove to myself that it is real? That it is worth everything I've sacrificed?

A rogue thought surges forwards: perhaps there is part of me that *wants* all this to derail. It is like I'm standing at the very edge of a train track, waiting to feel the churning rush of wind against my skin as it speeds dangerously close. All it takes is one more step.

I think of how Fiona would handle this situation. She wouldn't allow this bank manager to put something she loved, needed, under threat. I sit up taller. 'I've shown you the contract for my book deal. Next month the second half of my advance arrives. If you could just bear with me until then.'

The bank manager pushes his glasses up the narrow bridge of his nose as he scans the document.

'Yes, I can see that. But what concerns me is this clause here, where it states that if you don't deliver your manuscript on the specified date, then you would be liable to pay back the initial advance, which,' he pauses, looking up, 'is a considerable sum.'

Breathe. Just breathe.

'Can I check, Mrs Fielding, that you are indeed on track to deliver your book by the deadline, which, by my reckoning, is due in twenty-one days' time.'

I think of my waiting manuscript, the bones of a story that is haunting me, disturbing my sleep, pulling me back to a place I don't want to revisit. But I know I must. This needs to be finished.

I draw my lips into a smile. 'Yes, I am absolutely on track.'

★   ★   ★

I step from the bank into the cold bite of the afternoon. It is only two o'clock, but street lights flicker on around me, a dull orange glow breaking the darkening sky.

I should go straight home, straight to my desk. Write. But the meeting has left me anxious, my thoughts scattered.

I walk in the opposite direction to my car, skirting the proprietor of the key cutting shop who is bringing in a clapboard stand. I pause outside the florists, glancing at the wooden crates on the pavement stacked with purple heathers. There is something calming, grounding, about the gentle promise of flowers.

A bell tinkles as I push open the primrose-yellow door. The air smells of blooms and over-ripe pollen. The stiff formality of the bank washes away as I move beyond the displays, heartened by the beauty of the delicate petals, the fragile pink stamens, the sweet bursts of scent.

'With you in a minute, love,' the florist greets me, as she wraps a bunch of flowers for the customer who stands at the till.

The customer turns, too: Mark. He glances at me disinterestedly, giving no indication that he recognises me, and then resumes his conversation with the florist.

'Thought they'd brighten her room.'

'Course they will. How about I do them for a tenner?'

'Kind of you, Marg. Cheers.'

I move to the far corner of the shop and position myself by the buckets of single flowers: vintage blush roses, a spray of long-stemmed daisies, purple-stained freesias. I hear the stretch of tape, the crinkle of paper.

'How is your mum?'

'About the same. Still got no feeling in her right arm. They don't know if she ever will.'

'A bloody stroke. You just never know, do you?'

Enid had had a stroke? My God, the poor woman. It explains Mark's sudden return to Cornwall — and why I've not seen Enid or Frank in days. I'd like to send a card. Would that be appropriate? Despite our differences over the rebuild, I like Enid. She is my neighbour — of course I can send a card.

Mark's voice rings clear as he says, 'Apparently stress is a major trigger for strokes.'

'I've heard that. Your folks had all that

business with the cliff-top house, didn't they?'

I go very still.

'Bought up by an out-of-towner.'

'Could've guessed. Seen what they've done with it. Huge great thing, isn't it?'

'Blocked half their view. Stole their light.'

The florist makes a tutting noise in her throat. 'Well, listen, you send your mum my love. Once she's home, I'll bring over one of my carrot cakes, okay?'

I can hear the ring of the till, the slip of a receipt being pushed into a wallet, the rustle of paper as the flowers are gathered. I pluck several rose stems from a bucket, pretending to be deeply absorbed in them.

Mark's footsteps move purposefully towards the door. Then there's a side-step, and he's suddenly at my shoulder, leaning close.

'Pretty,' he says, gazing down at the roses in my hands. 'Are they for anyone special?'

'No. Just me.'

'You don't consider yourself special?' That dark gaze again, penetrating. 'That's definitely not the impression you give.'

Heat spreads from my neck, into my cheeks.

'Roses. A classic choice. They'll look perfect on your bedside table. Next to the cream lamp.'

My mouth opens in surprise, but before I have chance to frame a response, he is gone.

★   ★   ★

The Toad and Otter smells of the long-stale tobacco that is locked into the aged carpet. I order a large glass of white wine and wait at the bar, peeling back the edges of a drinks mat, thoughts whirring.

They'll look perfect on your bedside table. Next to the cream lamp.

He was implying he'd been inside my house — specifically my *bedroom*. But how? Enid and Frank haven't visited since the rebuild, so can't have described it to him.

My bedroom windows face the sea, so Mark couldn't have seen inside it from Frank and Enid's house. But what if he was standing on the beach?

'What did it do to you?'

I look up. The barman is smiling wryly, nodding towards the drinks mat that I've torn into a dozen pieces.

'Sorry,' I say, gathering the pieces, pushing them into my coat pocket. I carry my wine to an empty table by the flashing slot machines, aware that my hands are shaking. I try and lean back into the seat, relax, but my body feels tense, unyielding. I lift the wine to my mouth and drain half of it.

If Mark had known I was putting my house on Airbnb, he could have looked it up out of curiosity. I remember photographing each of the rooms, styling them carefully and choosing the right angles to give a sense of space and light.

Slipping my phone from my bag, I flick through the camera roll looking for the photos I'd taken for the Airbnb rental. Locating the image of my bedroom, my gaze travels over the smartly made bed with its fresh cream sheets and plumped cushions, but the angle of the shot cuts out my bedside table and lamp. I know I've never shared a picture of my room on any of my social media platforms, so Mark's comment must be a guess.

Unless, I think, seizing on something else, unless Mark had somehow been *inside* my house during the Airbnb rental. I think of the word LIAR carved into my writing desk. Had he done it? It was possible that he knew Joanna and her family. Maybe he was the person who'd suggested Joanna rent it. Even as I frame the thought, it feels unlikely.

I squeeze my temples. Perhaps Mark had introduced himself to Joanna's family, told them he took care of the maintenance for the property and wanted to check on the water tank or some other such detail. That is feasible.

But even if Mark had somehow found his way into my house, into my bedroom, into my writing room, the question that leaves me unnerved is: *Why?*

★   ★   ★

I shouldn't have ordered the second glass. Or the third. I've had to abandon my car and walk home across the beach. Drinking and insomnia are a toxic mix; everything feels distorted, held at distance.

I'm not dressed for the dark beach: my leather pumps are absorbing water from the damp sand, and beneath my thin jacket my skin is puckered with goose bumps.

I can hear the trickle and draw of the tide as rivulets flow beneath the sand. Is the tide coming in or out? I must get into the habit of checking the tables. From the low light of the moon and the glisten of the sea, I can see the water is still a little way off. I will keep going at a good pace. The house isn't far.

When Flynn and I bought the cliff-top house, one of the pulls of the location had been that we'd be able to grab a pub dinner in town, then walk home across the bay. The idea had seemed romantic, walking with clasped hands, the wind at our backs, the waves rolling against the shore.

Now fear beats in my chest as I hurry on, toes damp and icy within my sodden shoes.

I make good time across the beach and when I reach the stone steps, I take out my phone to use the flashlight. I see then how close the sea is — another twenty minutes and the access steps to the house would've been cut off. The sole of my foot slides across wet rock and I feel myself unbalancing, hinging forward. I put out my hands to save myself, but feel the smack of my knees against stone.

I cry out, my right knee scalding with pain. Struggling to push myself upright, I retrieve my phone, and hobble up the final steps, my breath short. Following the stone path to the side door, I fumble with the key, let myself in and stand in the kitchen in darkness, heart pounding, knees flayed. It was stupid and risky to walk along the beach at night. It could have been my head on the stone steps, not my phone.

I'm making bad decisions.

I slide my hand along the wall and flick on the lights, the kitchen gleaming in the bright downlights. I limp to the fridge and pour a large glass of wine.

I want to push away the feeling of the grate of rock against skin, the warm dampness of blood spreading, so I take out my phone, scroll through my Facebook page and focus on answering some new messages from readers.

I immediately see that Booklover101 has posted again.

I'm worried about you. You look like you're losing weight. Don't let this book kill you.

My back stiffens at the tone. The intrusiveness of the comment. The assumed intimacy between us.

I scroll back through the last few photos I've posted. There are shots of the indent of my footprints along the curving shoreline, the wingback chair in my writing room caught in a sunbeam, my side profile as I laugh.

No, I don't look like I've lost weight, or that I'm sinking under pressure. I've made sure of that.

My life looks idyllic.

I snap a quick picture of my glass of wine. Then I upload it to Facebook, adding, Celebrating a full-powered day of writing with a glass of wine. Three weeks and counting till deadline day! #book2 #almostthere

Then I delete Booklover101's post and push my phone back in my pocket.

★ ★ ★

Leaving the kitchen, I move along the hallway, flicking on the lights as I go. On the stairway, I pause by the window. I can see straight into Frank and Enid's house. I wonder how long Enid will be in hospital. Is Frank with her? If so, Mark will be in their house, alone. I imagine him moving through the silent rooms of the bungalow, coming to stand at the kitchen window in the darkness, a cigarette burning between his fingers. Watching.

If he looks this way right now, he will see me framed in the light. I step back and, as I do so, I notice something. On the window, there is a smear of a fingerprint. Looking more closely I can make out a word written in the faint condensation.

house

As I'm considering the word, something within me turns cold, like splinters of ice spreading and branching along the back of my neck, down my spine.

It isn't just a single word.

Three others are stacked above.

I'm
in
your
house

Everything goes very still. Saliva pools at the back of my throat. I remind myself to swallow. Breathe.

I blink, looking again at the words. My head feels like it is spinning, like the very ground is tilting beneath me.

I lunge forward, using the sleeve of my jacket to wipe at the glass.

There, it is gone. Nothing to see. I stare at the clear pane: it is almost as if I've imagined it.

The message could've been there for days, I tell myself. A joke written by a visitor. One of the book club members, even? Yet why would anyone write something so insidious, so perfectly creepy?

Above the rush of blood in my head, there is a noise, like the slide of wood against wood.

I wait, listening.

The pounding of my heart intensifies.

There. There it is again. The sound comes from upstairs. My writing room. Like a drawer is being closed.

Houses make noises, I tell myself firmly. There is no one in here. It is only my imagination. My senses are on high alert, amplifying things, that's all.

There are no further sounds from upstairs.

I let out the breath I'm holding.

As I turn away from the window, I catch it: the stretched creak of a floorboard pressing against a joist, then the low suck of air as a door is pulled open.

Someone is in my house.

Previously

I'm enjoying being in your house.

I drift through your kitchen, taking my time as I open each cupboard, inspecting the fine-stemmed wine glasses, the classic Wedgwood china, the heavy set of Le Creuset pans. I flick on your aerated tap to watch water sluice into the generous butler sink. No whiff of poor drainage here. No scorch marks from where a hot oven tray of chips was dropped.

I come to a halt only when I reach the window. I place my hands against the glass. I realise that the whorls and grooves of my fingerprints will be left here, as if claiming everything I touch.

This view. I feel like I'm standing suspended mid-air. It makes me draw my shoulders back, stand a little taller, a little lighter.

Feeling a stirring of hunger, I wonder absently whether there will be any food left in the fridge, or whether I'll need to supply everything myself. Opening the vast door, I can see you've arranged your food items onto the top two shelves, leaving space for my things. You have expensive tastes: orange-infused biscuits with a thick chocolate coating; a tub of garlic-stuffed olives; a generous slab of smoked brie, unopened; two small tubs of organic coconut yoghurt.

Your freezer holds half a dozen ready meals. You like feta, spinach and pine nut pie, and

161

chicken breasts stuffed with pesto and mozzarella. I slide open the bottom drawer and laugh: you have three lobsters in here. Most people have fish fingers and a bag of peas in their freezer — but you have lobsters! There are other fish, too; a whole bream; or perhaps it's a sea bass, and a bag of line-caught seafood mix.

One must be so careful with frozen seafood, I think, sliding my hand around the back of the freezer until it reaches the plug socket.

13

Elle

I am standing very still, barely breathing. I'm acutely aware of my own skin, the feeling of it pulled tight over my collarbone, the goose bumps raised on the backs of my arms, the pressure of my fingernails against my palms.

My hearing is alert, amplified.

Footsteps again, heavy, above me.

Blood throbs in my ears. *Do they know I'm inside?*

I need to get out of the house. My car is still parked in town, so I've got to go on foot. The tide is already coming in — I can't risk the beach again. That only leaves the laneway. It is half a mile long, flanked by hedgerows. There's nowhere to hide.

Slowly, slowly, I back down the stairs, my hand gripped to the bannister. Everything feels dangerously acute, the slide of the wood beneath my sweating palm, the tick of my pulse in my throat. I want to run, scream, but I force myself to move slowly.

Reaching the bottom of the stairs, I pause, listening.

Above, the tread of footsteps crosses the landing outside my writing room. Fear sparks in my veins. This is not my imagination: it is real.

163

Their footsteps pause.

I imagine the intruder standing still, listening. Have they heard me?

Then there is the groan of wood as they begin to descend the stairs, moving down through the house towards me.

Suddenly I am spinning away, racing towards the kitchen. I skid across the wooden floor, grabbing at the handle of the back door.

Shit! I locked it when I came in. My keys! Where are my fucking keys?

My heart hammers as I scan the kitchen side. No keys.

Is there time to double back, go out the front door?

I hear the change in the footsteps as the intruder reaches the bottom of the stairs. They've cut me off.

Firing on instinct, I grab a knife from the cutting block, the cold metal handle fizzing in my grip.

Fight, not flight, this time.

The tread of feet is growing louder, moving towards the kitchen.

Towards me.

Fear solidifies into rage, tightening my muscles, pumping blood hard through my veins.

I am strong. I am capable of anything.

I keep the knife close to my side, muscles coiled, ready.

They are coming.

★ ★ ★

As the figure fills the kitchen doorway, I lunge forward, knife raised. 'Get the fuck away!'

The figure stumbles backwards, hands raised. 'Elle, it's me. It's me!'

My name sounds so distant, so unfamiliar, that it takes me several seconds to realise it is Flynn.

'What are you doing?' I pant, knife pointed at him.

'I'm sorry, I didn't mean to scare you. I tried calling. I waited in the car for an hour. But I had my key still, so I . . . ' He lowers his hands. 'I'm so sorry I scared you. I didn't think. My car's parked outside. My shoes, my coat, it's all in the hall.'

'I came in the side door.'

'I'm sorry,' he apologises again. 'I didn't hear your car.'

'I left it in town.' I stare at him, heart still hammering in my chest.

'You're shaking, Elle.'

'You were in my writing room.'

'I was looking for our photos.'

'Why?' I ask, finally lowering the knife. Looking at him properly, I notice that his eyes are red-rimmed, the edges of his lips mottled.

Flynn squeezes his eyes shut, pinches the bridge of his nose.

I set down the knife and step towards him, my hands on his arms. He smells of wood shavings and something musky.

'What's happened?'

★ ★ ★

I sit back on my heels, arms hugged around my knees, watching Flynn as he selects another log from the basket. He turns it in his thick hands, then places it in the log burner. The flames stretch and flicker as he adjusts the spin wheel, light dancing across his face.

'I'm pleased you came,' I say, as he settles on the floor beside me, so that we are both leaning against the foot of the sofa.

'Looked like it when you came at me with a knife.'

We watch the weave of flames, listening to the crackling, sparking wood and embers.

When Flynn speaks, his voice is lowered, his gaze pinned to the fire.

'A heart aneurism. I'd never even heard of it. I was out on a job when the call came. The cutter was going, and I couldn't hear properly. I kept on saying, *What? What?* It wasn't the hospital that rang. It was James Fells, do you remember? The butcher.'

I nod.

'That's where it happened. He thought Mum had fainted as she just slumped against the counter. He called an ambulance. Said they were there in minutes — but it was all over.'

I picture Alison sliding against the curved glass counter, pink meats gleaming on ice; James's blood-stained apron as he fumbled with a phone; the clink of the shop's chain curtain as the paramedics rushed in.

Tears trail down the sides of Flynn's face, disappearing into thick, dark stubble.

'I've got to think about a funeral,' he says, his

166

eyes not leaving the fire.

'Did your mum ever talk about what she wanted?'

'A burial. Next to Dad.'

'Of course.'

'I'm going to wait till Rea flies in. Then we'll make plans.'

Flynn isn't brilliantly close to his older sister, Rea; there are seven years between them. She studied archaeology in California and met a man there who she'd married and followed to his family home in Minnesota. I've always liked her; she is forthright and serious but shares Flynn's sense of adventure.

'When is she arriving?'

'Tomorrow.'

'Have you told many people yet?'

Flynn shakes his head. 'I can't. It doesn't feel real.'

'I wish I'd been in touch with your mum recently,' I admit.

'She knew how much you cared about her.'

Alison was an intelligent, loyal woman, who adored Flynn, but was also aware of the challenges of being married to him. She never interfered, never voiced opinions unless they were asked for, yet her support was always implicit. We visited her in Truro at least once a month, Alison working through a pile of recipes pulled from magazines, insisting that she'd gone to no trouble. After the meals, Flynn would wash up, and Alison and I would sit together on the wicker chairs in her conservatory talking about books. She had every foreign edition of my novel on show in her lounge.

A log crumbles, tiny sparks bursting skyward.

'I know that everything is . . . different between us,' I say, 'but Flynn, I want to be here for you, okay? Even if we're rubbish at being married to each other, you're my best friend. That hasn't changed.'

He keeps his gaze on the fire, but I can feel the shake of his shoulder against mine. I take both his hands in mine and squeeze them.

I miss these hands. There is a scar across his thumb from where a chainsaw kicked back when he was cutting down a tree for Alison. I feel the raised ridge that stretches across his second and third knuckles where he'd punched a wall in a club toilet in a fit of frustration at one of the passionate arguments that glued us together in our twenties. I remember the slice to his fingertip from the spoke of my old bike he was repairing after I refused to give it up.

These hands, I think, holding them tight, how many times they've interlocked with mine. I'd once imagined his hands on the swell of my abdomen, feeling the kicks of our baby. I pictured them linked through a daughter's arm as he walked her down an aisle or clasping a son to him. I imagined these hands wrinkled and gnarled, still holding mine.

I trace the empty space on his finger where his wedding ring once was. 'Where do you keep it?'

He looks at me, gives me that lopsided grin. 'In the glove compartment of the van.'

I raise an eyebrow, then laugh.

'It's perfectly safe.'

168

'In amongst the car parking tickets, coins, CDs you don't listen to, road maps that you insist on keeping.'

'That's right.' He lifts my left hand, inspecting my ring finger. 'Yours?'

'In my jewellery box.'

'You ever put it back on?'

I shake my head. 'You?'

'Some days.'

I run my finger down the length of his. There is something incredibly touching and devastating about it. Without thinking, I lift his hand to my mouth, place my lips to the empty space where his wedding band once was.

I can feel his eyes on me.

Something shifts in the air, as if it has become charged. I feel our bodies draw towards one another, magnetic and irresistible, our lips searching, mouths soft and hungry.

I'd forgotten the exquisite feeling of his lips on mine, the brush of stubble against my cheek, those large hands moving to the back of my head, my neck. I can taste the salt of his tears.

We sink into each other, losing ourselves in a place so beautifully familiar, that I have no idea why we left.

*　*　*

I wake early, alone. It is the first night in weeks that I've slept through the night.

Downstairs I can place Flynn in the kitchen, the creak of a cupboard door opening, a mug being removed, the run of the tap.

169

I lie still, listening to the drift of sounds in the house. After the months and months of work I invested into the build, it still surprises me that Flynn has never lived here. In the planning stages — when the words *separation, divorce, unreconcilable* hadn't yet been spoken, when they were still words for other couples, ones who argued, ones who'd stopped making love, ones who'd felt a souring, of something turning bitter — I'd tried to picture the way Flynn and I would use the house. I'd imagined us padding down the rocky steps barefoot, still dewy at first light, to swim together in the bay. I'd imagined tiny wellington boots kicked off by the door, a trail of sand meandering across the wooden floors, a nursery filled with bright rugs, an understairs cupboard big enough to park a buggy. There would be barbecues in the summer, and roast dinners in the winter. There would be friends and family and laughter. And my writing room would watch over it all, a quiet space to retreat.

I snap the covers aside and climb from the bed. I slip on my dressing gown and go downstairs.

Pausing in the entrance to the kitchen, I watch Flynn who stands with his back to me, a screwdriver pressed into a cupboard hinge. I can see the veins on his forearms as he grips the door in position.

'Thought I'd sort the door out,' he says without turning.

I'd intended to fix the hinge myself with the aid of a YouTube tutorial and the oversized toolkit Fiona and Bill had bought for my birthday. But I'm grateful that Flynn is doing this small thing for me.

I move to his side. 'How are you?'

He takes a breath as if to speak, but then says nothing. It is too big a question, I know.

He tests the cupboard door, opening and closing it smoothly. Then he turns to face me.

Instinctively, I reach out, put my arms around him.

'Elle,' he says quietly, his lips against my hair. 'We shouldn't have let last night happen.'

The words are a physical blow. I step back, pretending to examine the door hinge. 'Yes, okay.'

'My head is too full. I can't complicate things . . . '

'Of course.'

Neither of us speak for a time. I busy myself making fresh coffee, taking part-baked rolls from the freezer and warming them in the oven.

We sit at the breakfast bar looking out over the view while we drink our coffee.

'The house looks good,' he says, surprising me. 'You've done an incredible job.'

'It wasn't just me — ' I begin, but he corrects me.

'It was. You drove it. You were the one with the vision. I couldn't ever see it. Wasn't sure that I wanted it.'

Or wanted me.

'Anyway, I just wanted to say — well done.'

'Thank you.' I think for a moment. 'It's funny. You think you want something — and then, when you have it — it's nothing like you imagined.'

171

He looks at me, a question in his brow.

'I still haven't delivered my second book. It's meant to be finished by next month.'

'You're not on track?'

I shake my head. 'Maybe you were my muse.'

He doesn't laugh. 'Elle — '

'I'm fine, honestly. It'll be all right. Anyway, you've got much bigger things to think about.'

He draws air into his lungs. 'I suppose I should get back. Start thinking about how to organise a funeral. You'll come, won't you?'

★ ★ ★

I go to the door with him, watch him shoulder on the coat I bought him two Christmases ago, which has a tear in the sleeve where it caught on a broken fence panel he'd been repairing for his mother. Will he remember that when he looks at the sleeve? Will it be one of a thousand triggers that will make him miss his mother?

He turns towards me. 'Thank you for being here.'

We hug, my fingers gripping the tough fabric of his coat. My chest aches with the wrench of having to let him leave.

'You're always welcome.'

'But maybe don't point a knife at me next time.'

I laugh, the quip softening the tension. We release each other.

'Flynn, really odd question,' I say, needing to check something before he leaves. 'Did you write anything on the stairway window?'

'Write something?'

'In the condensation on the glass.'

'Why would I do that?'

'There was a message there. It caught in the light last night. It could've been there for ages.'

'What did it say?'

I hesitate. Somehow saying it aloud feels ridiculous. '*I'm in your house.*'

Flynn's eyes narrow. 'Which window? Let me see.'

'I wiped it off.'

'A visitor was probably having a joke.'

I nod, although the only people I've had round in the past month are my book club. Unless it has been there since the Airbnb rental.

There is the clang of iron behind us as the post is thrust through the letterbox. Flynn gathers the pile from the floor and hands it to me. Then he opens the door and steps out.

The sun is up; it promises to be a beautiful day. I'm pleased. Flynn needs it for the drive back. I watch the planes of his face as the sun hits. The press of time nestled comfortably into the grooves at his forehead, the sunburst of lines around his eyes.

His gaze lowers towards the bundle of post I hold. Mine follows, noticing the capitalised red words *Final reminder* stamped across a brown envelope.

'Everything okay?' he asks.

I tuck the post under my arm. 'Fine. Everything's fine.'

He looks at me with his frank stare that says: *I see you, Elle Fielding.*

'I've been wanting to say this for a while.' He pauses, glances down at his feet.

I feel my heart rate increasing, hoping . . .

He looks up, right at me.

Yes?

'Are you being careful with all this social media stuff?'

I blink. 'Social media?'

'I looked at your feed. You share all these details about what you're doing, photographing corners of your house, or a place you're visiting, or a walk you're taking. You're inviting strangers into your life. They have this . . . this intimacy with you.'

I think of Booklover101's latest post and feel a shiver travel through me.

'That's what social media is all about,' I say in my defence. 'People want to have a glimpse of your life.'

'What if they want more than that? You announce that you're out jogging — then post a picture of the beach you're running along. It doesn't take much for someone who knows the area to work out exactly where you are — that you're alone. Or that your house is empty.'

'No one knows where I live.'

'No? You've shared dozens of pictures of the view. Anyone could recognise the bay, work out that your house must be on the cliff top.'

'What is this? Are you trying to frighten me?'

Hurt pinches his features. 'Of course not. I just want you to be safe. Everything you write or share, it's all out there for good. It leaves a trace.'

'Thanks for the safety briefing, officer.' I smile

in a bid to lighten the conversation. 'Anyway, what are you doing snooping around on Facebook? I thought you hated that sort of thing.'

'What do you want me to say? That sometimes I like to check in, see how you're doing?'

My heart wrenches at the thought of him having to access my life through a screen.

He pauses, shifting his weight. 'It's hard when friends of ours know more about your life than I do. I was hearing all your news from Heather and Nick. They kept telling me what you'd been up to — that you'd been out in France, that you'd joined a book club. That you're doing live writing videos, or something. They kept saying how happy you looked.'

'You know that's just part of the picture, don't you? I'm showing people what they want to see. Do you think I'd have half as many followers if I shared the mundane details of my life? If everything I wrote was the truth?'

A shadow passes over Flynn's face.

Truth. That was the wrong word to use. The word that had cracked open our marriage.

'All I'm saying is, no one wants to see photos of me looking haggard after a sleepless night, or of empty coffee mugs beside my flailing word count. I know it's all bullshit, this filter-perfect life, but it's part of my job. I have to do it.'

'Do you?'

Flynn always uses those two words — forcing me to pause, question myself. It irritates me enough to not answer him.

'If your publishers didn't need you to do it,

would you come off social media tomorrow?'

'Does it even matter?'

'I'm not criticising your choices. I'm just questioning whether it's good for you — good for any of us. Because, really, do we need it?'

'It helps connect people.'

'That's the line we're being fed: connect more. I don't know, Elle,' he says, shaking his head, 'I think people seem more disconnected than ever. You go out to a bar or a restaurant, and people are sitting right in front of each other, but their attention is on their phones. You see people — not just teenagers, but adults — walking down the street, necks curved towards their screens. Is that healthy?'

I don't answer, and he doesn't expect me to.

'When something like this happens — something like losing Mum — everything else just feels so flimsy. So pointless.' His eyes are shining. 'Life shouldn't be reduced to filtered images and captions, should it? It's about birth and death and that beautiful, brutal stretch of time between.'

Previously

Now that I am in your house, I find it interesting re-looking at the photos of it you share on social media. You favour the detail shot: a conch shell placed artfully on a stack of books; a water jug and glass on the edge of your desk; a vase of flowers on the bookshelf beside an oil burner. I can see how you've cropped certain photos, cutting off an aesthetically awkward radiator or plug socket or door jamb.

What other things do you choose to crop from your life?

I read an interesting study about how social media is making most of us miserable. Scientists reported that one in three people felt dissatisfied with their lives after visiting Facebook. It encourages seeking behaviour, greatly affecting dopamine levels and the neuropathways of the brain after just a few minutes' use. Imagine that. Mark Zuckerberg has made something so powerful that it can change the chemistry of the brain.

It concerns me that self-worth is increasingly becoming measured in Likes, or Follows, or little hearts popping up on the screen. Attention spans are shrinking. Advertisers are using terms like Jolts Per Minute, to inundate us with more information.

I've a feeling that there's going to be a time in the future when there's a backlash against social

177

media, when people want to strip the web of these intimate details they've shared. Don't they realise that the information will always be out there, somewhere? I picture spiders crawling through the Web, searching for husks of information, which lie there like crisping flies.

I'm still surprised about what people share. How much people give of themselves. You particularly, Elle. Why is it? I think it's the ego winning out against common sense. Do we need to know about the little habits and rituals of your day? I suppose the answer must be yes, because why else are we all hooked?

For anyone who had the inclination to scroll back through your posts, here's what you've told us: We know what car you drive. We know that you have two coffees a day from the Nespresso machine in your kitchen. We know that you hand-painted the dresser where your mugs hang. We know that your writing room is your retreat, your creative lair.

I want to tell your followers not to be dissatisfied with their lives, because what most of them don't realise is that your posts are little more than scenes you've created.

They are not the real you, are they Elle?

In fact, they are your greatest fiction of all.

14

Elle

I feel the curve of the road, the grip of tyres against tarmac. Hedges whir by, thick walls of green. As I approach Fiona's house, I flick through my mental diary of her week. Bill will be away. Drake has nursery. She'll be home, working. I won't disturb her for long. I just need to be out of the house. I need to talk to her about Flynn, his mother.

As I pull into Fiona's street, I imagine the kettle being flicked on, the comfort of her old sagging sofa. I park on the road in front of the house and climb out.

I've almost reached Fiona's front door, when it opens and a man steps onto the pavement — not Bill, someone slighter, who is pulling on a dark jacket, head ducked.

Fiona is saying something to him from the doorway, her feet bare, face flushed.

When the man turns, my lips part in surprise.

Mark's face breaks into a lazy smile. 'Morning,' he says to me with a slight nod of his head.

I watch as he climbs onto his motorbike, pulls on a helmet, then guns the engine, disappearing down the street.

Fiona is standing with her arms folded across

her chest, chin raised. 'Mark was just helping me with something.'

'With *what*?'

'My dishwasher is broken.'

I stare her down. I recognise the steely, determined look, the slight flicker in her eyelids.

'Bullshit.' I step through the doorway and move past Fiona into the kitchen.

She follows.

'Bill's away, I take it?'

'Yes.'

'Drake's at nursery?'

'Yes.'

'Precision scheduling.' I'd guessed that there'd been other men since Bill — but I've never seen the proof, haven't wanted to.

'Before you get on your high horse, it's just sex.'

'And if it were Bill saying that?'

Fiona waves a hand at the comment as if it were ludicrous.

'I know you don't like Mark. If it helps, I had no idea he was your neighbours' son.'

'When did it start?'

'Nothing's *started*. It's been a handful of times.'

'How many?'

'Three, four. I don't know. It's over. It was nothing.'

'How did you meet him?'

'Yvonne's birthday.'

Fiona had invited me to the party, but it was the day I flew to France for the writing retreat.

'He's what, ten years younger than you?'

'Thank you for that. It's seven, actually.'

I fold my arms, my gaze leaving Fiona and moving to the montage of photos on the fridge. I find myself looking at a picture of Drake grinning from beneath a golden party hat.

'Don't do that face,' Fiona says.

'What face?'

'That one. You're doing it right now. Your lips are pursed. Your shoulders are giving a little righteous wiggle. You're thinking about Drake and Bill and you're judging me.'

'I just think it's a lot to risk. Isn't what you've got enough?'

Fiona laughs. 'Oh, Elle. You've always romanticised the idea of motherhood. Drake is unquestionably the most important thing in my world — everything would be irrevocably less without him — but motherhood itself isn't always 'enough'. Being a mother is a huge part of who I am, but I also need my own part, just for me. And that is hard to carve out. Bill is away more than he is here. I've had to readjust myself to try and work out who I can be in that small section of time when Drake is asleep, or the occasional morning he's in nursery. The idea that it is 'enough' is so limiting, Elle. It makes anyone who wants more — who wants to work, who wants to have time for themselves, who wants to enjoy days away with friends — seem lacking. What I want is to feel whole. I want to feel like *me*.'

'So you need to fuck Mark to feel like *you*?'

Several beats of silence pass. 'It was a mistake. And it's over. I've told Mark.' She shakes her head. 'I love Bill — you know that.'

The tension in the kitchen eases back. I move to the sink, taking a glass from the draining board and filling it. Something is snagging in my thoughts to do with the timing. Where would Fiona have slept with Mark that first time? He was staying at his parents' house, and Bill would've been at home with Drake — so, where? At the party?

Then it clicks. Fiona had the key to my house. The rentals didn't move in until the following day.

I swing round. 'You took Mark to my house, didn't you?'

Fiona blinks, a flash of panic passing over her face. She opens her mouth as if to speak, then shuts it again. I'm surprised to see two blooms of colour spread across her cheeks.

'You had my house keys. You dropped the high chair off that night, didn't you? You told me you'd put it there the evening before the tenants moved in.'

Fiona holds my gaze. Very slowly she dips her head, nods.

'You brought him into my house. You let a fucking stranger into my home, without asking me, and — '

'Elle — '

'Jesus! That's how he knew what my bedroom looked like. He knew I had a cream lamp on my bedside table, because you had let him in!'

'No, no. He didn't even go upstairs. We were only in the lounge. It wasn't . . . I didn't plan it. I had the high chair in my car. Told him I needed to drop it off. He came in with me. Said it was a beautiful house. I wanted to show him the view — how it looks out over the bay. And then we ended up . . . ' She looks at her feet.

'Where?'

Fiona presses her lips together.

'Where did you have sex?'

'You're really asking me that?'

'Yes.'

She sighs. 'In the lounge.'

'Did you go into my bedroom?'

'No!'

'Did you leave him — even for a moment?'

'No. We were in and out,' she says, then grimaces at the choice of phrase. 'I mean, I . . . I freshened up in the bathroom. But it wasn't long — '

'It's Mark. I know it.' My hands are clenched, and I can feel a knot of tension in my jaw. I can imagine him prowling through my rooms, loping up the stairs and pausing to trace a message on the window. *I'm in your house.*

While Fiona was in the bathroom, he could've pushed open the door to my bedroom. I imagine him trailing his hands along the edge of my bed. Did he catch his reflection in the mirror? Recognise himself as a trespasser? Or did he like seeing himself there, in my bedroom? Had he imagined where I lay?

Maybe he had the whole thing planned: seduce Fiona, get her to let him into the house. If Mark blames me for his mother's stroke, this could all be a game of intimidation. His end goal is suddenly obvious: he wants me gone.

183

'He went into my writing room — '

'Oh, don't be so dramatic! I was in the bathroom for minutes. Do you really think that gave Mark enough time to poke around your house, realise you kept one room locked, and then break in? And then what's he supposed to do? Smash a paperweight without me hearing?'

My mouth hangs open.

'I know I messed up by taking him to your house — and I'm sorry about that — but the rest of this, Elle, it's all in your head.'

It's all in your head.

The words are an echo from the past. I ignore the pull of memory. It's too dangerous.

I lift my chin. 'I want my key back.'

'Excuse me?'

'My spare house key. The one I gave to you.'

Fiona scoffs. 'You don't trust me? What is it that you think I'll do? Let myself into your house, use it as a shag pad whenever you're away?'

'Quite possibly.'

Fiona folds her arms. 'I take it you've asked Flynn for his key?'

I say nothing.

'Don't you think *he's* the person you should be asking? You know — the person who's so hurt and angry about what happened that he asked for a divorce. The one who lives in a bedsit, while you float about in your beachside mansion. That person.'

She's right. Flynn had let himself in. Walked through my house. Gone into my writing room — *Looking for photos*, he'd said.

'I intend to.'

'Anyway, you can tick me off your checklist — I don't even have your spare key. I left it in the dish on your bureau after you got locked out. I told you.'

I flush. Fiona is right. She had told me.

I'd forgotten.

'But thanks for the vote of confidence.'

★　★　★

I swing into my driveway, gravel spraying from beneath the tyres. I yank the handbrake, fuming with myself. The last thing I need is to fall out with my sister.

Fucking Mark, I seethe. When Fiona brought him into my house, he knew exactly who it belonged to. I bet he enjoyed snooping around, going through my things — and then he bided his time, waiting for the opportunity to insinuate that he'd been inside.

Slamming the car door, I stride across the drive to Frank and Enid's house, and rap hard.

Mark answers, a lightly amused smile playing over his lips. 'Always a pleasure.'

'I'd like a word.'

'Step this way.'

I pass the lounge, where a computer game has been paused, muscle-bulging men with crew cuts and guns quivering on screen.

He bends close to my ear. 'We can do two-player.'

I ignore the comment and make my way into the kitchen. It is neat and clean and smells faintly of toasted teacakes. There is a jug of filtered water on the table and a plate of biscuits. It looks so homely and unthreatening that, for a moment, I falter.

Then I turn and see Mark watching me — and my anger roars back to life. 'I know you've been in my house. Fiona told me.'

He says nothing.

'You should know it won't work.'

'What won't?'

'Your pathetic attempts to intimidate me. Turning up at my library talk — '

'You found *that* intimidating?'

'I know you tipped my bins and have been watching the house. It's fucking creepy. It's just odd.'

'If you say so.'

I can feel the last threads of self-control beginning to strain under his flippant attitude.

'And that message on my window — why would you bother?'

'Message? Now you've really lost me.'

'You wrote, *I'm in your house.*'

His eyes widen. Then he bursts into laughter.

My hands clench at my sides, red crescent moons left on my palms. 'I know it's you!'

'You don't know anything.'

'Don't lie to me!' I scream.

He lifts his hands in the air as if to placate me. 'You need to relax. You're coming across as a bit fucking mental.'

'How dare — '

'Look, I might have tipped your bins, yeah? I was pissed off and wanted to let you know about

186

it. I came to your library talk because I wanted to see what made you tick. By the way, you bombed.'

A nerve flickers below my eye.

'I'm not your biggest fan, Author. I know you're one of those people who feels outraged if someone doesn't like them — but get over it. You're a stuck-up bitch — and that's just not everyone's thing. You come down from the city with your wads of cash and snap up the cliff cottage. D'you know, Mum rang to say what lovely neighbours they had — a young couple who wanted to restore the cottage into a family home. You even told Mum how you were planning on keeping some of the original features. She got all excited about that. But then, surprise surprise, you knock the whole place down. Tried to bamboozle Mum and Dad with architect drawings, promising it'll all be in keeping. But in keeping with what?'

I hold myself very still.

'It's blow-ins like you who are ruining Cornwall, buying up all the properties, putting up your three-storey second homes, then disappearing for half the year so that all the little shops don't have any business. Another town down the drain.'

'It's not a second home.'

'Not at the minute — but I'd be interested to see what you think of Cornwall after you've spent a full winter here.' He shakes his head. 'The people who've grown up here, we're all having to leave. We can't afford to live near our parents, help look after them, because you've

187

outpriced us. Now my mum's sick and I've had to take all my annual leave just to be here. What happens the next time she needs me — or Dad gets sick?'

Tension makes his brow white as he speaks, his lips pinching around his words. I've never heard him say more than a sentence or two, and now it seems like he can't stop.

'So, yeah, you were right when you said I want you out. I don't want people like you living next door to my parents.'

'You know nothing about me.'

'No? I know Mum's had a stroke, yet you haven't even been around to ask how she is, offer to cook my dad a meal, check if there's anything they need. Because that's what neighbours around here do. She almost died!' Spittle flies from the corners of his mouth. 'I could've lost her!'

'Except you didn't.'

My gaze swings to the doorway.

Enid stands with a pale hand gripping the doorframe. She looks tiny and fragile in a white cotton night dress, her fine grey hair loose, like drifts of a spider's web.

'I'm sorry — I had no idea you were here. We've been loud.'

'Arguments tend to be,' she says slowly, her word endings soft and unpronounced.

Mark's posture softens in his mother's presence. 'Sorry, Mum,' he says, placing a kiss on the top of her head. 'We didn't mean to disturb you.'

I catch a glimpse of him as a young boy

188

— running along the bay below, a shell curled in his fist for his mother to inspect. I can picture the beam of his smile when he was told the shell would be treasured.

'I'm so sorry to hear about your stroke,' I say to Enid. 'Mark's right — I should have been over to see you. Offered to help. How are you feeling now?'

'Grateful to be home.' To Mark she says, 'I came to ask for a drink.'

'Sure thing. Water? Tea? No nurses spying, so I could even stretch to a sherry.'

She chuckles fondly. 'Water, for now.'

He fills a small tumbler, then helps his mother into a chair, setting the glass in front of her and placing a straw in it.

Enid takes careful sips. 'Sit,' she says to me when she's finished.

I obey, pulling out a kitchen chair padded with a floral cushion. I look up, out through the kitchen window, guiltily aware that the view is now partially obscured by the top storey of my house.

'Forgive me, but I overheard your conversation. I'm very sorry to hear about your bins, Elle. I'm sure Mark plans to apologise.'

He looks at me. 'Sorry.'

'And as for the rest of the business, did that have anything to do with you, Mark?'

'No.'

She considers her son, then nods, convinced.

'Then perhaps it was your visitor,' Enid says to me.

'Visitor?'

'The person who looked after the house while you were away.'

'Oh yes. I rented it for a fortnight.' Conscious of Mark's comments about second homes, I quickly add, 'But I won't normally be renting it out. It was a one-off. They were a nice family, I think. I hope they didn't give you any trouble.'

'A family? I am surprised.'

My brow dips. 'Why?'

'The place looked almost deserted. We never saw anyone using the beach. Not even a car in the driveway. I don't know how they'd have managed without a car around here.'

That doesn't make sense. In Joanna's email, she'd clearly stated that they'd be driving down from Winchester, which was why she'd asked for the key to be left out.

'You saw them though?'

'Only one of them. Mark and I were on the beach together, weren't we? It was the day before . . . the stroke. You'd mentioned you were going away, so I was surprised to see someone at your window.'

I freeze. 'What window?'

'At the top of the house. The glass room. It looked as if someone was standing with their hands pressed to the glass, staring out.'

I feel the beat of my pulse in my throat: someone has been in my writing room.

Previously

I take the stairs, bare toes gripping the wood. Careful, careful. A trip could be nasty, if not fatal. Not a single person knows I'm here. Who would find me if I fell?

You?

No, that wouldn't do at all.

I don't pause at the first floor — I've already explored each of these rooms — so I continue up the stairs until I reach the top. Stepping onto the landing area, I can see there are just two doors.

I push open the first, which leads into a bathroom. A floating bowl-sink is set below a porthole mirror with a brass trim. Two fisherman lanterns hang from either side of it. A painted white ladder doubles as a towel rack, with perfectly folded towels in complementary tones. On the top shelf, spa products are gathered in a rope basket, the light scent of vanilla in the air.

This isn't the room I'm interested in, so I pull the door shut and turn my attention to the second door. Behind it lies the view that you built this house around, that you've shared so many times on Facebook, tempting us with a glimpse into your world.

This doorway leads to your writing room.

I place my fingers around the handle, anticipation hot in my throat.

I push down — but there is no give.

191

I try again.

Locked.

Annoyance twists in my jaw.

I place my palms against the solid oak door feeling the press of wood.

Now you have my attention, because I've started to wonder: what is inside that you don't want anyone to see?

15

Elle

'Writing isn't an escape. When you look at a blank page, you are looking yourself in the eye.'

Author Elle Fielding

I stand at the edge of my writing room, palms placed against the cool glass, looking across the bay. The tide is out, exposing the ribbed seabed, punctuated by clusters of jagged black rock.

I was surprised to see someone at your window.

What window?

At the top of the house. The glass room. It looked as if someone was standing with their hands pressed to the glass, staring out.

When I was in France, someone else had been standing right here, as I am.

My pulse flickers in my throat, like a stray heartbeat.

How did they get in? I'd left the tenants a key for the main house, but I took the only key to the writing room with me.

On the morning I left, everything had been such a rush. It'd taken far longer than I'd thought to strip and remake the beds, to empty the final shelves of my wardrobe, to scan the house for valuables and breakables. Then I'd realised that I hadn't left any instructions, so I'd scribbled a set of notes about how to use the dishwasher, oven, and central heating system. When I'd raced to the top of the house to lock my writing room, I was already half an hour late. It was possible that in my hurry, I'd only *thought* I'd locked the room.

I toy with that idea for a moment — then dismiss it. No, I'd locked it. I know I did. I can almost hear the clunk of the metal bolt sliding across, feel my hand on the heavy pewter handle checking it was secure.

Which means Joanna — or whoever she had staying here with her — had broken in.

I recall the message Joanna sent the day before she arrived, saying that their travel plans had changed and they'd be arriving late at night, and *was it possible to leave the key in a safe place?* An innocuous request, I had thought at the time.

Yet perhaps it had been planned.

The day after Joanna's arrival, Fiona had visited the house to make the face-to-face introduction — but found the house empty.

Yet, what if someone *was* inside? What if Joanna had been watching from the stairway window, just waiting for Fiona to leave? What if she never had any intention of being seen?

I picture Joanna's profile shot: middle-aged, attractive, a feathery blonde bob that looked as if it'd been created at the hands of an expensive hairstylist. A photo selected to reassure, to suggest your home would be well cared for, in safe hands.

194

Now a different image forms: the silhouette of a stranger hunched in front of a computer setting up a fake Airbnb profile. It would be easy enough to type a false name into an online form, then scroll through Google images and select a photo of an unknown woman to use as a profile picture. Had this stranger then decided to add a husband and two children to the form, knowing that it would make the rental sound more plausible? Perhaps the stranger spotted that the dates were outside of the school holidays, so decided that one of the children was still in nappies, and the other would be starting school next year. Were they pleased with themselves for thinking of that?

My heartbeat quickens as I imagine the stranger reaching the final section of the form, where it asks whether they have any information they'd like to ask the owner. Maybe they were enjoying it by then, their fingers hovering above the keyboard wondering what Joanna would say, adding a simple question, easy to answer: *Do you have a high chair, or should we bring our own?*

I look through the glass wall, out to sea. Beneath its silver skin, the sea pulses with energy, lines of swell rumbling towards the shore. Seething, rolling.

The sea stares back at me, a watchful grey eye. *What have you seen?*

Standing here, I realise that it is entirely possible that Joanna doesn't exist — and that someone else has been staying in my house.

Something Flynn said resonates in my

thoughts. He'd urged me to be more cautious about what I share on social media. *Everything you post leaves a trace.* I picture my Facebook photos and captions like a trail of breadcrumbs in a fairy tale. Have I unwittingly laid a path that leads to my front door?

I take out my phone and open Facebook, scrolling through dozens of previous posts until I find the one I'm looking for.

There it is. I'd shared the flyer for the creative writing retreat in France.

Anyone fancy joining me for a fortnight of cheese and wine? And writing. Obviously writing, too.

The flyer shows the dates and location of the retreat; therefore, anyone would know when I was going away. My mouth turns dry.

I continue scrolling through my feed, looking for something else.

There. I read the caption twice, words which I'd casually typed into my phone without a second thought.

Spent the morning photographing my house for Airbnb. Definitely deserve a glass of wine.

I screw my eyes shut. *You idiot.* Any one of my followers could see the dates of my writing retreat, could work out the area I lived in, and that my house would be available to rent on Airbnb. I have more than fifty thousand followers. All it takes is one person.

If I am right and someone has set up a fake

Airbnb profile, and Joanna and her family don't exist, the question is: Who has been staying in my house?

In the glass wall, I see the rest of the writing room reflected behind me: my desk, the wing-back chair, the bookcase, the oak trunk. There. That's where my gaze stays.

I stand very still, eyeing it, thinking: *What do they know?*

* * *

I pace to my desk, snap open my laptop, brain firing. I've got to do something. I pull up the Airbnb page and scroll to the *Contact Us* tab. There is, of course, no phone number to call. Instead, I am directed to the Help Centre, where a series of drop-down menus fails to locate the issue I need resolved.

My fingers stab at the keys as I type my question into a rectangular box. *How do you get in touch with someone who's rented your house — and has now deactivated their account?*

I press *Submit*, then push my chair back and stand. No one is going to respond to me. This sort of lack of personal communication makes me want to scream. Why can't you pick up a phone, ask for help? Speak to a real human being. Is that asking too much?

Disconnected. That was the word Flynn had used. He is right. The whole bloody world is disconnected.

Airbnb are hardly going to help me track down the person who rented this house. If I want to find out Joanna's real identity, it is up to me.

'Who are you?' I say to the empty room, spinning on the spot, as if I turn quickly enough I will catch a glimpse of them.

I pace the length of the room, muttering to myself, 'Why? Why were you in here?'

As I twist back, feet pounding across the floor, my gaze meets the wooden leg of my desk, settling on the roughly carved word. *LIAR*.

I'm assaulted by a memory. I try and push it down, keep it sealed, but it shoulders its way forward . . .

A pile of post heaped on the doormat of my student house. A slip of cream card. LIAR slashed in red lipstick.

I lock down the memory. In a flash, I'm pulling open the desk drawer, searching through pens, glue, Post-it notes — until I find the scissors.

I crouch, setting one of the blades against the desk leg, scraping and scratching against the wood, digging out those grooves, sending tiny curls of wood shavings to the ground. I gouge the blade deeper and deeper, teeth pressed together.

My breath is ragged, snatched. I work frantically, sawing metal against wood.

I can smell the fresh sawdust tang. The veins in the backs of my hand strain against the skin.

Liar. Is that who I am?

That's what people told me.

That's who I've become.

I work faster — it needs to be gone.

Erased.

Finally, it's done.

I toss the scissors aside and slump on the floor, chest rising and falling heavily. I stare at the pale wound in the desk leg waiting to feel something — to experience a kick of satisfaction — but there's nothing.

It doesn't matter that it's gone from the desk. It's in my head.

I push to my feet, knowing I need to write. I need to tip out the thoughts, shake them onto the page, before they worm in deeper, feeding on the rot.

I pull myself into my chair, open my manuscript.

I must go back there.

2003

It was Elle who made the appointment to discuss her essay. She felt a small jolt of excitement when the date was set.

The door to Luke Linden's office was already open. She knocked anyway.

'Come in.'

'Do you want it open or closed?'

'Up to you.'

She shrugged. Closed it. Took a seat.

She could smell her perfume, and beneath it the faint sweetness of sun lotion. She had spent the afternoon in the park with her housemates, laughing about Louise being asked to leave the students' union on account of drunkenness — a hard feat to achieve at the SU.

When she looked up, Linden was watching her. 'You've caught the sun.'

She glanced down at her bare arms.

'On your cheeks.'

She placed her fingertips there. 'Oh.'

Her hair was loose, and she hooked it over one shoulder as she leant back in the chair. She crossed one leg slowly over the other, aware of her bare knees, tanned and smooth.

They talked about her essay, *The role of women in Shakespeare's tragedies.* Linden told her that the first draft had potential, but that she needed to be clearer in her position, write her argument with more conviction backed up by theory.

She watched him as he talked, admiring the confidence etched into the length of his pauses. He was measured, his words well placed, the theatrics of the lecture hall gone. He leaned forward — close enough that she could smell cigarette smoke on his breath — and continued to talk carefully, as if everything they were discussing were of great interest to him.

He was a shade too pale, she decided. His shoulders skinny compared to the boys who played sports that she hung out with. But there was something in his eyes that she liked — the way they never left hers.

He slid the essay across the desk. 'Let's schedule another meeting — to see what you do with this next draft. Three weeks' time. I've got a nine-a.m. slot on the Friday.'

'Perfect.'

It never got put in his diary. There was no formal documentation of it.

But there it was, the date that would divide her life into *before* and *after*.

16

Elle

In the breathless darkness of three a.m., the sound of scratching slides into my dream. I'm hurrying somewhere, feet on concrete. It's early, the light in the dream bright and vivid. When I look down, I see the hem of a dusky blue dress grazing my thighs. My legs grow heavier, the soles of my shoes scuffing against the ground. A park. I'm in a park. I know this park.

In my dream, I turn and look over my shoulder and see a gardener digging with a trowel, dark soil lifted from the earth, the metal scrape of the tool as it hits a stone . . .

I am bolt upright in bed, mouth open, panting.

A dream, a bad dream, I tell myself. I am home, in my bed. I am safe.

My pyjamas are stuck to my skin. I can feel the backs of my knees slick with sweat.

I push the duvet away and let air reach me.

I glance at the clock.

Three a.m. The dead of night. Hours until daylight.

Then I hear the noise again, a low scratching. Not in my dream. In my house.

Every cell of my skin tightens.

I am rigid, listening. I can hear the draw of my

breath, the distant rumble of the sea beyond the house as I wait for the sound again.

Alone in the darkness, fear coils tight, squeezing my thoughts into the darkest corners of my mind.

There. Scratching. Like fingernails against wood.

I'm on my feet, grabbing my mobile, moving towards the bedroom door. The plush carpet is soft beneath my heels, but I move slowly, tense, waiting for that moment of hot pain, a shard of glass against flesh.

I am at the door, a hand pressed to the wood, breath held as I listen.

I did my nightly check before bed. I know that the external doors are locked, the windows closed and secure. I looked behind sofas, pressed my hands against the curtains, stared right to the back of the pantry, the foot of wardrobes.

I checked. Double-checked. There is no one in this house, except me.

This is just the spike of my nightmare piercing into my waking thoughts.

That sound again, scratching. Or shuffling. Beneath me. At the very foundation of the house, as if something is under it, or within it.

Then I think of it: the wine cellar. That's where the noise is coming from.

I checked the door was locked, like I always do. But it's been weeks since I've been inside the cellar. I prefer to keep my wine in a kitchen cupboard so that I don't have to make the windowless descent underground. It's too cold, too concealed. A place for moths to live and breed in the damp darkness. It was a mistake to build it in the first place. The architect persuaded me, inferring that new builds of this scale should include a wine cellar as a point of saleability.

I know that if I want to sleep, I need to check it. I need to open that door. Look inside.

I take a breath, place my fingers on the door handle, turning it quietly. All the while, I'm telling myself it is nothing, there is no one here, yet my heart beats furiously. I can feel the force of it as if it's trying to burst from my chest.

I cross the landing in darkness, then begin descending the stairs. I'm acutely aware of the danger of slipping here, alone. The thud of skull against wood. A vertiginous sensation washes over me, and I cling to the bannister until I've steadied myself, caught my breath.

I make it safely to the bottom of the stairs. I still don't want to turn on the light — too exposing.

Tiptoeing into the kitchen, there is silence. Nothing. No noise or light from within the cellar.

I stand in front of the door and type 999 into my phone, careful not to press *call*. Then I try the handle. I am thinking of moths. Their dusty, winged bodies, sealed in the darkness.

I make myself turn the lock — then give the door a quick, hard shove.

It swings open with a loud clang. Light flares — it's on a sensor — and the brightness is momentarily blinding. It takes several seconds for my eyes to adjust, then I am looking down concrete steps, into a gloomy, narrow space. Cold air breathes from the deep.

I need to step inside, to check the alcove, be certain.

As my feet press the cold concrete, my heart is stumbling and tripping. Phone still gripped, I take three steps down into the cellar, and angle my head so I can see into the alcove.

Clear.

In the corner I notice a cluster of rat or mouse droppings and a shredded newspaper. Is it possible that that's what I heard upstairs — rodents climbing between the walls, tiny feet racing over pipework and timber?

There is nothing here. Just darkness and the earthy damp smell of below ground. I want to laugh, to say, *See, Elle, nothing!* But the fear doesn't abate. I am alive with it.

I turn, begin to ascend the steps. That's when I see it on the concrete step. A menthol cigarette, unsmoked. The brand *he* liked. You rarely see them sold any more.

The smell of cigarette smoke, overlaid with mint, fills my nose.

I close my eyes, hear the roar of blood in my ears. Panic tears through my body and I feel like I am sinking within it.

I know — I KNOW — it can't be him. Not here, in my house. Impossible.

Breathe.

The cigarette could have been in the cellar for weeks, most likely tossed to the ground by a builder. I know all this. I honestly do. And yet, it feels like a threat . . .

I can't even make myself pick it up, dispose of it.

I don't want to touch it. A cigarette. A fucking cigarette!

Because of *him*.

I need to get out of the house.

I need to get out of my fucking head!

I pull the door shut. Lock it.

Keys, coat, bag. I grab all three, then push open the front door, and then I am sprinting through the darkness to my car.

I slam the door behind me, depress the central locking button.

I start the engine, headlights beaming across my house, illuminating it like searchlights. I swing out of the driveway, heart thundering, with absolutely no idea where I'm going.

⋆   ⋆   ⋆

Thank God for twenty-four-hour supermarkets.

I drift down aisles, placing items I don't need into a metal trolley. There is something immensely reassuring about the day-bright overhead lighting, the orderly stacked shelves, the glossily packaged products I associate with cheery chefs, grinning models.

My knee-length coat is buttoned to my neck, but my pyjama bottoms are on show, the soft pink cotton juxtaposed against stiff leather boots.

A woman passes me in the aisle, her white plimsolls squeaking below a blue uniform. A nurse, I think. She smiles at me shyly, a collusion of sorts, because here we both are, in a

207

supermarket, at this strange hour of the night.

Eventually, when I can stretch out the shopping trip no longer, I steer my trolley to the till.

'Working late, or just about to start?' the girl on the checkout asks as she scans my items. She hasn't noticed my pyjamas. She's banded me with the group of legitimate late-night shoppers who work unusual hours — not, I think with relief, the other group who use this store, with its well-lit aisles and centrally controlled temperature, as a safe space. Somewhere to run to.

'Late,' I answer with a smile.

'Well, you enjoy your sleep then.'

I unload my shopping onto the passenger seat of my car, then climb in, lock the doors.

Now that my fear has dissipated, I can feel tiredness washing in. A tide of it, heavy and full. I pull a French baguette from one of the shopping bags, break off the crusty end, and chew it with a dry mouth. I open a carton of milk and swig it back, moistening the bread.

Wrapped in my coat, I sit here in the floodlit car park, allowing my head to tip back, my eyes to close.

Tiredness beats against my eyelids, sleep rising, towing me under. Here, in a supermarket car park, locked in my vehicle, I finally sleep.

★　★　★

A man's face is pressed to the window, inches from mine. I can hear the rattle of the lock as he tries the door handle.

I scream, startled. I try to rear away — but I

208

am pinned to my seat, restrained.

Disorientated, it takes me several moments to remember I am in my car. It is daylight. I'm strapped in by my seat belt.

The man is waving. Saying something.

Blinking, adjusting, I realise it is Bill. He is talking to me through the glass.

Heavy-thumbed, I fumble to locate the central locking button and release my seat belt, but eventually I am opening the door, stepping out of the car into daylight. I am trying to smile, to arrange my face into an expression that looks normal.

'I saw your car,' Bill is saying. He's dressed sharply in a navy suit, on his way to work. Shaved. Freshly showered. 'Are you okay? Were you . . . asleep?'

'Just taking a moment out,' I say, heat hitting my cheeks. I glance down, noticing the breadcrumbs dusting my coat. I brush them away.

Bill looks at me for a moment. 'Are you . . . wearing pyjamas?' He's half-smiling, bemused.

'I dashed out first thing. Didn't bother to change.'

'Let's hope the literary paparazzi don't spot you. They'd make all sorts of assertions about your writing habits.'

I make myself smile.

It must be unconvincing as Bill looks at me more closely. 'Is everything okay?'

I nod vigorously. 'Fine.'

'Well, okay then,' he says, sounding unsure. Bill tells me to have a good day, then hugs me. He holds me tight in his arms, the strength of his embrace squeezing the air from my lungs.

Back at the house, I place the bags of shopping on the kitchen counter.

I open the wine cellar door, the rhythm of my heartbeat barely altering. I walk right in, down through the cold. It's not tomb-like or terrifying. It's just a wine cellar.

To prove it to myself, I pick up the cigarette, snap it in two and throw it straight in the bin. It is done. It was never anything.

In the daylight, last night's actions seem utterly ridiculous, inflated.

Yet, at night it feels like this is a different house.

I feel like a different person.

A reminder beeps on my phone, prompting me that it's only fifteen minutes until my next Facebook Live author chat.

I drink a black coffee while putting on make-up, mask-thick.

Then I am in front of my computer, the camera on, smiling, talking.

'I'm author Elle Fielding, live from my writing room. Today I'm going to be talking about writing twists.'

As I talk, I watch my own face on screen, lips moving, eyes bright and animated, and it's as if there are two versions of me: the author I'm watching perform who seems so natural and confident, and the other me; the one who is awake through the night, who slept in a supermarket car park, who still wears her pyjama bottoms out of shot beneath the desk. The one who is slowly unravelling.

Previously

If one searches for, 'How to pick a lock', one hundred and nine million results pop up in 0.59 seconds, which seems marvellously efficient. I simply clicked on the first link and was taken to a website where I learned the precise skills required to pick a lock, and the tools needed to assist me.

So here I am, in your writing room.

Everywhere is light and ocean and sky. It breathes into the room. Just standing here, my feet on the wooden floorboards, I feel lighter. This is a space from which to create. Do you know — do you have any idea — how lucky you are?

I move to your writing desk. That's where it all happens, after all. I pull out the limed carver chair, and lower myself down, tucking my legs under your desk. I look up — out to sea.

That view.

I run my fingers along the smooth edge of the desk. There's no laptop — you'll have that with you, of course — but I can see where it rests on the desk, the slight scuff mark as it's pushed into place.

There's an old hardbacked thesaurus beneath the desk which you must use as a footrest. You have a beautiful water jug — it's deep cream, glazed with a simple black fern. The pottery has that cracked, aged look, and I'm beginning to understand more of your style, the way you put things together. You like both the modern touches of minimalism, coupled with muted pastels and aged natural materials. It's pleasing on the eye. Calming.

Strange to think that before you had almost nothing — and now you have all this.

I set my hands on the desk and allow myself a moment, just to sit here, to imagine what it must feel like to be you.

17

Elle

'Write. Even when it feels like you have nothing left in you: write. You must keep going. Keep pushing yourself — and your story — to the limit. That's when your narrative will rise from the page, alive.'

Author Elle Fielding

Time seems to stretch and constrict, the week passing in a blur of writing, of sleeplessness. Day and night have lost their boundaries, have become melded, indistinguishable.

My fingers hover just above the keyboard, waiting. I squeeze my eyes shut, blanking out the screen, and the silver shimmer of sea beyond it. The words are right there at the edge of my thoughts. I had them, just a moment ago.

What were they?

I open my eyes a fraction, re-read the half sentence on screen, willing the rest of it to come back to me. But it's vanished, a puff of smoke.

Chair legs scrape against wood as I push to my feet.

I tip back my head, a deep growling noise of frustration leaving my throat. I've been up here all day, but it's not flowing, not coming together. It feels like each word, each sentence, must be coaxed, teased, cajoled onto the page.

I'm fifty thousand words into the story — only halfway. I can feel the approach of my deadline as if I'm standing in rising water and it is reaching around my waist, climbing higher, until finally there will be no air.

I move to the glass wall, push open the window, letting cold, salted air blast through my writing room. My skin puckers with goose bumps, but the fresh bite of sea air doesn't shift the fog in my head.

I know the havoc insomnia wreaks on your mental capacity — I've read the depressing articles in the desperate hours of the night. I know that a good night's sleep is required for the consolidation of memories — and that without consolidation, there's no recall. I know that my reaction times will be slower, my functioning dulled. I know anxiety increases, depression can set in. I know all this — but what can I do about it?

I want to sleep. I am desperate to sleep.

I need sleep to write. To finish this book.

Or, maybe that's just another excuse to add to my list. *It's the house renovations. The book tours. My divorce. Insomnia.*

Maybe it's none of those things.

Maybe it's *me*.

When I was writing my first novel, I'd carved out time on the hoof: in my car on lunch breaks, my notepad balanced on the steering wheel; in my head during slow shifts when I'd lose myself in a conversation between two characters; late at night with the noise of the street flooding into

214

my room, thoughts buzzing with ideas. There was no publishing contract back then, no deadline, no expectations, no success to replicate. I had been writing for myself — and because of that I'd felt uninhibited.

But this book, this is completely different.

★ ★ ★

Food, I decide. I need to eat something. *Fuel the body, fuel the brain*, my mother used to say.

Downstairs, I dig through the freezer and pull out a bag of seafood mix, eyeing it half-heartedly. I'm guilty of cutting corners now that I'm only cooking for myself, and I've noticed that my cheeks are looking hollowed, my collarbone too prominent.

Despite my lack of appetite, I fry up some garlic and shallots, then stir in the seafood mix, adding a generous glug of wine and a splash of cream. I used to enjoy cooking with Flynn, the two of us moving around one another in the tiny galley kitchen in our rented flat. There was no extractor fan and the windows would quickly steam up, so Flynn would insist on stripping to his pants as he cooked.

I smile at the memory.

I take out my phone and call him. We've spoken twice since his mother's death, but the conversations were brief, perfunctory, distracted. Our dynamics have never been good on the phone. Flynn can seem reticent, and I prefer to see people's expression when they talk, to pick up on the subtleties and nuance of the communication. Phone calls strip out too many sensory layers.

The call goes straight to voicemail. I leave a short message to say I am thinking of him and that I plan to arrive early at tomorrow's funeral in case he needs me. I try to ignore the ripple of panic at the prospect of yet another day away from my writing desk.

I stir the seafood into the shallots and wine, then lower the heat and perch on the kitchen stool.

Fiona texts to ask how the book deadline is going — and I wonder if Bill has mentioned that he saw me last week asleep in my car. I type a quick reply, then scroll through my Facebook feed, looking at the post I uploaded this morning of my notebook resting on the shoreline, sunlight hitting the water in the background. It has over two thousand *Likes* and sixty-three comments.

SJBurns81: Wow! Beautiful beach.
DonnaG: Can't wait for the new book.
Booklover101: My favourite writer at my favourite beach.

I hesitate. Re-read the last comment.

My favourite writer at my favourite beach.

Unease trickles through me.

I look out through the kitchen window, dusk closing the light from the day.

Booklover101 knows this beach.

I've posted countless photos of the view from

my house. If Booklover101 does know this bay, it means he or she will also know exactly where I live.

I run a knuckle back and forth across my lip, beginning to see how incredibly foolish I've been.

★   ★   ★

Unsettled, I only pick at the seafood pasta while listening to the news on the radio.

I manage a few mouthfuls, before scraping the rest into the bin. As I'm leaving the kitchen, I catch a soundbite from a group of students being interviewed on the radio about the proposed rise in tuition fees and whether they think university is worth the financial investment. Their voices are bright and sparky, filled with the bravado of youth.

'You've just got to weigh it up, y'know. Whatever's right for you. But yeah, I'm loving uni. A degree certificate is only part of it.'

I picture myself at that age — hair to my waist, lips full, skin plump and unlined. What would I have said as a fresher when life still felt bright, untarnished?

I press that question into my thoughts, carrying it with me as I ascend the stairs towards my writing room.

I pause at the landing window, my attention caught by a movement at the periphery of my vision. I hover, letting my eyes adjust to the darkness outside. A fox perhaps, or a gull.

I'm about to move off, when I see a shadow at

the edge of the drive, as if someone is sitting low to the ground.

I keep very still, aware of my breath quickening.

There. A person. Rising, then hurrying along the perimeter of the drive. Tall stance, broad shoulders. A man, almost certainly.

Blood pulses thickly in my ears. I remember the figure I saw on the shoreline weeks earlier, a pair of binoculars trained to this house.

Am I being watched?

My favourite author at my favourite beach.

I'm pinned to the spot, breath held, concentration fixed on the moving figure.

He is wearing a winter coat, the hood pulled up, a strip of reflective panelling at his collar. As he moves, the floodlight is triggered.

The figure freezes. For a second, he turns his face towards the house, as if he is looking right at me. In that moment, just before he jogs away down the lane, I glimpse his profile.

My breath catches in my throat with surprise.

I can't be certain, but I think it is Bill.

★　★　★

My skin feels hot, head buzzing with confusion. What would Bill be doing outside my house? He would just come to the door, surely?

I squeeze my brow, trying to pinch clarity into my thoughts. I've been making mistakes recently, I know that. This is Bill, for God's sake! There's no reason for him to be lurking outside my house.

218

But something ticks, just lightly, at the back of my thoughts: Bill had been the one to suggest putting my house on Airbnb.

But what does that mean?

It means nothing.

Next time you rent it, give me the nod. Wouldn't mind escaping the chaos of this place . . .

A quip, that's all.

Yet I find myself taking out my phone, calling Fiona. It's Drake's bedtime, so Bill is probably home doing bath-time or stories. Just a quick call — to put my mind at ease.

I let the phone ring and ring.

Eventually Fiona answers in a rush of words. 'Can't talk! It's chaos here. Drake just crapped in the bath and I'm currently using a plastic boat to try and scoop it from the water.'

I laugh. I can't help myself. I'd forgotten how good it feels.

'I'm pleased you find it so funny. I'm not sure I'll ever be able to enjoy a bubble bath again.'

'Where's the little poo monster now? Is Bill doing story-time?' The question is so light, it's almost as if it's not been asked.

'He should be — except he was in such a foul mood all afternoon that I sent him out to fetch a bottle of wine. He must've gone to France to pick the grapes, he's taking that bloody long. The one time of the day when I could really — ' There's a crash in the background, followed by a high-pitch squeal of delight. 'Got to go,' Fiona says with a sigh.

The noise and vibrancy of her house

disappears as the phone goes dead.

I'm left standing in silence, looking out onto the empty, dark lane.

★ ★ ★

I return to my desk, thoughts agitated, tied around Bill.

Had I seen him?

I try focusing on my manuscript, pushing deeper into the story, but I can't seem to reach it.

I arch my back, stretching to release the tension. I can feel the pulse of pain in my left wrist, an old flirtation with RSI. My head feels hot and I am uncomfortable, my stomach knotted.

I take a sip of water — and as I do so, a wave of cramp grips my middle and I bend forward, arms hugged around myself. After a few minutes it passes, but the churning sensation in my stomach remains. It must be anxiety, I think, taking several long, deep breaths. It won't help me write if I am this knotted with tension.

I select a playlist I've created for my protagonist. The songs help me find my way into the protagonist's voice — to visualise the set of her shoulders, to hear the tone of her voice. I close my eyes and, as the music washes over me, I picture my character. A young woman wearing a loose cotton dress.

I find myself getting to my feet, moving across the room as my character would: the long back, the drift of her strides, the narrowed gaze. I need to *feel* her to transcribe her to the page.

I return to my laptop for a moment, bending to read the words on the screen.

'*I won't believe it,*' I say aloud to the room, trying on my character's voice. I close my eyes and repeat the words again, waiting to hear what she will say next. As I listen for them, feel them flowing out of my mouth, another wave of cramp clutches at my stomach. I reach for the back of my chair to steady myself. A lurch of nausea takes me by surprise, and I clamp a hand to my mouth.

My God, I'm going to be sick. The moment the thought strikes, I am turning towards the door — racing for the bathroom.

My fingers grip the cold ceramic sink, knuckles turning white as I heave, the contents of my stomach lifting, surging from my throat.

I know instinctively it is the seafood pasta. I can't remember how long it'd been in the freezer. Or maybe I didn't defrost it thoroughly —

The next punch of cramp obliterates thought.

It is only the grip of my hands against the sink, the curve of my back, the upwards thrust of abdominal muscles.

Afterwards, I cling to the sink, spent, panting. A strand of hair hangs loose, slick with vomit. I eye myself in the mirror: my skin is white, eyes bloodshot, lips mottled. There is a sheen of sweat across my forehead.

Running the cold tap, I lean close to the icy gush. I take a small sip — but my stomach knots into a fist, and again I'm sick, the tendons in my throat standing proud from strain.

On and on it goes — a deep cramping urgency to expel everything from my stomach. My thoughts disengage from my book deadline — from everything — so all I can do is concentrate on breathing, on keeping myself very still, from not further aggravating the twisting fist in the very centre of me.

The tiles are frigid as I sink onto the bathroom floor. I drag the bath mat nearer, laying my head on it. I curl onto my side, knees hugged to my chest. I'm alone. Alone . . .

Light bleeds from the bathroom as I drift in and out of sleep. Dreams and waking thoughts wash together, a flow of disturbing images seeping into my mind. I feel my mother's warm hands against my cheeks, but when I look up at her, I see a red pen has leaked in her breast pocket, as if she is bleeding from her heart. Flynn emerges into my dream in a black suit, eyes dead — but he can't hear me — even when I am shouting his name, he doesn't hear. I see the empty pages of my journal ripped clean out — blank pages at my feet, scattered, swelling like waves. I see a fan's face pressed to the window of the house, hands cupped, a moth's beating wings within the cage of their fingers.

My breath is ragged, shallow when I wake shivering into a heavy darkness. I reach along the floor, feeling for the base of the towel rail. My fingers edge up it until they meet the soft fabric of a bath towel, which I tug free, pulling it across my body.

I am vaguely aware of the sound of a door

opening somewhere downstairs. The tread of footsteps, perhaps. Or is it only the wind? I try to explore the shape of the noise, examine it more closely, but my eyes begin to close, the thought blowing free as I give in to sleep.

Previously

I've spent the best part of two days in your writing room. I'm drawn to it, there's something about the space that is intoxicating.

Sometimes, like now, I stand at the glass wall, looking out across the bay. I'm beginning to know the patterns of the tides, to expect a high in the late afternoon, just before the light fades. I don't know the names of all the shorebirds that visit — there are certainly oyster catchers with their long orange beaks and striking black and white jackets — but if I lived here, I would make it my business to learn.

I know there was a cost to building this writing room. I remember what stood here before — the quaint fisherman's cottage, with the old chimney puffing clouds of smoke into the sky. You made all those promises about keeping the original cottage, updating it with integrity. But once the deeds were in your name, it was bulldozed to the ground, dismembered for something newer and sleeker.

But now I can see why.

A couple are walking on the beach, the man's arm linked through the woman's. As they grow nearer, I decide from their postures that the man is much younger than the woman. She walks slowly, uncertainly, a curve to her shoulders. She looks this way and I wonder if she sees me standing here at the glass wall. I realise that I want her to. I have the urge to rap on the window, shout, 'Look at me! Look at where I am!'

I turn away, moving towards the back of the room. In the corner, angled to face the view, is a reading chair. It looks antique from the twist of its legs and the beautiful detailing of the carving, but it's been reupholstered in a quality duck-egg-blue fabric. I don't choose to sit there. Instead, I kneel beside it, positioning myself in front of the aged wooden trunk.

The wood is split in several places, the hinges rusted. A reddish nail sticks out from the back, bent and rusty. As I open the lid, I catch the faint smell of dust and old paper.

It is a treasure chest of you. It is as if I'm peeling back your skin and looking right inside because this chest contains everything. There are a dozen diaries and journals stacked in a cardboard box, a bundle of cards and letters tied with an elastic band, a tin of beads and buttons, a bag of dried flower petals with a slip of paper reading: From my wedding bouquet, a cluster of mix tapes — a childish hand detailing each song on the sleeve.

I could close the lid, move away.

But I don't. I'm curious.

I remove one thing at a time, careful to recall the exact location so that I can return it, like building a puzzle in reverse.

Your handwriting is neat, blunt — blades of grass mown short. I quickly work out that you've kept diaries between the ages of twelve and eighteen, and then there is a five-year gap, before you started again in your mid-twenties.

There is not a word written from your time at university. I find that particularly interesting.

★   ★   ★

I'm about to close the trunk when the sight of a white envelope catches my attention.

On its front, a date has been inked in your handwriting. There is nothing else on the envelope. Intrigued, I turn it over and open the unsealed flap.

The photographic paper is slippery and thin, it trembles lightly as I hold it, examining the shape of the foetus's head, the tiny curve of its nose, the unformed legs curled towards its chest. A computerised notation reads: 16 weeks, 3 days.

I turn the envelope around. Check the date once again.

I tuck the scan picture carefully back into the envelope, return it to the wooden trunk and shut the lid.

18

Elle

'When you're a writer, there are no bad situations — only material.'
Author Elle Fielding

When I next wake, daylight streams across the bathroom floor. My mouth feels dry, my tongue swollen. Lifting my head, I experience a deep throbbing sensation at my temples.

Water. I need water. I manage to stand, my legs weak and unsteady. I drink from the tap, forcing myself to take only small sips. My stomach is bunched and tender, but thankfully the water stays down.

Feeling more certain on my feet, I splash my face, refreshed by the gasping cold. I pat my skin dry, then glance at my watch. Three o'clock. I blink, confused. Three? I must have slept through the entire morning.

For me that is just . . . unheard of.

Something is nagging at my thoughts as I pick up the towel from the bathroom floor, folding it and re-hanging it over the rail.

The funeral!

Flynn's mother's funeral is today. The service was at two o'clock.

I look at my watch again even though I know

the time. Know that I've missed it.

My fingers push into the roots of my hair, squeezing. How could I have missed something so important?

Maybe there's still time to catch Flynn at the after-ceremony. It's a forty-five-minute drive to the pub where it's being held. If I leave now, I might just make it.

★　★　★

There is no time to shower. I brush my teeth, throw on a black dress, and race from the house.

I hurl the car along the narrow laneway. It jolts and rattles over potholes, the chassis complaining as it connects with a hump of gravel. Once I reach the main road, I put my foot to the floor, trying to ignore the banging headache reaching across my temples.

Forty minutes later, I pull up in the pub car park. I sit for a moment, dazed. I have no recollection of the second half of the drive. I got here on autopilot, I realise, unnerved.

My throat feels coarse and dry and I search the footwell for a bottle of water but find none. Locking the car, I enter the pub and go straight to the function room. The only signs of a funeral party are a stack of crumb-lined plates, and two trays of flagging sandwiches, the crusts already stiffening in the centrally heated air.

I cross the main bar, then turn down a flagstone corridor lined with gilt-framed prints of hounds wearing flat-caps. The headache has spread from my temples into the back of my skull, and I move tentatively, trying to limit the impact of my steps.

Turning a corner, I descend into the alcove at the rear of the pub — and there he is.

Flynn is dressed in a charcoal-grey suit that I last saw him wearing at my mother's funeral. The top button of his shirt is undone, his tie loosened. An elderly woman I don't recognise is clasping his face, as if trying to impart something of great importance. Then she presses a kiss to his forehead, before releasing him and shuffling from the room.

Flynn looks up and sees me. His expression is blank.

As he comes towards me, I clock the light stoop of his posture, the slackness at the edges of his mouth — and see immediately that he is drunk.

'Flynn.'

'So,' he says. 'You came.'

His sister, Rea, and her husband, Iain, are getting to their feet, moving towards me. Rea kisses me on the cheek.

'It's good to see you!' she says, squeezing both my hands in her own. The last time we were together was New Year's Day, two years ago, when Flynn and I were very much still married. Rea and I had got hopelessly drunk on White Russians.

'We're going for a cigarette,' Rea says. 'But catch you later?'

'Yes,' I say. 'I'd like that.'

She looks from me, to Flynn. She presses her lips together. Nods once.

Alone in the alcove, Flynn sinks onto a wooden chair, cradling a whisky. I draw a second chair close, sitting with my knees almost touching his. I try not to betray my shock at the hollows beneath his eyes, or the grey pallor of his skin.

I can't imagine I look any fresher.

'I'm so sorry I missed the service, Flynn. I wanted to be there. I've had food poisoning. I haven't left the bathroom in hours.'

'Do you mean your writing room?'

I flinch, the speed of the jab catching me by surprise. 'That's not fair.'

Flynn finishes his whisky and sets down the glass without care. He is a bad drunk — alcohol masking the best parts of him.

'Fiona and Bill both send their love. Bill said when he's next in Bristol, he owes you a pint.'

A flicker of a smile spreads across Flynn's mouth. 'And the rest. His squash debts go back years.'

I feel a glimmer of relief. There is the Flynn I know.

He looks at me. 'How's Drake?'

'Good. He's started nursery. Still talks about that wave you paddled him into on the bodyboard.'

'It'd be nice to see him again — see all of them.'

'I know.'

He sucks in a breath. 'We've started going through Mum's things. Thought we better get on it while Rea's over.'

I don't envy them the task. When I lost my

232

mother, I remember the heartache of clearing out her things. Fiona had handled it with brisk efficiency, masking the brutal depths of her grief. She came armed with cardboard boxes, storage bags and a plastic folder filled with labels and marker pens. A Sue Ryder delivery van was pre-booked for the larger items, and everything else was put into boxes.

I'd felt stunned, as if all I wanted to do was be in that space and remember, freeze each frame of it in my mind so that I could gather the remaining pieces of my mother. Each of her belongings — be it a necklace, a pair of hiking boots, a mug with a hand-painted feather — was a relic of our family life. I wanted to hold onto each item, re-read the story. Fiona had no patience for it. There was an argument. I called her unfeeling, which was cruel and inaccurate. Later I understood that Fiona simply couldn't bear being in the flat without our mother there.

During the clear-out, I filled my car with all the boxes that would fit. Flynn said nothing when the one storage cupboard in our flat was overtaken with my mother's belongings.

'Yesterday we tackled Mum's study,' Flynn tells me. 'Do you know how many copies of your book I found? Eleven.'

I smile. 'She'd chosen it for her book club to read. She must have bought copies for them all.'

Flynn says, 'Every time she went into a book shop, she always adjusted the displays so that yours was at the front.'

My smile widens.

'She was so proud of you.' His eyes lower, his

mouth turning downwards. 'I can't believe she's gone.'

I reach for his hand, but Flynn pulls away, gripping the sides of his chair.

'How did the service go?'

His voice has a harder, clipped edge as he answers, 'Hymns. Readings. Incense wafting around the coffin. Then they took her away. Put her in the earth. Held out a metal box filled with soil to sling at the coffin.' His expression is set.

'I bet there was a good turnout. Your mum was so loved.'

He looks up, right at me. Something in his expression has shifted.

'No grandchildren to wave her off, were there?' His eyes are shining.

I flinch, as if I've been slapped.

'That was all she really wanted. To be a grandmother.'

'Don't,' I warn. 'Please. Not here. Not today.'

Yet, of course, this is exactly the moment. The alcohol, the bleak depth of his sadness, the vindication that I didn't even make it to the service — it is all crashing together in Flynn's thoughts, the perfect storm.

A muscle in the side of his jaw clenches and releases. 'You know,' he says, leaning forward, and I can hear something sharp in his tone. 'I never told my mum.'

For weeks, for months, after Flynn found out, I'd tried to encourage him to talk about it — but it was like he'd parked that set of information in a room, pulled the door to, and no one could enter. Now I sense that that door is about to be

234

yanked open, and I'm not sure whether I want to go inside.

'I didn't want her to think *less* of you. Thought I'd reserve that mantle for myself.'

I keep my tone level. 'I know today is just horrible, and that you need someone to lash out at but, please, I'm begging you, Flynn, let's not talk about this now.'

'Would you prefer to wait another seven years? Shall I wait until I'm sitting next to you in a consultant's office, so that he can be the one to bring it up — because that was fun, Elle. That was a real party!'

Cold shivers along my spine at the memory.

I recall the way the consultant adjusted his glasses as he read through his notes, explaining, 'We've found a thickening of the uterus concurrent with scar tissue. It's making implantation harder.' He'd looked up then, asking me, 'Have you had a previous termination?'

I heard the strain of Flynn's chair as he shifted, turning to look at me. He must have read my hesitation. 'Elle?'

I didn't look at him. I couldn't.

'Yes,' I answered the doctor. 'When I was twenty-four.'

Instead I looked down at my hands, which were balled in my lap. *It was your baby, Flynn. Ours.*

Flynn lurched to his feet. 'I . . . I need to . . . ' He'd fumbled with the door handle. Cursed.

'Push,' the consultant said.

He pushed the door open with force.

I sat very still, listening to the thunder of feet

235

disappearing down the clinic corridor.

Now his gaze is fixed to me. 'Why didn't you talk to me about it?'

'We'd only been together for six months. You'd left to travel the world. I didn't know if you'd come back for me.'

'But I did. Three months later — because I loved you, I didn't want to see the world without you. And you said nothing. Actually, no — that's not right. You said vows to me in church, about trust and love. We talked about a future with children in. We tried and tried to make that a reality — but all the time you were keeping this from me.' His voice is gaining volume. 'We kept an ovulation calendar, we cut out alcohol, we had sex on a monthly schedule, you did post-coital shoulder stands — and throughout all of that you never once thought to mention it?'

'I didn't want to hurt you.'

'You aborted *our* baby!' He is shouting now. 'It was eighteen weeks old. I looked into it, did I tell you that? By that age, it would have been moving — tiny dance-like movements in your womb. Did you feel it kick?'

'Please — '

'I read that it would've been the size of an apple. Its features would have started to develop — perfectly formed little ears, lips, eyes. It would have had eyebrows. Can you believe that? Our baby already had eyebrows!'

'Flynn — '

'I read an account about a late termination — a baby a few weeks older than ours — and when it was removed, the mother heard a sound.

Her baby was alive. The sound was its unformed lungs gasping for air. It took thirty minutes before — '

'STOP!' I am on my feet, lips drawn back across teeth. 'Don't you say another fucking word!' My fists are gripping the lapels of his suit jacket, pushing him back in his chair so that it teeters on two legs.

'It was *my* choice! Mine! And I am the one who must live with it! Don't you think I regret it? Have you ever wondered what it was like for me to put my hand on Fiona's stomach and feel Drake kicking? Or to cradle him when he was born? Thousands of women have terminations, but only a handful of those terminations ever lead to what's happened to me, to my uterus. And do you know what I think about that? I think I *deserved* it. I *deserved* to be punished, to be childless, because I chose not to keep that first baby. That only baby.'

I release him, twisting away. Hot tears streak my face.

This, I remember, is why we are over.

2004

'Have a good shift!' one of her housemates called from the lounge, as Elle opened the front door, stepping out into the night.

Pushing her arms into a too-thin coat, she set off in the direction of town, her trainers beating a steady rhythm against the pavement.

She realised with a sigh that she'd forgotten her book. The only enjoyment in her cloakroom shift was the dead hour between midnight and one o'clock when few people arrived, and even fewer left. With no coats to check in or out, she could disappear into the world of her novel, while bass thundered through her chest. She was thinking about this when she heard them: footsteps.

They were slow, purposeful. Leather soles against concrete some distance behind her.

She'd never liked the walk into town. It was poorly lit, the roads uncared for, the parade of shops mostly unoccupied or else inhabited by takeaway joints.

Reaching the end of the street, she turned right.

The footsteps followed like an echo.

This stretch of road ran along the back of the university buildings, which were vacant at night. She scanned the dark street and saw that she was alone.

The footsteps were a little closer now. A heavy

tread. A man's footsteps.

Her fingers searched out her mobile in her coat pocket, met the heavy rectangular shape of it, felt the curve of its buttons.

She wanted to stop, turn around, face whoever was behind her, but she was afraid that it would confront something, put something in motion.

Her heart rate increased as she picked up her pace. Blood pulsed in her ears as the footsteps behind her sped up, too.

In the darkness, her imagination flamed. Had someone been waiting outside her house? Were they following her?

At the end of the road, the next street was wider, well-lit, lined with houses. She could knock on someone's door. Call out.

Her heart thundered as she strode on, telling herself not to run. That she was fine, strong, safe.

Turning onto the next street, she was relieved to see a middle-aged couple walking towards her, arms linked. Emboldened, she spun round, looking over her shoulder to see who'd followed her.

A man was several paces away, his concentration not on her — but on the mobile phone pressed to his ear. She stared into the darkness, trying to make out his features.

For a moment, she thought that it was Luke Linden, but then he'd taken a sharp turn, disappearing down a narrow walkway between two houses, and she couldn't be sure.

19

Elle

'At the heart of all good stories is character. Your reader doesn't have to like them, or even trust them, but they must be rooting for them.'

Author Elle Fielding

Standing outside Fiona's house, I check my watch. It is after eight — Drake will be in bed. I knock quietly.

It is Bill who answers. I'd assumed that he'd be working away.

'I'm sorry — I didn't know you were home.'

'Elle,' he says, brows lifting. 'Is everything okay?'

'Yes, I was just . . . passing.'

He considers me for a moment. 'Then come in, m'dear. Have a glass of wine.'

As I step inside, I have a prickling sense of unease, remembering the figure moving along the dark perimeter of my house.

'Where's Fiona?' The question comes out sharply.

'Working upstairs.'

'I thought the brochure copy was finished.'

He shrugs. 'A new project, I suppose.'

I unbutton my coat and drape it over a chair.

241

When I turn, Bill is looking at me.

I need to ask him while it's just the two of us. 'Bill, were you over my way last night?'

'Your way? No. Why's that?'

'No reason, really. I thought I saw someone who looked like you, that was all.'

'Were they also marvellously handsome and well-dressed?'

The comment makes me smile and I feel the tension easing back.

'Anyway, what's with the black dress?'

'I've been at Alison's funeral.'

'Of course! I'd forgotten it was today.' He steps towards me, placing his warm hands on my shoulders. 'How are you?' His eyes — an indistinct brown, with a short spray of lashes — hold me comfortably in their gaze.

How could I suspect Bill? I feel like I can't trust my own thoughts. I'm fighting with Flynn, distrusting Bill, worrying about comments from readers. I'm letting things get out of control. Ridiculously, tears well in my eyes as I struggle to frame a response.

'A difficult day,' he says gently, removing my need to answer.

Behind me, the stairs creak as Fiona descends. My sister's dark hair is loose and kinked as if it's been recently taken out of a hairband. Her glasses are pushed onto the bridge of her nose and she is wearing pyjamas. She reminds me so much of our mother that, for a moment, I can only stare as I study the straight line of her nose, the loosening of skin beneath her eyes.

'Thought I heard your voice.'

'Sorry to show up unannounced.'

Fiona bats away the apology with a flick of her fingers. 'The funeral. How did it go?' She kisses me on the cheek.

'I missed the actual service — '

'What?'

'Food poisoning, I think. Seafood pasta. I've been sleeping on my bathroom floor.'

'Oh Elle! You should've called us!'

'I couldn't even make it downstairs to the phone.'

'Would you like something to eat?' Bill offers. 'I could do you some toast?'

'Thank you, but I'll grab something when I get home.'

Bill looks unconvinced, but he doesn't push me. He checks his watch, announcing, 'Right, I'm going to leave you girls to it. I've got shirts to iron for the week.'

'Don't go making me look bad,' Fiona says.

'I think your sister knows that I didn't marry you for your home-making capabilities.' Bill places a kiss on my cheek, telling me, 'You take care.'

We listen to the tread of his footsteps up the stairs, and creak of the bedroom door closing, then I sink into the armchair, drawing my legs up beneath me.

'You look terrible,' Fiona says.

'Don't hold back, will you?'

'Bill told me about your starring role in Supermarket Sleep.'

'The gossip. I was tired. I just needed to close my eyes for a moment before driving back.'

243

'Is it even safe to be driving when you're so exhausted?'

'I'm fine,' I say firmly.

Fiona eyes me for a moment, then lowers herself onto the sofa. She changes the subject. 'How was Flynn?'

'I arrived at the pub about four whiskies too late.'

'That bad.'

'He brought up the abortion.'

'Jesus, you've been trying to get him to talk about that for the past two years — and he decides the funeral is the right time.'

'I know.'

'I take it his view hasn't mellowed.'

I shake my head. 'The thing is, I understand. I do. He's not anti-abortion . . . he's just . . . '

'Anti-lying?'

I nod.

'If it wasn't for the abortion, do you think you'd still be together?'

This is trademark Fiona: sending a bullet direct to the heart of the issue. I know marriages rarely end because of a single incident. But maybe one event is enough to shine a light on the cracks you hadn't paid attention to before.

'Yes,' I answer eventually.

'Do you regret it?'

My eyes widen. 'You're asking me if I regret having an abortion?'

'Yes.'

'I've spent my thirties trying to get pregnant — but I can't because of a decision I made a decade before. My marriage has collapsed. I'm

244

living alone, and childless. Of course I regret it!'
I shake my head. 'I came over hoping you'd
cheer me up.'

'Cheer isn't my forte.'

'You're not kidding.'

'I take it you didn't tell Flynn that you'd like
your house key back?'

'Not quite the right time.'

'Suppose not.' Fiona gets to her feet to adjust
the position of a candle on the mantelpiece, then
uses a fingertip to prod at the softening wax at its
edge. She glances at me sideways. I can tell she
wants to say something further.

I wait.

'Sometimes I think about the abortion. You
asked me what you should do, didn't you?'

I nod. I'd gone to London to see Fiona, waited
on her doorstep until she had finished work,
watching the traffic and buses crawl by, people
nipping into stores to buy cigarettes or
newspapers. I'd only visited Fiona once before in
her south-east London flat, which she shared
with two other male journalists. It had an air of
neglect, as if the importance of the work
undertaken within it was highlighted by the lack
of time they had for domesticity, Fiona's room
pointedly the untidiest.

As I'd sat on the concrete step watching a
woman sweep the shopfront opposite, I'd tried to
picture Flynn somewhere in the South Pacific.
He had no idea that, safe in the warm folds of
my body, there was a cluster of cells with his
DNA, growing, beating.

Pregnancy was so far off my radar that I'd

been slow to connect the dots between my tiredness, the weight gain, my missed periods. I'd finally taken the test earlier that day, gripping the stick that contained my future, while a housemate barrelled up the stairs, shouting, 'Where the fuck is my phone?' As the blue cross materialised, a vertiginous feeling overwhelmed me. I'd found myself on my hands and knees, forehead pressed against the swollen lino.

I'd no idea that, several years later, I would find myself on a different bathroom floor, another pregnancy test gripped in my fist, the pale blue cross markedly absent. For the twelfth time, the thirteenth time, the fourteenth . . .

I'd no idea that the yearning to have a baby growing inside me, to feel the butterfly kicks within my womb like a secret, would be so powerful that it would seem like a hunger.

I'd no idea that it would strike me almost daily — when I would see a heavily pregnant woman sitting at the table next to me in a café, or when I'd watch a mother buttoning her small child inside a coat, or when I'd have to celebrate a friend's news that she was pregnant with her second child, her third.

I'd no idea, as I waited outside Fiona's flat, that the person I was about to take advice from — someone who claimed they would never marry, never wanted children — would in fact have her own family one day.

Fiona eventually arrived wearing a black military coat buttoned to her collar. She'd drawn me along the hallway, straight into her room, which was littered with books and reams of paper bearing scribbled annotations. Wherever Fiona lived, her desk had always been awash with paper, books, Post-it notes.

'I don't know what to do,' I'd said, head in hands.

'You've got no partner. No job. No qualifications.' Fiona had a blunt fringe at the time, cut an inch above her brow line, which lent an extra degree of severity to her face. 'Can you imagine living in your house-share with a baby?'

I couldn't. It was already cramped — five of us squashed into three rooms, with only one bathroom between us. But it was all I could afford on my barmaid's wage.

'What would you do?'

'If it were me, my body,' Fiona had said, unfolding her arms and setting them at her sides, 'I'd have a termination.'

Terminate. Abort. They were brutal, abrupt-sounding words. Endings.

I'd tried to picture Flynn with his sun-struck skin, snorkelling over coral reef. He felt so impossibly far away — as if we were living in different universes. Why would anyone leave all that, come back for me?

There had been a long stretch of time in my early twenties — before Flynn — when I used to feel a quickening in my chest, a heavy darkness moving in, the weight of memory pressing against my ribcage. I would do things to alleviate it: drink through the night; blast music into headphones to drown out thought; walk the streets of Bristol until my feet blistered and my mind turned blank. And then I had met Flynn.

There was something about him — an openness, an intrinsic sense of integrity, of goodness — that somehow rebalanced me. I couldn't bear to lose him, to sink back into the person I was before.

Fiona had booked the appointment, holding a brick-like mobile to her ear, speaking in a calm, clipped manner as she said the words, 'It's for my sister.' She had sat beside me on the tube as we sped underground, my gaze straying to the pregnant woman sitting with her eyes closed, hands locked beneath her bump.

Fiona had made sure I walked through those automatic doors even when I'd hesitated in front of them, the glass opening and shutting impatiently as I said, 'I don't know . . . I just don't know.' Fiona's practicality and efficiency and certainty had created a momentum that had carried me with it.

Fiona looks at me now and asks, 'Do you blame me?'

I've often wondered that same thing. If our mother hadn't been abroad visiting her aunt, if I'd gone back to our family home and been brought mugs of steaming hot chocolate as we'd discussed not options, but feelings, would the outcome have been different?

'You influenced my decision,' I reply simply, because it is true. 'But I don't blame you. I asked your opinion — you only gave it.'

Fiona nods, her expression serious. 'But now I have Drake — and you don't have . . . '

'Anyone.' I look away. 'I know.'

Fiona goes into the kitchen to fetch two wine glasses. I slip my phone from my pocket, hoping for a message from Flynn.

There is no word, just a text from Jane. She typically emails or else calls — and she rarely gets in touch outside of work hours. I open the message.

Just a thought on your latest Facebook post — might be an idea to create a bit more buzz about the new book. Don't want your readers getting cold feet! Cheers, Jane.

I know Jane keeps up-to-date with all her authors' social media channels. She is great for sharing posts on the publisher's main page, or circulating them with her team, but she's never commented negatively on the content. It seems a strange thing to write: *Don't want your readers getting cold feet!*

I open my Facebook author page to refresh my memory of my most recent post. My eyes widen as I read it.

Can you still call yourself a writer when you can't fucking write?

I stare at the screen, a wave of panic rising. I don't remember posting this.

I read it again, but this time the words feel familiar.

'Fiona,' I call, my cheeks blood-hot.

She comes into the room, brows dipped. 'What?'

I'm on my feet, turning the screen towards her. 'Did I text you this?'

She pushes her glasses up the bridge of her nose, reads the message. 'No, but I haven't checked my phone in a couple of hours.'

'Not today. I would've sent it yesterday. You texted me and I replied.'

'What, yesterday afternoon? When I asked how the book was going?'

I nod.

'You didn't reply.'

'I did. I thought I did. But . . . ' A hot flush of humiliation suffuses me as I realise what I've done. I'd been writing all afternoon — I was exhausted, on edge. I was rushing, switching between texting and using Facebook. 'I must've typed it into Facebook by mistake.'

'Just delete it. People will forget.'

'Except thousands of people have already seen it.' I scroll through some of the comments.

MattH: We all have crap days, you'll get there.

ChrissieEdge: I still call myself a writer and I've had five manuscripts rejected.

SueRTerm: You've got this!! Loved your first book.

Booklover101: Swearing doesn't suit you, Elle.

Fury spikes in my throat. Of course Booklover101 would have an opinion. And that tone — like a parent remonstrating a child. Booklover101 doesn't have a clue who I am! None of them do. I want to scream at the screen, tell Booklover101 — tell everyone — that my last post is the only truthful thing I've written in weeks!

Fiona is staring at me.

I realise my fingertips have turned bloodless where I'm gripping my mobile.

I soften my expression, put the phone away. 'Sorry . . . I just can't believe I did that. My editor has seen it. She's just messaged to ask me to create 'more buzz' about the new book.'

'You're exhausted, Elle. That's when mistakes happen. I'm not sure I knew my own name for the first three months of Drake's life. Try not to worry too much. It's easy to resolve: delete the post, apologise to your editor, and write something chirpy about your book.'

Smart, sensible advice. I take a deep breath. Then I follow each of Fiona's instructions.

When I'm finished, Fiona places a glass of wine in front of me.

'You'll be laughing about it by tomorrow.'

★   ★   ★

I throw down my handbag, then kick off my boots. My stomach still feels tender from the food poisoning, and exhaustion is closing in. I should have come straight home after the funeral; the visit to Fiona's has only delayed me getting to my desk.

I try to ignore the acceleration of my pulse as I begin my nightly check of the house. I start in the kitchen, testing the back door, the windows, pulling down the blinds so that not even a sliver of glass is exposed. I switch on the radio, comforted by the chatter of a presenter's voice as I go next to the wine cellar, unlock the door. I don't cross the threshold as I peer inside, the earthy cold air filling my nose. I lock it again swiftly, then move through the hallway into the lounge, switching on all the lights as I travel.

I'm aware that this routine is growing longer, more elaborate as I look behind the sofa, the tub chairs, draw the curtains, check behind the door. I should stop it, I know that. It's not good for me. I barely recognise the nervous, fearful person I'm becoming.

No, that's not true. I recognise that person all too well. I'd let that young woman dictate my early twenties, telling me I was weak, vulnerable, afraid. Now I feel the presence of those strange distorted years catching me up. It is a rising sensation, like being followed, stalked.

Once the downstairs is checked, I climb the stairs. My feet meet something wet. Looking down, I'm confused by the sight of a small puddle of water on the wooden step. I haven't spilled anything.

As I'm considering where it has come from, I feel something land lightly on the crown of my head. I press my fingers there.

I look up. Beads of water are dripping from the ceiling.

I continue climbing, my heartbeat quickening. Where is the water coming from?

My feet sink into another puddle, and another, as water slides down the staircase, trickling over the varnished wood.

Disorientated, I reach out to put a hand on the wall but find that it, too, is wet.

'What the — '

I can hear the gush of water coming from somewhere above. I force myself to move, to continue climbing the lethally flooded steps. At the top, I flick on the light, illuminating the scene. The door to the upstairs bathroom is wide open and I can see the sink tap running on full. The overflow is unable to drain it quickly enough, so water is pouring over the edges of the basin, streaming across the bathroom.

I wade forward through icy, ankle-deep flood water, and twist off the tap.

'My God,' I say, clamping a hand over my mouth, surveying the devastation. The entire bathroom is flooded. It has flowed out across the landing. I slosh my way through it and open the door to my writing room. There is a large puddle in the doorway a metre wide, but the rest of the room thankfully is dry.

I turn back towards the stairs, wondering whether the water has leaked through other parts of the ceiling into the rooms below.

I pick my way carefully down the flooded stairway and onto the first-floor landing. I go to my bedroom first and, as I flick on the light, I freeze. Water is coming through the ceiling. Dark drips streak my duvet, like splattered blood. I feel myself retracting, wanting to turn, run.

But I can't.

I draw in air, telling myself to keep it together. I need to be logical, calm. Try and minimise the damage.

I push myself into action.

Grabbing a mop and bucket, and an armful of towels, I start at the top of the house in the flooded bathroom. I work systematically through the rooms. The scale of the damage is overwhelming, water pooling on carpets and furniture, marking the walls, leaking into light switches and plug sockets.

When I run out of dry towels, I have to wring them out by hand, my arm muscles burning with the effort. I've nowhere to put all the wet towels and sodden bedding, so I push open the balcony doors from my bedroom and hang them over the railings in the darkness.

The moon is high tonight, edging the tops of the waves with silver. I pause, taking a moment to catch my breath. As I look out onto the beach, I have the unsettling sensation that someone is out there, looking back at me.

★   ★   ★

It is three in the morning when I finally climb into the spare bed. The guest bedding feels starched and unyielding against my skin as I toss from one side to the other in a bid to get comfy. The foetid smell of damp wool pollutes the air.

Somewhere in the house I can hear the steady drip of water. The sound seeps into my thoughts till I can focus on nothing but the slow, insidious repeat of it.

How can I have been so stupid? I can't afford this sort of mistake. My thoughts spiral into panic as I think of the damage — the carpets will

254

need to be ripped up, the wooden flooring is going to be watermarked, the paintwork will need to be redone . . .

I can't believe this has happened. I remember waking on the bathroom floor earlier, the side of my face pressed into the bath mat. I'd staggered to my feet, clinging onto the sink. I recall splashing water over my face, the cold shock of it against flushed skin. Then I'd cleaned my teeth. Had I left the tap running? It was possible. I'd been disorientated, frantically rushing to get to the funeral.

Yet something niggles. If I'd cleaned my teeth, why was the plug in the sink? I almost never used the plug. I try to zoom in more closely to the moment I turned on the tap; had I first reached for the plug, slotting it into the hole? I don't think so.

But can I be certain? There have been so many mistakes recently, lapses in judgement.

I sit up in bed, pressing my fingertips into the arch of my brow. Beyond the walls of the house, I hear the distant heave of waves collapsing onto the dark shore.

If I do trust myself, if I believe unequivocally that I didn't put the plug in the sink or leave the tap running, then it only leaves one explanation: someone else did.

20

Elle

The following morning, I pick up the still-warm pages of my manuscript from my printer and draw them towards my face. Ink, toner, fresh paper. This is where my thoughts need to be. I can't think about the damp smell permeating my house, or the damage the flood water has caused. All of that is for later.

My mobile is on silent. The internet is switched off. There are no distractions. In this room there is only my story.

I stack the pages into a smooth pile and secure a bulldog clip to the ear of them, then settle into my reading chair beside a steaming mug of coffee.

Book 2, by Elle Fielding, the title page announces. I have just a fortnight till my deadline — but I still don't know how I'm going to end the novel. My job as the author is to pull together the threads, tighten them, drawing the reader towards the climax, the moment of reveal.

My chest rises as I take a deep breath, feeling a tremble in my ribcage.

I'm scared to read my own story, I realise.

I grip the pages tighter. I need to sit here, read the draft in one long gulp, and assess the story afresh. The ending will show itself, I'm sure.

But what if it's not the ending I want?

I've got to finish this. If I don't, I will lose this house. This life.

Everything I've done — every sacrifice I've made — will be for nothing.

★ ★ ★

I stare at the horizon, eyes glazed. Sea and sky merge in a shimmer of silver-grey.

I'd been certain that the ending of the story would present itself, the petals of a flower opening to reveal the brilliant pollen-dusted stamen at the centre. But there is nothing — no indicator of where to go next, how to tie it together in a meaningful resolution.

You're useless.

A fraud.

I snatch up my empty coffee mug and launch it at the wooden floor. A burst of china cracks open the silence, shards pinwheeling across the room.

I curl forward, arms clamped over my head, eyes squeezed shut. After all this time, this is all I have. It isn't enough.

Write the truth, I'd said on Facebook Live.

Can I?

Do I want to?

I begin gathering the broken china, feeling the sharpness in my palm. My thoughts slide towards my lead protagonist, the smooth, youthful skin of her hands. I am picturing those hands as I tighten my own fist — feel china bite into my palm.

Opening the pedal bin beneath my desk, the china clatters against the plastic drum. Then I look at my empty hand, examining the pale heart of my palm. The idea is shaping itself, I can almost feel the weight of it. I open my laptop, and type, 'A burst of china cracks open the silence . . . '

★   ★   ★

Later, there is a loud knock. I look up from my laptop, surprised to find the room in darkness.

I check the time: seven p.m. I'm not expecting anyone.

A ripple of unease moves across my skin.

I glance towards my manuscript. I don't want to break the flow, leave the pages. I'll ignore whoever is at the door, keep writing.

My fingers move back to the keyboard, finding their places, my gaze pinned to the screen. I try and slip back into the story, into the world on the page.

Knock. Knock.

My hands clench, frustrated.

I realise that whoever is at the door will have seen my car in the drive, the lights on in the house. They'll know I'm home.

Reluctantly, I push back my chair and cross the room. On the landing I pause by the window, looking out over the floodlit driveway. Strangely, there is no car in the drive except for mine. The visitor has come on foot?

I angle my head to try and see more, but the doorstep is concealed from view by an overhang and I can't identify who it is.

I'm so immersed in this story, living and breathing the tension, that it feels as if one of my characters has stepped off the page, is waiting at my door. I think about the coldness in their eyes, thin lips pulling back over long incisors.

I jump back as the knocker raps again, hard, insistent.

My heart is beating hard as I creep down the stairs, the wood still swollen and damp from the flood. I slide my fingers into my pocket, feeling for my mobile. I take it out, ready.

Reaching the front door, I place a hand on the latch. My fingers are trembling.

I don't want to be the person who cowers behind her own door. I'm not that girl any more.

I'm not.

I yank open the front door.

'Mark.'

His hands are stuffed into the pockets of his leather jacket, shoulders hunched to his ears as if fending off the cold. 'I came for Mum's fleece.'

It takes me a moment to realise what he's talking about. The purple fleece I'd borrowed when I was locked out.

'I dropped it back a while ago.' Or had I? I know I'd planned to.

'Mum was looking for it earlier.'

'Was she? I'll have another look later, make sure I don't still have it.'

'I don't mind waiting.' He shifts, moving forward a step, so his foot is at the threshold of the door. He is looking at me directly, his dark stare unnerving. He would only need to take one more step and he'd be inside this house.

Tension pushes through my veins. I want him to leave. I want to get back to my manuscript — I can't afford to lose my train of thought. Cold air is snaking through the open doorway. I'm dressed only in jeans and a thin jumper and can feel my skin turning to gooseflesh.

'I'm in the middle of something, so if it doesn't inconvenience your mum, I'll look for it later.'

It is a sign-off. Yet Mark makes no move to leave. He takes his hands from his pockets and folds them across his chest. He looks past me, into the house.

'Ever get to the bottom of your mystery visitor?'

'Sorry?' The word emerges as something tight, defensive.

'You know, the car-less, childless *family* who rented your pad. The person who left a message on your window.'

I remember the accusation I'd levelled at him. 'It was nothing.'

He looks at me, suppressing a smile. 'Didn't seem like it when I saw you last.'

'You must be returning to London soon?'

'Still got a bit of time.'

My fingers grip tighter to the door latch. I recognise him for the type of man he is: someone insecure who gets a kick out of attempting to intimidate people.

'I need to get back to my desk now.'

'Course. Stories to weave. Lives to imagine.'

'Something like that.'

'You know,' he says, leaning close, his voice lowering a notch, 'you're nothing like your sister.'

'What, married? With a child?'

He laughs. 'It was a bit of fun, Elle. You can relax — I'm not in the wife-stealing market. That's over.' He pauses, looking at me closely. 'What I mean is, the two of you are very different. Your sister is direct, strong-minded, there's a straightness about her. Whereas you,' he says, his gaze turning contemplative, 'are a mystery.'

Is he flirting with me? Is that what this is?

'I'm still trying to figure you out. The international author with the grand designs house — who falls apart at a little local library talk. No offence,' he adds. 'You lock yourself away in your cliff-top palace — and yet you seem like the sort of person who thrives on company. You share all these details of your life on social media — but it strikes me that it's not *your voice*. That none of it is *you*.'

My breathing shallows. I can feel my skin flushing beneath the neckline of my jumper.

'Interesting pop psychology,' I say with all the lightness I can muster, 'but like I say, I need to get back to my desk now. Goodnight.'

As I begin to pull the door to, I hear the crunching of wheels on gravel. I turn as a glare of headlights beam into the drive.

'You're popular tonight.'

I squint into the dazzling headlights, trying to make out the car. The engine is cut and as the car door opens, my sight adjusts to the darkness.

Bill is crossing the driveway.

I wrack my brain. Had there been an arrangement? Something I've forgotten? No, I don't think so.

'Evening,' he says as he approaches. 'Fiona told me about your flood. Thought I'd come and lend a hand.'

'Bill. Hi.'

His attention turns then to Mark, taking in the leather jacket, the narrow set of his eyes, the hands stuffed into pockets.

'This is my neighbour, Mark.'

Bill nods. There is no offering of his hand, none of his usual warmth.

'Better get back,' Mark says, lowering his gaze. He crosses the dark drive with quick, taut steps.

I watch him all the way until he reaches his door.

When I look up, Bill is staring at me. 'Everything okay?'

'Fine,' I say brightly. 'Come in.'

★   ★   ★

'Nice of you to pop over, Bill.'

'Fiona said you needed to move your bed off the wet carpet. Thought you could use some muscle.'

'Who did you bring?'

He grins, then follows me upstairs.

'Sorry if it smells like wet dog,' I say, pushing open the bedroom door, the carpet damp beneath my feet.

He grimaces. 'More like a pack of wet dogs

263

have been rolling in a brackish stream and are panting in the back seat of a car with all the windows closed.'

'That bad?'

'It's going to be sunny tomorrow. Whack the heating up, open the windows, and let the moisture escape.' He nods towards the bed saying, 'Right, what are we doing with this?'

'I just want it moved onto dry carpet — let this side breathe a little.'

He nods and gets into position. 'On three, then?'

My back protests as we heave and drag the oak bed, eventually managing to place it at the far edge of the room.

Beside the skirting board lies a pair of my lace knickers; they must've slipped down the side of the bed. I swiftly pick them up, tucking them into my pocket. When I look up, I know Bill has seen. I expect him to make a quip, but instead he flushes and looks away.

I fetch an armful of towels and busy myself spreading them over the wet carpet. Bill helps me walk off the worst of the moisture, sinking our heels into the towels to draw up the wet.

'I must come over more often,' he says.

I smile.

He nods to the book on my bedside table, a novel by a Nobel Prize winner, which I've already given up on twice, but am determined to read all the way through.

'Third time lucky, is it?'

'How did you know?'

'You must've posted about it. These days I can

264

never quite remember what you've told me, or what I've read about you.'

'I didn't know you followed me.'

'I like to keep one toe in the literary world.'

I grin.

'Time for a quick drink before I go? It'd get me out of bath-time.'

I'm eager to get back to my manuscript, but Bill has been so helpful — and it's an intense relief to have company after another day on my own, the silence of the empty house breathing around me.

'Course.'

★ ★ ★

Bill stands by the lounge window with a glass of whisky, looking out over the dark water. It has begun to rain.

There is something different about him that I can't quite place — a tension in his manner, or the sense that he's preoccupied. Perhaps there's been an argument at home.

'Even at night, this view is still incredible,' he says. 'It's the sense of space, I think. That feeling when you look out that nothing else needs your attention.' He pauses, allowing the lull of waves and rain to wash through the room. 'The sea always makes me feel so small. It's just there, this huge watery mass. People say it's beautiful — but I don't see that. It's treacherous.' Bill turns and looks at me. 'I can't swim. Did you know that?'

'No,' I answer, surprised.

'Never learned as a child. Somehow as an adult I didn't find the need to learn. Always lived in cities.'

'So why Cornwall?'

He looks at me as if the answer is obvious. 'Your sister.'

Fiona has always maintained that it was Bill's idea — that he was ready to get out of the city. That they wanted to bring up Drake by the coast.

Outside, there is a loud vibration as a motorbike throttles to life. Bill turns in the direction of the noise, his brow tightening, lips thinning. Then he lifts his glass and finishes the whisky.

'Mind if I have another?'

'Sure.' I fetch the bottle and hand it to him.

The neck clatters against his glass as he pours a generous glug. I watch, uncertainly, wondering about the car he needs to drive home. I can't think that Bill has ever been here without Fiona or Drake. I have the strange feeling that Fiona doesn't know he is here.

He swirls the whisky around his glass. 'So,' he begins slowly without looking at me. 'He drives a motorbike.'

'Sorry?'

'Your neighbour. Mark.' He looks up. 'The man Fiona's been fucking.'

Shock pinches my features.

'I see that you know.'

'I . . . well . . . I found out . . . by accident. How did you . . . '

'Drake got hold of her mobile, somehow

266

found his way into her messages.'

My stomach drops at the thought of it — the awful shock, the cruel struggle for Bill to hold it together in front of Drake.

'Have you talked to Fiona?'

He shakes his head.

'You and Drake — you're her world. It was a fling. Not even that. It's over. Fiona told me. He meant nothing.' Everything I'm saying feels wrong. I'm speaking in clichés.

Bill finishes his drink and carefully sets down the glass.

'What do you do, Elle, when the person you love confounds you completely? When there's something about who they are that is destructive?' He is looking at me intently.

I don't know the right answer.

'I worried about the move to Cornwall,' Bill says. 'I thought Fiona might find it too quiet after the city. She loves it here. She likes walking the beaches. She loves Drake having all this space to explore. But she misses her work, I know that. There are certain things Fiona needs — we all need — to feel good about who we are. I just wish they didn't include having sex with twenty-something-year-old men.' His laugh is bitter.

'It was a mistake. A one-off.'

'You believe that'll be the last time?' He looks at me. The set of his face is altered, distorted. It is like looking at a stranger. I can't help thinking of the person I glimpsed crouching outside my house a few nights ago. 'People don't change, Elle.'

'She loves you, Bill. Please, talk to her.'

'If we talk, it blows the game apart.'

'Then what?'

'Maybe I fuck someone else.' His voice is dark, angered. 'Even the slate.'

Unease spreads down my spine: something about the moment echoes back to my past. I feel the strange flicker of dislocation, a sense that something has changed. That I have underestimated or misjudged.

There are moments in life when a situation or an individual that has previously felt known to you will swing round and surprise you so completely that it knocks the very breath from your lungs. Those moments — if they come — alter you, cause you to doubt yourself, your judgement, your safety.

I feel this moment turning on me — as if I'm standing in the shallows, watching a rogue wave rising. I find myself being dragged from the present, towed out into the past, into a small office with a wooden desk and a metal filing cabinet.

I know what it is like for fear to reduce you to something static, vulnerable. I had always thought that if I were in danger, I would claw and rage and fight and kick.

Only I didn't.

Now, when Bill comes towards me — when I feel that first touch of skin, uninvited, fingers brushing my throat — something primeval overtakes me. Rage pumps through my veins and I react instinctively, powerfully. My muscles fire and I shove my hands hard into his chest.

There is a backwards step, a deep thud, an explosion of glass.

Then stillness.

I stand blinking, staring at the space where the coffee table had previously been. It is difficult to comprehend its former shape as something solid because now only the wooden base remains, the glass top shattered into thousands of glinting pieces that stud the lounge floor.

And in the centre, him.

Bill.

Not a stranger.

Bill, my brother-in-law.

As he moves, shards of glass tinkling to the ground, it is like I've been startled awake. My fingertips tremble. The floor feels as if it is liquid, moving beneath me.

I watch as Bill's mouth begins to twist around words, but I cannot hear them beyond the roar of blood in my ears.

Then he is standing, glass raining from his shoulders, as he glares at me, white-faced.

My hearing comes back in a rush — like exiting a tunnel, ears popping.

'What the hell?' he booms.

'I . . . I thought . . . you were going to . . . ' I stop.

'To what?'

'I don't know.'

'You were crying, Elle. I went to hug you.'

My fingers lift to my face — explore the hollows beneath my eyes — and come away wet. I shake my head, bewildered. 'I didn't realise . . . '

He dusts his trousers, empties out his shoes. Glass fragments are bouncing from him. Then he turns from me, moving towards the door.

'Bill, wait!'

He stops. Swings back. 'You thought I was making a pass, didn't you? And THAT was your reaction! You threw me halfway across the room. I never realised quite how repellent I am.'

'Bill, I'm — '

He lifts a hand, cutting me off. Then he turns, leaves.

I hear his footsteps travelling towards the front door. Hear the suck of air as it opens, then the slam of it shutting.

I listen. There is the faint double beep of a car alarm, then the more distant sound of a car door opening then closing. I don't catch the engine starting, just the low crunch of gravel beneath tyres and the scrape of the underside of the car against the pothole just beyond the edge of the drive.

He is gone.

I squeeze my eyes shut. The memory is crimson-fresh, like blood that hasn't had a chance to clot.

A fragment of glass, caught in my jumper, falls onto the wooden floor with the lightest clink. I bend down to examine it between my fingertips. Strange to think this had once been part of the table top. Its very form has shifted, altered irreconcilably.

It was Bill, but also not Bill.

Me, but not me.

I leave the room, crossing the hallway. As I

pass the gilt-framed mirror, I do not look up: I don't want to see the bloodless tone of my skin, or the darkness in my pupils.

Strangely, my mind is locked on how I would write this. The power in my hands, my wrists, my shoulders as I'd pushed.

I ascend the staircase to my writing room.

2004

Elle tipped back the shot glass, a fiery red liquid sliding down her throat. She slammed the empty glass on the bar top, grinning at Louise. Then she led the way out onto the floodlit terrace of the nightclub, the cool spring night refreshing against her flushed skin.

There, standing near the exit, smoking, was Luke Linden.

Elle felt a flutter of excitement, the night holding fresh promise.

'There is no such thing,' he said, pausing to draw deep on a cigarette, 'as an anonymous night out in this town. Now you'll forever know my weakness for grungy bars and Welsh reggae singers.'

Beside her, Louise's voice turned skittish as she enthused about the band, how she *loved reggae*, that he should check out this new group she'd discovered a few months ago . . .

Elle wasn't listening. She was concentrating on the pleasing feeling of her palms skimming the hem of her short dusky blue dress. Her body had that warm, boneless feeling that came when she'd been drinking, making her feel light, loose-limbed.

As Louise turned, pointing over her shoulder towards the band, Luke Linden's gaze moved to Elle, to the hem of her dress. His eyes lingered there for a moment, then rose to her face.

She enjoyed the way he was looking at her, not with the darting eyes of the boys her age, but with a steady, unapologetic stare.

She found her lips parting lightly, her mouth turning into a smile that she'd not worn before — a pursing of her lips.

Then Luke Linden made a small movement with his head, a nod, as if an agreement had been made, something decided between them. A thrill shivered through her body.

Louise turned back to them. 'Want to watch the band?'

'I've got an early meeting,' Luke Linden said, 'which I need to be fresh for.' Then he stubbed out his cigarette and bid them goodnight.

Maybe it was the noise out on the terrace, or perhaps it was the alcohol coursing through her, but Elle had missed it — the clue he'd handed her.

★　★　★

With her mood dampened by Linden's departure, Elle returned to the bar and ordered another round of drinks for her and Louise. They drank and danced, bodies glistening with sweat, balls of their feet burning. At close, they stumbled out onto the street, their skin chilled by the late spring air.

Their ambling, drunken path home took them down a stretch of road inhabited mostly by students. One of the houses was illuminated with strobing lights, the front door lolling open, a group of students spilling onto the pavement.

Elle tugged Louise's hand, following the pulsing music into the house party.

Inside, a disco ball spun above a crowd of cramped bodies. Two girls danced on a sofa, heels sinking into the depths of the cushions, raised hands brushing the ceiling. The air smelled of spilled beer and sweat, bass drilling through the thin walls.

Elle squeezed out into the hallway, feeling the beat of the music change as she climbed the stairs. The rhythm was mellower, sexy. She felt her hips slink from side to side as she squeezed past a tiny girl with bright blonde hair wearing vivid pink lipstick.

Upstairs, a bluesy voice belted from a speaker somewhere. The smell of weed was heady and thick, drifts of smoke tinged purple by the hypnotic formations of a lava lamp. Behind another door there was a small group of people huddled around a desk where a line of coke had been cut, its path lit by a study lamp.

'Elle! Hey! Didn't know you were here! Cool!' It was a boy — Carl — who took one of the same modules as her, Fiction of the Indian Sub-Continent, and had read Arundhati Roy's *The God of Small Things* and declared, 'Not much of a page-turner.'

He grabbed her by the hand, saying, 'This line's yours.'

She looked at the group of people standing around, shrugged, then bent over the desk and pressed a finger to a nostril, feeling the coke zing through her system, making her eyes blink, then widen as a golden beam shone into her chest.

Later there were shots — of absinthe, of tequila, of a sickly red liquid that tasted like cinnamon and burnt sugar — and then later still, there was that elfin girl with the pink lips, who tasted of cherry and cigarettes as they'd kissed to a roar of cheers.

And then, all at once, the sun had risen, the light revealing the bare springs of the sofa she was lying on, the threadbare patches of carpet, the chipped polish of her nails.

She stumbled into the morning, intent on getting back to her house, to a bed with clean sheets, where she could pour a long glass of water, line up the painkillers for the hangover she knew she deserved.

As she moved through Bute Park, dog walkers and joggers eyeing her in last night's dress, her heels clacking along the concrete, she glanced at her watch. Just before nine. She had a vague recollection of an appointment. Something she was meant to be doing. No, not an appointment, a meeting.

With Luke Linden.

21

Elle

'Don't be afraid to draw from personal experience — it's the richest resource you have.'

Author Elle Fielding

Pushing open the door of the writing room, I pace to the far wall, swing round, stride back again. Back, forth. My feet thud against wood, thoughts flashing dangerously: Bill's face up close to mine, so close I could see the open pores of his nose filled with tiny beads of grease; the crash of glass, high notes of sound as it shattered; the twist of Bill's lips as he swore; the knock at the door moments later —

No, wait! I halt, fingers outstretched as if pushing at something. That isn't right. That was before. That was a different room, a different man.

The images are stretching and blurring, the heat of emotion melding them together. Bill's features distort, reshape into a thinner face, darker eyes. Eyes I can't read.

I push off again, feet drumming across floorboards.

The narrative isn't clear. There are question marks, patches that seem as if they have two versions: his, mine.

I stop pacing and place my hands on my hips, breathing out hard. I can't unpiece it all.

Seized by an idea, I'm drawn towards my desk. I stay on my feet as I open a Word document and type something.

No. Wrong.

I delete it. Type a different sentence, then another.

I continue typing as I lower myself into the chair, knees folding beneath the desk.

My fingertips race over the keys, a dance, feeling my way into the story, my eyes never leaving the screen.

★   ★   ★

It is gone midnight when I lean back in my chair, fingertips sliding free of the keyboard.

I've been at my desk for hours, not daring break the writing momentum to so much as fetch a drink.

The room is in darkness, except for the glow of my laptop. I flick on my desk lamp, blinking against the sudden light. I'm aware that if anyone is standing in the dark bay, they would be able to look up and see me spotlighted. Alone.

My thoughts swim back to Bill's earlier visit and swirl there, a dizzying eddy.

People don't change, Bill had said.

But I'm not sure that's true. We do change. I have changed. I'm no longer the carefree student of years ago, who had a restless energy, wanting to tear through the skin of the world and go explore. Nor am I the girl of later, the one who got lost for years, who walked the streets searching for something, who barely ate, who didn't sleep. I'm not sure I'm even the woman who gradually emerged — the one I liked best — who married a good man, who once lay on her back in a warm ocean, hair fanning around her, weightless, marvelling, *It's all so beautiful.*

No, I'm a different woman altogether now.

I drag my focus back to my screen, saving my work and shutting down my laptop. I stand, stiff-legged. The heating must have turned off an hour or two ago and I'm chilled to the bone. I can feel a tension headache tightening at the front of my skull. I must get in the habit of bringing a jug of water to my desk.

I've barely eaten since the food poisoning and I can feel the waistband of my trousers gaping as I cross the room. I must eat something — keep up my strength.

I reach the door, my fingers sliding around the cold pewter handle. I push downwards, but there is no release in the door mechanism. I try again, assuming I've made the movement incorrectly. But again, there is nothing. No click. No releasing. The door stays shut.

Unease scuttles down my neck, like an insect falling beneath the neckline of my jumper. The door is jammed.

I try a third time using both hands.

The door doesn't move. There is no give.

I flick on the main room light, then crouch to look more closely at the mechanism of the handle. I blink. It is impossible — yet I can see it.

There is the rectangular block of metal pushing into the mechanism: the door is bolted.

★ ★ ★

My palms are flat against the door. I hold myself very still, listening.

All I can hear is my own breath, quick and shallow.

My mind is racing. The key for my writing room is downstairs in the bureau. It's an externally locking door — I couldn't lock myself in, even if I wanted to.

Have I been locked in?

My throat turns slick with bile.

I talk myself clear of the idea, focusing on the possibility of a broken spindle, or loose bolt.

I spin away from the door, pacing across the room. The hurried tread of my feet echoes through the silence. My mobile is in the kitchen. The Wi-Fi router I keep downstairs is switched off. There is no way of calling anyone.

What do I do?

I will have to force my way out. I face the door, my eyes mapping it: solid oak, no weak points. There's no chance of me shouldering it open. Even if I use my office chair as a battering ram, it'll crack and splinter long before the door gives.

The lock mechanism, that's what I need to focus on.

Yanking open the desk drawer, I search through potential implements: pens, a pair of scissors, paperclips, a metal ruler. I grab the latter and hurry back to the door, crouching low as I try to slide the ruler between the gap in the frame and the door.

Too thick! There is no space to slot it. Even if there was, I've no idea how I'd jiggle a metal bolt out of position.

I drop the ruler and flatten my hands against the door, smoothing them over the sanded planes, as if I can intuit some divine answer.

My mouth feels dry, my tongue thick against the roof of my mouth. The thought of a tall glass of water becomes an acute desire. Thirst lights a flame of panic: what if I *can't* get out?

It could be days before anyone realises I'm missing.

I grab the handle, pulling, pushing, jostling.

Nothing fucking works!

I launch myself at the door, slamming my shoulder against it. A deep pain ricochets down my arm. I pull back and throw myself at the door a second time.

I do it again and again, till the bones and muscles and skin of my shoulder feel hot and flayed.

★　★　★

I shiver at the foot of the door, arms hugged to my chest. The wind is beating against the glass wall, breathing the cold night into the room. It must be around one in the morning. The heating won't be on again until six.

As I'm rubbing my arms to keep warm, somewhere below there is a noise. A single clunk, like a book being dropped or a picture frame falling to its back. Something with weight.

Panic shoots through me. I'm aware of my own breath, shallow and rapid.

I wait, listening. There is the push of wind against glass, and far, far below, another sound — like the strain of wood beneath a footstep.

I hold myself very still, listening.

Nothing more.

After a minute or so, I am about to move when I catch the light creak of metal, like the hinge of a cupboard or door opening.

Someone is downstairs.

My head whirls.

Who?

Flynn still has a key . . . He's let himself in before.

Or, has Mark been watching the house. Found a way inside?

What about Bill? He could've taken the spare key from my bureau on his way out.

I squeeze my eyes shut, thoughts spinning dangerously. I'm thinking of him. Luke Linden. I tell myself it isn't possible. It can't be.

I picture that faint, insidious message written on my window: *I'm in your house.*

Then it comes to me, a dark thought swooping down. Whoever rented this house had a key. What if they've had it copied? Let themselves back in.

I grab the thick arms of my reading chair, pulling and dragging it towards the writing room door. The solid legs scrape across the floor-boards, scratch marks clawing across the wood. I heave it firmly against the door, the chair back slotting beneath the handle, barricading the entrance.

I stand there, hands on hips, breath ragged. *Now what?*

Shivering hard, I rush to the glass wall. Shoving aside my laptop, I scramble onto my desk, then open the window as wide as it'll go. Wind-lashed rain rips into the room, the pages of my books flapping wildly on the shelves.

Standing on tiptoes, I push my head out, rain biting against my scalp, the rush of wind filling my ears. It would be useless to shout for help: there will be no one out in the bay at this time of night, and my voice is no match for the weather. I squeeze my shoulders through the window, rain sliding down the neckline of my jumper. I could just about fit through this window if I had to.

Below on the second storey, a balcony wraps around my bedroom. The lights in my room are on, spilling onto the balcony and illuminating the sheer height of the drop. Is it twelve feet? Less perhaps? If I don't land correctly, it could mean a broken leg — or worse. I'm not certain that I'd even land on the balcony area. If I misjudge the drop, or am buffeted by a gust of wind, I could miss the balcony altogether.

I would hit the rocks.

Rivers of rain slide from my forehead, my chin. I'm shivering hard, the window frame digging uncomfortably into my back. I grip on harder, my fingers numb with the cold, angling myself so I can assess my options, look for any struts or points of purchase that I could use to climb down — but there are none. There is absolutely no way out.

My attention is snatched by a movement below. Rain blurs my vision, but I am almost certain I see the swing of material — perhaps the hem of a coat — as a figure crosses my bedroom, then disappears.

Previously

It's my second-to-last day in the house. I'm ready to leave.

I'll miss certain things. The view will be the hardest thing to give up. I've kept the windows ajar most of the week — the novelty of fresh, sea air blowing through the house has not dimmed. I'll also miss the coffee machine. An expensive little habit those coffee capsules, though.

Do you know what I won't miss? All the space. The rooms feel empty enough to echo. Your own voice, your own footsteps, following wherever you walk. I don't know how you bear it.

I look down at my hands, studying the three carefully selected items they hold.

I go to the lounge first, edging the toy giraffe beneath your sofa, so just a hoof protrudes. Next, I take the stairs to your bedroom and place a small pot of men's hair wax at the back of your bedside drawer. Finally, I make my way into the smallest room — the would-be-nursery — and leave the nappy rash cream on the shelf below the porthole window.

There. Done.

Satisfied with my thoroughness, I climb the stairs to the writing room. I press down the handle, considering whether I'll need to attempt to relock this door before I leave.

I decide that no, I won't. People see what they

want to see. When you slot the writing room key into this door, you'll assume it was always locked, just as you left it.

I cross the room and position myself before the oak trunk. The lid is open from my visit earlier this morning. Finding myself in a strangely reflective mood today, I decide to take a final look at the photos.

I leaf through the albums, thinking I've probably examined all of them, when I find another tucked right at the bottom of the trunk. Not hidden, but not easily accessible. I imagine you can't have looked at it in a long time.

I pull it out. The cover is sturdy, bound in tan leather that is soft and timeworn. As I open it, I immediately see my mistake. This is not a photo album, after all.

★   ★   ★

Dusk gathers around me, the floorboards turn to ice, yet still I don't move. I stay there in the muted darkness, with this new knowledge surrounding me.

I cannot believe it.

Except — it all makes complete sense.

My knees are stiff as I stand, pins and needles fuzzing through my feet.

This changes everything. I feel winded, foolish.

I should have known!

I move to your desk, anger spreading through my chest, twitching down my arms, causing my fingers to curl into themselves.

286

Right in front of me there is a paperweight — solid, glistening, a glittering jewel in your office. I reach for it.

LIAR. LIAR. LIAR.

I launch it at the floor, the dull thud of solid glass against wood. There is no pleasing smash or ringing glass. Instead, it lies cracked, a chipped fragment splintered from the whole.

22

Elle

The window frame scrapes my hip bone, as I pull myself back through it. I yank the window shut and clamber from my desk.

I fumble through my desk drawer until my fingers meet the hard metal blades of my scissors. I grip them close to my body, then cross the room, searching for anything else I can use to defend myself.

Blood pumps hard through my veins. I'm firing with energy.

I crouch by the vintage case where I store electrical items and, opening it, I find an old power cable. It is a metre-long, thick, kinked in places. I pull it out and wrap one end around my hand. Yes, I could use this. I picture it tight against a throat, veins bulging.

I will do whatever it takes.

Then I notice it: an old router, dusty and tired. It's been relegated here because of a loose connection in the wiring. I wasted hours of my life having to wiggle and adjust the cable every time the connection dropped out. There's a chance I can get it to work. I heave my desk away from the wall to access the phone point behind it. My hands are shaking so hard, it takes three attempts to plug in the cable. I set the router on the desk and watch for the green light to flash, indicating that there is internet access.

Nothing happens.

This router came with me from Bristol and must be six or seven years old. I lightly jiggle the cable in a bid to realign the loose connection. I used to have a technique that involved wrapping the cable around the router itself. I try it now, my hands unsteady, breath laboured.

A single green light begins to flicker and wink. 'Yes!' I hiss.

Glancing over my shoulder, I check the door is still secure, then I open my laptop. My hands are clammy, and I wipe them against my thighs before navigating to the Wi-Fi settings. I have to position my desk lamp near to the router to read the minuscule code. Breathless, I stab the code into my laptop, then hit *Return*.

I sit very still.

There is not a beat of noise from downstairs.

Please, please.

The Wi-Fi icon appears on my toolbar. I am connected!

I work quickly now, fingers racing over the keyboard as I open Skype and dial 999.

A message pops up on my screen informing me that this service isn't permitted to make emergency calls.

No!

I rarely use Skype and have no contacts listed. I squeeze my eyes shut trying to think.

Fiona. I know Fiona's mobile number. I tap it into the computer, then listen to Skype dial.

Answer, will you? Answer!

'Elle?' Her voice is muffled.

'I'm locked in my writing room. Someone's in the house. Please. Call the police.'

'What?'

'Call the police, Fiona. I'm in my house. Locked in my writing room. I can hear someone downstairs.'

'I'll call them now! Then I'm coming over.'

'Is Bill there?'

'Bill? Of course. He's asleep right here. He'll stay with Drake.'

The call ends. I sit very still at my desk picturing Fiona ringing the police, imagining them getting into their cars, blue lights flashing.

What if something happens to me before they arrive?

Fear is circling me, gaining ground.

I remember the advice I gave in my Facebook Live video a few days earlier. *When you're a writer, there are no bad situations — only material.*

I eye myself in the dark glass wall. I am a character. This is a setting. The plot is unfurling around me. That is all. I am here, and I am not here.

My gaze lowers to my open laptop. I flick the cursor to the next line, set my fingers above the keyboard and begin to write.

★   ★   ★

I catch the faint wail of a police siren in the distance. The sound blows in and out of earshot, buffeted by the wind.

Thank God, they're almost here.

The sirens grow louder — then cut out. The lane, I think. They must be on the lane. They don't need sirens on the lane.

There. The sound of tyres on gravel as a car enters the drive. There is the slam of car doors, the tread of feet. Muffled voices. I suck in air with relief.

Then there is a sudden, violent bang, and I feel the house shake. Then a second one.

The door, I realise. They are breaking down my door.

On the third crash, the door must swing open, as I hear it whack into the oak settle.

'Mrs Fielding?' A police officer is calling from downstairs.

Then Fiona's voice. 'Elle?'

'Up here!' I cry. I drag the wingback chair away from the door, as the tread of footsteps rises through the house.

'I'm locked in!' I shout. 'The key is in the bureau down — '

The door opens wide.

A male officer with a thatch of auburn hair steps into my writing room, eyes sweeping across the space. 'Are you okay, Mrs Fielding?'

I stare at the open door, my gaze fixed to the lock. There is no key in it. 'How did you do that?'

The officer is looking at me. 'It wasn't locked.'

I rush towards the door. 'Of course it was! I've been in here for hours! I tried to get out . . . I did everything . . . It was completely locked.'

Fiona is stepping forwards, asking, 'Are you okay?'

292

I don't answer. I step out of the writing room and pull the door closed. I need to test it, to show the police that it was locked. But when I press down on the handle, it opens easily.

Everyone's eyes are fixed on me.

'It was locked,' I whisper.

The male officer introduces himself as PC Steven Cart. 'Is it possible you made a mistake?'

'No. Someone locked me in!' I hold his eye, my jaw clenched. 'The key for my writing room, did you check in the bureau? Someone used it, I know they did.'

Pushing past everyone, I race downstairs. I open the bureau, reaching into the clay pot — but the key for the writing room is there, exactly as I'd left it.

I rake my fingers through my hair. They don't believe me — but it was real. I was locked in. I'd seen the bolt across the door, felt the resistance of the handle.

I catch my reflection in the hallway mirror. My eyes look sunken in the shadows of their sockets. I press my palms to my cheeks. My face feels hollow, as if lack of sleep has carved flesh from bone.

I smooth my hair, tucking it behind my ears, and straighten my jumper. I will go back upstairs, make the police understand.

On the staircase, I pause, hearing my sister's voice, low, confiding.

'Listen, Steven, she's been under a lot of pressure recently. Elle doesn't sleep well. She's going through a divorce. There's work stress, too.'

There is something else said, which I can't quite make out. I climb the stairway to get closer, fingers trailing the cool wall.

'Has anything like this happened before?'

There's a pause. Then I can hear Fiona's voice, low, urgent — but I can't make out what she's saying.

I keep very still, my breath held, straining to listen.

The moment is broken as the female officer descends the stairs, passing me and saying, 'I'm going to check the house for signs of forced entry.'

When I reach the top, I arrange my expression into one of composure. Fiona smiles at me, gives my hand a quick squeeze.

PC Steven Cart says, 'I'd like to get an account of what happened.' He removes an electronic notebook from his pocket. 'How long were you in this room for?'

I note the absence of the word *locked*.

'I don't know . . . I came up here in the late afternoon. It was still light. Maybe four o'clock. But then I went downstairs again to answer the door. My neighbour visited briefly, Mark. Then my brother-in-law, Bill. It was probably about eight o'clock when I returned to the writing room.'

'What alerted you to the idea there was an intruder?'

'I work with my headphones on. It was only much later, when I'd finished — when I went to leave the writing room and couldn't — that I heard something.'

'Heard what?'

'It sounded like something was dropped — a book, maybe. And I'm sure I heard a door being closed.'

His expression remains impassive, but I can tell he's unconvinced.

'I caught sight of someone, too. I saw a movement through the window. Someone was in my bedroom.'

'Through this window?' PC Steven Cart says, walking towards the glass wall.

'Yes.'

He examines it, as if this will offer the clue as to the intruder's identity. 'You saw into your bedroom through here?'

'I was leaning out.'

He climbs onto my desk, knees creaking as he pulls himself up, the full weight of him on my writing desk. He opens the window, rain and wind rushing back into the room.

'Mind my laptop,' I say, but he is pushing his head out of the window, peering into the night.

After a few moments, he withdraws his head and closes the window.

'My bedroom is the one directly below, where the balcony is. I saw someone move across the room. I could see their silhouette in the light.'

He looks at me. 'The light is off.'

I hesitate. 'It was on. The light in my bedroom was definitely on. Maybe . . . maybe the other officer turned it off? Or maybe the intruder did. I don't know.'

PC Steven Cart climbs carefully from the desk. He pauses there, gaze on my open laptop.

When he turns back to me, his expression has changed. 'What's this?'

'Oh . . . just . . . I'm a writer,' I say, as if that is explanation enough.

His eyes narrow minutely as he considers me.

The female officer returns, saying, 'There's something you should see.'

I feel a stab of satisfaction. There will be evidence — something to make everyone take me seriously.

The female officer leads the way downstairs, the fug of damp carpet surrounding us as we move past the first-floor landing, then receding again as we continue down to the ground floor. Turning left at the bottom of the stairs, the female officer pushes open the door onto the lounge.

Under the beam of the downlighting, the floor glints with fragments of broken glass. The wooden frame of the table looks exposed, as if poised to take a weight. The rest of the room is otherwise immaculate.

PC Steven Cart asks, 'What happened here?'

I hesitate, thoughts tripping to Bill. I glance at my sister. Her expression gives nothing away. Has Bill told her what happened?

I turn back to PC Steven Cart, looking at his pale, puffy skin, the red veins at the edge of his nose. The last time I'd talked to a police officer was more than a decade ago. Under fluorescent strip-lights, I'd sat on a plastic chair in an interview room, the smell of other people's sweat stale in the air.

Just like then, this man will be analysing me,

wondering whether I am reliable, whether my word holds weight. I wonder what he sees when he looks at me?

If I stick to the truth, will I be believed?

I look at the shattered table. 'I've no idea what happened.'

PC Steven Cart moves carefully around the room, examining it.

His colleague says, 'There's no sign of forced entry. Everything's secure.'

'Does anyone other than you have a key?'

'No one,' I say, clearly.

'You've not given anyone a key recently? A neighbour? A friend? Or left a spare under a plant pot or anything like that?'

'Last month I rented the house on Airbnb. It's the first time I've done it. It's possible that the tenant got the key copied, let themselves back in.'

PC Steven Cart asks, 'Who rented the property?'

'A woman named Joanna Elmer. I've been trying to get in touch with her actually, but her Airbnb account has been deactivated.'

He nods. 'Do you have any reason to think she would want to return to the property?'

'Not that I can think of.'

From behind me, Fiona says, 'What about Flynn? He still has a key, doesn't he?'

'Flynn?' PC Steven Cart repeats.

'My husband. Well, sort of ex-husband. We're separated. Yes, I forgot. He has a key.'

His brow lifts, as if this is the first point of interest. 'And are things amicable?'

I can feel Fiona's gaze on me. 'Well, not exactly, no. But he wouldn't break into my house.'

'Didn't he use his key a fortnight ago?' Fiona queries.

I shoot her a look. 'His mother had just died,' I explain to the officers. 'It was unusual circumstances. He let himself in a few minutes before I arrived home.'

'I'd like to take his details, just to follow up.'

'No, I don't want you calling him. Flynn wouldn't break into my house. I know that.'

I've made a mistake lying about the table. Now I just want the police out of my house.

'Thank you for coming over, but I'd like to get some rest now.'

I can feel Fiona watching me.

PC Steven Cart glances at his colleague, then says, 'The latch on your front door is broken from where we forced our way in. It may be a good idea to have someone stay with you tonight, and then you can organise a locksmith tomorrow.'

★   ★   ★

'You don't have to stay,' I tell Fiona, arms hugged to my middle. I've pulled on a thick jumper and switched on the heating, but still can't get warm.

'Course I'm staying.' Fiona fetches a bottle of gin and two glasses. She moves swiftly around my kitchen, sloshing gin into the waiting tumblers, scooping ice cubes from the freezer drawer. She selects a knife from the cutting rack and slices two pale discs of cucumber, dropping them into the glasses, tonic fizzing. She slides my drink towards me.

It is the last thing I want, but I take a sip, the bitter kick hitting the back of my throat. I set down the glass.

Fiona is leaning against the kitchen side, considering me. Her steady gaze is unnerving. She pinches the slice of cucumber from her glass and drops it into her mouth, chewing measuredly.

'Here's a question, Elle. What I'm wondering is: why did you lie to the police?'

'What?'

'Your coffee table wasn't smashed by an intruder.' Her gaze is direct and unflinching. 'When your husband returns home and there are fragments of glass caught in the weave of his jumper, you tend to ask why.'

There it is, her journalist's instinct for the story.

Fiona picks up the knife from the chopping board. She turns the handle through her fingers.

'We gave you these. Bill and me. They were a wedding present. Bill spent ages researching the right ones, the best ones. The strongest blades. They are ceramic so that the knife doesn't react with the food.'

A cold silence spreads like creaking ice.

Fiona takes a step towards me — I'm aware of my body stiffening — but Fiona merely passes, moving to the sink, where she flicks on the tap and lets the water run down the blade. She takes a tea towel and carefully dries the knife, before setting it back on the wall mount. She leans against the sink, folding her arms.

'Why did you lie to the police?'

'I wanted them to believe there was an intruder.'

'Was there?'

'You don't believe me?'

'Should I? You call saying you're locked in your writing room — but the door was perfectly open. Then you lead the police to think this mystery intruder smashed your coffee table, when in fact you pushed my husband through it.'

I swallow hard. I think of the explosion of glass, the shock-white of Bill's face.

'Is Bill okay?'

Fiona studies me. 'You thought he was making a pass at you.'

'I . . . '

'Not everyone is smitten with you, Elle.'

I flinch, stung. 'It was a mistake. I just reacted.'

'Overreacted.' A pause follows. 'All this — believing you're locked in your writing room, distrusting Bill, fixating on smashed paperweights and stolen brooches — it's all in your head.'

She looks at me for a long moment. I don't know what she sees, because the hardness in her expression loosens and is replaced by something else, something worse.

Pity.

As she steps forward, squeezing my hands, reassuring me that things will get easier, I can feel the reverberation of those words, *It's all in your head*. They ripple outwards, washing over a memory, loosening the silt from it, so when I look down into the pool of my past, the memory is there, hard and certain.

2004

Elle opened the door of her student house, forcing the mound of post to one side. She'd been walking for hours, right out beyond town and over to the docks, her feet pounding across concrete. It had begun to rain — she'd gone out with no coat — and now her hair was soaked to her scalp, her trainers sodden.

Squeezing past Louise's bike in the hall, she moved into the lounge, the stale drift of cooked food lingering in the air. From the kitchen, she could hear the rumble of a kettle boiling, her housemates' voices. She called out a hello, pausing by the radiator, where she slid along a gym-towel to make space to dry her socks. As she peeled them from her feet, she caught Louise's voice. There was a hushed quality to it, alerting her that this conversation wasn't meant to be overheard.

'His wife is eight months pregnant. Can you imagine how she must feel?'

'It's so awful. How long do you think he'll be suspended for?' This from Claire, a quiet girl from Northumberland who Elle had comforted through fierce patches of homesickness.

'I suppose until it's resolved.'

There was a pause. Then Claire asked, 'Did you tell them? What she said?'

Elle stayed very still. She heard a cupboard opening, the clink of two mugs being set on the side, the drag of the cutlery drawer.

Louise must have nodded, because Claire was talking again, her voice gentle with sympathy. 'Don't feel bad. You had to.'

'I know, I know. It's the police.'

Claire asked, 'Do you believe her?'

There was a long silence. Elle felt her pulse flickering in her throat as she waited.

Then Louise's answer. 'It's all in her head.'

23

Elle

In the violet-bruise dark of five a.m., sweat beads between my breasts. I drag the duvet free and sit up, pushing my hair from my face. My breathing is shallow, like I have just finished a race.

I wish I hadn't sent Fiona home. I should have accepted her offer to stay.

I go to the bedroom door, depress the handle. It opens with ease. I needed to check.

Had I been locked in my writing room?

Since the Airbnb, something about this house is different. I know it, even if I can't articulate it clearly. There is a feeling of coldness in the very bones of the place. The atmosphere is . . . changed. That is the only way I can describe it. It is as if the house is trying to communicate something.

Whoever stayed here moved through my rooms, slid open my drawers, looked through my cupboards, drank from my mugs, slept in my bed.

This bed.

What else have they done that I don't yet know about?

Every smear of fingerprints is a reminder that a stranger has been here.

Is still here.

I'm

in
your
house.

⋆　⋆　⋆

Exhaustion burns like a bright light behind my eyes. I'm not sure I'm safe to drive, but I do anyway. I need to be out of the house. I keep the windows down, damp morning air rushing against my face. The radio blares as I grip hard to the steering wheel.

The locksmith came first thing and replaced the locks on both the front and side door, while I wrote him a cheque that I can't be certain will clear.

I'm relieved I didn't give Flynn's details to PC Steven Cart. The last thing Flynn needs is to be hassled by the police. I dial Flynn's number on the car phone and listen to the empty rings, the click as it trips to voicemail, the low drawl of his request for the caller to leave a message.

'Flynn, it's me. Again. I need to know that you're okay. That *we're* okay. Please, ring me . . . '

⋆　⋆　⋆

I park outside the chemist. I check my face in the rear-view mirror — see the deep shadows circling my eyes, the bloodless look of my skin. I snap the visor closed.

The scent of antiseptic mingles with perfumed soaps as I enter the shop. Sleeping pills, that's what I've come for. I can't put it off any longer.

306

I need help of the chemical variety.

I select a pack, along with a few toiletries, then take them to the till. The checkout lady, a woman in her sixties with a short fuzz of black hair, smiles at me.

'Elle Fielding, isn't it? The author.'

I blink rapidly, feeling so far away from that role right now.

'Yes,' I say, adjusting my expression into a smile.

'My daughter lent me her copy of *Wild Fear* in the summer,' she says, ringing my items through the till. 'I loved it. Couldn't put it down. I've ordered half a dozen copies to give to my friends for Christmas.'

'That's so lovely of you. Thank you. When I next pop back, I'll sign them for you, if you like?'

'Really? You're so kind.'

I hand over my credit card.

After a few moments, she looks up, flushing lightly. 'I'm sorry, but the machine's saying your card has been declined.'

'Has it?' Colour rises to my cheeks. I rummage in my handbag. 'I'll pay cash.' Pulling out my purse, I dig through the coins and realise I don't have enough. 'I'll leave these,' I say, pushing aside the bottles of shampoo and conditioner.

I hand over a fistful of coins for the sleeping pills, but I'm rushing, flustered, and they spill across the counter.

'Oh sorry!' My cheeks grow hotter as I scrabble to gather the spinning coins.

It's a relief when the transaction is finally over. As I move off, I hear the patter of footsteps behind me.

'Auntie Elle!'

Drake is running across the shop floor, arms swinging at his sides, his face beaming with delight. I crouch down, wrapping my arms around him. I breathe in his sweet, biscuity smell. The sudden physical proximity of him loosens something and I feel tears welling. I focus firmly on a point beyond Drake's shoulder to keep myself from crying.

'It's Auntie Elle!' Drake announces giddily as Fiona and Bill approach.

'So it is,' Fiona says.

There is a strained moment where no one seems to know quite what to say. Bill concentrates on the carpet tiles of the shop floor.

'Thought you'd be writing,' Fiona says.

'I'm on my way to the library. Working there today.'

She raises an eyebrow. 'Because of last night?'

'Just a change of scene,' I answer without meeting her eye. I can't admit to Fiona that I don't want to be at home right now. That I can't bear the thought of another day, another hour, on my own. I need to be around people. I need to focus. I . . .

Fiona's hand is on my arm. 'You okay?'

I realise my breathing is loud, ragged. It's like there is not enough air in the room. I concentrate hard on taking a deep, slow breath.

'Fine,' I manage eventually.

She glances at the sleeping pills I'm still gripping. Says nothing.

I don't want to have this awful tension with Fiona — or Bill. They are both too important to me.

'Thanks again for coming over last night. Sorry

that I've been a bit off form lately. Once this dead-line is out the way, I'll be back to normal, I promise.'

Fiona's expression softens. 'Listen, we're going for an early lunch at the pizza place. Fancy it?'

I'd love to join them and listen to Drake's chatter about diggers, to watch him pull apart his pizza, painstakingly removing any flecks of oregano in case they are, in fact, vegetables.

'I'd love to, but — '

'The book.'

'Sorry.'

Drake tugs at Fiona's hand, saying, 'Come, look, Mummy. Calpol!'

The two of them slip off, leaving Bill and I standing together.

Bill pretends to be deeply focused on the contents of the shelf nearest him, which is filled with incontinence pads.

'Listen, yesterday . . . it was . . . ' I begin, not sure how best to explain. 'Completely mad.'

'You don't have to apologise.'

'I do. I want to. I'm sorry, Bill. I'm all over the place. It's like . . . I don't know, like sometimes I get locked in my head and — '

'It's okay.'

'No. No, it's not. I freaked out — and you were on the receiving end. It wasn't fair.'

'If we're going for a clean slate,' he says, glancing over his shoulder towards the far end of the shop, where Fiona is nodding at something Drake is saying, 'then you should know that you were right about seeing me outside your house a few nights ago.'

I blink.

'I was waiting for Mark. I planned to have it out with him — but I saw his mother was home. Didn't feel quite the right thing to do.' He shrugs. 'Probably for the best. I've decided not to tell Fiona that I know about Mark.'

'Really?'

He nods.

'If that's what you want.'

'It is.' Then his face brightens as if he's relieved to have cleared the air. 'Back to being mates?'

'Absolutely.'

Bill steps forward, opening his arms. 'I'm about to hug you. No shoving, okay?'

It's just a joke, but it feels too fresh, the words stinging.

★ ★ ★

The still air inside the library gathers the fusty scent of paperbacks. Laura and Maeve are both serving at the main desk. Laura glances up, sees me, waves. I wave back. As I'm moving away, I catch them exchanging a glance, the registering of surprise on Maeve's face.

For a moment, I wonder about that look. Perhaps they're questioning why I'm working here, not at home.

I find a table tucked away against the far wall. I want to be around people — but I don't want to be disturbed.

Grabbing my mobile, I take a photo of the library desk and upload it to Facebook. Working at the library today because sometimes you need a change of scene.

I go to press *Post*, then hesitate. Something Flynn said echoes in my thoughts.

Everything you post leaves a trace.

In sending this, I'm not just telling the world I'm working from the library — I'm also telling them that I'm not in my house.

An idea swims, fish-quick, into my thoughts. An experiment. I save the post, knowing I won't need to upload it until tomorrow.

Then I snap open my laptop lid and clamp on my headphones.

One week to go.

Panic spreads along the cartilage between my ribs, tightening, compressing.

I need to stay calm, focused.

I select my writing playlist. An ethereal neo-classical track pulses into my ears and I set my hands on the desk. My eyes sting, feel gritted as I blink, staring at the screen.

Some combination of the swirling notes of music, the library setting, the absence of my house, seems to unite and I, thankfully, gratefully find myself beginning to write, crawling back into my story.

★   ★   ★

I'm not sure how long I've been working for when the soft tread of feet passes behind me. With my headphones on, I'm not immediately alerted to the presence of someone — it is only when I catch a reflection in my laptop screen

311

that I pause, look around.

Maeve is standing a few steps back. Her gaze is on my screen.

I pull off my headphones. 'Maeve?'

'I wasn't going to disturb you when you looked so focused. Is book two another psychological thriller?'

I nod, lowering my laptop screen.

'It must be hard, having to hold yourself in a state of heightened tension, of suspense.'

Odd comment, I think. 'I leave the suspense firmly on the page.'

Something in the way she is standing — the way she is looking at me — feels familiar, but I cannot place the thought. Everything is slow to form, the lag of another night of bad sleep, of pacing the spare room for an hour in the blue-black of night, of twisting in tangled, hot sheets.

'How are you feeling?' Maeve ventures. 'After last night?'

'Sorry?'

'Just that Steven mentioned the call-out.'

Steven?

I'm about to tell her I have no idea what she's talking about, when it clicks. Maeve is married to a police officer. Steven. PC Steven Cart.

Surely it is against some sort of confidentiality code to go home to your wife and share details of a call-out. What has he told her? That I am a hysterical writer who thought she'd been locked in her writing room?

'It's all fine. A misunderstanding.' I smile, but I'm thinking about who else Maeve may tell.

Laura? The other book club members? I add brightly, 'Things always look different in the light of day.'

'Yes, they do,' she agrees in a tone so weighted, that I can't help wondering what those words mean to her.

24

Elle

*'Trust in your readers and only whisper
them your clues.'*
                    Author Elle Fielding

In the closed-tomb dark of three a.m., I listen to
the thunder of my heartbeat. It's too fast, as if I
have run a race. Like I cannot get enough air.

I have the strong sense that something is out
of alignment.

There are winding lists of things that trouble
me at this hour: my book deadline, the mortgage
payments I'm failing to meet, the increasing
possibility of losing this house.

But what pins me here, keeping me from sleep,
causing a slick of sweat behind my knees, is deeper,
more fundamental than each of those things.

I feel as if my past is catching me up.

It's like a current running through the darkest
channels of me. It is an acute sense of apprehen-
sion, of expectancy.

A feeling that there will be a price to pay.

⋆   ⋆   ⋆

The house is filled with sunlight; it streaks into
the rooms, making everywhere airy and bright.

But I stand in the shade of the hallway, looking at the closed front door.

It's locked. I've checked it twice. So is the kitchen door. The windows. The wine cellar. All of it, double-checked and secure.

No one can get in.

My car is parked on a side road a mile from the house. I left it there this morning and jogged home across the bay.

No car in the drive.

Right, then.

I slip my mobile from my pocket and open Facebook, scrolling through to the draft post I'd saved yesterday. I amend the caption and press *Publish*.

I'm working from the library all day. I'm armed only with my laptop, a pair of headphones, and a bottle of water. Austerity measures in place. I am not allowed to leave this desk, look at my phone, or disappear for a coffee until I've written three thousand words. Wish me luck!

If someone is following my movements via my social media posts, then I am handing them an open invitation.

★   ★   ★

I spend the morning trying to lose myself in the lives of my characters, but every noise the house emits — the sigh of the heating turning off, a creak of timber, the vibrations of the glass panes as an aeroplane passes overhead — causes me to

316

freeze, my head turning towards the sound.

Maybe it was ridiculous to park my car away from the house, pretending I'm working at the library. Now I'll have to fetch it later in the day.

If I could just manage one decent night's sleep — even four or five hours in a row unbroken — it would be like pressing a refresh button. I took a sleeping tablet last night, but it had little effect, leaving me drowsy rather than rested.

I tap my fingers on the edge of the desk, then stand. I need a break. Need to move. Get out of my own head.

I descend the stairs, the wooden floorboards watermarked and stained. The damp stench of the carpets is worsening, and I know they need to be pulled up so the floors can breathe. It feels too much to deal with. Everything feels too much.

In the kitchen, I fill the kettle. As I wait for it to boil, I stare out to sea. Lines of swell are running towards shore, the neoprene-clad bodies of surfers dotting the line-up. On the shoreline, a walker moves with languid strides.

It reminds me that I've not been keeping up with my sea swims. Everything is sliding away from me. I'm forgetting to do the things that make me happy, that ground me. My circle of reference is shrinking, coiling tighter, so that now it feels like it is only this house, and within it my book, my characters. Me.

When the kettle boils, I make myself a cup of tea. My gaze returns to the figure on the shoreline. I watch with detached interest as they walk towards the near end of the bay, below my house. Rather than turning and retreating the way they've come, the figure moves closer to the cliff line, pausing at the small wooden sign by the rocky steps that reads: *Private access only.*

Perhaps it is Mark. I saw his motorbike earlier, so know he hasn't yet left for London.

The person begins climbing the rocky steps with strong, purposeful strides, gaze turned down. It is only when they reach the top and look up that I catch the angle of their face, the dark stubble on the jawline, the curve of their brow: Flynn.

My first impulse is to lift my hand, wave to him through the window. Flynn is here!

But something holds me back. I can't help wondering why he's chosen to park so far from the house, or why he's used the steps rather than the front entrance to the property, or why he hasn't been in touch to tell me he is coming.

As he moves along the side of the house, I find myself ducking behind the kitchen table, my gaze fixed on the window.

I can hear his footsteps along the path — then they stop at the kitchen door. I can just see his face pressed close to the glass, a small cloud of condensation forming.

I remain precisely still, my breath caught in my throat. He hasn't seen me yet.

'*Does anyone other than you have a key?*' PC Steven Cart had asked.

I think now of the evening I'd returned home and found Flynn had let himself into my house. I'd heard him upstairs in my writing room. What was it he'd said about that? Something to do with looking for photos of his mother — but I hadn't seen him with any.

My mind trips to the word *LIAR* carved into my desk. Flynn had dedicated hours to restoring that desk to show me how deeply he believed in me. Maybe I hurt him so very badly that he wanted to replace that message with a new one.

A flash of memory explodes. '*You lied to me, Elle,*' Flynn had said. He'd been leaning close, his chest pressing into the edge of the restaurant table. I'd been the one to suggest meeting out so we could talk. It had seemed like a good solution at the time; being in public would keep things in check, whereas the intimacy of our flat would allow conversation to swerve into raw territory.

Flynn had come straight from a job, wearing steel-toed boots and a T-shirt that was ripped at the collar. I knew he'd have had time to return to our flat, shower, put on fresh clothes, but I also understood that he was making a point. He was showing me, *See, I'm not the one who's changed.*

I had been in New York for five nights on a book tour, signing hundreds of copies of my novel in brightly lit stores, while at home my marriage was crumbling. On the return flight, I wrote a list of the things I could talk to my husband about. I'd tell him that I found a doughnut shop that sold a different flavoured doughnut for each state; that my US publicist was also married to a tree surgeon and — *Get this — his name is Woody!* I'd tell him the builders had been in touch, and they'd be clearing out tools by the end of the month. I'd gently enquire whether he'd had a chance to look for any work nearer to Cornwall.

But when I'd reached that part of the conversation, Flynn had pushed his plate aside, looked down at his clasped hands and said, 'I'm not sure.'

'About what?'

'I don't think that's what I want. Cornwall.'

'Excuse me?'

My tone was wrong. The question came out haughtily, a teacher pulling up a pupil. I saw the shift in Flynn's features, the way his head snapped up, a darkening in his eyes.

'That's not what I want,' he reasserted. 'The big house. The fancy kitchen. The bloody king-sized bed. When was any of that ever what we wanted?'

I blinked, staggered by his sudden outburst. I'd been working tirelessly on the house, pushing aside my writing so I could make decisions about lighting and tiles and heating systems.

'Then you should have said.'

'When? I don't see you. You've been in New York. And before that it was Frankfurt. Then back and forth to Cornwall — '

' — to check on the house. To make it ready for *us*.' The jet-lag combined with wine was lending a surreal edge to the conversation, as if I were watching it at a distance.

'It has five bedrooms, Elle,' he said looking up at me, pupils dark, retracting.

The restaurant setting was useless; I knew where the conversation was headed. The same destination that underlined every interaction.

'I thought we'd live in a jumbled little house

full of kids and chaos,' Flynn said.

My hand slammed against the table. 'I made a mistake!'

'It's not about the abortion. It's never been about that. It's that you could lie to me with . . . with such ease.' He leaned close, the table rocking. 'You lied, Elle. Over and over and over.'

Now I hear the clod of Flynn's boots as he moves along the stone pathway.

Does he resent me so deeply that he wants to unpick the life I'm making here? Cause me to leave the house? I know he'd benefit in the divorce settlement if I sell the house. In the end, does it come down to money?

There is a loud rapping at the front door. Three thuds of the knocker: one slow, two fast. Flynn's knock.

I remain very still.

Flynn doesn't know I've had the locks recently changed. I wait for the sound of a key, the rasp of metal.

After a minute, he knocks again.

When I don't answer, I hear his retreating footsteps. The movement of him along the side path. This time, he doesn't pause at the kitchen door, he simply returns the way he came, climbing down the stone steps towards the bay.

He is leaving.

I move out from behind the table and cross to the kitchen window. I watch as he reaches the beach, his hands pushing deep into his pockets, his shoulders rounded against the cold.

It is just Flynn. My Flynn. He's come to see me — and I've hidden from him.

I hurry down the rocky steps. 'Flynn! Wait!' I call once my feet reach the sand.

He turns, his face lit with surprise. 'Elle! You were in. I knocked . . . but . . . '

'No car?'

'I parked at the other end of the bay. Wanted the walk. Needed to get my head straight, work out how best to tell you I was a complete idiot at Mum's funeral.' He grins sheepishly.

'So did you?'

'Not really, but how about we walk for a bit while I figure it out?'

It rained heavily overnight, but this morning the landscape looks scrubbed clean, the sky a bright, crisp blue. Everywhere is teeming with moisture, steam lifting from the glimmering sand, rising beyond the dunes, the long fingers of grass catching the golden winter light. The temperature has dropped and there is a clarity to the air and I catch the saltine notes of wet rock, the aerated ozone of sea spray, the chalk scent of damp sand.

I feed my hands deep into the pockets of my coat, my feet falling into an easy rhythm with Flynn's.

'How have you been? I'm guessing Rea's left.'

'She flew home a few days ago. We managed to sort out the house while she was here. It goes on the market next week.'

'That soon?' I say, surprised. 'Was it hard going through your mum's things?'

He looks out over the water. 'The hardest

322

thing was stepping inside, knowing she wasn't there. Would never be there.'

I nod.

'We've stored a lot,' Flynn says. 'Reminded me of all those boxes of your mother's that we shunted up to our flat.'

'Flynn,' I say, turning to him. 'I just want you to know — I truly am sorry that I wasn't there for your mum's funeral — '

'Don't. Please. It'll make me feel even worse. It's me who needs to apologise. Those things I said,' he pulls a woollen hat from his head, running his fingers through his hair and then resettling the hat into place, 'they were inexcusable.'

We walk in silence for some time. A sentence from my novel comes to me, then a paragraph — and I want to hold them in my thoughts, examine them — but I also want to let them pass, so I don't absent myself from this moment.

Flynn breaks from the line we are following, bending to inspect something on the sand. I see the knot of fishing line, the bright flecks of a jig, the rusted snag of a hook. He gathers the knotted tackle, tucking it into his pocket to dispose of later.

In that wordless gesture — one he's made hundreds of times over as he removes bottles, plastic bags, food containers from any beach we visit — I see him for the man he is.

Mellow waves fold onto the shore, and everything around us becomes visceral, sharpened. I can hear the rub of fabric between Flynn's arm and his side, the cinder-crunch of the sand beneath my boots, the suck of retreating waves as they roll pebbles and shells, the fizz and burst of white-water.

Moving through this sharpened beauty, I am acutely aware that something has gone very wrong. My life is meant to be full of the things that are surrounding me right now: Flynn, the sea, writing — but not like this. Not at all like this. The needle has slipped from the record and the wrong song is playing. But no one else in the room has noticed. Everyone continues to dance, and I am standing here in the centre, waiting for someone, anyone, to realise that my smile isn't real.

'Elle?' He has turned, is watching me, his head angled to one side.

There are tears on my face.

'What is it, Elle?'

Ahead of us, a crow struts across the damp sand, its black beak jutting forward as it caws. I catch sight of my house at the edge of my vision. I am suddenly struck by the size of it, the scale. It looks obscenely pristine on this rugged, natural cliff top. A stamp of wealth, of desire, of ownership. I feel as if I'm wearing new lenses, everything coming into sharper focus. It's not spacious, but empty. All those unused rooms for the people missing from my life.

'I'm not sure I'm where I'm meant to be.'

He looks at me for a long moment. 'You know something that I've always admired about you, Elle? The way you turned your hand to all of those crappy part-time jobs we both did in our twenties.'

I laugh at the swerve of conversation, the

randomness of the compliment. 'What do you mean?'

'You did them uncomplainingly — chambermaid, till-worker, receptionist, barmaid — but you never loved any of them. When you started that creative writing night class, it was different. You came home one evening with a notebook — and you said you didn't want to watch a film, instead you wanted to write. It was like a fire had been lit. You'd found what it was that you were meant to be doing.'

Flynn has always encouraged me, believed in me. *Don't call it a dream, call it a plan*, he used to say.

'I knew you'd get published. I never saw any other outcome. You wanted it. You were driven. You had talent.' He pauses, drawing in a long breath. 'But then when it happened, it wasn't how I imagined. I suppose I'd thought of writers as mostly being underpaid yet filled with this passion about what they're doing. I could see how that would work for us. That we could travel. Work anywhere. That I could pick up the slack if there were stretches while you were between books. But then . . . you got that deal, all those foreign contracts started rolling in — and Jesus Christ, Elle. The money! It was crazy. Neither of us could have predicted it. Then there were the book tours, the press conferences, the photo shoots — and part of me was just bursting with pride, wanting to tell everyone — *Look what Elle's done!* But at the same time, I felt this distance opening between us.'

I had felt it too, a void of my own making.

Because of what I'd done.

'And then . . . and then I found out about the abortion . . . ' he shakes his head, and I feel everything in me tighten. 'When I realised that we'd had a chance to be a family — but I'd never known about it — I guess I felt like you didn't want that life I'd envisaged for us. That this new one, with the big house on the cliff, the writing room with a view, was what you had been wanting all along. And I suppose I didn't know how I could fit into that any more.' He swallows. 'I blamed you for it. Held you responsible. Because I could see the Elle I knew, changing. And I couldn't keep up.'

He looks up, his gaze set on the cliff top. 'Maybe this is where you are meant to be. But maybe I'm not the person you are meant to be here with.'

Previously

I zip up my holdall, swing it over my shoulder. Time is up.

I open your front door, then pause.

Soon, you'll return to England, to Cornwall, to this house.

As you step inside, I wonder whether there will be a beat of time where you feel like it is you who is trespassing?

I think of you alone in this house. Just you and the silence. You and the knowledge of what you've done. Does it come to you in the dark hours of the night, the weight pressing down on your chest until you're forced to push back the covers, stand, pace the room?

Perhaps it'll be tonight, or another evening as the light grows dim and your senses prick alert, that you'll start to wonder about me.

I close the door behind me, and stuff your keys back through the letterbox, hearing the clatter of metal against wood as they hit the floor.

I'm out of your house. Now it's time to get in your head.

25

Elle

In the comfortless dark of two a.m., I am still awake.

Three a.m. Awake.

My thoughts loop around Flynn. Flynn. Flynn.

There is so much I want to tell him.

So much I can't.

Trapped in the silence of my own secret.

Five a.m. Awake.

I'm slipping deeper and deeper into the sleepless abyss of insomnia.

Six a.m. Seven a.m.

Awake.

I do not sleep.

★ ★ ★

To go to bed — but to not wake, because there was no sleep to wake from — is so disconcerting that I feel as if the ground is tilting, the walls are too close, my chest too tight.

Caffeine, a shower, fresh air — my hat trick of defensives — does nothing. So I am here, in the library again with my laptop. Staring at the screen.

It takes time, an hour, maybe two, but eventually I slip into my narrative. Classical music plays through my headphones as I write. My fingertips swim over the keyboard and I daren't take my eyes from the screen. The library blurs around me; I don't notice the shelves filled with books, the faint beeps of the copier machine, the slow press of feet against the carpeted floor as a gaze drifts over me, my laptop.

All I can do is write.

Meeting this deadline has become everything. It is my way through.

Once I get this story on the page, it will be out of my head.

I need to make things right.

I can almost see the ending of my novel at the edges of my vision — but if I try to look too closely, the idea floats away. I need to wait. I understand that at this point in my story, I can't prescribe each turn and swerve of the plot; I must trust in my characters, let them lead me there.

★   ★   ★

I unwind my scarf, warm now. I've written three thousand words this morning. I don't know how. If I can stay focused, keep up the pace . . . it is possible, just possible, that I'll make my deadline.

I stand, stretch, feeling the knot of tension between my shoulder blades.

I move away from my desk for a moment, get the blood circulating.

Across the room, Laura is serving customers at the main desk, and Maeve is stacking books onto a trolley. I regret not saying hello when I arrived earlier. When the customers have thinned, I'll go over, ask how they both are.

Drifting down an aisle in the Fiction section, I decide there is something immensely comforting about libraries. Perhaps it is that book-warm smell that's linked to the nostalgia of my past — me and Fiona racing down the pavement ahead of our mother to be the first into the library. On wintery weekends, the library was a prized outing — we'd choose books, then go to the café on the opposite street, which served hot chocolates in mugs as big as bowls, sprinkling tiny marshmallows across a snowdrift of cream. Afterwards, the three of us would return to the flat, and Fiona and I would make the afternoon's reading den, an elaborate production involving sheets and cushions and layers of thick blankets, which would quickly become dusted with biscuit crumbs.

My fingers trail over book spines until I reach *Fielding, Elle.* There are two copies of *Wild Fear.* I pick one up. I've never liked the cover — the woman on the front bears no resemblance to the character I picture. The font is wrong, too. Large and shouty compared to the subtlety of the text. I didn't fight for alternatives, still too bowled over by the whole process to feel like I could take ownership. I'd allowed myself to be swept along by a tide of decisions that other people assured me were correct for the current market. Turns out they were right.

I open the jacket to see how recently the novel has been borrowed. A flash of red stretches across the title page. A handwritten word right beside my printed name.

The book slips from my fingers, crashing to the floor, the pages splayed. An elderly man in a tweed waistcoat turns to look.

I hastily gather the book, heart hammering. I open it again. The word is still there, accusatory in its glare.

Liar.

Dry page edges brush against the pad of my thumb as I flick through the rest of the book, searching for a further hint of red. The remainder of the novel is unmarked.

I pick up the second copy, my pulse flickering in my neck as if something is trapped there, trying to push its way from beneath my skin. There, in the same place on the title page, is that one devastating word: *Liar.*

Dread grips me, pins me to the spot.

I snap the cover shut.

Someone knows.

★ ★ ★

I become aware that someone is watching me. The hairs on the back of my neck stand on end. I turn. The waistcoated man at the edge of the aisle has disappeared.

There is movement beyond the shelves, in the next aisle, just the lightest shift of colour from dark to light, a shape moving away. I side-step, trying to make out who it is, but the shelves are too densely stacked to see. Hurrying to the end of the aisle, I peer down the next — but it is empty except for a book trolley.

My skin feels clammy, hot. I didn't imagine it. Someone was there, watching. I move along the next aisle, and the next, my footsteps rapid in the hushed space.

There are people browsing. A middle-aged woman in tights and cherry-red boots. A skinny young man wearing a baggy jumper and pale jeans in an unfashionable cut. No one is looking at me — yet I'm sure that moments ago someone was right there, on the other side of the shelf, watching.

He comes to mind as he always does. Linden. The library setting. The pulp and mint scent of him in my nose. He feels so present, so real, that it is as if I can feel his breath against my neck.

But it isn't possible. Of course it isn't.

Looking down at the books in my hand, I realise that if I return them to the shelf, whoever loans them will see the word *Liar* written on the title page, right beside my name.

I could ask Maeve or Laura to check the system to see who the last person was to borrow them. No, not a good idea. It will invite attention, speculation.

Dispose of them. That's what I need to do. Tucking them underarm, I hurry to my desk, push them into my handbag, then shut down my laptop.

'Elle?'

I swing round to find Mark behind me. 'What are you doing here?'

He holds up a clutch of hardbacks. 'Returning Mum's library books — if that's okay with you?'

'Sorry,' I mumble. All I can think about are the graffitied books. Did Mark see? Was it him, earlier, watching me through the shelves?

'I'm heading back to London tomorrow,' he says. 'I'd ask you to look in on my folks, but . . . '

'Of course I will.'

He considers me. 'All right, then. That'd be good.' He shrugs. 'Well, see you next time then. Unless your place is shuttered up.'

'Excuse me?'

'February — that's the month that people dread the most. We'll see if you hack it.' He smiles.

Then he crosses the library and places his mother's books in the deposit box. I wait a full minute, then pack up my laptop and belongings and make for the exit, too, keeping my head down.

As I move through the doors, I'm startled by the hammering beeps of an alarm. An automated voice commands: *Please see a member of staff.*

I freeze, heat rising to the surface of my skin.

'Elle! Hello!' Laura is coming towards me. 'Our security system seems to be working: we don't allow authors to leave the building without saying hello!'

It takes me a moment to realise she is joking. I adjust my expression. Smile.

'Yes, sorry!'

'I did see you earlier, but I didn't want to say hello and interrupt your flow. Looked like you were beavering away. It's coming up soon, isn't it?'

I blink.

'Your book deadline. The library follows your Facebook account. Your deadline is next week, isn't it?'

'Oh. Right. Yes.'

'Well, good luck with it! We're all so excited to read the second book.' She takes a breath. 'I suppose I should let you go. Sorry about the gates. They must have taken a disliking to you. Sometimes they do that, don't they?' she says to Maeve, as she approaches us.

'Nice to see you again, Elle. Yes, sorry, the gates can be a little oversensitive. Do try them again.'

The man in the waistcoat is lingering nearby, pretending to browse. I can feel myself overheating beneath my jumper as I approach the gates. The alarm immediately beeps as I pass through them.

'Oh,' Laura says, bewildered. 'I really don't understand. You've not got any books stashed in your bag?'

I remind myself to keep smiling. 'No books. Just here to work this time.'

'I saw you.'

My head snaps round.

The man in the waistcoat is pointing at me. 'You put two library books in that bag.'

My face flames.

'Would you mind serving this gentleman?' Maeve says to Laura. Then, to the man, she adds, 'I assume you want to borrow those books in your hand?'

He looks chastised as he follows Laura towards the checkout desk.

'This is mortifying,' I whisper to Maeve once we are alone, 'but he's right.' I pull out the two copies of my novel.

If Maeve is surprised, she doesn't show it.

'They've been defaced. I was too embarrassed to bring them to the counter, so I was going to . . . well, take them home.'

'Defaced?'

I feel my fingers tightening around the books. I don't want her to see what is written. I don't want anyone to see.

'May I?' she asks, holding out her hand.

I have no choice. I pass them to her. 'At the front.'

I watch her expression as she turns to the title page, sees my name with the word *Liar* beside it.

She goes to open the second book, but I say, 'It's the same. On both books.'

Her gaze slides to me. She looks as if she is about to say something — but then changes her mind. She glances away.

'Nothing like this has ever happened to any of our books. I'll try and get to the bottom of it.'

'No, please. Don't worry. It's not a problem. I don't want to make a fuss.'

'We'll order fresh copies for the library. I'm very sorry this has happened. I hope it won't put you off visiting us here.'

I step from the library, grateful to be outside, to feel fresh air against my cheeks.

As I am moving away, that's when I think I hear it, the low whisper of Maeve's voice from behind me: *Liar.*

But when I turn, Maeve already has her back to me, her head bent over the copies of my book, examining them.

2004

Elle heard the door slam, the last of her house-mates leaving for the day's lectures. No one called out to ask if she was coming. No one checked if she was all right. It was as if she no longer existed, as if the Elle they used to drink with, laugh with, study with, had just — vanished.

She climbed from her bed fully dressed. She hadn't changed in days. Her hair felt matted and lank, her skin puffy beneath her fingertips. There was no danger of catching sight of herself in the mirror as she'd obscured the glass by draping a scarf across it.

She opened her bedroom door a crack, peering out across the narrow landing. They were gone. The house was completely empty. She needed a glass of water, but even that felt like a task that required more energy than she had.

At the bottom of the stairs, post spilled across the doormat. Her eye was caught by a thick cream envelope that looked out of place amid the glossy flyers about contents insurance and pizza loyalty vouchers.

She turned it over, her heart kicking against her chest as she saw her name handwritten on the front. Hesitantly, she slid her finger beneath the envelope corner, tearing it open and pulling out an A5 slip of thick card.

Written in a slash of red lipstick, the word *LIAR* filled the space.

Blood drained from her face.

Her fingers shook as she shredded the card, tearing it over and over, until a confetti of cream paper lay at her feet, the red smear of lipstick left behind on her fingertips.

26

Elle

In the tar-black dark of two a.m., I lie with my eyes closed, ears alert to the shifting sounds of the sea. If I could just keep my mind there, pin it to the water, the changing rhythm of the waves, then perhaps I would be okay, perhaps sleep would arrive.

Instead, my thoughts swim to shore. Drag themselves across a dark beach, up jagged rocky steps, they press their darkness to the windows of this bedroom and peer in, searching for me.

They ask questions that I don't want to answer.

Why did you lie, Elle?

Is this the life you want?

Even when I try to explain, they are not listening.

Instead, they gather a crowd, until at my bedroom window I see the faces of Flynn, my mother, Fiona. They are staring as if it is not me in this bed, but a stranger, someone they do not recognise.

★   ★   ★

Five days until my deadline. Time is a noose, tightening around my neck. I need to retain focus, stay calm.

I'm halfway through composing a sentence when the door knocker raps. The sound jolts me — the words I need billowing tantalisingly out of reach. I squeeze my eyes shut, hands still poised above the keyboard, imploring my brain cells to grasp them before they are lost completely.

The knocker raps a second time — and with it, the sentence vanishes like smoke.

I place my palms on the desk. Groan. I may as well answer now.

I hurry downstairs and pull open the front door, blinking into the sun-bright December sky.

Laura is on my doorstep, smiling, her skin flushed pink, her hair windswept. She is holding up something — a piece of material in ivy and ink swirls.

'Your scarf,' Laura beams. 'You left it at the library. I found it beneath your chair.'

'Oh. Right.' I take the proffered scarf. 'Thank you.'

Just behind Laura, I notice a mint-green bicycle propped on its foot stand, a satchel heaped in a wicker basket.

'You cycled here?'

'I try and get a little exercise on my days off.'

'It's kind of you to return my scarf, but you really shouldn't have gone out of your way.'

'No trouble,' she says, brightly. 'Gave me a reason to get some fresh air.' Laura smiles, sets her hands at her sides, giving no indication that she plans to leave.

'I would invite you in, but I'm writing. Deadline time.'

'Course! I wouldn't dream of holding you up.

340

Although I do have a very quick favour to ask. I'm going to see my sister this afternoon. She's just had a baby. He's three days old. Alfie. I wanted to take her a present. It's always the baby who gets all the fuss, isn't it? But I think *she* deserves something, just for her. She's had a bit of a hard time of it . . . So I was thinking about what might be nice, and I decided a book could be a good thing — to keep her company during the night feeds — and then I thought of you! Helen will totally love your novel. I don't suppose I could buy a copy, and have you sign it? I went to the bookstore on the way here — but they've sold out, of course! If you had a spare, I'd be so grateful. Helen would love it.'

After the solitude of my writing room, the hurried thrust of Laura's speech leaves me dazed. I widen my eyes, trying to focus on Laura.

'You know, if that would be okay?' she says, uncertain now.

It is such a small request — a signed copy of my book — and Laura has cycled all this way.

'Yes. Of course.'

I usher Laura into the hallway. 'Wait in the warm for a moment. I'll just fetch the book from my office.'

'Is that on the top floor? I've never been in a writer's room. Mind if I nip up with you?'

I hesitate. 'Sure.'

Laura bends to undo her trainers. 'Don't worry, we'll only be a moment.'

She seems to miss my hint as she removes her jacket, hanging it on a hook above the settle with

341

a familiarity that causes me to pause. As Laura's hand lowers, it brushes my winter coat, and I think once again of my missing brooch.

Everything feels too visceral, too pointed. I don't trust the sharpened edges of my thinking right now, yet, as we move up the stairs, I can't shake the feeling that the deeper I lead Laura into the house, the harder it will be to remove her, a worm burrowing.

I regret the churlish direction of my thoughts when I see Laura's giddy delight on entering the writing room. She claps her hands together.

'This is literally the most beautiful room ever. And look! Your desk! It's like it's floating in the air. Oh, Maeve was right.'

'Maeve?'

Laura startles at the abruptness of my tone. 'We watch your Facebook Live videos — you know, where you talk about writing tips? Maeve said that lovely, pared-back feel to the room would probably feel so calming to write in.'

They both watch me?

Going to my bookcase, I remove a spare copy of *Wild Fear*.

'Your sister's name — was it Helen?' I ask, taking a black marker from a drawer.

'Yes. She will just be completely thrilled about this!'

I scribble a brief message, wishing Helen luck with the new baby.

'There,' I say, handing the book to Laura.

'How much do I owe you?'

'It's on the house to say thank you for returning my scarf.'

'Really? That's so generous. Thank you. I don't know what to say. Helen will love it — we always like the same books. It's that funny thing with sisters. One of us will be describing a book to the other — and half the time, the other one is reading the same book. Not surprising though; we're both such book lovers.'

We're both such book lovers. I turn the words over in my mind.

Something is trying to connect in my thoughts.

I concentrate on that comment — and eventually it comes to me. Booklover101. I think of their profile picture, a shot of a bike, its wicker basket filled with books.

Laura?

She is looking out at the view. 'It's mesmerising here. So nice to see the view in the day time. I can see why you built your office at the top. It really must feel like you're a million miles from real life.'

She is standing very close to my desk, where my laptop is open, part of the manuscript on screen.

'Although,' Laura continues, 'must be a bit eerie at night. No curtains. All that dark water right there.' She shudders. 'That was so odd about your library books, wasn't it? *Liar,*' she says, whispering the word. 'Wish I'd spotted it first, so you didn't have to. I've been wracking my brains about it. It's so pointed, so direct. To do it on *both* copies of your book. We occasionally see the odd bit of vandalism — but that, that felt directed. Personal. Why specifically write, *Liar?*' She fixes her gaze on me. It is as if she is trying to read the explanation in my expression.

'No idea.' I clear my throat and say, 'I'm afraid I need to get back to work now, Laura, so I will see you out.'

She follows me downstairs.

When I open the front door, I stare at her bike again.

'Laura,' I say, turning to her. 'What profile name do you use on Facebook?'

There is a pause. 'Laura Allan, of course. Why?'

I shake my head lightly, saying, 'No reason.'

She looks at me, her face unreadable. Then shrugs.

As she moves down the flagstone steps, she calls, 'See you Thursday!'

I must look blank, as she adds, 'Book club. It's at Maeve's.'

'Right, see you then.'

I pull the door closed with a sense of relief. Picking up the scarf she returned, I wind it loosely around my neck, then begin climbing the stairs to my writing room.

I hesitate, a hand on the bannister. Lowering my chin into the scarf, I breathe in. Caught in the weave of the fabric is the distinct smell of Laura's perfume.

★　★　★

Back at my desk, I try to recapture my focus, but Laura's visit has left me agitated. I read back over the previous scene to try and feel my way into the story.

It is a relief to note that the language is crisp and the pacing feels taut. The protagonist steps from the page, vivid and alive. I can hear her voice in my head, can visualise the small details of how she moves, from the expressive curl of her lips, to the tension she holds in her shoulders.

It is only when I reach the end of the scene that I find myself sitting back heavily, my fingers pressed to my mouth.

I have no recollection of doing it. Embedded within the novel, instead of my protagonist's name, there in black and white, is my own.

2004

She felt the slide of gazes as she gathered her final things — the pile of DVDs in the lounge, the candle-holder on the windowsill, the crockery pushed at the back of her cupboard — while her housemates made vague excuses before disappearing to their rooms.

She loaded the back seat of her mother's car, aware that only months earlier they'd been making this journey in reverse. Her mother's voice was lined with confusion as she asked, 'Are you sure?'

Elle nodded. Tried to smile for her mother.

'I'm not enjoying the course,' she'd said on the phone when she explained why she was dropping out of university.

When the final box was packed into the car, Elle went to climb in.

Her mother looked at her, brow furrowed. 'Aren't you going to say bye to your housemates?'

She swallowed. 'Oh, yeah.'

Inside, she climbed the stairs for a final time. The door to Louise's bedroom was open, and she found her sitting cross-legged on the single bed facing Claire.

The two of them turned to look at her in the doorway.

Elle cleared her throat. 'I just came to say bye.'

'Bye, then,' Claire said.

Louise said nothing.

Elle shrugged, was about to leave, when she

saw a shift in Louise's expression, her shoulders jostling as she folded her arms, her lips pursing. Elle had seen this look before — knew that she was gearing up, readying herself.

'We're never going to see each other again,' Louise said, 'so I may as well tell you. What you've done isn't right.'

Elle stood very still, felt the raised beat of her heart.

'You're the worst type.'

She waited.

'A wolf-crier.'

Her cheeks burned with a shameful heat. A flash of memory scorched her thoughts — the slow cross of her bare legs, the glint in her eyes as she'd smiled at him.

'You might have withdrawn the allegation, but you've ruined everything for him. Mud sticks.'

Elle turned away.

She was already on the landing when she heard Louise's voice calling after her, 'It will stick to you, too.'

27

Elle

'Inspiration gets you off the starting blocks, but to make it to the finish line you need tenacity, determination, and grit.'
Author Elle Fielding

Maeve's house has a glossy red door with a simple brass knocker. It is mid-terrace, set in a row of narrow, traditional Cornish houses. A window-box with still-flowering plants stands proud from the pebbledash wall.

I raise my hand to the knocker, then hesitate. I can't hear any voices inside and wonder if I've got the correct evening for book club.

I curse under my breath, realising that I've forgotten the wine. There's a bottle of Sancerre chilling in the fridge that I'd intended to bring. I can't arrive empty-handed. I take it as a sign that I should just go home. I'm bone-tired, preoccupied by my deadline. The only place I should be is at my desk.

Returning to my car, I mentally compose the text message I'll send Maeve, apologising and citing my book deadline. No one will mind.

I'm reaching for the car door handle, when there is a rush of feet behind me. Hands grip my waist.

'No, you don't!'

Startled, I twist around.

On the dark pavement, it takes me a few seconds to recognise the face beaming at me from within the fur-trimmed hood of a duffle coat.

'Hope you weren't thinking about slipping off,' Laura says.

'No . . . well, I just . . . I left the wine at home.'

'Lucky I've got two then, isn't it?' She opens the tote bag at her side and pulls out one of the bottles. 'Anyway, this one was for you.'

I must look confused as Laura adds, 'To say thank you for signing the book for my sister. She was so happy. She cried! Although that could be the hormones.'

'You really needn't have,' I say, embarrassed by the gift. As I accept the proffered wine, I notice the label: Sancerre.

'Your favourite.'

'How did you — '

Laura taps the side of her nose. Then she tucks her arm through mine and steers me firmly towards Maeve's front door.

⋆   ⋆   ⋆

'Welcome.' Maeve ushers us into a narrow hallway lined with black-and-white prints of iconic 1950s items: a jukebox, a typewriter, a pair of platform patent shoes.

Maeve hangs our coats from a stand, then directs us into the lounge, where a cherry-wood dining table has been pushed back against the wall to maximise space.

Fiona isn't here yet, but most of the book club are already seated, and the room feels hot and stuffy, a small electric fire pumping out heat.

'Speak of the devil,' says Ana, who is sitting on a pale blue Ercol sofa, looking stylishly casual in high-waisted trousers. 'We were just talking about you, Elle.'

'Oh?' I say, joining her.

'I wasn't sure you'd make it. Thought I'd read it was deadline time on your Facebook page.'

'Forty-eight hours to go.'

'Wow. Are you on track?'

'Nothing like a bit of pressure to focus the mind.'

Maeve pours the wine and hands me a glass, saying, 'If you ever need any early readers, you know you'd have a team of volunteers here.'

'She sure would,' Laura agrees.

The knocker raps again and Maeve slips out. I hear Fiona's voice from the hallway.

'Last one here? I'd hate to lose my mantle. Fucking lasagne. It always takes three times longer to make than you think.'

She strides into the room, and I smile, pleased to see her. Perhaps it is the lighting, but she looks tired. There are new lines etched into her brow, and her face looks pale and drawn.

'Have you read it?' Laura says to Fiona. 'Elle's new book. We were just offering to be her early readers.'

Fiona puffs air from her lips. 'You are joking? This one,' she says, nudging me in the ribs, then squeezing onto the sofa next to me, 'is a master of secrecy. I don't even know what it's about.'

'I don't like to give away any spoilers.' I smile, then say, 'Did you really make lasagne?'

'Don't sound so surprised. Occasionally I do actually feed my family.'

'Where's Steven tonight?' Ana asks Maeve.

'Late shift. Phoebe's upstairs — purportedly doing homework.'

It's a relief to know he's out. Can't say I'm eager to face him after the humiliation of the call-out.

I take another drink, surprised to see I've almost finished my wine. I lean across the low coffee table and pick up the bottle. I scan people's glasses looking for someone's to top up, but no one needs a refill. I tend my own, deciding that I could leave my car here overnight, get a lift with Fiona.

'I'm only about a quarter of the way through,' Katherine, the assistant headteacher, is saying. 'Things have been manic at school. Ofsted came last week. I keep falling asleep as soon as I begin reading.'

Sleep. Wouldn't that be a delicious thing? In the heat of the lounge with the wine softening the muscles in my back, I feel exhaustion washing over me. It would be so tempting just to close my eyes, right here.

I blink rapidly in a bid to stay alert. I could really do with opening a window. Glancing around, roman blinds are covering the bay window. On the shelf below, I admire the cluster of succulents in terracotta dishes. In the centre

352

of them there is a framed photo of two women sitting beneath a blossom tree, on a carpet of petals. The younger woman looks like Maeve, and her arm is wrapped around another woman — her mother, possibly. In the background is a pale, regal building, fronted by large pillars. It takes me a moment to place it: the Bute building from Cardiff University. I remember walking in the park beyond it on a spring morning, tears stinging the corners of my eyes. A rush of heat rises through my body as Luke Linden pushes so suddenly into my thoughts that it is as if I've been shoved hard in the stomach.

When I glance up, Maeve is watching me closely.

'The Bute building,' I say, nodding at the photo. 'Do you know Cardiff well?'

'I used to live there.'

'Really? Whereabouts?'

'On the outskirts of the city, near the docks.'

'Didn't you work at the university library?' Laura asks.

'Yes, for a time. That was before I had Phoebe.'

Maybe we crossed paths in the year I studied there. I wonder whether Maeve had heard the rumours about me, which spread like wildfire through corridors and lecture halls.

Ana sits forward, saying, 'On the subject of photos, is anyone friends with my ex-husband on Facebook? Have you seen his pictures from Goa?'

'He went with *her*, I take it?' Maeve asks.

'Yes. I think they've had some sort of joining

operation, so they can't physically separate or their internal organs begin to fail. After all he said about public displays of affection, he took a photo of them mid-snog. Thank God we don't have children to humiliate.'

'Pete? I don't believe it!' Fiona says.

Ana takes out her phone. 'I'm warning you, it may put you off your wine.'

'How little you know me.'

Ana finds the picture she's been describing and holds up her phone.

'I mean, he's wearing a beaded necklace, for God's sake. He's forty-two.'

Then she turns the screen towards herself and continues scrolling. A few moments later, her brow dips and she glances sideways at me.

'That's weird.'

'What is?'

'In my news feed it shows you're live on Facebook right now.'

'Must be an old post.'

Ana shakes her head. 'No. It shows you went live at 8.05 p.m. this evening. What's that, quarter of an hour ago?'

'You must have accidentally pressed it in your pocket,' Laura says. 'Oh, we're probably all live right now!'

'No. I'm looking at the feed,' Ana says, her voice low, serious — causing the room to fall quiet. 'It's live from your house, Elle. From your writing room.'

28

Elle

I'm aware of a quickening in my chest, heat spreading up my neck.

I stare at Ana's phone trying to absorb what I'm seeing.

My writing room is lit by my desk lamp, the beam of light fanning towards the back wall. The room appears exactly as I left it. My chair is empty. My notebook is open on my desk, a pencil resting in the spine.

Beside me, someone is asking a question, but the words drift away. The world feels as if it is slowing down, grinding to a halt. My focus shrinks to the rectangular screen in my hands.

The live feed almost looks as if I'm staring at a photo, as everything is static. When I look closely, I notice something else. In the corner of the room I can see my oak trunk. It's not right. The wooden lid is open, hinged wide, like a screaming mouth.

I did not leave it open — I haven't looked inside it for days.

Have I?

I swallow, moving my tongue across my inner cheeks, trying to get some saliva working.

There are dozens of comments running alongside the screen.

Hello! Hello! Anyone there?

Think you're having technical problems — we can't see you!

Nice room — but, where are you?

Everything okay?

Accidental live? Lol! Sort of thing I'd do!

The wine is flooding darkly through my head. I press my fingertips to my lips, thoughts swimming. I am distantly aware of the phone being removed from my grip.

The open trunk, I'm thinking, *Why?*

Fiona studies the screen. 'Did you accidentally set it to Live before leaving?'

I shake my head. 'No, definitely not.' I'm working hard to keep the panic from my voice, but I can feel the other women exchanging glances.

'Did you shut down your computer?'

'It was on sleep mode.'

Across the room, Maeve says, 'Perhaps there's some sort of glitch, a self-start thing, and it logged you back into Live mode.'

I want to believe that is possible, yet I've never heard of anything like that happening. Computers don't simply wake themselves up, unprompted, and set off a live video.

'Can you log in through your phone? Switch it off?' Ana asks.

I pull my handbag onto my knee, hands shaking as I take out my phone and open Facebook. When I log on, there is a message to say my account is in use. There is an option to override it and end the live session. I click.

A beat later, the live recording has disappeared.

I sit in silence, blinking at the empty screen.

'Probably one of those weird, unexplainable computer-type things,' one of the women offers.

'Yes,' I say, rubbing at my neck where my skin has flushed red. 'I'm just going to get a glass of water.' I leave the room, aware that everyone is watching me.

I follow the hallway into a brightly lit galley kitchen.

Fiona is a few steps behind. 'You okay?'

I turn. 'No. That was so fucked up. You saw it, didn't you? A Facebook Live from my house when I'm not there. What the hell is that? The trunk in my writing room was open. I didn't leave it like that. Someone's been in there. Someone's been through my things. I — '

Fiona steps closer, placing her hands on my shoulders. 'Breathe.'

I suck in air, tipping my head back to exhale. Between breaths I say, 'There was the cracked paperweight, the tap left running, getting locked in my writing room . . . It's like there's a fucking poltergeist in my house.'

'Did you just use the word *poltergeist?*'

'How do you explain it?'

'I've no idea how these things work, but it's probably like Maeve said, some random technical hitch.'

I don't respond.

'On the plus side, at least your writing room looked groomed. If I'd gone Live from my desk, everyone would've spent half an hour staring at the mould growing from my coffee cups.'

I fail to muster a smile.

357

'Look, weird stuff happens. Fact. Don't let that brain of yours over-process this, okay? I don't want to hear the word *poltergeist* ever again, and if you begin suspecting anything along the lines of your Airbnb renter morphing through the walls to set up a Live feed, then I'm going out myself and buying you that dog.' Fiona smiles. 'How about we pour you a big glass of wine, then go back in and pretend like we're remotely interested in whatever book they're about to discuss?'

I'm grateful to Fiona for rallying. I know she's trying her best to jolly me away from anxiety. But she can't. My head is crowded with everything I've not shared. I feel like I'm creaking under the pressure of it all.

'There's more to it,' I whisper.

She looks right at me.

'I think . . . someone set it up. As a message.'

'Please tell me you recognise how paranoid that sounds?'

I look at my hands. 'There are things I haven't told you, Fiona.'

When I lift my gaze, her eyes are pinned to me.

The air in the room constricts, feels harder to draw.

There are footsteps behind us. 'Everything okay?' Laura asks brightly.

I look away, nod.

The moment is gone.

★ ★ ★

I climb Maeve's narrow staircase in search of the bathroom. I need to splash water over my face. I

358

breathe deeply, working to bring down my heart rate.

Reaching the landing, I open the bathroom door and find myself stepping backwards, startled.

'Sorry!' I apologise to a teenage girl, who is sitting cross-legged on a single bed, a mobile in her hand. 'I was looking for the bathroom.'

'Next door.' The girl considers me for a moment. 'Are you the writer?'

'I am.'

'Cool,' she says, smiling a little.

'It's Phoebe, isn't it?'

'Yeah.'

Her room is a contrast to the rest of the house, a teenage den filled with baskets of nail polishes and cotton balls; bottles of perfume and colourfully packaged body lotions jostle on a dressing table; beaded necklaces hang from the corners of a mirror. Somehow, it's calming being in here, normalising.

'Hope our book club isn't disturbing your night?'

She shrugs. 'I read your book. I liked it.'

'Oh. Thank you,' I say, a little taken aback. Phoebe can be no more than, what thirteen? Fourteen?

'There's my copy,' she says, pointing towards the top shelf of a bookcase, which is adorned with tiny star-shaped fairy lights.

'You read a lot,' I say, my gaze travelling along the titles. '*The Girls*. I loved that book. And you've got *Eleanor & Park*!'

'It's one of my favourites,' she tells me, eyes sparkling.

'Have you read *We Were Liars?* It's beautiful — reminded me a bit of *The Girls.*'

Phoebe moves to the bookcase and pulls out a copy of that very book.

'You have excellent taste! Maybe you should recommend the next choice for our book club,' I say, and Phoebe grins.

As she sets the book back on the shelf, my gaze is drawn to a photo housed in a silver frame. I find myself looking at a face that I haven't seen in fourteen years, a face that visits me in dark, tangled dreams, a face that causes my stomach to fall, my breath to shatter.

Luke Linden.

⋆　⋆　⋆

In the photograph, he's wearing a brown corduroy jacket, the same jacket he used to wear when he stood at the front of the lecture theatre, moving easily across the space, the soles of his brogues squeaking on the polished wood.

In the photograph, he's holding a baby, a round-faced little girl with a mass of fine black hair. The baby's head is cushioned in the crook of his elbow, her gaze turned towards him.

In the photograph, he's smiling, the corners of his eyes creased as he grins at the camera, a look of contentment filling his expression.

'Who?' is all I manage.

'Me and my dad,' Phoebe answers. 'He died when I was four.'

I don't say that I know this. That I know he

drowned in the Gower during an unusually warm October. That I learned of his death from a newspaper article.

I was on a train to Bristol with Flynn when I found out. We were sitting opposite each other, talking about our plans for Christmas. We could escape somewhere — hole up in a B&B in the Lake District.

I'd glanced out of the window, picturing walking over a frost-jewelled hillside, or going to a thatch-roofed pub for lunch. In the train window, an open newspaper, discarded by another passenger, was reflected at me, a face smiling into the dark glass.

I snatched up the paper, surprising Flynn.

There he was. A black-and-white picture of him sitting behind a desk, dark eyes peering through that thick hair, one leg crossed over the other. I hadn't seen his face in years.

A man's body washed up on Llangennith beach in the early hours of Sunday morning. He has been identified as Luke Linden, a lecturer at the University of Wales, Cardiff.

I skimmed over the rest of the article, each word sharp and dangerous, like broken pieces of glass: *accidental drowning; dangerous currents; leaves behind a wife and child.*

I began to shake. It was the unexpectedness of it. I'd been so careful not to allow him into my head.

Flynn had called my name as I'd pushed away from the table, running through the carriage. I slammed my palm against the illuminated exit sign. *Let me out!*

361

The door remained locked. The carriage began to move, rocking over the track, sliding out of the station.

★　★　★

'I'm sorry,' I'm saying to Phoebe — and then I am moving, stepping backwards, my hands feeling for the doorway, my eyes not able to leave the photo until I am on the landing, pulling the door behind me.

Blood roars in my ears as the realisation hits: Luke Linden was Maeve's first husband.

★　★　★

My feet seem disconnected from my body as I take the stairs, legs trembling. A voice somewhere within me is giving concise instructions. Coat. Keys. Leave.

At the bottom of the stairs, I can hear chatter from the lounge, the bark of my sister's laugh, the clink of a wine bottle against the lip of a glass. Tugging my coat from the stand, I pull it on, digging in the pockets to retrieve my car keys.

I should tell Maeve that I'm leaving, I know I must, because otherwise it will be cause for speculation. I take a breath, force a smile to stretch across my face, then I lean my head around the door.

'Sorry everyone, but I've got to slip off early tonight. Deadline looming.'

There is a collective murmur of surprise.

Really? But you've only just arrived.

Fiona is saying, 'I'll come with you.'

But I am shaking my head, holding up a hand, saying, 'No, I'll be fine.'

And then I am out of the lounge, reaching for the front door, stepping out into the night.

I feel the pavement beneath my feet, air in my lungs.

At my car, I pause, heart hammering. I place my hands against the cold bodywork, breathing in deeply. The wind has got up, gusting through my unbuttoned coat.

It feels as if the ground is spinning, veering. I lower my head, concentrating on breathing.

'Elle.'

I tense, as if my name on Maeve's lips is a blow.

Slowly I turn.

Maeve is standing behind me, her head tipped to one side. 'Everything okay?'

'Fine. Sorry for rushing off. I just need to get this book finished.'

Her gaze is steady as she looks straight at me, something knowing in her expression. 'Thought I heard you talking to Phoebe.'

I swallow. 'Wrong room.'

Maeve looks at me for a long moment, then nods. 'Go safe, then.'

I turn and fumble with the key fob, setting the alarm firing to life — the pavement flashes orange, a staccato of beeps bursts into the night. I swear beneath my breath as I press it again, managing to silence it.

I climb into my car, pull the door hard.

As I push the key into the ignition, Maeve's cool expression is sealed in my mind. I realise: *Maeve knows exactly who I am.*

29

Elle

'Endings are one of the greatest challenges for the author. But remember: the clues for the ending are always there, tucked within the pages of your earliest drafts. One must simply look for them.'

Author Elle Fielding

I pull into my driveway and park facing the house. I remain in the car, lights turned off, keys in the ignition, the engine ticking as it cools.

The cliff-top house looks lonely, imposing. The security lights cast gnarled shadows of the potted bay trees framing the front door, shapeshifting the coastal entrance into something gothic.

Looking up, I can see the lights are on at the top of the house. I think of my empty writing room live on Facebook, the lid of my oak trunk hinged open in the background.

I don't want to leave the car, go inside.

Everything is tangling together: the house . . . my book . . . Maeve . . . Linden.

He should have been my lecturer, me his student. That is all.

Forked-tongue. False allegation. Liar.

In the depths of a Cardiff police station, I'd

turned a corner and seen Luke Linden and his wife moving towards me. I'd known he was married in that vague, faceless use of the word, 'wife'. I'd heard a rumour that she was older than him, petite, attractive. I noticed her purple ankle boots first, suede, a stylishly placed zip, a flat heel. Her hair had been different back then — dyed raven black, pixie short. As she came nearer, I saw the round, distended bump of her pregnant stomach. One of her hands rested beneath it, as if trying to support some of the weight. She was talking to her husband, but a shift in atmosphere must have alerted her to my presence, as suddenly her gaze was swinging towards me, a blast of ice coming from her pale stare.

It was new to me — the feeling of being hated by another woman. I thought about that look for a long time. What did Luke Linden's wife think of the student with the narrow hips, her wide fawn-like eyes licked with mascara?

What did she think of the same girl who swooped into her life just four weeks before she was due to welcome a baby into the world, making an earth-tilting claim about the man she'd chosen to begin a family with?

What did Luke Linden's wife believe?

What would she be prepared to do for justice?

★ ★ ★

I sit forward, eyes lifting to the rear-view mirror. A car is approaching, headlights bouncing as the driver navigates the potholes in the dark, narrow lane. I watch as the vehicle passes the entrance to Enid and Frank's driveway. They are headed for my house.

The car pulls up directly behind me, sealing off the exit.

My heartbeat quickens.

Behind me, the headlights flick off. The driver's door opens — the wind snatching it wide. An interior light is triggered, illuminating the driver as they step out.

Maeve.

A cold feeling of dread reaches down into the pit of my stomach.

There is the slow crunch of gravel beneath feet. I'm pinned to my seat.

But the footsteps continue, passing my car.

Maeve hasn't seen me. She is heading towards the house. The hem of her red coat is lifted by the wind. She pauses on the floodlit doorstep, raps on the knocker.

It was Maeve, I think. Maeve who vandalised the library copies of my book, branding the word *Liar* beside my name. And, it must have been Maeve who, on the day of my library talk, circled the two words in my novel, subtle but pointed: *You Lied*.

As I watch her standing on my doorstep, chin lifted, I think about the lone figure Enid saw in my writing room. Something is unravelling from my memory, a thread of conversation . . . Maeve had talked about returning from a week-long retreat at the end of October. That was during the same period I was in France.

But what if there was no retreat? What if she'd

discovered that my house was available on Airbnb? What if she'd set up a fake profile, called herself Joanna?

Trapped here in the dark box of my car, blood pulsing thickly through my veins, I see it all now.

I left out a key. I left her flowers and a welcome note. I let her in.

★ ★ ★

Maeve lifts her fist to the door and knocks. Then she returns her hand to her pocket, rooting for something.

A key?

I wait, barely breathing, pressed into the seat.

My mobile phone flares to life, rattling across the dash, its flashing light reflecting in the windscreen. I snatch it up in a bid to silence it — and catch the name of the caller.

Maeve.

Slowly, I lift my gaze.

On my doorstep, Maeve has turned. Her face is in shadow, but I know her eyes are fixed on me.

'Yes?' I whisper into my mobile.

I hear the crunch of footsteps as Maeve moves towards my car, her voice strangely distended on the phone as she says, 'There you are.'

★ ★ ★

I could hit the central locking button. I could end the call and dial 999.

I don't.

I can feel something hardening in my chest.

My fingertips find the handle of the car door. Pull.

I step out into the bitter darkness, heart thundering. The wind whips my hair across my face.

The two of us eye one another. Maeve's lips are pursed. There is no smile in her expression.

'You were in Phoebe's room.'

'Yes.'

Her tone is steel. 'You saw his photo.'

'Luke Linden.' I've not spoken his name aloud in a decade.

Maeve must have known who I was since the day I arrived in town. But she said nothing. She watched. She waited.

For what? I wonder, panic beating in my chest.

The events of the past have become so distorted, I'm no longer sure of anything. The truth is something murky and changeable, a winding river, never still.

Did I lie?

Did he?

The security light flicks off and the driveway falls into sheer darkness. Behind me the sea rolls and shifts, churning waves breaking against the beach with a booming roar. If I turn, I know I'll see the grey-black expanse seething with white-water, smell the edge of a storm on the salt-wind.

Then I feel the grip of a leather glove against the bare skin at my wrist. 'I know the truth.'

The words buckle me, send me hurtling back,

through year upon year, to when I was a different girl, living in a different city, believing that truth was just one thing: a single line, either black or white, not anything in between.

2004

Why would anyone book a meeting before midday with a student? Elle had thought idly as she weaved towards the humanities block, her fingertips working through her bag to locate a stick of chewing gum. A burst of mint filled her mouth and she tossed her hair back as she climbed the stairs towards Luke Linden's office, practising the feeling of sobriety.

She knocked once, then sauntered in, still high on the effervescence of partying through the night, toxins rushing through her bloodstream.

She closed the door behind her.

Luke Linden wore a fresh shirt, his hair was clean, he smelt of aftershave and cigarettes. He seemed markedly older than the boys she'd left at the house party.

From behind his desk, he considered her, perhaps noting last night's dress, or the smudges of kohl beneath her eyes, or the fading scent of perfume on her skin.

'Good night, I take it?' A smile in his voice.

'Absolutely,' she'd said, twisting her lips around each syllable. 'Welsh reggae was only the start.'

She slouched in the plastic chair, like she was sitting with a friend in a coffee house: intimate, relaxed. There was a discord in the change of environments — just an hour ago she'd been lying on a sofa beneath a light projection on the ceiling, while around her people danced into the morning, and now, somehow, she'd been transported to the formality of her English lecturer's office.

She was aware of his gaze on her.

She looked up, met his eye.

'You're smiling to yourself.'

She touched her lips. Linden was watching her intently, mouth parted, eyes alert. She saw then what she had only half-guessed before: he was attracted to her. The certain knowledge of it was strangely deflating, like at a fairground, when the playing for a prize is more exciting than the winning of it.

He smiled slowly, revealing long incisors. The image of a wolf came to mind.

Her head had started to pound, and she wished she had skipped the meeting, gone straight home to bed. She wanted to eat something, shower.

The airless confines of the room were causing her head to spin. Pushing to her feet, she moved to the far wall, which was dotted with black and white prints of Shakespearean quotes. She looked at the nearest one.

'And though she be but little, she be fierce.'
A Midsummer's Night Dream

'Are you?' he asked.

She hadn't heard him move, slide out of his chair, come around his desk so that he was standing right behind her, his mouth close to her ear.

Uneasiness spread through her: the proximity

of him, the shut door, the suggestiveness of his tone. She wanted to step back but was hemmed in by a filing cabinet to her right, a wall to her left, and behind her, was him.

She could feel his breath against her neck.

She thought then of the oddness of being offered a lift home by Linden a few weeks earlier. Of the strange night she'd been followed to work and had turned and seen him. Of the shadowy figure down by the train tracks, his gaze on her window. Her stomach tightened with the sudden understanding.

'I need to — '

Her words were cut off by the twist of his fingers in her hair, wrapping the length of it around his fist.

Her head snapped back. There was the sensation of burning across the centre of her scalp, the scrape of fingers against her thigh as his other hand lifted the hem of her dress, yanked down her underwear.

Her throat was stretched so far back that her cry of 'No' came out as a whisper. She felt the sharp corner of the metal filing cabinet against her hip, smelt the spearmint bite of mouthwash, overlaid with cigarettes. Then pain, white and flooding.

Her thoughts seemed to detach from her body, rise to the ceiling. Her eyes fixed on the edge of a strip light, where a moth lay trapped in its plastic casing. She felt the beat of its wings as it tried, over and over, to take off into flight, the soft fibres of its body working against the ungiving plastic. She was willing it to find the gap it had entered by, but it was trapped, useless. She imagined the light sticky grip of the moth's legs as if it had landed on her chest, the dusty cover of its dark wings as they settled silently over her heart. It would die there, she knew.

There was a grunt, a sigh close to her ear.

A moment later, her hair was released from his fist. He stepped back. She heard a zip. A buckle. The squeak of leather as he re-seated himself behind his desk.

There was a knock at the office door. Luke Linden looked at her, smiled, then held one finger to his lips.

'Sssh.'

He clasped his hands together on top of a sheaf of papers, before saying, 'Yes?'

A secretary had a message from a student's mother. The secretary didn't cross the threshold into his office. If she had, she would have seen Elle still pressed against the filing cabinet, her face white, the sleeve of her dress falling from one shoulder.

'Thank you, Lynn,' he'd said affably. 'You can leave the door open, thanks.'

What amazed her was that, after the secretary had left, Luke Linden had signalled to the seat in front of his desk and said, 'So, about this essay of yours . . . '

★   ★   ★

She drifted through Bute Park, every sound startlingly acute — the rasping voice of a passer-by talking into a phone, the yip of a small

374

dog nosing a ball closer to its owner's feet, the dig of a trowel through the dark earth of a flowerbed.

Reaching her student house, she went straight to her room, locked the door. She heard the rattling of a train along the track beyond the house — and pulled the blind. She threw a scarf over her mirror, concealing the full length of it. Her whole body shook as she undressed. She put everything she'd been wearing into a bin bag: dress, underwear, shoes. Knotted it three times.

In the shower she lathered soap over every inch of her body, while Claire banged on the door, yelling, 'Hurry the fuck up!'

Elle turned the dial further until water scalded her skin like hot needles. She angled her face up into the stream of liquid, letting it pour into her nostrils, her open mouth, the corners of her eyes.

Afterwards, she dried herself carefully. And then . . . then there was no other plan. No what to do next. She took out a book, tried to read, but couldn't. She sat in the lounge and stared at a day-time television show while her housemates went to and from lectures, in and out of the kitchen, made cheese toasties and countless mugs of tea. She told anyone who asked that she was hungover — and they laughed and said no more.

That night, she didn't sleep. The television kept vigil, repeats of *Friends* playing through the dark hours, canned laughter like a drill in her head.

The following morning, she stayed in her room until her housemates had left for lectures, and then she pushed her feet into trainers and began to walk.

There was no route, no plan, no direction. Just her feet against pavements, turning down paths, walking in the shadows of buildings, rising over a bridge, passing a dock, a cement yard, a parade of shops.

The beat of her steps finally stopped. Her heels were blistered, calves tight. She looked up at the building. Grey breeze blocks, weather-stained and blunt. From the flat roof, a flag whimpered in the breeze. A sign read:

Police
Heddlu

She climbed the concrete steps, pushed open the doors. Disinfectant, stale sweat, reheated food. A reception desk. Plastic chairs. A vending machine.

Then, later, a windowless room. Two officers, one male, one female. The male officer leant back in his chair, pushing aside a thinning curtain of auburn hair. He looked at her carefully.

'It's a very serious allegation.'

In that one sentence, she realised that was all it was — an allegation. Not the truth. Not a lie. Simply an allegation.

30

Elle

Maeve faces me in the dark driveway, her fingers curled around my wrist. 'You lied.'

I'm aware of the sea behind us, the flicker of my pulse beating beneath her grip.

'That's what I thought — that you'd made it up. Wanted the attention.' Her hand drops away. 'But I was wrong, wasn't I?'

I blink. Her question is distant, as if being pitched from a far-off place.

'When I asked Luke what happened, he looked me in the eye and told me, unequivocally, that he didn't touch you.' She swallows. 'I believed him. He was my husband. His baby was growing inside me. I had our future as a family mapped out. I had to believe him.'

I hold myself very still. I do not speak.

'And then, days later, you dropped the charges. Left the course. Quit university.'

I remember the sidelong glances of my course-mates, the hushed whispers within the walls of my student house.

'No one believed me,' I say at last, my voice thin, a shadow.

Maeve stares at me.

'I told the police that I thought he'd been following me. That he'd been lurking outside my

377

student house. I told them he'd picked me up once in his car, but he denied it. He had an alibi.'

'Me.'

I nod. 'You lied for him.'

'I worked in the humanities library — I saw all the young students flirting with him, trying to impress him. I listened to the whisperings beyond the bookshelves.' She pauses, eyes fixed on mine. 'Do you know, I heard you once? You were talking to another girl. I was standing nearby stacking books on a trolley. The girl you were with asked if you'd fuck him.'

The comment makes me flinch. I remember the day, remember the librarian standing nearby with her back to us. I know every word of the answer I'd given.

'In my mind, you were a girl who'd let her imagination ride wild. I believed so deeply in my husband that I wanted everyone else to have the measure of you.'

I blink. 'What do you mean?'

'I made sure I discussed the situation with colleagues loud enough for students to overhear. I wanted the wind of favour to shift, for people to suspect *you*. To doubt *you*.'

My head shakes from side to side as I begin to understand. 'You posted an envelope through my student door, didn't you?'

Maeve looks at me as she nods. She says the word that was written inside with red lipstick. 'Liar.'

I can feel tears leaking from the edges of my eyes. 'When did you find out the truth?'

She shifts, gravel crunching beneath her feet. 'Four years later. A girl came into the library — must have found out I was Luke's wife. She said, *Get your husband to stop stalking me!* She told me they'd screwed a couple of times, but he'd become obsessed, kept following her between her workplace and student house. That he'd had her pinned up against a wall.'

A slick of bile rises in my throat.

'I knew then he'd lied about you.'

I cup my fingers around my mouth, breathing the warm, moist air trapped in my hands. The ground seems to sway.

'I thought,' I whisper, 'that I was wrong. That I had . . . remembered it incorrectly. No one believed me. Not the police. Not my friends. I didn't even tell my family. I was scared they wouldn't believe me either.'

When I'd gone to the police, I felt like it was my word thrown into question. They had focused on the alcohol and drugs, the outfit I'd been wearing, the flirtatious comments I'd made the weeks before. But not what happened in that room, not the moment I said, *No.* It had confounded me so deeply, cast such a dark shadow of doubt that I'd questioned myself, my ability to recall the specific details of what had happened, my own culpability.

If I'd amended the truth — not told them that, *Yes, there had been a point at which I was attracted to him; Yes, I'd snorted coke just hours before; Yes, I'd flirted with him in a bar the previous night; Yes, I'd curtsied to him in a lecture hall filled with students* — if I'd missed out those details, shaped it into a clearer storyline that pointed more firmly to 'Truth', then perhaps I would have been believed.

I've learned in the years since that truth is something varying and slippery, and that lies sometimes help shade in the harder areas of the truth. That knowledge has altered me, caused me to misjudge situations, make wrong decisions — bend a fact so far that it can no longer return to its former shape. Black and white have become layers of grey.

'I thought about trying to locate you, telling you I believed you,' Maeve says. 'But I didn't. I feared dredging it up — for Phoebe's sake. Then, all these years later, I saw your photo on the back of a book I was unpacking in the library. I couldn't believe it was you. A bestselling author.' She pauses, shaking her head. 'You had turned your life around. He hadn't robbed you of that.'

My teeth meet my lower lip, pressing down into the warm flesh.

She has no idea how he has changed my life.

'I want you to know,' Maeve says, 'that the day that second girl visited me in the library, I left him. I packed our things, collected Phoebe from pre-school, and drove straight to Cornwall to stay with my mother. I left Luke a note and said if he came looking for us, I'd go to the police myself.'

'Did he?'

She shakes her head. 'We never saw him again.'

'He drowned.'

Maeve sets her hands in the deep pockets of

380

her coat. 'It was suicide.'

My eyes widen.

'I received a letter from him at my mother's the day his body was found. He wrote that he couldn't reconcile the two men that lived in him: the father, and the 'other' as he referred to himself. I didn't tell the police about the letter. I've told no one, not my mother, not Steven, and certainly not my daughter.'

She pauses, looking me straight in the eye. 'I do not want Phoebe to find out who he really was. Ever. In her mind, Luke Linden is a loving father who tragically drowned. That is the story.' She takes a breath. 'I know you don't owe me a thing. But I'm asking you — begging you — to keep it that way.'

I think about the manuscript saved on my laptop, the story of a girl who wasn't believed, of a man who misused his position of power. I think of the pregnant wife I've written about, the scenes that I've laboured over, crafted.

Lived.

'Promise me,' Maeve says.

31

Elle

'Shift the lens on your characters. Adjust the angle of the lens to reveal — or expose — the truth of their character.'
Author Elle Fielding

The sea lies before me, flat and unruffled by wind, glassy in the thin morning light. Behind me, tall fronds of dune grass neither sway nor shiver. Footprints on the sand remain cemented there. A stillness pervades the air and I feel suspended, held by it, as if each moment is stretched.

I drop my towel and wade forward. The sea parts and folds, enveloping me in its icy embrace. I can't regulate my breathing and I fight against the cold with jerking uneven strokes and frantic kicks, my muscles contracting, shrinking.

The light refracts through the water, so my limbs look distant, ghost-white.

It takes me longer than normal, but eventually I find a rhythm. With each stroke, each kick, my breath begins to regulate. The clarity of my thought becomes centred, sharpens.

I think of Luke Linden. Out here in the water, this is my space, my terms. I wonder where life would have taken me if I'd been believed. If I'd believed in myself. Would I have stayed at university, completed my degree? Would I still have met Flynn? Still travelled? Still walked into an abortion clinic? Or would I have had the confidence in myself, in my decisions, to think differently? And what if there'd been no Luke Linden at all? Who would I have been then?

My mind drifts to my unfinished manuscript. I've weaved a story out of the dark places that I've never spoken about, of the nineteen-year-old girl and the lecturer in a corduroy jacket.

I think of Maeve's request.

I have no intention of hurting Phoebe. I've worked with fake names and locations, a new timeline. It will appear to readers as a work of fiction. Only Maeve and I will know the truth in the pages. After all, this is my story. It is up to me how I tell it.

I swim to shore with a burst of kicks.

Now I know exactly how my novel will end.

★ ★ ★

This novel, which has tormented and eluded me, which has seeped into my dreams, caused me to tear reams of paper from my notebooks and crush them into pellets — now opens up. I can see precisely how I will draw the threads together.

I have two days left to do it.

I hurry upstairs to the writing room, bare feet pounding against wood. Pushing open the door, I don't even glance out to sea as I move into position in front of my desk, hair still wet, no coffee to prop me up. I feel the burning heat of inspiration. It is like being lit from the inside.

Somewhere downstairs, I'm aware of my phone ringing. I ignore it. There isn't room for anything else. Only this story.

My fingertips fizz with anticipation as I log in to my computer and open my *Author* document folder, then click on my manuscript. When it opens, a sheer white screen eyeballs me.

I scroll down — but the entire document is blank.

I blink, confused. It can't be. I'd been writing yesterday afternoon. I'd saved my work. This must be a file permission error.

I snatch a breath. Close the folder, and then reopen it.

The Word document is there, but once again, when I click on it, the pages are completely blank.

It's fine, I tell myself as panic begins to spill through my chest. Everything is automatically saved to the Cloud, and I also have a folder called *Errata*, where I save previous versions of the manuscript so that I can see the changes throughout the drafting process. I go there first, looking for the most recent draft I've saved.

But when I open the document folder — it, too, is empty. There is not a single version of my manuscript, not even my earliest copy.

My teeth press into the flesh of my lips as I think of the Facebook Live that had broadcast last night from my empty writing room. *As if someone has been in here.*

My palms are sweating as I log in to the Cloud to access the online version of my files, but as I open it up, I have the awful sensation that the manuscript won't be there either.

I click on *Author, Book 2*.

Blank.

The back-up of my *Errata* document folder: blank.

Everything: blank, blank, BLANK!

I slam my hands against the desk, making my water glass jump, liquid sloshing over the rim.

Stay calm, I instruct, fighting against the panic that is ricocheting through my chest. *Just think*.

I take several deep breaths, feeling my ribcage expanding. This is a mistake. Just a mistake. My novel will be somewhere. My computer could have a virus and it has spread to my back-up files. I've saved my work. Of course I have. It'll be somewhere.

At least once a week, I email my manuscript to myself, so that the document stays on a server, not only my hard-drive. It is a failsafe. I probably haven't done it for a few days, but at the very least, the previous version will be there, tucked away in my archive folder of sent emails.

I open my email account, ignoring the latest batches of messages that flood in, and go straight to *Archives*.

'No . . . ' I whisper as I look at the empty screen. There is absolutely nothing there. Not a single saved email. I click on my *Sent* folder — but it, too, is empty.

I'm blinking rapidly as I trawl through my *Deleted* folder, then my *Recycle Bin*, but there are no messages from myself in there, either.

I push away from my desk, standing. I pace across the writing room, hands clenching and unclenching, trying to make sense of what I'm seeing.

Have I even written a fucking novel? Is this . . . all in my head?

I laugh at the sheer lunacy of the thought. Of course I have written it! I was writing yesterday. I've lived it. Breathed it. I was sitting right here, adding to it, shaping it, coaxing it nearer to an ending.

I have written a book. And now it is gone.

* * *

Maeve. Her name appears in my thoughts like a shot being fired.

I can hear the steel in her voice as she'd warned that Phoebe must never learn the truth about Luke Linden. Would she have deleted the manuscript?

She was capable of falsifying an alibi, and of sullying my name to protect her husband. What lengths would she go to in order to protect her daughter?

When I was writing in the library, I'd left my laptop for several minutes — long enough for Maeve to read a scene or two, decide she couldn't let my manuscript be published.

I press the heels of my hands hard into my eye sockets, trying to think. I revisit the idea that Maeve had rented this house under the fake profile of Joanna. Was her husband, PC Steven

Cart, somehow involved? My thoughts are spinning faster and faster, none of them quite connecting.

I need to speak to Maeve. It can't wait.

I hurry downstairs, shove my feet into boots, yank my coat from its hook. As I am pushing my arms into the sleeves, pulling the collar to my neck — that is when I feel it. Something solid, yet fragile beneath my fingertips.

I glance down.

Then scream.

I tear at the coat, ripping it from my body, pulling my arms free. I wrench open the front door and fling it out of the house. It collapses on my doorstep, deflated, inanimate.

I slam the door, then stand in the hallway, hands clasped to my throat, heart skittering.

A dead moth, its powdered wings sealed against its body, has been pinned to my coat.

A guttural cry leaves my throat.

I press myself back against the wall. My legs are shaking, threatening to buckle.

I hear a noise, spin around. But it is just my own breath, ragged and uneven.

I catch sight of myself in the mirror — I am ghost-white. The balance of my face seems altered: my cheekbones are too prominent, my eyes sunken. I press my palm against my forehead as if checking a child for a temperature — but the skin there is cool to touch.

I think of Maeve taking my coat at book club last night, hanging it on her wooden stand. Has she done this? Or someone else who was there? The whole book club knows about my mottephobia.

I screw my eyes shut. Maybe it is all in my mind. Other recent mistakes spread like heat in my thoughts: the missing author talk notes; the bathroom tap I left running; the funeral I missed; my utter conviction that I'd been locked in my writing room.

I open my eyes, instructing myself to move. My fingers grip the door latch. I open it, heart hammering. My coat lies puddled on the step. I inch closer, as if expecting it to lurch awake. The collar is obscured. With my foot, I nudge the material. I need to be sure.

I peer down.

There it is. A dead moth attached to the collar. Its wings dusky brown, its body barred with pink and black. A safety pin pierces its abdomen, pinning it in the exact place of my missing brooch.

This isn't in my head.

It is real.

32

Elle

'Can you come over?' I whisper into my phone.

There is no hesitation. No question. 'I'm on my way.'

Fifteen minutes later, Fiona is standing on the front step, my coat dangling from her hand.

'Having a clear-out?'

I step back. 'Look at the collar.'

Fiona pulls the material closer — then her face screws up. 'What the hell is that?'

'Someone pinned it to my coat.'

'You are bullshitting — ' She stops when she sees my expression.

'Leave it outside,' I instruct.

I pull my sister into the house, hurriedly telling her about the deleted manuscript. I'm aware my explanation sounds surreal, breathless, as words spill from my lips.

Eventually Fiona holds up her hands. 'I need to see it. Let me look at your computer.'

* * *

Fiona peers at the screen, her brow furrowed as she examines the blank documents where my manuscript should have been.

'I don't understand . . . '

I feel vindicated that she is witnessing this, too.

Fiona's head shakes from side to side as she says, 'I just don't see — '

'How this could've happened?'

★ ★ ★

We go downstairs.

Daylight has faded into dusk, but the kitchen feels overly bright, everything too vivid, the sound of my footsteps beating against wood, the tick of the clock, the roar of waves through the open window.

I talk, pace, talk.

Fiona watches me, saying nothing.

'My deadline is tomorrow. There's no book to deliver — not even part of one.' My head shakes as I race through the implications. 'The novel is scheduled for release next summer. The copy editor is booked. The production plans are in place. The design team are poised and ready to begin work on the jacket. All that wasted time, wasted money. They'll drop me. The contract will be void. I'm going to lose this house. Lose everything.'

Fiona goes to the fridge and I watch her take out a pint of milk. Then she finds a pan in a lower cupboard. She is, I realise, going to make hot chocolate. It is what our mother always did when we were girls.

'Sit.'

I park myself on a kitchen stool. There's something vaguely comforting about my sister

392

clattering around the kitchen, sprinkling chocolate powder into the pan, searching out a
wooden spoon.

'What do you think is happening?' I ask.

I want her to make a joke, something dry and
barbed to cut through my anxiety, but instead
her gaze slides away from me — and that's when
I realise.

I stiffen, my voice lit. 'You don't believe me.'

She turns slowly, looks right at me. Her gaze is
searching, as if she is looking for something
recognisable in my face.

'You think I pinned a dead moth to my own
coat? Deleted my own manuscript?' My
fingertips turn white as I press them into the
granite counter.

After a moment she says, 'Why, Elle? Why
would anyone do these things to you?' She is
looking at me expectantly.

Because, I think, *I deserve it.*

Tears threaten to spill from the corners of my
eyes. 'I don't want to stay here tonight.'

She nods slowly. 'I'll make up the sofa bed.'

'Thank you.'

She takes out her phone, sends a quick
message to let Bill know I'll be coming, then sets
her phone on the counter.

'Do you want me to drive you?'

'I'll follow. I need to pack a few bits.'

Fiona looks at me. 'It's going to be okay,
Elle.'

I swallow, nod.

She hands me the wooden spoon. 'Now, stir
that. I need to pee.'

I lean against the range cooker, stirring methodically. The smell of warming chocolate reaches me and is followed by a wave of exhaustion. All I want to do is shut my eyes, sleep, let everything else fade away.

Ringing cuts across the kitchen. It's Fiona's phone.

'I'll get it,' I call, swiping at the screen. 'Hello?'

'Is this Fiona Henley's number?'

'Yes, it is. I'm her sister, Elle.'

'Elle with the cliff-top house?'

'Yes . . . '

'Joanna Elmer. From Airbnb. I was meant — '

'Joanna?' I say, staggered. I'm filled with a burst of sheer and brilliant relief that she is real, that she exists. 'I've been trying to get in touch with you,' I rush. 'I messaged you, but your account has been closed down.'

'Yes. That hacking problem. Very frustrating.'

Her voice is crisply articulate, well-educated — a voice that fits her profile picture exactly. All those dark-winged thoughts about the mystery person who rented my house scatter. Joanna and her family stayed here, in this house.

'I'm pleased I got through to you,' Joanna says, and I notice the tightening in her tone. 'I've been talking to some friends who've used Airbnb a great deal, and they've led me to realise that it was incorrect for me to pay the full amount. I don't want to be difficult — and I should have thought of this at the time, but with everything that was happening, my mind was elsewhere, as I'm sure you can understand — but anyway, I've had a chance to look back through the terms and conditions, and they do clearly state that in the case of a cancellation more than twenty-four hours before, that fifty per cent of the original balance should be paid.' She draws a breath. 'It was more than twenty-four hours before, by the way. I checked. It was twenty-six hours if we're being pernickety.'

'A cancellation?' My heart stalls.

'Yes. When I rang to cancel, your manager didn't tell me that I was entitled to a partial refund.'

I'm staring into the pan, a milky skin forming on the end of the wooden spoon.

'Are you telling me that you *didn't* stay in the cliff-top house?'

'I explained it all to the manager,' she says, a hint of exasperation in her tone. 'My sister-in-law had appendicitis, so we had to go up to the Midlands to look after her children and . . .'

'And you told all this to my . . . to Fiona?'

'She was very sweet about it, said it wasn't a problem. But there was no talk of a refund or rescheduling. In the heat of the drama, I didn't question it. It's only now that I think it was, well, rather unfair.'

I turn very cold. If Joanna and her family didn't stay here, why hadn't Fiona told me? Had she kept the rental money for herself?

No, of course she hadn't — the payment had come directly into my account. I'd seen the transaction on my online statement.

Why, then?

I recall the evening I arrived back from France. The house was clean and much as I'd left it, save for a few items Joanna's family had left behind — a pot of nappy rash cream, a toy giraffe, and some hair wax. If they hadn't belonged to Joanna's family, whose were they?

'The refund?'

My attention is jolted back to the call. Joanna is waiting for some sort of answer.

'Yes ... yes, you can have the refund. I'll organise it right away.'

I end the call and set Fiona's mobile on the counter.

Directly above me, I can hear Fiona's footsteps. Hadn't she said she was going to the bathroom? Only the bathroom isn't above the kitchen: my bedroom is.

My heartbeat gathers pace as I listen to her crossing the landing, descending the stairs. I am still standing by the counter when Fiona returns to the kitchen.

'Did I hear my phone go?'

'It was mine.'

I glance up and find Fiona looking at me carefully. 'Everything okay?'

I force myself to nod, smile. I move to the stove, keeping my gaze on the pan.

'You get off. I'll drink this, pack my stuff, and follow on.'

Fiona steps closer, so that she is standing at my back. She leans her head over my shoulder, so our cheeks are almost touching.

'Oh,' she says. 'You ruined it.'

I freeze.

'The hot chocolate. You let the milk burn.'

I take the stairs, keeping the lights off. I pause at the landing window and watch my sister cross the driveway towards her car.

Air leaves my lungs in shallow puffs. My face is pressed so close to the window that a small cloud of condensation forms on the glass.

Why didn't Fiona tell me that Joanna had cancelled her reservation?

Someone stayed here, that I am certain of. Had Fiona double-let it? Taken the money from a second family and kept it?

Another possibility comes forward: Drake had been staying with Bill's parents the same week that I'd been away. Fiona had been on her own. When she learned that Joanna was cancelling the booking, maybe she had decided to stay here instead.

As I watch Fiona climb into her car, I recall Enid's remark that she'd seen someone in the room at the top of this house.

Fiona?

As a child, I remember the way Fiona would wander into my room, casually looking through my things, her fingers flicking through the pages of my exercise books or turning over my pencil case to examine the doodling on the back. She'd pluck free a letter I'd written to a friend, reading it with her back against the wall as if my property were hers.

If Fiona had found her way into my writing room, her curiosity would've been piqued. I picture her moving across the room, glancing at the titles on my bookshelf, pulling open my desk drawers. And then what? Where did she stop?

The skin across the nape of my neck tightens as I picture the word carved into the leg of my writing desk. *Liar.*

A single thought ticks back and forth: *She has found it.*

★   ★   ★

I race to the top of the house, taking the stairs two at a time.

My palm smacks at the light switch. I rush straight to the oak trunk, yank open the lid, and begin pulling out journals, diaries, old notebooks. I'm looking for a tan leather cover, timeworn and soft.

I cast aside the bundle of cards from Flynn, an old mix tape, a notebook covered in Polaroid images, a file with a geometric pattern of daisies.

Where is it?

It should be right here at the bottom of the trunk, hidden beneath photo albums and notebooks. I haven't looked inside the file for months — it makes it easier to pretend it doesn't exist.

The floor around me is a spill of letters and photos and diaries. Then I spot it — an edge of leather, the mark of time showing in the softened corners of the file. It is still in the trunk! My heart skips with relief.

I draw out the file, but as I do, I'm aware that

something is wrong. The weight of it in my hands is off-beat, the thickness incorrect.

My breathing is shallow as I open the cover. No . . .

The file is completely empty.

⋆   ⋆   ⋆

I turn sharply, alert. I haven't heard the crunch of gravel beneath tyres.

Getting to my feet, I cross the writing room, moving swiftly down the dark stairway. Reaching the landing window, I pause there, leaning close, hands pressed to the cold glass.

Fiona's car is still parked in the drive. The interior light is on and I watch as Fiona takes out her mobile, the screen casting a cool glow on her face. She is checking something on her phone.

Then my sister lifts her gaze, until she is looking right up at the house, as if she knows I am standing here against the dark window.

A beat later, the car door opens.

Fuck!

The floodlights burst to life. A shiver peels down my spine as I watch my sister approach my front door.

I brace myself for the sound of the knocker. I don't have to let her in. I could pretend I haven't heard — that I was in the shower.

I need time to think. Need to get everything straight.

But there is no knock at the door.

There is the sound, faint and low, of a key in a

lock. Then a cold breeze travelling up the stairway. I can hear the edges of the blinds in the hall move, the cord tapping against the window pane. And then it stops. The door has been shut.

Fiona is inside.

33

Elle

'Have a sense of how your story will end — but allow yourself to step into your character's shoes and be surprised.'
Author Elle Fielding

I wait by the window, barely breathing. Blood pulses in my ears as I listen to the rhythmic clack of boot heels as Fiona rises through the house.

I catch the swish of her long coat on the staircase, the slide of her bracelets against the polished wood bannister.

I move then, turning, lurching upstairs to the top of the house, reaching for the light. I stand in the illuminated doorway, arms outstretched, blocking the entrance of my writing room.

Fiona emerges slowly from the stairway: the crown of her head, the dark rise of her brows, the straight line of her nose, the black fall of her coat with her handbag strung from one shoulder. On the landing, she halts. She looks straight at me, eyes glittering, a white, pinched look to her face.

She says nothing.

Silence wraps around us, pulling us deeper into each other's gazes. We are exactly the same height, I think, her eyes matching mine.

My heart is beating hard, fast. It feels as if

something is straining beneath my skin, a pressure against a seam that is threatening to tear.

Eventually I say, 'You let yourself into my house.'

'I have a key.' Her voice is nothing I recognise. Flat, emotionless. A dead voice.

'I had the locks changed.'

'You keep a spare in your bureau.'

My God.

Fiona places her long-boned hands into the wide pockets of her coat. 'You answered my phone to Joanna.'

My voice emerges as something strange, thin. 'She never stayed here.'

'That's right.'

'Who did?'

Fiona's mouth curves into the lightest of smiles. 'I think you've already worked out the answer.'

I look at my sister. 'You.'

A single nod.

'Why?'

'Joanna cancelled. The house was completely empty — all paid for. Why not?'

'That's not a reason.'

'I need a better one, do I? Then, how about this: Drake was with Bill's parents. I had brochure copy to finish and knew I'd be distracted working at home, so I decided to stay in your house. The *writer's* house.'

The coldness of that last sentence hits like a spray of ice.

'If you'd asked, I'd have let you stay.'

'I called you in France. Three times.'

'I didn't have reception. But you could have told me afterwards — '

Fiona laughs, a sharp brittle note. I expect her to say something further, but there is nothing more.

I listen to the distant roll and crash of waves breaking beyond the house.

'Your car wasn't here,' I pitch into the quiet.

'I took a taxi. I wanted everything to be different. I wanted to walk into this house on my own — not as your sister, not as a wife, or a mother — but just as *me*.' Her voice is emotionless, a knife turned blunt. 'I wanted to come here, into this serene, quiet space, and experience the privilege which you live with daily: to sit at your own desk, looking out over the water, and write.'

'This room was locked.'

Fiona shrugs, and in that gesture I understand that my sister thought nothing of breaking in. Dread tightens in my chest: once Fiona stepped inside my writing room, I know exactly what she'd have found.

★   ★   ★

She comes towards me — and I step back.

Fiona skirts me, hands pushed deep into the pockets of her winter coat. I watch her enter my writing room, and I'm reminded of the way she would wander into my childhood bedroom, her gaze sweeping along my shelves, moving across my wardrobe, running over the soft toys huddled at the head of my bed. She would seize upon something — a favourite picture book, a pen in a glittering shade — and decide to take it back to her own room, just to borrow it, because *We must share, Elle*. Had that been the assertion of an older, strong-willed sibling? Or had there always been a sense of entitlement — as if Fiona knew she could take whatever she wished from me?

'Do you know,' Fiona begins, chin raised, voice steely, 'since you've had this house, I've only been up to your writing room once? It was before you'd finished it completely. You wanted to show me this desk.'

She sets her handbag on top of it. Her fingertips trace the grain in the wood.

'I can imagine how hard Flynn must have worked to restore it. A writer's desk — for his little writer. He believed in you so completely.' She eases out the top drawer, as if admiring the smoothness of the runners, the craftsmanship. She doesn't close it.

'I wondered why you never brought me up here. I guessed it was because you felt awkward. Here you were with the ultimate writer's room. The resplendent oak desk with the sea view. The wide, open space uncluttered by crap. The beautifully upholstered reading chair. It's perfect, Elle. Truly. You've created a sanctuary. Perhaps you were being tactful in not wanting to shove this down my throat, that's what I thought, because who wouldn't feel a little whisper of envy?'

I stare at my sister, aware of the unevenness of my breathing.

'I sat right here, at your desk. It was the first time since Drake that I'd had time to myself, to write. Of course, I don't get the freedom to write what I want, like you. That — to pull a story together from images in your mind — that's a magician's trick. A privilege.'

She pauses, her gaze sliding to my bookcase.

'Do you remember those books I used to make as a child? I'd take a pile of paper from Mum's printer, and fold the sheets in half, stapling the centre to make the spine of a book. I'd write endless stories, then line them up on my bookshelf, imagining that they were mine, published.'

I listen closely, my senses keen to the inflections in her tone.

'I finished writing the brochure copy in two days. It's incredible quite how much one can achieve without distractions. Once I was finished, I sat at your desk, looking out, feeling a strange absence of purpose. It unsettled me — Drake being away, Bill working, you in France, Mum gone.'

She pauses again, as if her thoughts are wandering in a new direction. 'When we cleared out Mum's flat, I barely kept anything. A couple of pieces of her rose-gold jewellery, some photos, that peacock-print scarf I loved. I'm sure you thought I was ruthless when I boxed up the rest. But I didn't want her clothes or her books or her furniture or her record collection: I wanted her.

'I wish someone had told me that, later, I may want those things. I knew you'd kept more and so I went over to your trunk,' she says, crossing the room towards it. 'I wanted to look at some photos of Mum or see if there was anything special you'd kept.'

Fiona kneels in front of the trunk among the sprawl of photos and notebooks.

'There's an album in here that I hadn't seen in years. It was from one of our trips to Cornwall. We came to this bay. Picnicked here.'

She reaches for a navy photo album, pale fingers turning through the sleeves until she locates the photo she is after.

'Look,' she says, holding it up. 'You can see the original fisherman's cottage that stood on the cliff.'

Fiona is right. I haven't noticed it before and now feel a strange sense of connection, a gossamer thread running between our past and present.

'Mum always wanted it. She pointed it out to us as girls, said how much she'd loved it, couldn't imagine any better place to write.'

I blink slowly. *Had she?* I have a vague childhood memory of sitting on a red tasselled blanket in the bay below, our mother looking up at the cliff.

'But you had to knock it down. Build something bigger, grander.'

I go to speak, but Fiona has picked up another photo. It shows our mother perched in the window seat of the caravan we used to rent, a notebook balanced on her knees, a curtain of hair falling to one side of her face as she writes. It is clear she hadn't known the photo was being taken, and I can't recall now whether it'd been me or Fiona behind the camera.

Fiona looks up, her gaze unflinching. 'Mum always wanted to be a writer. It was her dream, wasn't it?'

I say nothing.

'I carried on looking through the trunk. There are so many precious things in here — photos and letters and diaries and notebooks. And then I came across something that caught me completely off-guard.'

My breathing is shallow now, harder to draw.

'It was a leather-bound file. At first, I thought it was another photo album.'

Tan, timeworn.

'But when I opened it, I realised it was something completely different. I don't need to tell you what was inside, do I?'

It is as if all the blood is draining from my body. My arms feel heavy and cool; my fingertips tingle.

Fiona's voice doesn't change, doesn't hurry.

'Do you know how much it hurt to discover you'd been writing a book, but hadn't thought to tell me? You didn't come to me for help, or encouragement — you did it in secret. When I complained to Bill, he told me to let it go, that it was natural for you to want to strike out alone, wait until you had something solid to share. But I found it hurtful. It was embarrassing when friends asked about it — and I had to admit, *Actually, I had no idea.* It showed up the cracks in our relationship.'

I remember calling Fiona to share the news of my book deal. My palms had been sweating so much that the phone had felt slippery within my grip. My voice was unnaturally casual as I'd said, 'Hey, I've got a bit of news!' I'd not mentioned I was working on a novel previously, because I'd worried that she'd say something, or simply deploy one of her looks, which would give away exactly what she was thinking: *Elle, you're only playing at it.*

'So, I admit that I was intrigued,' Fiona continues, 'to see the starting point for the story that launched you. Because, one moment you are my little sister — the wanderer, the part-time barista, the light-hearted free spirit.'

She draws a breath, steel entering her voice. 'But the next moment, you are an author. A bestselling, internationally-recognised author. An author whose debut novel won a host of awards. And I wondered to myself: how does one make that transition? It was like I'd missed some essential part of the plot.'

Fiona has risen to her feet. She stares intently at me as her next words cut through the room:

'And I had, hadn't I?'

I hold myself completely still. From the very moment it began, I have been waiting for this. Waiting for the truth to be cracked open and the hundreds of tiny lies I've told to come wriggling out, like maggots feeding on the rotten core.

'Because it's not your book, is it, Elle?'

34

Elle

Readers always want to know how it happened. To understand the journey from aspiring writer to published author.

For me it was a series of moments, a string of interactions, tiny pearls of excitement, of anxiety, of choices, which, when strung together, finally became the weight that hangs at my neck.

It happened when Flynn was abroad. He'd accepted a four-week job on a film set in Spain creating a haunted wood for an indie movie. It had been arranged through a tree surgeon friend and was too good to turn down. If he had remained in Bristol, would it have changed things? Probably.

As Flynn kissed me goodbye, he'd clasped the tops of my arms, dipping his head so he could look me straight in the eye.

'Good luck with the publishers. Ring me the minute you're out of the meeting. I want to know everything.'

So I had. I'd stepped from the revolving doors onto a busy London pavement, already reaching for my mobile. I was eager to share every detail: the receptionists in their tailored black uniforms and headsets; the glass lift rocketing through the building; the view from the twelfth floor over the snaking brown Thames. I would tell him about how the senior commissioning editor had loved my story, how we'd talked about my characters and, for the first time, the story felt real. And then I'd tell him: *I've got to think of another book idea by tomorrow!* They want to see '*the scope of my ideas*'. Flynn would laugh, congratulate me, tell me this was incredible news.

But Flynn hadn't answered.

Back at our Bristol flat, I made a coffee and settled myself on the sofa, a notepad on my knee. An idea for a second book by tomorrow! It was absurd, but also strangely energising to have a sudden goal — a deadline of sorts. It made my dream feel excitingly close.

I began jotting down thoughts, digging deep into the recesses of my memory. Old ideas fluttered past, like birds soaring across the edge of my vision — too quick to see their full plume.

I recalled a glimpse of an idea about a woman driving a dusty pickup across the Canadian plains, a baby strapped into the passenger seat, a smear of blood on the headlights, a clump of human hair caught on the bumper. But when I tried to examine the idea more closely, I couldn't see the woman's expression, couldn't zoom in on any details to reveal how the plot may unfold.

I made another coffee and paced the flat as I sipped it, scalding my top lip. I only needed something loose, a paragraph or two would do. Just a concept. As my agent had said, it was simply to display breadth of ideas.

'Even if they offer you a two-book deal, you won't be tied to the idea.'

A two-book deal. My God, the thought of it!

I sank onto the sofa, pushing aside a cardboard box filled with my mother's photo albums. A fresh wave of grief reared up, fierce and sudden. I would have loved to speak to her, to stay up late into the night bouncing around ideas, pulling out threads from other stories we'd loved, discussing ways to weave them into something fresh.

I considered — then dismissed — the idea of ringing Fiona. I could imagine the clipped edge to her tone, her surprise that I had been to see a publisher without her knowledge. No, I had come this far on my own.

A ten-minute break, then back to my notebook, I decided.

I reached for one of my mother's old albums and flicked through the photos in their plastic sleeves. It was a Christmas album filled with winter pallor, me and Fiona sitting on a pink carpet, surrounded by a sea of used wrapping paper. I picked up the next album, covered in soft, tan leather, but as I opened it, I was surprised to find, not photos, but a sheaf of papers filled with our mother's sloping handwriting. My first thought was that they were a collection of letters, but as I began looking through the pages, I noted the chapter heads.

I drew it onto my lap, expecting it to be one of my mother's stories that I'd seen before; yet, as I began to read, the words were completely fresh, unfamiliar. It felt like treasure, a piece of my mother that I hadn't worn smooth by stroking the memory of it.

411

Within minutes, I was lost in the story. It was like disappearing into an effervescent dream — the characters so real that I wanted to reach into the pages, sit with them, talk with them, cry alongside them.

The light faded from the room, hours slipping past. I moved only to turn on a lamp, to pull a blanket over my knee. The story consumed me, the deft beauty of it, the plot that weaved so many strands into a single, textured narrative. The breathless pace.

It was morning when I finished the final page. Outside I heard birds chirping, the beep of a van reversing, the huff of a bin lorry. I was exhausted, yet utterly elated. Look what our mother had done! I couldn't wait to share this with Fiona.

I set aside the manuscript, deciding to take a quick shower, clear my head, and then push on. I only had a few hours to get back to my agent.

As steaming water sluiced over my scalp, I saw it: the fresh bloom of blood. I watched the hypnotic pattern it made as it fanned outwards before making a path to the plug hole. I knew the rhythm of my cycles, was acutely tuned to the minor fluctuations of my body — a dull ache in my lower back, or a slightly bloated feeling around my middle — that signalled it was coming. I found that it was better to know in advance that my body had, yet again, failed me, rather than having to bear witness to the red proof of it.

But somehow that month — perhaps in the rush of a particularly busy set of shifts at the coffee house, or the excitement of the publisher meeting — I had missed the usual signifiers, and instead allowed myself to feel a tiny heartbeat of hope.

Two years and five months we had been trying for. Twenty-nine cycles — each ending the same way. I began to see that the future I'd mapped out, a future that orbited around me becoming a mother, was going to have to shift. It would need to make space for the possibility that I would become someone else, someone who didn't fold tiny sets of dinosaur pyjamas beneath pillows or hold a small pudgy hand on a pavement repeating, 'Look both ways.'

I snapped off the shower, twisted my damp hair within a towel, and returned to my laptop. *Maybe*, I told myself as I read the waiting message from my agent — 'Ready with an idea I can ping across?' — *just maybe, what I am meant to be is a writer.*

In that moment I felt viscerally connected to my mother, as if she had been watching over me, gifting me those pages, saying, *Here! Go make this dream real!*

And anyway, two paragraphs, that was all I had to send my agent. Just the essence of my mother's story. I wouldn't have to take it any further — it was simply to display that I had ideas.

It didn't feel momentous. It didn't even feel like a path had been chosen. I typed out those two short paragraphs, then pulled on my uniform, and went to work.

★ ★ ★

'I went to work,' I continue to explain to Fiona. 'I didn't feel guilty about sending over Mum's idea because it was the book I'd already written — the book I'd spent eighteen months working on — that the commissioning editor was interested in.'

Fiona is still, her gaze pinned to me.

'My agent called later that day to tell me that the editor wanted to make an offer.'

I'd taken the call in the stock room at work, my back to the door, the phone pressed to my ear. I could recall the exquisite excitement, as if something inside me was rising, reaching for air, filling my lungs with the glorious possibility of a new future. One that didn't involve the black apron fastened above my hips, or the dishwasher that needed filling with dark-ringed mugs.

As I'd listened, nodding intently, hoping the reception didn't falter during this call that was a lifeline, my agent said, 'The acquisitions team liked your novel and said your writing style is fresh and beautiful — but, they didn't think the concept was quite strong enough for the current market. Essentially, they felt the story was too quiet and lacked the hook that would help them sell it through to readers. However, what they did fall in love with was your second book idea. They think that's the one.'

The beautiful sensation of something lifting, rising — was pricked. It collapsed around me.

'So, what do you think?' my agent asked, bright with the expectation that, of course I would say, *Yes!* This was what every aspiring writer aimed for — a solid book deal with one of

414

the largest and most respected publishers in the industry.

How could I tell my agent that the second story idea — the one the acquisitions team had fallen in love with — wasn't my own? I would not only lose the book deal, but my literary agent, too.

What I wanted was *my* book published. I had done the work. I had written a ninety-thousand-word story. But in that high-rise, glass-fronted office in London, a team of people had sat around a table discussing fiction trends and packaging, and decided that the story I had written wasn't the one that would sell. It was the other idea, that tiny concept sent to them via a hastily typed email.

And they had been right.

I look at Fiona. 'I accepted the offer. I told myself that it was just a starting point. Mum's book would secure me that first publishing contract, and then after that I'd be writing my own stories again.'

It had been a small deal. They had offered me a fifteen-thousand-pound advance. I'd had no idea that my agent would then sell the rights internationally, that my mother's story would cause a bidding auction in Germany with twelve publishers going to three rounds. That in Holland, editors were sending what my agent called 'love-letters', extolling why I should pick their publishing house. Or that in America, an editor in a New York skyscraper was already briefing her team of designers about how best to package the novel tipped to be their biggest-selling title that summer.

'I felt like I'd pressed *Start* on something I couldn't stop,' I explained. 'People wanted interviews. Book tours were arranged. I had to talk about my inspiration for the novel, how I brought my characters to life.'

Submitting my mother's manuscript was only the first lie. The others unfolded one after the other, digging a hole so deep that I couldn't escape.

'My insomnia flared back to life. I had panic attacks before interviews because, how could I stand in a roomful of people and talk about a book I didn't write? Everyone was congratulating me, telling me how proud I must feel, what a beautiful novel I'd written.'

I look at my sister. 'I trapped myself in a life I never wanted.'

Fiona's stare is unflinching. 'Didn't you?'

35

Elle

'Mum worked two jobs,' Fiona says, looking straight ahead, eyes dark, almost unfocused. 'Yet she still set an alarm every morning, so she could write before work.'

I've anchored myself by the oak trunk. Below the tight set of my jaw, I can feel the flicker of my pulse.

As a girl, if I woke early, I'd often find my mother sitting at the kitchen table, head bowed over a notebook. I recall the perfect stream of her handwriting as it flowed across the page, the knit of concentration in her brow. If my mother noticed me, she'd glance up, pen hovering above the page as she'd offer to make breakfast — but I could see it in her eyes, the cost of leaving behind her story.

'Mum put everything into her writing,' Fiona continues. 'She didn't have the privilege of going to university, or the luxury of financial support. She squeezed every moment she could from each day and used them to write.'

Turning to her handbag, she removes a large manila envelope. From it she withdraws a set of pages that I recognise: our mother's manuscript.

'Mum never told us she was working on a novel,' she says, laying the manuscript on the desk, like an exhibit. 'Why do you think that was?'

The question hasn't been pitched for an answer.

'Mum never truly believed she was any good. She referred to her writing as her *silly hobby*. She didn't tell anyone about it. Beyond having a couple of short stories published, she wrote for herself, for pleasure. She wrote because she couldn't not.'

Fiona places her forefinger in the centre of the manuscript, an arrow pinning it to my desk.

'When Mum died, she had no idea that she'd left behind something of such startling beauty that people all over the world would go on to read it, to fall in love with her characters, to recommended it. She never got to see any of that, or to know that all those years she dedicated to her *silly hobby* — meant something.'

I feel the rise of guilt, sticky and hot, crawling into my throat.

'When you found her manuscript, you could have seen it as a chance to honour her. You could have published the story on her behalf, posthumously, and brought her dream to life. It would have been Mum's legacy — the stamp *she* left behind.' She pauses for a fraction of a beat. 'Yet you claimed it for yourself. There was no one to stop you, so you thought, *I'll have that.*'

My teeth press against the insides of my cheek, clamp to the warm glossy flesh. The words sound so dark, so calculated.

Ever since I submitted my mother's manuscript, I've fought to push away the disgrace of

418

what I've done, to squeeze it to the back of my mind. The sensation is like an immense pressure, building and expanding.

Fiona's words puncture something. Guilt and regret come rushing out. I cover my face with my hands, a raw sob escaping into the room. The hot slide of tears streams from my eyes.

My mother loved me, believed in me.

But I betrayed her.

★　★　★

Fiona's expression remains motionless, rigid. 'Does Flynn know?'

The question is simple. Answerable. I wipe my face with the back of my hands.

'No.'

'Flynn never read your original manuscript — no one did — so you thought you'd get away with it.'

'It was never about getting away with it. He was abroad when the book deal happened. By the time he flew home, I was in too deep. I didn't know how to undo it. I was — '

'I remember you calling to tell me the news,' Fiona says, cutting me off. She leans against the writing desk, one ankle crossed over the other. Chin raised, lips pursed. 'I was eight months pregnant, kneeling in front of my holdall, trying to work out what the hell one puts in a hospital bag. I wanted so very, very badly to talk to Mum, for her to tell me what to pack, what to do, that this was all going to be okay. And then you called.

419

'I felt this surge of relief to hear your voice. I began to tell you about my hospital bag dilemmas. You listened — listened for ages — and it was only right at the very end that you said, 'Hey, I've got some news.''

Fiona's expression tightens, a muscle working in her lower jaw. 'I was floored. A *book deal*? A fucking book deal! Writing had always been my career. It was part of how I defined myself, how other people saw me: *Fiona the journalist*. But when I put down the phone, I realised that, somehow, we had switched lives.

'You visited after Drake was born. You saw how hard I found it adjusting to motherhood. I had expected to be filled with this instinctive, body-rocking love that new mothers talked about, but I just . . . I wasn't. I didn't have a clue what I was doing. And this whirlwind of success you were riding — the praise from critics, the sudden surge of wealth — all of that just compounded everything I was lacking. All I knew was that I was somehow failing. Failing Drake. Failing Bill. Failing myself.'

She pushes away from the desk, turning and positioning herself in front of the glass wall, her back to me. The beach is shrouded in darkness, except for the white trim of the waves that surge towards the waiting shore. In the reflection, I can see the stony set of Fiona's face.

'A few weeks after Drake was born, you decided you were going to move to Cornwall. I wanted to be happy about it. Truly, I did. I knew how much you loved Drake and wanted to be near him — but I also felt like, somehow, this space I was trying to establish for myself was being compromised.'

Fiona lets her head tilt forward, until her forehead connects with the glass.

'Jealousy is so dull, so fucking predictable. I hated myself for being jealous — but that's what I was. After being in your house with all the space, the light, this sense of calm you created, it's hard to return to your own house and not notice the cracks in the paintwork, or the threadbare patches of your carpet.'

Fiona turns, faces me. 'Your being in Cornwall should have been something positive and wonderful, but instead, it just . . . wasn't.'

A deep sadness spreads through my chest.

'Since you've moved here, everyone new I meet says to me, *You're Elle's sister, aren't you?* You are the reference point for who I am.' Bitterness raises her voice a notch higher as she says, 'Half the town follows your social media accounts. We're all there looking on at your picture-perfect house, this fabulous career, the serene lifestyle you've created — but it's all one big lie.'

She steps forward, jaw set, eyes narrowed. 'You knew Bill and I had been struggling to make ends meet on one income, that our house was falling to bits — and there you were putting in your granite work surfaces and bifold doors and glass-fucking-walls, all of it with money that wasn't yours.'

'I tried to give you some . . . I offered to pay for your bathroom renovation . . . to pay off your mortgage — '

'A handout! I thought you were giving us a fucking handout! Of course I said *no*. I didn't realise that money really belonged to our mother.' Her lips pull back over her teeth. 'What about Drake? You could've put money aside for him, for when he's older. But instead you ploughed it all into the house. And now you're on the cusp of losing it all — when you had everything.' Her mouth twists. 'You took Mum's dream. Made it your own. You cheated her. You cheated all of us, Elle!'

She is so close now that I can smell the sour tang of her breath, muddied with a hint of perfume. I can hear the draw of air into her lungs, quick and low. *Your face*, I'm thinking. *Who are you?* Veins straining to escape her neck, teeth bared, a lock of hair caught in her mouth.

But then Fiona's expression seems to shift, alter. The twist of her mouth loosens, the creases above her brow release. Her eyes turn blank — not filmed, but vacant — and her expression shutters, entirely impenetrable.

I'm no longer looking at my sister, but a distant version of her.

'You,' Fiona says, her voice a steel whisper, 'deserve everything you're going to get.'

36

Elle

We could be strangers.

I try to reconcile this Fiona with the one who used to braid my hair while she sat cross-legged on the floor, humming. Or with the teenage Fiona who would take me to the park when our mother was working. Or the Fiona who'd lift the corner of her duvet and let me slip in beside her if I woke from a nightmare.

Yet the Fiona standing in front of me, moved into my house, broke into my writing room, pried through my possessions . . . And then what?

My thoughts are travelling back through the events of the past few weeks, rippling over the unsettling things that have felt different in the house, the paranoia and doubt that have lit up my mind.

'You locked me in here. I didn't imagine it. You had the key.'

Fiona looks straight at me. 'Yes.'

'Why?'

'Bill came over earlier that day, helped you move your bed.'

That is right.

'Before he paid you a visit, he showered, put on a clean shirt, patted his jaw with aftershave. I

423

had to watch my husband dress with as much care as if he were meeting a date. Except he was meeting you.'

Beyond the writing room, the wind gusts across the water, rakes over the cliff face.

'I'd guessed months ago,' Fiona says.

'Guessed?'

'That he is infatuated with you. Oh, it's so obvious; it's the way he lingers when you visit, or this alertness he has when you're in the room. He tries to hide it, of course — tries not to look at you for longer than necessary — but he can't help himself. I found him watching one of your Facebook Live sessions a few weeks ago. He went scarlet, like I'd caught him watching porn.'

'Fiona — '

She holds up a finger, silencing me. 'Bill told me what happened in your lounge.' She draws breath. 'That night I came over to talk to you. I don't know what I was planning to say. I knocked on the front door, but you didn't answer. I could see the light was on in your writing room and guessed you were working with your headphones on,' she says, 'so I let myself in.'

Goose bumps travel across the backs of my arms.

'I climbed the stairs — and there you were, writing your next novel with absolutely no clue what you'd done to me. I was so furious, so hurt, that I simply pulled the door shut. Turned the key. There was no plan. No big idea.' She laughs then, a short, bitter note. 'But of course, you tried to get out, and when you couldn't, you called me.'

Fiona had been in my house the whole time. I remember hearing the police siren, the crunch of tyres on gravel — but now I realise that I'd only heard one vehicle arrive. Fiona's car must have already been in the drive.

I stare at my sister, utterly confounded. 'You locked me in — and then you *unlocked* the door before the police arrived.'

My thoughts are accelerating, tripping and scrambling in my hurry to piece it together.

'All the things that have been happening in the house . . . the words circled in my novel, the smashed paperweight . . . I thought I was going mad, imagining things. That Facebook post that I sent you as a text message . . . was that . . . did you — '

Fiona sighs, impatient. 'Do you know how nauseating it is to read all that crap you post? The filtered shots of this house, the soft-focus selfies, the captions about your word counts and your inspirational view. And let's not forget your Facebook Live writing tips.' She takes off my voice perfectly: ''I never feel qualified to give advice . . . ' *but here's a shit load of the stuff anyway.* It amazes me that thousands of people tune in to watch. That you can sit here, in your glass writing room, blathering away, giving people — real writers, hard-working writers without six-figure advances and international deals — your advice. What a fucking joke!'

She arrows a finger at my chest. 'I listened, Elle. To them all. There was one piece of advice that resonated.' She pauses for a beat. ''Shift the lens. Adjust the angle of the lens to reveal — or

425

expose — the truth of their character.' ' She looks right at me. 'Smart advice.'

Fiona's bitterness is so overpowering that I take another step back. 'How did you know my password?'

'Your hard-drive,' she says, inclining her head towards the case where I store all my electrical items.

I suddenly understand how Fiona has managed it. The hard-drive contains all my passwords, including details of my Cloud account, my Facebook account, the login for my emails. With a feeling of dread, I realise that it would have allowed Fiona access to absolutely everything.

★ ★ ★

Thirty-three years of knowing her. Running to the shops to select cola cubes together. The way she always amends her food order at the last moment. Her girlishness when she swims, head bobbing high above the waterline.

Part of my brain rebels, tells me, *This can't be your sister!* Except, of course, it can. It is. Her ruthlessness as a journalist. Her ability to park emotion and focus on the task at hand. Her determination to succeed, to win.

It is all moving into sharper focus. My fingers clench and release as I realise that it was Fiona who set up the Facebook Live feed of my deserted writing room, trunk lid open. A message, a little prelude of what was to come. Creative in her malice. She must have done it before coming to book club.

'My God,' I say, the sudden unfurling of understanding. 'The dead moth.' I picture her standing on my doorstep, examining the collar. 'You pinned it to my coat.'

'Yes,' Fiona says, eyes dark, her expression as blank, as masked, as I've ever seen.

'You positioned it exactly where Mum's brooch used to be.'

'You don't remember, do you? Mum bought that brooch when she had her first short story published. She never treated herself to anything. Every penny was saved for us — so that we could have new shoes, or the bags that the other kids were wearing. I was so happy that she'd treated herself. I asked why she'd chosen a silver swift, and she said that when she wrote, she felt like she was soaring.' Her lips pinch tight to the words she directs at me: 'You didn't deserve to wear it.'

'So you took it.'

'Yes.'

'But that's not all you did,' I say, voice rising, throat throbbing with anger. 'You pinned a dead moth in its place! It's so . . . so completely messed up.'

On my desk, light reflects in the curve of my paperweight. I reach for it, turning the cool glass through my hands, feeling the jagged crack that runs through it.

'And this . . . ' I say.

I'd told Fiona about my fear that someone had been in my writing room, chipped the paperweight. Her laugh, dismissive. *It's all in your head*.

Except it wasn't.

'You cracked it.' My grip on the paperweight tightens as I think of the missing shard of glass that found its way into my bedroom. Not walked in there on the heel of a shoe, but purposefully embedded in the plush weave of the carpet — right in front of my bedroom mirror. 'You planted the shard in the exact place you knew I'd stand.'

'Yes.' The word is delivered firmly, without apology.

The passive violence of it, the utter cruelty in her planning, the implicit threat . . .

The air in the room feels impossibly dense, hard to draw. Everything is tilting, spinning away. My sister has purposefully, wilfully hurt me. Over and over . . .

The hard weight of the glass globe in my hands, my thumb pressing into the jagged groove.

The darkness of her irises, the hatred I see reflected at me.

My arm draws back, tendons tightening.

She registers the paperweight, the angle of my wrist. I see her brows rise in surprise even as she begins to duck, arms reaching up to shield her face.

I launch the paperweight with force — but in the moment it leaves my fingers, I twist.

The glass wall shatters. A perfect icicle of broken fragments cling together, as if strung from the web of a spider.

★ ★ ★

428

There is silence. The room fills with it, so only the sea wind breathes in through the ruined glass wall, twisting between the tiny gaps.

Fiona's voice emerges as something smaller than it was before. 'You were going to throw it at me.'

I am thinking about all the hours I've spent in this room, attempting to write a novel that atones for the one I've taken from my mother, the words I've laboured over, crafted, doubted and rewritten.

'My manuscript. Did you delete it?' I ask — but I already know the answer. Fiona has been through my files, my emails, my Cloud account. She has waited until the day before my deadline to be sure my book deal was ruined.

'Every copy.'

My teeth grind together, pressure building in my jaw. I tip back my head and open my mouth, a low throttle of a groan escaping.

'What do you want?' I cross the room, grabbing my mother's manuscript from the desk. 'Are you keeping this as some kind of collateral? Are you waiting to show it to the press — to bring me down publicly so that everyone can see I'm a fraud? Or is there something else you want? Money? Revenge? What is it, Fiona?'

'Look at the envelope.'

Beneath the manuscript, I remove a manila envelope, turn it to face me. It is addressed to Jane Riley, my editor.

'What I want,' Fiona says, 'is for *you* to send it to her.'

I squeeze my eyes shut, picturing how it will

unfold. All copies of my book in circulation will have to be withdrawn. There will be a legal case. Financially I'll be ruined. I will never be able to publish again. Everyone I know and care about will hear.

'Do you think,' I say, opening my eyes, staring down my sister, 'that this is the life I would've chosen? I wanted to write — but not like this. What I wanted was a home, children, marriage.'

'You made a series of choices. Told a thousand small lies. Lived and perpetuated a deception that affected all of us. Don't try to rewrite the story to make yourself the victim.'

'If that's what you want to believe, then do; tell yourself that every move was orchestrated and planned. But I think you know that's not what I did.' I pause, look her hard in the eye. 'That's what *you* did, Fiona.'

I grip the manuscript to my chest. The handwritten pages contain hour upon hour of our mother's thoughts, the moments where she'd paused to think, the pen nib resting against the page so that the ink spread into the weave of the paper.

When I had begun typing the story, I'd intended to change things — make some of it my own — but it was impossible. The voice was so distinctive, each word crisp and perfectly placed, sparse yet haunting. The story was complete as it was. The manuscript became the most important thing in my possession — it showed the brilliance, talent, and empathy of our mother.

But it was also the one thing I know I should never have kept.

37

Elle

Fiona holds out her hand. 'Give it to me.'

I don't move.

Fiona's brows arch sharply, as if to say, *Now*.

Turning my back to my sister, I slide open the desk drawer and reach inside. I know it's in here. My fingers brush its plastic casing and I draw it swiftly towards the bottom edge of the manuscript, flicking the metal coil with my thumb.

A perfect blue-yellow flame springs to life and I hold the lighter steady. A few seconds will be enough . . .

The paper catches alight, the lower corners of the manuscript beginning to curl and blacken. The flames lick higher, swallowing words, sentences, paragraphs. The metal bin is beneath my desk; I just need to let it flame for a beat longer.

I expect my sister to launch herself at me. To yell at me to stop. But she does nothing.

'Do you honestly think that's the only copy I have?'

Of course she would have other copies! Everything would be meticulously planned. No stone left unturned. Suddenly flames are licking at my fingers — and I cry out, dropping the manuscript.

Lit pages soar like burning wings. I watch transfixed, as they flame and curl through the air, drifting downwards.

As they settle on the wooden floor, the room looks set alight.

I lurch into action, stamping out the flames. Heat singes at my ankles as I press the soles of my shoes over the burning pages.

When one sheet is put out, I hurry to the next, pressing my heels to the floor — but each time a flame is suffocated, another seems to rise.

There is a fire extinguisher in the kitchen. I can get downstairs and back in under a minute. I rush towards the door — then halt. Behind me, Fiona has begun to scream.

I turn. The hem of Fiona's long coat is on fire. A flame has caught the synthetic material, heat streaking upwards. She is yanking her arms free, her movements jerky and frantic, eyes wide with terror. I rush to help, dragging the coat from her, the flaming material collapsing to the floor.

I stamp across her coat, smoke rising from the smouldering fabric, catching at the back of my throat.

'You okay?' I ask, breathless.

Fiona says nothing, shock etched across her face.

In the corner of my eye, I see a page of the manuscript has caught the base of my reading chair, which is beginning to flame.

I seize my water jug from my desk — there's no more than a cup of liquid in it — and I slosh it against the material, which sizzles, the flames dampening immediately. A small drift of smoke rises from it, a final flame flickering, which I suffocate with the sole of my shoe.

I set down the jug, catch my breath.

'Elle . . . '

In the reflection of the glass wall, I can see Fiona standing with her hands pressed to her face. I swing around.

'What?'

And then I see it.

In the corner of the room, by the door, something is aglow. At first, I don't understand. But as I focus, I see a mouth of flames seething from my bookcase. The fire has spread across the lowest shelf of the bookcase, where paperbacks, maps and travel books are burning like kindling.

'My God . . . ' I whisper as the whole case is set alight.

I turn and see the fire has spread towards the oak trunk. Blue and green flames are curling relentlessly from the plastic sleeves of photo albums, acrid smoke pluming upwards.

'No,' I cry, running towards it, falling to my knees and trying to grab for an album, save it. But the heat forces me back. I stagger to my feet, watching helplessly as the fire consumes everything — the pile of cards from Flynn, photos of our mother, my journals and diaries. All of it ignited in seconds. The room is alive with noise, the creak of wood expanding then cracking, the roar of flames.

'We've got to get out!' Fiona cries, grabbing my wrist, pulling me away.

A hot, dark cloud of smoke rises towards the ceiling. I feel it burning into my airways.

Instinctively, I pull my jumper over my mouth. We hurry towards the doorway, but a searing heat pushes us back. The flames have already burned through the frame creating a deadly ring of fire.

Black plumes of smoke thicken and deepen at the ceiling.

We crouch low, Fiona shrieking, 'What now?

I whirl round, mind racing. I look at the shattered pane of the glass wall — and know it is our only option.

'Help me with this,' I shout, picking up my desk chair — a heavy oak carver with solid legs.

We lug it towards the glass wall, and then raise it so the chair legs are angled at glass.

'On three,' I shout.

We draw the chair back and launch it hard against the glass. A leg pushes through the weakened centre, widening the hole.

We batter the glass a second time and a third, then I kick out the rest of the glass, fragments bouncing off my jeans as I smash through it.

I can taste the fresh salted air — but as it breathes into the room, it angers the flames, and the smoke and heat seem to be sucked towards the glass wall.

'We've got to jump,' I yell.

Peering down, I can see the balcony off my bedroom. It overhangs the writing room, but there is a gap of a few feet. We need to jump out far enough to ensure we reach it. If we get it wrong, the drop is onto the jagged rocks below.

'I can't!' Fiona cries.

I grab her hand, pulling her to the edge, glass

crunching beneath our feet.

'When I say, we're going to jump! You've got to launch as far as you can, okay?'

Fiona doesn't respond. Her eyes are glazed with fear.

I help her into position at the edge of the glass wall, but it is awkward; we are half crouched among the shattered glass, smoke pouring around us. I reach for the metal frame to steady myself, but it is searing hot against my palms.

There is no time — we must go.

'Ready?'

I grip my sister's hand tighter.

'One . . . two . . . three!'

In the moment that my feet leave the building, I feel Fiona's hand slipping free. The night rushes at me. I hear a scream leaving my throat. Another behind me.

I am alone as I fall through the darkness, the writing room lit up behind me with flames.

★ ★ ★

I land badly, the breath punched from my lungs.

It takes me a few seconds to come around, to feel air filling my chest again. I stagger to my feet, dazed, a hand pressed into my hairline feeling for blood.

When I look up, at first, all I can see is the roaring blaze. The flames have spread across the room, swallowing my reading chair, my book-case. I cannot see my sister . . .

'Fiona!'

Has she jumped — and missed?

Please, no . . .

And then, slowly, slowly, my eyes begin to focus. I can just make out a figure crouched at the edge of the shattered glass wall, arms clamped over her head. The flames are right behind her, a black stream of smoke pouring into the night.

'You have to jump!'

Fiona makes no sign of having heard.

'Please, Fiona! Now!'

A gust of wind pours from the sea, pushing over the cliff face and billowing into the writing room. The flames seem to reach out of the broken glass wall.

Fiona screams, a burning cry.

It all happens so quickly. Suddenly Fiona is on her feet, stepping out into thin air.

Immediately, I can see it is wrong. The angle of her body is tilted too far forwards, her limbs are flailing. She hasn't pushed hard enough. Gone far enough.

I can only watch as she falls through the night, hair lifting from her face, eyes wide, terror-struck.

Her legs pedal empty air.

She's dropping, reaching out — and then somehow, somehow, her foot just reaches the balcony rail and catches there. All I see is Fiona falling forwards, crashing to the balcony floor — knees first — with a sickening crunch of bone against wood.

A scream rips through her.

She is down, splayed on the balcony, head turned to the side, face bleached in the moonlight. I lurch to her and see blood on her lips, the whites of her eyes as they roll.

'Fiona!'

She groans, a deep wail resonating from the base of her throat.

I look over my shoulder, through the bedroom. Beyond the door I can see smoke filling the landing, billowing towards the stairs. We need to move.

Hooking my arm around Fiona, I try and heave her up — but she screams, her legs unable to bear weight.

I lower her again, catch my breath. Above us, a burning piece of material drops from the writing room, soaring downwards. It catches the edge of the balcony, showering us with embers. I dust at them frantically. There's no time. I've got to get Fiona out.

I circle my arms around her chest and, using every reserve of strength, I drag her backwards, heaving her from the balcony and into the bedroom. My arms and back scream with the strain, but I clamp my teeth and continue to drag her until we're in the hallway.

I pause, just for a second to catch my breath, but the smoke is too thick and heavy, I'm choking, coughing. I sense the blaze above is penetrating doorways, moving through unseen structural shafts, spreading through the interior walls.

Gripping Fiona tight, I haul her down the stairs using the momentum of the descent. With each thud of the wooden steps, I expect to hear fresh screams — but she makes no sound at all now.

Finally, we reach the ground floor. I pause only to grab my phone from the bureau, then I yank open the front door and, with a final surge of effort, I pull Fiona through it, out of the house and onto the fresh, beautifully cold driveway.

★   ★   ★

I call 999, talking as I press my fingertips against Fiona's neck. Her pulse is faint — but it is there. My coat is still heaped on the doorstep from earlier, and I fetch it, draping it over Fiona. I crouch beside her, talking softly as I wait to hear the wail of the ambulance, for blue flashing lights to streak the dark lane.

Beyond the dancing scorch of flames, the sea wind twists and sucks, waves groaning and echoing against the cliff. I adjust the coat tighter around Fiona's shoulders.

My sister lies motionless on the ground, her skin deathly pale.

I squeeze my eyes shut, willing the ambulance to hurry. Out to sea, the relentless surge of waves continues to pound.

I think of my mother's dream: a place to write with a view of the sea.

Her dream.

My dream.

My sister's dream.

Opening my eyes, I see the dead moth pressed against the clavicle of Fiona's throat, and beyond her, the writing room burning red.

Epilogue

One year later

I hear the creak of the letterbox as something is pushed through the metal mouth. There is a low thud as the package hits the doormat, followed by the snap of iron as the letterbox hinges shut.

Flynn continues his story. He is telling me about one of the apprentice tree surgeons he is training as he fills a water bottle at the tap, a stream of clear liquid locked within the twist of a lid. He tosses it into the backpack along with an apple and a packet of biscuits.

He bends to kiss me. Our lips connect, and I feel the charge between us. Neither of us will forget our separation — how close we came to losing each other for good. I grasp the neckline of his T-shirt as I pull him deeper, cotton bunched within the heat of my palms.

I've told Flynn everything — each tangled thread. It's taking time, but we are slowly unravelling things, working our way around the knotted centre of it, in the hope that we can begin stitching our relationship together again.

I listen to the heave then stamp of work boots being pulled on, the clatter of keys as he fishes them from the windowsill, the suck of the door as it opens.

'Package for you,' he calls, before the door shuts.

Then he is gone, disappearing into the blue thrust of the morning.

As I look out through the window, I contemplate the day that lies ahead. There, beyond the stretch of farmland, is the glimmer of sea. North Island, New Zealand, is where we've chosen. We will move on eventually, but for now I find I am happier than I have been in a long time. I write, I swim, I fall asleep beside Flynn.

I think back, as I often do, to the night of the fire. I'm working hard to own the memory of it, to not push it into a corner of my mind where it would fester. So I think about it, I talk about it with Flynn.

I wonder if Fiona ever talks about it, too.

She, Bill and Drake are still living in Cornwall. We're not in touch, but I've heard on the grapevine that her recovery has been good. She broke both her legs jumping from the writing room. I can still hear it, her burning cry, the terrible crunch of bone.

The cliff-top house is gone. Sold to a wealthy buyer from London who I hear has rebuilt the destroyed writing room and turned it into a gym. I've discovered that I don't miss the house. Perhaps that's telling — the clearest indicator that it was never meant for me.

After the fire, my editor got in touch. She was sympathetic about my novel being destroyed in the blaze, although I could tell she was surprised there was no back-up copy on a remote server somewhere. But how could I explain? I suppose I could have grovelled, asked for an extension, a chance to rewrite the book. But I didn't. That

440

story was a piece of time, a piece of me, and I must let it go.

So I've begun a new novel. Just loose seeds of ideas, not something that has rooted into a full narrative yet. But I am cutting my teeth, learning my craft, and I will get there. I'm enjoying writing without a publishing contract, without a deadline. The pressure has lifted, and I feel uninhibited, free to create.

Nowadays I don't have a desk: I write sitting cross-legged on the lounge floor, or at a café table, or leaning against the peeling bark of a eucalyptus tree. I care little where I am. Writing feels almost like a form of meditation, a way of working my way through the pages and out of myself.

Deciding I'll work in the garden this morning, I'm passing the hallway when I remember the package on the doormat. We do not get much post out here — I've only given our address to a handful of people.

I bend to retrieve the padded envelope, feeling the familiar weight and shape of it: a book. An advance proof copy, most likely. A British postmark. My agent still sends these with waning frequency. I rip open the package and look for the publisher's typed letter, but there is none. Strange. I pull out the book and examine its jacket. A proof copy, published by Harper-Collins.

The cover is unsettling. In stark grey and white tones, it depicts an empty staircase running through the centre of a house. Only when I look again do I notice the shadow of a figure lurking at the edge of the stairway. Watching. Waiting.

Hackles of fear rise.

Tucked into the dark edge of the image is the author's name.

My heart skips, then accelerates; my breath quickens.

It can't be.

The letters swim and waver, shimmering in the heat of my shock. Hesitantly, I open the cover. The pads of my fingertips are damp as they grip the book, pressing into the weave of the paper.

As I begin to read, I experience something like déjà vu — a vague familiarity, a reality slightly distorted as if it is being held at a distance or seen through a lightly fogged lens.

The words have a rhythm to them that I know. My gaze snaps through the sentences, paragraphs, pages. I barely blink. I find my legs have carried me to the bedroom, lowered me onto the edge of the mattress. My concentration is directed solely on the book.

The story is about a woman who lives in a cliff-top house. A woman whose first novel was not her own. A woman who has lived a kind of fiction for years because of one startling event in an English lecturer's office that changed her sense of who she was, of what was believable and what should be omitted. That story — the one I had written — is tucked within these pages.

As I read with my head bent, the story unfolding before me, I remember each of these words as I wrote them. I can almost feel the firmness of my desk beneath my forearms, the wooden floorboards against the soles of my feet. I'd spent hours in my writing room, attempting to create something worthwhile, a novel to stand shoulder to shoulder with my mother's manuscript, a novel to absolve me.

This is my story, the deleted manuscript.

Except Fiona has kept a copy of it.

But it is not solely my story about Luke Linden. Blended within my deleted manuscript is a second narrative — one I did not write — but lived.

Everything is in here. The discovery of a jagged shard of glass from a broken paperweight; the carving of the word *Liar* on a desk leg; a walk on a beach with a little boy who wore a beard of sea foam; the way the Cornish coast holds a particular quality of light in the early morning.

I recall Bill saying that Fiona was busy working on a new project — but that was long after the brochure copy had been finished. I realise that this book I now hold in my hands was Fiona's project. She has been biding her time, working out her narrative, structuring the plot, waiting — with a journalist's instinct — for the full story.

Fiona has always been the one who can see three steps ahead, a master chess player with each move thought out. Of course an author only controls part of a story: they have an idea of its arc and direction — but there is a point at which they must allow their characters to step forward and direct things. When the characters begin to live and breathe.

Fiona has watched. Waited.

The story in this book is a depiction of us both. The names are changed, the details have been altered, the locations are fictional — but the truth of us lies in the pages.

I wonder at what point Fiona decided that she would use part of my manuscript to blend with her own? It would have appealed to her unwavering sense of fairness: to have taken my words and put her own name to them.

An eye for an eye.

I feel the echo of it, the pull that would have drawn Fiona with its neatness, the symbolism, the payback.

After all, who owns a story? The person who tells it? The person who reads it? The person whom it is about?

Or all of them?

★ ★ ★

As I finish the final page, I turn back to the beginning in search of a notecard or a message from my sister.

But there's nothing.

Looking out through the window where the day now burns away, a sense of stillness settles within my chest. This story has been threaded together from a series of moments belonging to me, my sister, our mother. It is a story about choices and mistakes, truth and fiction, dreaming and failing — and all the other messy things that life delivers and removes, waves falling and receding.

444

My words haven't been deleted or lost. Those truth-lined pages have been set free — just like my mother's — to soar in someone else's imagination.

Dusk presses close to the window causing me to reach for the lamp. Light hits the pages of the book — and that's when I notice the dedication.

As I look at the three words that frame the novel, I wonder whether they were typed with venom, Fiona's parting shot, her final word?

Or perhaps, I hope, as my fingertip runs beneath them, they were fuelled by a deeper curve of emotion.

Understanding.

For my sister.

Acknowledgements

Thank you to my editor, Kim Young, who heard this story idea when it was no more than a suggestion in a phone call, and told me, 'I've got goosebumps.' Kim, and the brilliant Charlotte Brabbin, have worked with me on every draft, raising questions, encouraging me to dig deeper, to explore further. This book is so much better because of you both.

I am fortunate to have the most wonderful literary agent, Judith Murray, along with her team at Greene & Heaton. I've worked with Judith from the moment I stepped into this author life, and her advice, support and friendship are invaluable. Thanks also to Kate Rizzo for handling my foreign rights — and for providing such insight and thoughtfulness on her read of this manuscript, and many before.

Thank you to my early readers — Faye Buchan, Becki Hunter, Laura Crossley, Maria Evans and Rachel Trotter. Your thoughts were so helpful in shaping the story.

A big thank you goes to YOU, my readers, for cheering me on and recommending and sharing my books. Honestly, it's your excitement that keeps me lit.

Thank you to my parents and parents-in-law for being such a brilliant support team while I write. When deadline time was fast approaching, and stress levels were high, they simply asked, 'What can we do?'

My husband, James, is my frontline in every way. On hand for brainstorming ideas or chatting through issues, he knows each layer of every book I've written. He also makes it possible for me to be both a writer and a mother — and I'll always be grateful for that gift.

Finally, my children, Tommy and Darcy. Thank you for the mid-scene cuddle breaks, the noise and chaos and colour. You are my very best creations.